In the Land
of Dreams

In the Land of Dreams

Lawrence Swaim

TOP HAT
BOOKS

Winchester, UK
Washington, USA

First published by Top Hat Books, 2017
Top Hat Books is an imprint of John Hunt Publishing Ltd., Laurel House, Station Approach, Alresford, Hants, SO24 9JH, UK
office1@jhpbooks.net
www.johnhuntpublishing.com
www.tophat-books.com

For distributor details and how to order please visit the 'Ordering' section on our website.

Text copyright: Lawrence Swaim 2016

ISBN: 978 1 78535 599 8
978 1 78535 600 1 (ebook)
Library of Congress Control Number: 2016952465

A CIP catalogue record for this book is available from the British Library.

Design: Stuart Davies

Printed and bound by CPI Group (UK) Ltd, Croydon, CR0 4YY, UK

We operate a distinctive and ethical publishing philosophy in all areas of our business, from our global network of authors to production and worldwide distribution.

Chapter 1

Being of sound mind and disposing memory, and not acting under duress, menace, fraud or undue influence of any person whatsoever, I do hereby make, publish and declare this to be my Last Will and Testament, revoking all other former wills.

This document is not about California *feelings*, nor even the sure and certain *hope* of anything, and certainly not a better world; its subject is the honest nuclear-grade fuel of our country's East Coast, the *loot*, the *booty*, the very *pelf* of a Last Will and Testament! *Money*, and lots of it—that's what this Will is all about, and what you will soon receive!

For this reason, I am pleased to examine the odd spectral evidence that has already manifested itself to me. Who would have *imagined* I might suddenly receive these visitations of the literal *essence* of the immigrant ancestor's son—in a residential treatment program such as this one, in Lower Manhattan of New York City?

Could it be because of its physical *proximity* to Staten Island, where Thys Barentsen first served as magistrate under Pieter Stuyvesant?

I know the lies you've been told—that the much-discussed Old Money of the family is *so old* that it's already been *spent*! But the money exists, and it exists in amounts that would stagger the imagination!

Did I mention that it would *stagger the imagination?*

2.

I currently live in reduced circumstances, in a residential treatment program in Lower Manhattan, in New York City. There was once a farm where this residence is situated, I am reliably informed; after that there was a church, most likely Episcopal or Dutch Reformed. Then, for reasons unknown, the two houses here today were built—perhaps to house an extended family of some kind, huddled together in an increasingly nonresidential neighborhood. Today, the two abodes are surrounded by lofts, small- and medium-size businesses, a day-labor agency, a heavily padlocked space where professional dancers practice, a Chinese restaurant and a laundry—the latter two owned by the same family—and a three-story parking garage. At some point a catwalk was built between the two houses, bedrooms were renovated, a staff office was created in both residences, and *voila!* . . . an aging but thoroughly respectable residential treatment program was created, just shabby enough to suggest the distress of its clients, but without such seediness as might add to it. At some point its funding nonprofit ennobled the two houses into a single mental health program, called Voyager House.

The house where I now live is set aside for transitional housing, whereas the house next door is an acute care program. Our neighbors were told a variety of things about the two abodes, including a vague story that the residents received advanced vocational training of some unspecified nature; but in reality, both houses constitute nothing more than a residential mental health program. (By the time I arrived, the appellation "group home" had fallen out of use.) I am not crazy enough for acute care, and my referral to transitional housing served my purposes in many ways—it is a long-term program, lasting from twelve to eighteen months, which means I might be able to remain a client for the full eighteen months, as long as I follow the rules.

My intake into Voyager House was done at night by a competent young counselor named Neil, who identified himself as a psychology student at City College of New York. He was the single overnight staff person in the transitional housing program on the night I arrived. Throughout my intake he shared small bits of information about himself, even as he extracted somewhat more substantial nuggets of information about me. The objective was to create the illusion of a conversation; but the difference between our situations, I quickly saw, was that his life story was in the present tense, whereas mine either resided comfortably in the past, or was experienced partially or wholly in my own imagination.

At some point, Neil mentioned that I had been accepted into Voyager House because of a municipal program for homeless seniors with chronic mental illness. There were currently five other clients in transitional housing, three men and two women. I was apparently the only person in the transitional housing program who didn't take psychotropic medications.

"Do the psych meds really help the clients?" I asked.

"Sure, when they're appropriately prescribed," he said, "but when a lot of these clients start to feel better, they stop taking the meds. Then they decompensate, and end up in acute care. Once we get them stabilized and back on their meds, they either go back to their lives in the community, or—if they've burned enough bridges—they come to transitional housing, where you are now."

"How does your program get away with dispensing medications? I thought only doctors and nurses were allowed to do that."

"We hand over their med boxes, and let them self-dispense their own meds. Then we check off the meds in the med book. That's how we get around the state regulations."

"And when they're discharged into the community, they go off their meds?"

"Well . . . not always, but it's fair to say that most of the clients living here went off their meds at some point. But going off your medications isn't what got *you* into this program."

I wondered how much he knew about what I'd told the staff at Bellevue. To get a good referral to a community-based program, you had to talk about self-harm—or "suicidal ideation," as the Bellevue shrinks like to put it.

I told the psychiatrists at Bellevue Hospital Center that I had suicidal feelings, but that I would never act on them—or at least, I didn't *want* to act on them. That last twist was improvised, but effective, I'm happy to report, and I had good reason for using it, beside the fact that it was mainly true. It was November, and the chilly winds were blowing, so a referral to a decent residential program was my ticket to ride; it would enable me to survive the winter, and that fact alone would contribute greatly to my mental health. It was a simple, time-tested formula: you had to cop to suicidal feelings to gain admittance to a decent residential mental health program, but you had to be careful not to talk *too* much about it—or get too dramatic in the telling of it—or you might be put in a jacket and sent off to one of the forgotten backwards of Bedlam-by-the-Hudson.

It was a nervy play, but damned if I didn't pull it off. I was now in a reasonably nice residential program with actual beds and toilets and all the other accoutrement of civilized life.

"What are you thinking?" Neil asked.

"That I'm grateful that I still have enough balls to punch my own ticket."

He laughed. "Man, *you* don't need psych meds."

3.

The clinical director was a funny, somewhat manic woman named Clarissa Rowland. She came bustling in on the morning after I was admitted to the program. Neil, the young man who had done my intake, had apparently snoozed a bit during the wee hours, but had thoughtfully deployed three alarm clocks—not to mention his so-called "smart watch"—and was up and writing in the charts long before the boss lady arrived. She, in turn, was sporting what looked like an expensive but extremely well-worn brown pants suit, once the universal uniform of management women in human services, and still capable of sending the message that advancement came, in her world, from expertise rather than somebody's impression of her. Her weapons were words, the brown pants suit said, and for her the good fight had nothing to do with appearance. That's what the handsome brown pants suit of yesteryear said.

I came up from the kitchen, where I had been trying unsuccessfully to operate the steaming dishwasher, and made my way to the staff office. "I'm afraid the dishwasher is hopeless," I announced.

"Never mind," Neil said. "We have a client who specializes in repairing it." My eyebrows must have gone up a good inch, because he added, "We can't afford the repairman."

Rowland introduced herself, then took up my chart, which was lying on the table, and expertly flipped the pages open to survey Neil's intake note. "Yes, you were expected here," she said, reading. "EMS told us you were coming."

This magical acronym EMS referred to the Emergency Management Services at the world's most notorious insane asylum, Bellevue Hospital Center.

"I'm glad you have a bed for me," I said.

"Yes, well, the census has been down lately." That was exactly the kind of proprietary information she shouldn't be sharing with a new client, I thought, but the fact that she had done so made me trust her.

"I'll try to be an asset to. . . to your—"

"Whatever."

"Transitional housing program," I said.

She immediately went back to my chart. "There's no age here," she observed. "How old are you? You *do* have an age, don't you?"

"That's—well, I'm not legally required to give my age, am I?"

"If you don't want to give it, you don't have to."

"Nobody knows for sure when I was born, you see, except that it was in the state of New Jersey. After a certain time, I got tired of trying to ferret out the chronology."

"Well, I'm not sure I really buy that, but who knows, maybe you're better off not *having* an age." She exchanged a quick smile with Neil, as though they shared a fascination with the exigencies of aging. "The first group is at ten o'clock in the morning," she said to me. "It's the regular Tuesday check-in group, where we talk informally about . . . you know . . ."

"Feelings," I suggested.

"Ha, yes," she said brightly. She looked at her watch before hurrying off.

"There's coffee downstairs in the pantry," Neil said, by way of explaining the clinical director's sudden departure. "I make the coffee early, about an hour before anybody gets here. But watch out, if you decide to drink a cup. It's strong."

"Do you make it that way on purpose?"

"The coffee *has* to be strong, after you've been here all night."

I nodded in the direction of the vanished clinical director. "I wouldn't say that that she needed any coffee."

"Clarissa?" He shrugged. "High energy. It's built-in with some people."

A moment or two later Rowland came hurrying back to the staff office, clutching a large cup of steaming coffee. She smiled brightly at me. "Whatever it is, I'll answer all questions when I'm awake!"

I interpreted that as a polite request for me to leave, so I went to my room. Later, when I went to shave and clean up in the second-floor bathroom, I saw Clarissa and Neil counting meds in small plastic med-counters, pushing them around in groups of five with wooden coffee stirrers. A short time later, as I returned from the restroom, I saw that Neil was gone and that Clarissa was alone in the office, burrowing through the charts. She glanced up, smiled brightly, and returned instantly to the charts. It occurred to me that perhaps she'd had a long weekend and was trying to get caught up.

Or perhaps she simply relished work. There was something

about her manic style that I found oddly comforting. I am in awe of those who are mad to work; it is a Protestant value, and a full-fledged emotional orientation, one that I unashamedly embrace—in the lives of others. As for myself, I have on occasion sought the easy way. You might well ask, have I sought—as one might say—to "beat the system," even to malinger a bit now and then? Is the Pope a Catholic?

Yes, it is true that I admire others who are mad to work, but as for myself, I am agnostic on the issue. There's a lot more to it, I say, than meets the eye, and besides, each case is different. Work won't kill you, as a favorite great-uncle of mine used to say, but why take a chance? And the reality is, as you may already have guessed, I am currently on a mission that involves a more formidable kind of work than even the most hardened reader might imagine. It is dangerous, and it is demanding, but if I am successful it could change the world as we know it.

4.

We ate a simple, healthy breakfast downstairs in the dining room. My fellow clients referred to Director Rowland by her first name, and appeared to like her. The clientele were appropriately shabby—actually rather slovenly, I thought—but it was early in the day, and in a treatment program such as Voyager House there would be no dress code. Therefore, the threadbare appearance of the clients did not surprise me. (And it was a break for me, as well, since I lacked anything in the way of an adequate wardrobe.)

At breakfast I sat next to an older client who intermittently described the residential repairs to our building he was obliged to make, which included the daily rehabilitation of the dishwasher. I found out later he was a former building contractor who fancied himself still employed, and regarded himself as specifically required to make appropriate home improvements at Voyager House. Two of the older women at breakfast carried large bags with knitting supplies—interestingly, however, they did not actually knit until well into the afternoon or evening. Maybe, I thought, they were unable to fire up the knitting needles until the second cup of coffee, or were perhaps waiting for the proper signal to begin, a signal known only to them.

I had decided to wear some old slippers I'd found deep in a drawer in my room—they were too large for me, but flopped delightfully as I walked down the hallway. I had no robe, but by way of an unfettered and comfortable eccentricity that I imagined as natural to this place, I wore all of the three shirts I owned, leaving them all to hang out of my trousers for added verisimilitude.

After breakfast, I—like several of the others—took my cup of coffee into the group session. The group was held in a room that was once a parlor, but was now extremely rundown, as though it had been used for storage.

After the group settled down, Clarissa Rowland set her coffee down long enough to introduce me. "Would you like to tell us about yourself?"

"I was referred here by—well, the Emergency Management Services at Bellevue Center."

"Why?" a middle-age black man asked.

I was delighted to see that both he and the former building contractor had not once taken their hats off throughout breakfast, and continued to wear them in group. The hats were of the workaday cloth kind worn by longshoremen, and were virtually identical. Wearing their hats in the house gave both clients the appearance of serious persons who were pondering the wisdom of leaving, but hadn't yet made up their minds about it.

"They said that this program at Voyager House would be appropriate for me," I said, by way of answering the black man's query.

He chuckled. "Did they say *why* it would be appropriate for you? Might could be they have a reason they haven't told you about yet."

"No, I have a pretty good idea of what opened the door for me," I said.

"Self-harm," said a young male client knowingly. His notebooks, which he carried with him, were full of violent drawings of weapons and fully armed space vehicles. "They keep asking you to tell them how you *really feel*. Then when you tell them, they punish you."

"No, no," I said, "I don't feel punished. I'm lucky to be here, I think."

"Maybe you can start out with some general background about yourself," Clarissa Rowland interjected firmly. "I mean, where you come from, what your interests are, what your family was like, things like that."

"Actually, I don't mind talking about why Bellevue sent me to Voyager House. In fact, I *need* to talk about it, if the group has no objection." I glanced at Rowland, and she nodded, so I continued. "From the moment I awaken in the morning, I have this terrible feeling that I'm cursed," I began, avoiding eye contact with the others, "but I *don't* mean cursed by being referred to Voyager House—I'm happy to be here. Maybe I should say that I am struggling with the feelings that my *life* is cursed, that no matter which way I turn I will encounter insurmountable problems that I don't fully understand. I believe I am being followed—shadowed, you might say—by a man who has some detailed knowledge of my situation, a man who may actually be an ancestor of mine, and who can therefore explain to me why I feel this way . . . that is, why I feel that my entire life is cursed, compromised, booby-trapped by dangers I cannot control."

"An *ancestor*?" somebody asked.

"It's a feeling I have. I can't explain it."

"Ask him to come over in the afternoon," said the eldest of the non-knitters. "The afternoon would be good."

"No, no, no," the young male client said. "This man, the man he's talking about, is dead."

"What?" said the woman, stricken. "How do you know that?"

"This man was his ancestor, so he must have lived a long time ago; therefore, he must have *died* a long time ago."

I was taken aback by the stricken look on the woman's face, so I quickly interjected: "I believe that the person in question lived around here—or if he does not *live* here, he once came here often, somewhere here in lower Manhattan; and suddenly began appearing here every month since the horror of 9/11." I turned to the elder knitting person. "It's not entirely out of the question that he—or some essence of his personality—might visit today, but when he is likely to come, I can't say."

"A ghost or revenant of some kind, then," Director Rowland asserted. "Like a ghost making the rounds in his territory, sort of like Hamlet in lower Manhattan?"

"More like 'Lear' or 'Macbeth,' if you have to drag in the Bard. The scapegrace scion of some squandered Manhattan fortune, late of the Upper East Side." Actually the block on which Voyager House was located was quite dangerous at night—for one thing, there was a perennially rowdy homeless encampment in an empty lot on the next block. Only the lack of a nightclub made our block even marginally safe, but it was still not quite safe enough to walk at night. "I don't believe in ghosts. But it's almost like this man is stalking me, and that's really of some concern to me."

"But you said—"

"I know what I said. I may have implied that he lives around here, but I know that's wrong. Yet, I just can't stop believing that from time to time—at least once a month—he shows up around here, since a long time ago he periodically came to a place in this neighborhood. In short, the neighborhood has some meaning for him that I don't yet understand. All I know is that he wants to talk to me."

Rowland was leaning forward, tapping her forefinger on the table. "You don't believe in ghosts, but you complain that a ghostly figure is haunting you."

"That's accurate."

"Let me tell you what this sounds like to me." Rowland shifted in her seat. She seemed to have momentarily forgotten the other clients. "I mean, you have this delusional system, is what it sounds like; and sometimes you're in it, and sometimes you're—you know, when it's not convenient, you're out of it."

"Not exactly," I said, "although I know there's something weird about what I'm telling you. And most of the time it's not an active delusion, but more like a story—but it's a story that I can't stop thinking about. In fact, I often hear the words themselves, repeating themselves in my mind."

"Good," Clarissa said, looking expectantly with raised eyebrows around at the group. "Obsessive thinking? Is that what we're hearing?"

"Yes," I answered, although the question had been addressed to the group, and not me.

"And the *curse?*" Rowland seemed simultaneously irritated and fascinated, a feeling I knew well. "What is it with this *curse?*"

"It can be different things, and has been different things, in different time periods—different historical periods, I mean. It has manifested itself to certain members of my family in ways that are highly specific to that time period, but deeply personal. I can't stop the story that's playing in my head until I figure out how it ends—until then, I can't turn it off. But to understand the ending, there is some part that I have to play in the story. I still don't know what that could be. When I figure out what I'm supposed to be in the story, I'll have a better idea how the story ends."

"The answer has to be inside you," Rowland said.

"This man who is following you," said the older of the two non-knitting ladies, "he can come pretty much anytime in the afternoon, as far as I'm concerned."

"I'm sure he will want to visit sometimes," I said, "but I think he wants to visit *me*. Why don't we wait and see how many people he can see in one visit?"

Now the younger of the two non-knitting knitters raised a tremulous hand. "Does he have any, like, previous felonies?"

Later on, I found out that this lady had witnessed a mugging in the neighborhood, and had overheard the police questioning both victim and suspects. The horrifying details of that interview had created in her mind a clear and present sense of the world's dangers, and also functioned as a controlling metaphor for how seemingly disparate circumstances could work together to do harm.

"These are things that happen that stay in our memories," Rowland was saying soothingly, "and after a while they fade away."

"Not the felonies," said the black man. "The cops got a *big* computer where they keep that information. If they got a jacket on you, might could be they'll turn you every way but loose."

I paused to consider a way to express my next point, and found myself appealing directly to Clinical Director Clarissa Rowland. "I didn't invite these difficult feelings to invade my personality. But the feelings are there, and I'm willing to try to figure it out. But I'm not in control of any of this. At least not yet."

"How can this stalker possibly help you?" There was the barest hint of sarcasm in Rowland's voice, a sarcasm of which she was almost surely unaware. "Does he play a role in this? Can you guess which character he's supposed to be in the story?"

"I think there's something this man wants to give me," I said, "and I still don't know whether it's good or bad. But I'm pretty sure it has something to do with a considerable amount of money that belongs to me."

The clients were impressed. After a brief pause, Rowland said: "Okay, let's get to the bottom of this. What is his intent in following you? What does he want from you?"

"Maybe he wants to give me something."

She hesitated, briefly flummoxed. "We're running on fumes here. We have no idea what this imaginary man's reasoning is. Or what he wants to give you. For all we know, it might be a bomb. Or a"—Rowland was temporarily overcome—"what the hell *does* he want to give you?"

"Treasure!" said the fraudulent building contractor sitting next to me. "Money, gold, it could be anything!" He leaned forward to regard me with a gaze that was intense but not unfriendly. "Now that you've told us, sir, be careful where you go with this. I mean that in a nice way."

Rowland was not amused. "If there were treasure here, it would have been discovered long ago, and I would have put it to good use!"

"His opinion is as good as any," I said, nodding to the faux contractor, "although in the case of hidden treasure, there is always the possibility that it could be a trick. In some perverse minds, a treasure could be—well, a bad thing, a kind of sabotage."

Clarissa Rowland rolled her eyes and looked at the ceiling, and briefly appeared to be appealing directly to me to disavow the idea of hidden booty; but I found that I rather liked the idea of hidden treasure, and what it implied of some dramatic and previously misunderstood fate.

"Treasure!" insisted the wannabe building contractor. He lifted his hat up and gestured at me with it, then put it back on. "You have no idea how much hidden stuff is out there, hidden in walls and under floors." He surveyed the group triumphantly. "It might not even be buried, you understand—just hidden."

"Yes, of course," Clarissa Rowland said in a low voice, "and now I will tell you what *I* think it means. This is classic. *Classic.*"

She leaned back and once more looked at the ceiling. "There is this fantasy, a generic delusion that keeps popping up in the literature. It has sometimes been called 'the Lost Estate.' People in the midst of hard times believe that they, or their family, were once fantastically wealthy . . . and of course, it's just a matter of time until the *true heir* to the estate is discovered, and the proud, foundling prince, the rightful recipient of the fortune, is escorted to his palatial family estate where he proceeds to live in the very lap of luxury. Or perhaps our harried pilgrim's family had titles in Europe, or once enjoyed every manner of aristocratic privilege—"

"White privilege," murmured the African-American man.

"Well, as a matter of fact," I said, but Rowland interrupted. "No. *No.* Keep your stories of lost estates until tomorrow. I'll give you a one-on-one session then. Now let's talk about somebody else's problems." She looked around the room. "Who wants to start?"

Chapter 2

On May 9, 1661, Thys Barentsen van Leerdam sailed into the colony of *Nieuw Nederland* on the *St. Jan Baptist*, skippered by the capable Captain Jan Bergen, and presented himself at Fort James, on the very tip of the island called Mannahattas by the tribal people, and Nieuw-Amsterdam by the Dutch colonial administration. The name Thys Barentsen van Leerdam was patronymic, literally meaning Thys, the son of Barent, with Leerdam being the Dutch town that he came from. He was accompanied by his wife Scytie Cornelis and their three children, age 15, 10 and 1 year old . . . also accompanying them were family friends Jan Teunissen, Walraven Luten, and the outspoken Pieter Billiou, a French-speaking Huguenot originally hailing from the Canton of Vaud. Two months previously, all had departed Amsterdam looking for a new life in the Dutch colony of New Netherlands.

Thys Barentsen from Leerdam almost immediately bought land on Staaten Eylandt, and was appointed a *schepen*, or magistrate, by the Dutch General-Director of New Netherlands, Pieter Stuyvesant; this automatically made him part of Stuyvesant's governing council. His friend Billiou became the sheriff of Ould Dorp, the first town on Staaten Eylandt. Thys Barentsen's ascendance to magistrate was seemingly automatic and done without opposition, either by prearrangement or—more likely—because nobody else wanted the job. The established colonists in Nieuw Nederland were already too familiar with Stuyvesant's temper to attend his rare council meetings unless absolutely necessary, or unless ordered to do so by Stuyvesant himself. No doubt it was thought by most that he would do whatever he wanted anyway.

From studying related documents of the time we can determine the identities of the three children of Thys Barentsen van Leerdam. The fifteen-year-old would be Bernard or Barent (or "Barnt," as he was usually called); the ten-year-old would be the daughter Beleyte; the toddler would be Anthony. Barent and Beleyte were the children of a first wife, from a French Huguenot family that had immigrated to the Netherlands; the clever Anthony was the son of the second wife, Scytie Cornelis. (His brother Willem would come later.) There had been other children—perhaps many of them—that did not survive; nor did children linger at home when able to work or marry. Boys were expected to help their fathers tend crops and animals, to become apprentices and learn a trade at twelve or thirteen, or attend one of the harsh schools of the Dutch Reformed Church. The average age for marriage of girls at that time was about sixteen years of age. All of Thys' children were literate, however, including his daughter Beleyte.

They had come to a good place for crops and grazing cattle. Staaten Eylandt was eight miles wide at the widest point, and a good thirteen miles long. It was bounded by the Atlantic Ocean on the east, the "Narrows" on the north, and on the west by Kill Van Kull and Arthur Kill, with Raritan Bay to the south. The first settlement consisted of Thys Barentsen and eighteen other families, which settlement became known as Ould Dorp, or Old Town, not far from South Beach.

And so it was that on August 22, 1661, Thys Barentsen, Peter Bielliou, and Paulus Direck stood before Pieter Stuyvesant and coolly announced that "the locality of Staaten Eylandt suited them well, and they requested therefore that some of the lands on said Staaten Eylandt might be allotted and given to them as property for farmland, meadow and pasture, and that lots for houses and gardens might be *laid out at a convenient place.*"

Amazing, the casual arrogance of it, when seen in retrospect! They did not posture themselves as humble partners in the precarious experiment of New Netherlands; they simply arrived and claimed that part of it they coveted. Note that they not only wanted living quarters, but *lots* for gardens as well—at a *"convenient place."* A convenient place! The dream, you see—which is to say *their* dream, was of a bourgeois but tasteful comfort, abutted and justified by a thoughtful and unalienable Constitution, in their case the Constitution of the United Provinces of the Dutch Republic. As supporters of the Dutch Republic they styled themselves good republicans all, but there is no mistaking the imperial—that is, the *imperious*—nature of the way they established themselves in this New World place.

And partly because of that imperious attitude, this is a story of how a curse, a *maldición*, is allegedly made—or *laid*—against an entire offending family, either by those offended, or by those who have witnessed some great wrong; and how such curses can become secret over generations, making the curse ever more malignant when entire families are not conscious of it. But it was not Thys Barentsen van Leerdam who caused the curse, but rather his son Barent, the privileged young *Barnt*, who was everywhere at once in various struggles real and imagined against authorities both British and Dutch. The nightmare of which he would become the unknowing, sleepwalking protagonist was a dream of infinite land ownership; in time it was precisely this dream that would morph into a nightmare, to such an extent that those lost in its wastelands could no longer tell the difference between a succubus and a pleasant reverie, between normal ambition and irrevocable evil.

Thirty years after arriving in New Netherlands, Barnt would take one side in a civil conflict, for reasons both of pride and an insane love, thinking he was doing something good and necessary, and instead doing something terrible. It is an old story, variations on the sins of Adam and Cain, criminals who, if the Bible is right, were also our first family. If a butterfly's wings in China can change the course of a whole epoch ten thousand miles across the world, so can an egregious crime continue to victimize people after many centuries. I am, as the reader may have guessed, a descendent of Thys Barentsen van Leerdam, so this entire matter is more than academic to me.

It was a dangerous gamble of Barnt—Thys Barentsen's oldest son—that resulted in the fact that I, and several thousand other Americans, use the same surname. And why, once a month or more, he now appears in downtown New York, on this very same street, not to drink at his tavern or carouse with his roustabout friends, but—as I believe—to at last apologize, and make his case to me, and explain his reasons for acting out the perfidy that named, branded and claimed us. I do not know why he chose me, but I do know that by making his case directly to a descendent, he sought to at last be free of the sin of 1691. But at the same time, I could not be sure to what extent his atonement might, by its violent and disturbing nature, compromise me as well.

Chapter 3

I went out on the morning of my second day at Voyager House to shop for clothes at a local secondhand place. The place was quite disorganized; in the 1950s such establishments were known as "jumble shops," and in this case the name fit admirably. I got some basic items of clothing, nothing too old or too new, in order to avoid attracting attention to myself. Best of all, I was able to purchase a beautiful, rust-colored smoking jacket, appropriately shabby but with remnants of a shawl collar, front pockets, turn-around cuffs and intact tie belt—the perfect garment for lounging about in one's residential mental health program.

I feigned indifference to the jacket—which the owner immediately noticed, having seen such gambits every day of his working life—but I was able to buy it for only twelve dollars. "Where on earth did you get this beautiful smoking jacket?" I asked the owner after he had put my money away in a wooden drawer.

"We have a deal with Trinity. With their used clothing shop."

"Trinity Church, you mean."

He looked at me over his twisted-wire reading glasses, of a kind that has, for at least the third time in my lifetime, become quite popular. "Well, if it's got Trinity in the name, it's bound to be some kind of church. That's the only Trinity I know about in this neighborhood."

"Not only a church, but a very famous one," I added.

I noticed that the shop-owner's clothes were not at all secondhand, but doggedly fashionable, and he exuded cologne. I repressed the desire to tell him that his small teeth were far too well-maintained for his jumbled secondhand station in lower Manhattan; furthermore, I could already imagine, and in fact could not stop imagining, the neo-Dickensian character that might with much more verisimilitude inhabit this disordered place, instead of this self-conscious dandy in a new suit. These were not delusions, I point out, but merely pleasant fantasies.

But I did not share these particular fantasies with the shop-owner. "Do you also get garments from Saint Paul's Chapel?" I asked.

"That's part of Trinity Church, isn't it?"

"Yes, yes, of course. I'd forgotten."

Since the wind-hawk of the Hudson River was shrieking just outside the door, I also bought a battered leather bomber jacket which was far too big for me, but warm. I thought about how nice it would be to go to Trinity Cemetery, but I knew I didn't have the energy to get there. Too bad, because there is a collateral ancestor of mine buried there, a loyalist who abandoned the American Revolution in New Jersey to go to New York, where the British were still firmly in control. Then, unexpectedly—just after making a place for himself in British-controlled territory—he gave up the ghost. I've always felt this was somehow rather clever of him, to die so quickly after abandoning the patriot cause. For me there has always been a bizarre integrity about it that eludes all attempts at analysis.

"I thought I'd visit one of the burial places, but I've changed my mind now," I said, putting on the bomber jacket. It was so old the leather in front was almost white, but the zipper worked. "I just don't have the energy these days to get to the Trinity burial place, even if I hop the bus. Some days my body hurts all over. It's the weather, maybe."

And now the owner of this secondhand shop, the reigning monarch of a secondhand world, sighed and nodded. "When we get old, there are some things that can't be done anymore. If we tried, we'd run the risk of getting seriously hurt."

"I mean, I'd like to walk there, but—"

"That particular Trinity Cemetery is quite a way uptown, if it's the one I'm thinking of."

"I'm afraid so."

"Ed Koch is buried there," he added mysteriously.

I pondered that for a moment before deciding to let it go. "Well now," I said, "there you are."

Having had enough of the secondhand shop, I quickly gathered up my new-old garments and started back to Voyager House. I was scheduled for a one-on-one counseling session with the director, Clarissa Rowland, right after lunch; and I looked forward to it, because I liked everything about this endlessly energetic woman, including her name.

As a child I was able to avoid grade school through the fortuitous intervention of severe asthma, and it was at this time that I read the epistolary novel *Clarissa, or, the History of a Young Lady*, by Samuel Richardson. The Clarissa of this novel was driven mad by her family, whose New Money caused them to obsessively pursue men with titles, resulting in Clarissa's death in a brothel. That deliciously horrific story—with its delicious denouement—came across to me even then as a garish parody of Jane Austin–type ambition and social climbing. But the beauty of the name stayed with me.

2.

My one-on-one counseling session with Clarissa Rowland was to be held in a small room at the end of the hall on the second floor, a place once probably intended for a servant or cook, or perhaps (or so I imagined) the enforced confinement of the occasional young girl in a family way. I say "enforced confinement" because there were no windows in the room; it had probably also been used for storage at some point. I do not know how old the house was, but I'd place it somewhere in the late Victorian era: it was not well-constructed, but it was not badly constructed either. Interestingly, just across from the small room a red, neon EXIT sign had been recently installed above a steel door leading to a fire escape.

As the time for my one-on-one psychotherapy session with Director Rowland approached, I poured an especially strong cup of coffee and took it with me into the small room. There were photographs of clients push-pinned to the wall, and an abandoned computer over in the corner; it was all oddly cozy. Therefore, the small room did not make me feel claustrophobic, despite the fact that the first thing Rowland did was to close the door.

"Confidentiality," she said by way of explanation.

"Speak freely—I'll never tell."

"No, no, no, it's not like that," she said, sitting down across from me and briskly opening my chart. "You can say whatever you want to about *me*. I just don't want other clients hearing what you say about *yourself*."

"Thank you."

I had worn my tattered new-old twelve-dollar smoking jacket to the counseling session, and Rowland noticed it. "Well," she said, "a new garment. What style is it?"

I was delighted that she asked about its style, not what it was. "It's called 'shabby genteel,'" I explained. "Also 'genteel poverty' and 'threadbare gentility,' stylistic conceptions originating amongst poor and overly ambitious intellectuals anxious to pass themselves off as landless gentry. Thackeray wrote a very nice story about it called 'A Shabby Genteel Story.'"

"Can you remember anything about it?"

"Not really."

"Well, there you are." This greatly amused her, and she cackled pleasantly. "Isn't posturing oneself as a 'type' invariably somewhat pretentious?"

"Yes."

"You are pretending to be someone or something, then."

"I have no reason not to—I enjoy it, and I don't see that it hurts anyone."

She went back to reading my chart. "Have you by chance

remembered your age, and if you remember, are you willing to tell me what it is?"

"Old."

"Do you care to tell me what your *numerical* age is? Ballpark?"

"As strange as it may seem to you, I experience that as a violation of my privacy."

"I suppose it is, in a way." She closed the chart and looked at me. "I think that knowing someone's age could be helpful in a medical emergency."

"Again, thanks."

"The EMS doctors believe that you are delusional, but they also wonder if by chance you are suffering from a short-term reactive psychosis. Basically, they deferred diagnosis so that you could be observed at Voyager House. They also said that you had fantasies and dreams of killing yourself . . . at least enough to recommend an emergency referral to residential treatment."

"Yes," I said.

"What really worries me, though, is the speculation by some of the doctors at Bellevue that you're experiencing some kind of extremely late onset of bipolar disorder, which has now developed psychotic features. I've never heard of somebody getting bipolar onset so late in life . . . which is one reason why I wanted to know how old you are."

"Okay."

"The Bellevue shrinks were wondering if some of these delusional thoughts were brought on by your intensive genealogical work at this . . . this"—she consulted the chart again—"genealogical library of this Netherland Society, on Forty-Fourth Street. They say you told them that you believe you are being stalked by an ancestor of yours who was somehow responsible for everything bad that's happened to you. Couldn't that obsession have been generated by reading about your ancestor in this genealogical library?"

"No, you've got it ass-backward, just like the psychiatrists.

The delusion, as you call it, came in long before I started the genealogical work. The genealogy in no way generated the delusion, but was an attempt after the fact to determine why it takes the form it does."

"Ha." She thought about this. "Okay, but you're aware that it's delusional."

"I'm aware that you *call* it a delusion," I said. "Use a clinical word to describe it if you wish—that doesn't in any way make it less problematic to me, any less difficult to get into perspective. Call it an obsession, if you wish. Surely it is to some extent an obsession."

"And along with that, you *do* have some fantasies of self-harm."

"Because I get tired of it. I can't turn these thoughts off. I want to stop the story that keeps playing in my head, but I don't believe I can until I bring the story to some kind of conclusion. And I don't know what that conclusion is."

"But this ghost—this guy—who's stalking you, doesn't he know how the story ends?"

"Not definitively. He simply understands that I have a role to play in the story, as though it's a kind of real-world, real-time theatre, set in the present moment in New York City. You could even say *improvisational* theater. After I figure out what my role in it is, then I will be able to move the story toward some kind of conclusion. Whether it will be a good ending or an apocalyptic one I do not know. But I get damn tired of it all because—well, so far I'm not in control of any of it."

"So you feel like putting a period to the story by killing yourself?"

"Sometimes."

"Instead of ending the story, why not simply try participating in it?"

"That may come down to the same thing. Once I get into the story I might not be able to see the larger narrative arc."

"What about the treasure that the errant ancestor is supposed to bring you?" Rowland was starting to smile again. "Isn't it worth sticking around to see what that will be? Maybe you can trade in that shabby genteel jacket for a good four-hundred-dollar blazer at Brooks Brothers."

"You sound like a telemarketer." I drank from my coffee, and took my time answering her. "To tell you the truth, I don't know what to make of my situation. It's scary. I mean, I'm simply too old for some transcendent, overwhelming new experience, no matter how wonderful. Besides, the million-dollar goldmine usually involves brand-new responsibilities, things that you don't see at first. And my so-called 'treasure' might end up being nothing more than a series of garish punishments for a lifetime of self-centered irresponsibility."

"Uh-huh." She smiled. "Maybe an old wife or lover will make an appearance."

"I hope they come in my dreams, so I don't have to get up and socialize with them."

She laughed mightily and then shook her head slowly. "My God, what great insight you have. Who wants to socialize with someone who may be a ghost, and a judgmental one at that?" She continued to shake her head. "But insight is only a beginning. It's never enough by itself."

"That's been my experience as well."

There was a very long pause.

"What on earth is this Holland Society?" she wanted to know.

I explained that the Netherland Society was a group of Americans descended from Dutch immigrant ancestors who had arrived in New Netherlands before 1675. They kept a low profile, held irregular meetings, and boasted a genealogical library with a professional genealogist available to assist members. I spent a fair amount of time there, but did all of my research myself, and went out of my way to be courteous whenever approached by staff, since—being homeless—I presented as less than respectable. On the other hand, nobody bothered me as long as I minded my own business, showered before visiting, and didn't doze off. The people who had over the years come to be regulars at the genealogy library were mildly eccentric, but not unbearably so; actually they were a quiet and studious lot, and most of them kept their distance from me, and from each other.

"Is it, like, a snob organization?"

"No," I said, "I don't believe so. The Netherland Society's members tend to be ordinary middle-class Americans that are interested in the history of New York, which was once New Netherlands. But they are free to think of themselves as they will, I suppose. They keep a low profile and certainly don't advertise themselves in the media, and I happen to know they do some good work."

"And you are a member of this organization?"

"Yes, but I haven't paid my dues for this year." My Social Security check was supposed to go directly into my bank account every month, but had stopped arriving some time ago. "So what do you think? Am I obsessive, or am I still delusional, in your book?"

"Both, I'm afraid. Or maybe you're just a gifted malingerer."

"Everybody is a malingerer," I said rather loudly. I had expected this objection, and had my answer prepared. "In fact malingering is itself a pathology deserving of treatment, according to—"

"Never mind," she said, "you don't have to convince *me*. If malingering wasn't pathological, I'd have no excuse for not finishing my housework on the weekends."

3.

This session with Clarissa Rowland was fairly typical of all the one-on-one counseling sessions we had during the time I was a client at Voyager House. There were a few changes as time went on, however. At first, Clarissa was most interested in my belief that I had been cursed. Then she gradually began to give more importance to the phantom ancestor, which she increasingly called a "ghost" (because she believed he was haunting me). Then she began to give more importance to the 'treasure' I was to receive or inherit, since she thought it could be transformative, a kind of salvation from the curse. But who could say it might not be a death sentence? I, for my part, began to see fleeting signs of my vagrant ancestor when I went out . . . quick glances of him turning the corner, or popping suddenly into a house or alleyway down the block. It did not seem threatening or strange—at least, not yet.

Interestingly, when I reported these sightings Clarissa Rowland asked me to sign a No Self-Harm Contract. This was a gambit I wasn't familiar with, so I asked her to explain.

"I write something out on a blank piece of lined notebook paper to the effect that you won't harm yourself, and we both sign it."

"How could *that* work?" I wanted to know. "If a suicidal client wanted to kill himself, wouldn't he sign the contract in order not to raise suspicion, and then go ahead and kill himself anyway?"

Clarissa explained that everybody had the same reaction, but for reasons that nobody completely understood, mental health clients actually made an effort to adhere to the wording of the contract. Sometimes they made a big deal of saying they wouldn't harm themselves while on the premises, which was a tip-off that they intended to engage in self-harm somewhere else—by jumping off a bridge, for example. So it was important to word the contract correctly. Clients developed relationships with the staff in residential programs, Clarissa said, and they didn't want to "get the staff in trouble" by breaking the contract.

"For example," she said, "let's say you signed this contract, and I also signed it, and you were depressed and feeling like ending it all. Would you go ahead and kill yourself?"

"No."

"Why not?"

I thought about it, and the truth of the matter was astonishing: *I wouldn't violate such a contract because I wouldn't want to cause unnecessary trouble or anxiety to the staff*, especially Clarissa Rowland. It was just that simple. The No Self-Harm Contract formalized my affection for Rowland—for her slightly manic laughter, for her unpredictable cackle, for the fact that she really cared about the clients in her program. It was astonishing that a simple, handwritten contract could have such power. All of it was based on daily associations in Voyager House, on the fact that in those daily interactions we had gotten to know each other, and in so doing saw that the other person's humanity as potentially just as important as our own.

There were a few other important themes that she harped on in our one-on-one counseling sessions. The things that most fascinated her, I noticed, were exactly the things that I tried not to think about. For example, Clarissa could not stop asking and talking about the importance of the "treasure," the money or valuables that my vagrant ancestor was likely to bring me. Once she suggested it, it came to feel like something new and unheralded in my life—perhaps some new insight, or new psychic power that I had not had before. My first reaction was that Rowland probably focused so much on the money because Voyager House was perennially short of funding, and therefore scorned its importance in my fantasy system; yet I increasingly came to assume that the money, if it manifested itself at all, would be of such an enormous amount as to be beyond my wildest imaginings.

I gathered that the idea of treasure came from beyond one's consciousness, from spiritual and psychological powers over which one had little control, and were for that reason a special idea to Rowland, a kind of controlling metaphor, as a literary critic might say. I gradually came to agree with her regarding the important of the treasure, partly because of her own enthusiasm for the idea . . . in any case, was not life itself—or at least consciousness—a mysterious benefaction from well beyond our own daily intentions?

It was natural that I would associate the idea of treasure with Old Money, since my father was disinherited for marrying my mother. The loss of an inherited fortune was an enormous reality in our family, although rarely discussed. Thus, the interesting paradox that my father certifiably came from Old Money, but had no access to the money itself—a dilemma not unlike my own. I did not mention this to Clarissa, wishing instead to hear her fantasies of the treasure I was to inherit.

"You yourself say that these things I'm struggling with are part of a delusion," I pointed out reasonably. "I try not to think about what comes next. Would you have me believe my own delusions?"

"No, not believe them, but listen to them. What we dream, what we imagine, are often signals of something that is coming up over the horizon. They prepare us for the next step."

"Or warn us that something bad is on the way."

"More often they prepare us, whether the thing is good or bad. That way, it may start out as bad, and evolve into something good."

Perhaps, she suggested—or at least I remember her as suggesting this—there were two or three opportunities in every life to do something supremely important. One was the opportunity to change history for the better, which usually involves great risk and sacrifice. But it could also be a more private gamble, with lowball odds but with seemingly unlimited applications. What it all meant in my case, I could not say. But I was grateful for Clarissa's sure and certain idea that for me there was indeed a boundless treasure waiting outside the limits of my previous experience, which I associated rather vaguely with the idea of Old Money. But inherited from whom? How was the contract negotiated, and according to what terms? The idea scared me a little, but to anticipate something that was completely unknown was one way, I had to admit, to take the story to the next level.

4.

I saw him on my street in the late afternoon, first hurrying away from me, and then into an alleyway between two buildings. I hadn't been sure before, but now I knew. It was Thys Barentsen's oldest son, Barnt, the reckless young adventurer and scapegrace son of the magistrate. But why the hell was he here, and why did he keep appearing? Why was he hurrying away from me? What was he afraid of, or was he afraid of *my* fear? I didn't know, but this was how I always saw him, in my first few sightings of him, always turning a corner or dodging behind an iron fence or a building. The big question, however, was this: why did he continue to avoid me, when I *knew* that he was seeking me out? Was I supposed to do something to cause him to change his mind? Or was that part of a paradox that I would simply have to live with?

That night I was quiet at dinner. Clarissa Rowland had joined us for the evening meal, as she did twice a week, and was giving a great deal of attention to Harley, our young paranoid schizophrenic, whose passion was intergalactic war, and the weapons by which space warriors killed each other. "What do you mean," Clarissa was saying, "*Star Wars* was tacky? Could you have designed better weapons than Lucas?"

"No comparison."

"I'd like to see your sketches, then."

"I can't show them to anyone, because you-know-why." He nodded toward the rest of us at the table.

Harley sought to patent all his space weapons, but so far the US Patent Office had not answered his inquiries. He was pretty sure that meant that someone had stolen his ideas, or was about to do so. So he had decided not to take any chances. Although he carried his sketch notebooks with him, nobody knew where he kept them at night, or on those rare occasions when he did not bring them to the table during meals.

At a certain point in the meal Clarissa announced some interesting news. "I think we're going to get a new client tomorrow." She was sitting next to me, and now she turned to smile directly at me. "You will be getting a new roommate. Lucky you!"

"Great," I said. I wasn't necessarily thrilled with the idea, but it was only fair—I was the only client without a roommate. "Being able to talk to someone on a daily basis is itself therapeutic, especially to a semi-recluse like me."

"That's very gracious of you," she said.

I was thinking I might go to bed early this night, by way of enjoying my solitude one last time, so I went upstairs after doing chores. At the head of the stairs I saw Neil puttering around in the staff office, preparing for his last overnight shift of the week. "How's the psych classes?" I asked. "Are you being sufficiently challenged?"

"Not so much. I'm thinking of changing my major to anthropology."

"Why?"

"I'm going for the big money." He laughed a little too hard, as though he'd been living with this particular joke too long.

"You can always teach," I said, trying to sound helpful.

"Everybody says that."

"Never mind—I absolve you for whatever failures you have incurred. This mental health client absolves you."

"You're probably the only person that could."

"I mean, look how successful I've been."

As I came down the hall I decided I needed a quick consult with my aging bladder, and ducked into the bathroom. Afterward, as I washed my hands, I experienced a touch of vertigo, and noticed something bleary about the mirror, as though my reflection was under the influence of occult forces. As

I came out of the bathroom, I saw a movement down the hall. It was just a few feet away from the neon EXIT sign that was across from the room where I normally met for counseling with Clarissa Rowland.

It was a man standing there with his back to me. It was as though he was trying to make up his mind whether to exit or not. I remember wishing that he would turn around, so I could see his face.

"Hey," I said.

I wanted to say, *Can I help you?*, but couldn't get the words out.

He turned in the uncanny slow way that often happens in a dream. It even occurred to me that I was *in* a dream—or if not a dream, an illusion or daydream, as if I was dreaming with my eyes open. Or maybe I was slowly waking up, but the dream I'd been having was still going on. I had heard about epileptics having temporal lobe hallucinations, and that's what this felt like. It was like slow motion, something outside of time.

Then I saw his face. I felt a shudder pass through me, and an impulse to run. But I couldn't run, because I couldn't move.

He was smiling. I had the feeling he might be about to speak; instead he slowly shook his head. But he was still smiling.

Sorry, I thought he was saying, except not with words. *I won't hurt you.* That's what I thought he was saying, although there were still no words, and no sound.

He was moving very slowly, and then faster, like a reflection of a mirror—and then, suddenly, like a bat out of hell, he slammed open the EXIT sign door, and shot outside. The steel door slammed open against a fire escape, and then instantly slammed shut; but these two things occurred without any noise, like something seen in a silent film. It wasn't a frightening thing, necessarily; it was just shocking, that something so dreamlike could happen without making any noise. Nothing had prepared me for that. But I had seen enough to know, now, that this was the young man of whom I'd been catching glimpses of for several weeks.

But now — well, now he'd appeared in the hallway at Voyager House, and he had been smiling, smiling, smiling. It seemed to me he had gone out of his way not to frighten or alarm.

I went into my room and sat down on my bed. I was trembling all over, but what had just happened settled in my mind in the sequences in which it had occurred. I thought about all the things I had just seen, and what they meant. Things were happening very fast, but now I understood something important about it.

Now, I thought, I knew who my new roommate would be.

Chapter 4

It might seem that Bernard, son of Thys Barentsen, would be a total stranger to me, given that he lived so long ago. But because of my interest in genealogy—and American history of that time—there were already a great many things that I already knew about Bernard (or the man who claimed to be Bernard) before he came to Voyager House. I knew that in the two decades after Bernard's arrival in Nieuw Nederland at the age of 15 in 1661—this is, during the 1660s and 1670s and finally the 1680s—people saw him as wild and unpredictable. I knew also that he was called Barnt by family and friends, and that he appears in documents under a variety of names. Overall, you get the feeling, when studying relevant documents of that time, that on some level he was perpetually engaged in trying to win the attention and possibly the affection of his father.

But after the Conquest in 1664, as Nieuw Nederland suddenly became New York under the English, there was a great deal that was going on, so much that it was difficult to keep it all straight; and one can understand that perhaps Barnt's father, Thys Barentsen, might have been more focused on protecting his various businesses than giving more attention to his oldest son (or any of his children, for that matter).

Thys and his family had arrived on May 9, 1661, the reader will remember; but in September 1664 the English took New Netherlands. Suddenly New Amsterdam was New York—and if that weren't confusing enough, in 1673 the Dutch actually won New Amsterdam back. But then—in 1674—in a *second* unthinkable reversal of fortune, it became English again under the *Second* Treaty of Westminster. The Whale Road that the Dutch had bravely dominated for so long had become a boulevard of broken dreams. Despite the fact that Dutch currency continued in New York for many decades after the Re-Conquest, slowly but surely the Dutch *riksdaalder* began to give way to British currency; and much later—after their own war with Britain—the new country America would embrace the "dollar," a distant echo of the *riksdaalder*. But for Dutch families in Nieuw Nederland after 1674, the republican dream of elegance and beauty under the United Provinces of the Netherlands gave way, of a painful and probably unavoidable necessity, to living in the English dream of empire.

How could it have happened, that a robust, ocean-going nation such as the Netherlands could have been defeated by such a race of shopkeepers, religious versifiers, starving yeomen and minor gentry? It was still the same New Amsterdam on the day after the Treaty of Westminster changed everything; everybody felt the same, it was the same place, with the same people sailing in with the same goods and selling them to the same people. So how could it be that now another nation claimed it? It had happened for the simplest of reasons: the Dutch had long believed their own dreams of superiority on the sea, whereas the British had carefully counted up how many ships the Dutch had, and built more of them. Yet, to the Dutch families on Staaten Eylandt it all seemed like a dream for a long time after the reality imposed itself. After all, *Staaten Eylandt* had been named after the *Staaten-General*, the government of the States-General in Amsterdam. Now it was required of them to live in the empire of another country.

But the fact was, the reality was—and those who thought for more than a moment or two had long known this—it hadn't been a wholeheartedly Dutch colony before the 1674 English Re-Conquest changed everything. People in Nieuw Nederland had known in their bones that they were something new, something different than anything in the Netherlands, something that really didn't belong to any European country. It had been from the beginning a polyglot riot of people from every country in the world: Dutch, French, English, German, Flemish, low Saxon—

there were languages from everywhere, spoken by people from everywhere, including Africans, Jews and people from every imaginable port in the Caribbean.

The Dutch dream of endless elegance, accompanied by a flourishing economy and a just, well-regulated political establishment, had been inherited by all Dutch-speaking people in the colony; but those Dutch who were republicans had an especially high opinion of themselves, as the unacknowledged saviors of Europe and humankind generally. Had they not defended the lowlands—and therefore Europe itself—against the corrupt French and Spanish Bourbon monarchies? Interestingly, this loathing of the Catholic monarchies created a significant area of agreement between the English and Dutch, since it was not so very long since the English themselves had fought and defeated the Spanish Armada.

Nieuw Nederland had been a success story for very different reasons for all the others, because for many reasons it had become a kind of refuge for non-Dutch of many nations who were homeless, including those with missing arms and legs but still able to beg or work or sail, slop hogs or clean out ovens, many of whom were running from a past they mostly declined to talk about; and it was therefore a home also for hard-drinking roustabouts and whores in taverns on the lookout for sailing men, not to mention some young men who were unafraid to seize life by the collar, sometimes by marrying strong-willed, exotic women whose languages they could not even speak particularly well.

They were, consequently, a people who all ended up speaking a little of every language, at least enough to do business; and very shortly not many spoke High Dutch at all, except in a few families who loved the sound of it, and partly because the Dutch Reformed Church used it for liturgical purposes. Even Thys Barentsen from Leerdam was more likely to speak French with his Walloon neighbor Billiou, who was now the sheriff of Staten

Island, and English with the merchants who now brought fine things from Paris and London. Meanwhile, Jersey Dutch was becoming the colloquial lingua franca among traders in East Jersey and many parts of Staaten Eylandt, a wild mixture of Low Dutch, English and the language of the Lenape tribal people. Jersey Dutch was a home language, wild, colorful and attuned to survival and the things of the earth, whereas High Dutch was for church or for the denunciation of one's political enemies.

The Dutch families that had risked everything to come to this place were not persecuted, but they were no longer deferred to as before. After 1674 they no longer had power, or the same kind of power, even though Thys Barentsen remained magistrate of Staaten Eylandt. It was a great coming down in the world, to be sure; but prison and disgrace and death did not await them, as it had for many another people who lost wars in the pursuit of empire. The Dutch families knew how to work hard, to support themselves well, and to above all to make good marriages— sometimes with the English that now flocked to the colony. The kind of people who had wanted to live in a rough colony like New Netherlands were likely to land on their feet no matter what happened in the struggles of the great imperial powers.

Thys Barentsen was the first to graze large herds of cattle, on his own land and much of the unsettled and unclaimed lands as well, his cattle-brand becoming the first on Staaten Eylandt. His ambition was already becoming the goal of all whose countries have been defeated in seagoing wars, to become wealthy and establish his family in the new world they had already been engaged in inventing. If the dream of an enlightened *national* exuberance was to some extent now lost, Thys had already internalized much of it and made of its rich sensibilities a driving force of his personal dream.

At first the Dutch agreed, those that talked among themselves, that the reversal of fortune was only temporary. Surely the Dutch, whose ship captains were the cleverest on earth, would win back the colony. The Dutch and English were not even at war when the decisive loss occurred, in 1674; it had happened as the result of treaty negotiations, an afterthought on the part of the English commanders. New Netherland had, after all, been bracketed on both sides by much larger English settlements, the Puritans of Massachusetts and the planters of Virginia. But it was not long until the older Dutch settlers stopped talking about the Conquest of 1664 and the Re-Conquest of 1674. For one thing, they did not want their children to hear it, and repeat it among their English friends, since that might make them seem like enemies of the colony's new administrators, who after all were taking many steps to accommodate the Dutch clergy and traders.

When it was all said and done, there were many times more English people than Dutch in this part of the New World; England was itself twice as big as the Netherlands. England was consciously pursuing an ambitious imperial strategy, whereas the Netherlands had taken its smaller empire for granted. And the Dutch were, when it came right down to it, a trading and commercial nation and not a warlike one: the hard-working Dutch farmers, merchants and traders did not have an appetite for a prolonged war against the British in the New World, especially since the English crown could recruit troops from the settlements on either side of New Netherlands. Serious resistance would end catastrophically for the Dutch-speaking minority.

The truth was, the English triumph over the Dutch in 1664 had been to some extent inevitable; and due to the growing ascendancy of England on the seas and in the European religious wars, it gradually began to seem irreversible. Barnt's father, Thys Barentsen, was wise enough to see this, and dealt with it in the classic manner of those living in recently defeated nations: by retreating into the world of memory, of family, and of religious speculation, sweetened by the comforts of wealth. Barnt well understood his father's attitude in this matter. Barnt had been eighteen years old the first time the British took over New Netherlands, at a time when he had become aware that his father's fortune was to some extent his also. But although the oldest son might have a certain prestige among siblings, Dutch estates were divided equally among children, including girls, at the death of the patriarchs.

So Barnt sought something else, something wilder, something bigger, something (to be honest) without the limits associated with the rule of law. And so it was that he fell in with a group of wild young men who were dreamers, but also heavy drinkers and fighters, although with enough republican ideas that the gruesome habit of dueling had not become an obsession among them, as it had in some quarters of Europe. That was lucky for them, for otherwise a good half of them would have perished on the dueling fields.

They regularly gathered together, partly to mourn in their various youthful escapades the disappointment attached to the loss of the Dutch dream of New Netherland; but Barnt had grown up speaking English as well as Dutch, and spoke it regularly after he was fifteen with very little accent. And he was not alone in that regard. So you cannot call what he felt exclusively a form of Dutch nationalism, as some have said. It was something else, a dream without outer limits, and because Barnt and his friends did not always have words to describe it, it became for some a narcissistic dream that corrupted the dreamer; something with a certain aggression in it, something self-serving, something a bit insane, and something that consciously or unconsciously sought out—as projects of young males very often do—its own doom.

To some extent this darkness had always been in the land where they had settled, the word for Staaten Eylandt having always been "the bad woods," in the language of the Raritan tribe of the Lenni Lanape, the tribal people that had preceded the Dutch on the island. The thickest part of the woods was a place to be avoided by the Raritans, but therefore the Bad Woods was also a magical place and a place of dangerous wonders, a place that young braves would dare each other to enter; and the brave that entered it, and spent the night there, would quite naturally brag about it, if indeed he survived and came home to his clan.

When Barnt and his friends had to describe what they wanted in words, the band of young adventurers spoke of the tradition of the patroonship, or a revival of same, both in a sort of defused cultural sense, but also in the original political meaning. They spoke, that is, of a bold new application of this patroon system, stretching not just across Staaten Eylandt but inland, unlimited by modern ideas and designs, and unlimited also by the ability of government to regulate or govern them; and unlimited also in the way that Europeans coming to America were starting to comprehend the unlimited expanse of the land, and of the availability of that land to the bravest and the foolhardiest who would risk their lives in it.

The patroonship that Barnt and his friends idealized was the largest kind of manorial estate, and on this oversized estate the Dutch patroon was literally the Lord of the Manor. He was a landed aristocrat in everything but title. Those that lived in his fiefdom were under his authority, and could be tried in his court, as he was automatically magistrate of his own estate. Such patroonships were awarded in Amsterdam, beginning in 1629, but were also awarded by the British after 1674, for the same reason that the Dutch had done—to stimulate settlement. The patroon was optimistically expected to attract at least fifty families through his own efforts; these families would pay taxes to him for ten years, and afterward rent. Some patroonships had their own churches, and the settlements had the potential of becoming towns or trading villages.

If Barnt and his reckless young friends had spent more time asking the advice of those who knew what they were talking about, they would have discovered that there had already been an attempt to establish a patroonship on Staten Island, one that failed miserably. This campaign was launched by Cornelis Melyn, who was driven out of Staaten Eylandt in 1655, only six years before Thys Barentsen arrived with his family.

Cornelis Melyn, a violent misfit who was also a dreamer, was defeated in three decisive battles by the Raritan tribe that had inhabited the island for the previous several thousand years. The Raritans were a very old part of the larger Lenape people, and fought fiercely and unremittingly; but by the 1650s their ranks were so depleted by the fighting that they became easy targets for other tribes that wished to displace them. Despite their victory over Melyn, it was necessary for the remaining Raritan to fall back to East Jersey to defend their ancestral lands there.

Over the course of several major battles on Staaten Eylandt, as many as a hundred people lost their lives. Disgusted by the ineptitude of the Dutch colonial administration—which had him imprisoned without trial—Cornelis Melyn left Staaten Eylandt in disgust with his family, swearing an oath of allegiance to the English crown in New Haven colony on April 7, 1657. It was these defeats, the last of which occurred in 1655, that caused Thys Barentsen and the eleven other families of Ould Dorp, or Old Town, to hastily build a blockhouse in case of further attacks when they arrived in 1661. As for Cornelis Melyn, he relinquished his right to the patroonship of Staaten Eylandt in 1659.

Although they were victorious, the Raritan sustained too many casualties, which robbed the tribe of its energy and confidence, and was so weakened that they were mainly displaced in East Jersey by their tribal enemies. Staaten Eylandt was the location of the Raritan burial ground, the oldest burial place in the colony, so there was no doubt they had good reason to defend it; but they did not have the fighters to do so. Since the patent-owner Melyn had retreated to New Haven colony, and therefore given up his right to the patroonship of Staaten Eylandt, the idea of the island being ruled by a single person quickly became an absurdity. Melyn came to be seen as a quixotic failure, another example of the sin of pride, and therefore a grisly joke in the taverns of Mannahattas to be roundly laughed out of court.

Besides, after 1661, when Thys Barentsen and this group of eleven families finally succeeded in settling Staaten Eylandt at Ould Dorp, a single patroon for Staaten Eylandt would never have been permitted by the Dutch-speaking republicans themselves, not to mention the French-speaking Walloons who arrived on the same boat; all considered themselves progressive supporters of the Republic of the Seven United Netherlands. They had no objection to a patroonship located far inland, where only tribal people hunted and lived; but *they* had paid good money for their own land, and to be governed by some jumped-up fool with a patent would have struck them as an unseemly joke.

Meanwhile, Barnt and his friends apparently learned nothing from poor Melyn's fate, even though it was precisely the kind of cautionary tale they needed to hear. The very idea of Staaten Eylandt as a patroonship was enough to drive some people to fits of laughter; and in two or three recorded instances, elaborate toasts to the unfortunate deceased Melyn were made by certain drunken souls whose names are lost, and only to be guessed at. Why did Barnt and his crew not hear this, and understand just a little of what Melyn's failure meant? Because they were young and stupid, full of pride, and for those reasons attracted to perilous and self-destructive things.

Let us say this for Barnt: he could put in a full day's work. The land was being bought up at a ferocious rate in the 1670s, but Barnt managed to get his own place in 1676, on land given to him by his father at Karle's Neck near Fresh Kill. He got this land in the way many young people of that time did. He was obligated to stay home and help his parents for the rest of his adulthood if he was unattached, especially since his stepmother and father had become parents to other children. The winters were ferocious, and he was obliged to sleep on the floor in front of the fire. So how could Barnt ever get a place of his own?

He did so by introducing a sturdy Dutch girl to the passions of the flesh, which Barnt explained to her were designed by God to be irresistible, helpfully adding that it was the sacrament of an eternal love that would bind them both. Wide-eyed but unresisting she watched him as he took off her many garments and undergarments; her reasons for sexual congress were probably like his own, to get out from under the parents' roof. Within three months she was in a family way. The parents rushed to get them married: and it was now clear to everybody that Barnt *had* to have his own land, in order to support his new wife and a new grandchild waiting in the wings.

So he went to work raising corn, but that was not the real money crop; what made the most money was raising cattle near the unclaimed land where his father also grazed his livestock. The two of them could tell their stock apart by the cattle brands; his father had gotten quieter with time, apparently defeated by the march of events, but he concentrated marvelously on increasing his wealth. Barnt could see the wisdom of accumulating money, since it enabled his father to hire a few hands to help him with the chores.

It was the bi-weekly get-togethers with his roustabout friends during the warm summers that Barnt really enjoyed. They made a kind of rickety summer house on land owned by Barnt, with long tables and benches, and met there on Saturday afternoons to drink, plot, discuss the deaths of kings, and to be wild and irresponsible. As I have heard it, they adopted the camouflage of a secret fraternal order, of the kind that was popular in Europe, and even had a little oath of sorts that they took at the beginning of their meetings. During the late 1670s and early 1680s all the best subversive gossip was about the power the Catholics were accumulating in England, and the subsequent divisions within the English government.

Barnt and his friends were a group that had organized themselves for the defense of religious liberty, which at that time meant opposition to the Church of Rome, which they believed to be the Antichrist. And there were any number of rumors that this same Church of Rome, led by a calculating Pope and the Cardinals of France, was supposedly infiltrating and gradually taking over the government of Britain. If they succeeded in taking over the monarchy, that would mean Catholicism imposed on the colony of New York, and the destruction of the Dutch Reformed Church, not to mention the religious freedoms formerly guaranteed by the Dutch Republic. Nobody living at that time could have predicted the Glorious Revolution of 1688, a revolution within the very heart of the English monarchy; nor could they have imagined that spectacular circumstance in which the Dutch champion, William of Orange, would play the hero's part, to save the Protestantism of both Dutch and British in one fell swoop.

But in the late 1670s, the Glorious Revolution was not only unimagined but unimaginable, most of all by Barnt and his friends. The reality was, Barnt and his followers were young males spoiling for a fight. The Masonic-sounding oaths they took were overly imaginative play-acting of young men in a wilderness: in reality, their Dutch Protestantism was in no immediate danger. They could smell a fight, these disreputable young bloods; but they had not yet learned that when people look for a fight, the fight they find—or that finds them—often takes a form they would be incapable of imagining at the outset of their quest. The fight that found them would turn their world upside down; and would—among other things—cause Barnt and his brothers to think long and hard about what they were, and what their destiny in the New World really was.

It was, at least in part, about choosing a surname in place of the usual Dutch patronymic, without attracting too much attention to it. The ideal became a name that sounded English, yet not *too* English, or to invent or embrace a name that nobody could quite place—*that* could be politically useful, because you could discard it for another name if it was politically expedient to do so. You could find another name that was not so aggressively Dutch, but not unreservedly English either; so that politicians, pastors and merchants would be forced to say it respectfully, just to be on the safe side.

After 1674 a name that sounded overly English was seen as a too-eager accommodation to the English colonial administration. Therefore, it remained a kind of seventeenth-century dilemma of the Dutch in America: to use or not to use a Dutch patronymic. Barnt would continue to use a patronymic based on his father's name—Thysen, which meant son of Thys—until a violent and revolutionary turn of events made a different destiny necessary, for him and for his brothers.

Chapter 5

This was the day that Voyager House staff was scheduled to do their intake of my new roommate. This new roommate had, I believed, some insight into my burning conviction that I labored under a curse, as well as the mysterious treasure I wanted to know more about; therefore, I felt I was probably about to enter a new phase of my life, and was grateful to whatever powers were taking me into it. I awoke before 6:00 AM and shaved and showered with the speed of light, even before the night counselor had started writing in the progress notes. Instead of coffee I enjoyed a cup of tea in the gray-lighted kitchen, giving a silent toast to my loyalist ancestor buried in Trinity Church graveyard, a tea-swilling Anglican if ever there was one. In that kitchen I could hear—or felt that I could hear—the morning sounds of New York all around me, and gave thanks for New York as a *place*, not just in saga and song but as a location that one could find on a map, which was yet capable of generating sudden storms of powerful emotion, some dangerous and all challenging.

My collateral relative William Sydney Porter, also known as O. Henry, had looked deeply into the peculiar attraction of New York City and its multitudinous energies, perhaps never so tellingly as in the following story: a man thinks obsessively of nothing except escaping from New York, which he regards as a hellhole of corruption; but when given the opportunity to leave, he discovers—to his surprise and disappointment—that he is unable to do so. He is too attached to New York City; he is, in fact, a slave to it. His very existence depends on being somewhere in its domain.

O. Henry was the first to understand New York City *as an addiction.*

And it was exactly through those penetrating energies that I felt my salvation entering, as I stirred sugar substitute into my Irish Breakfast Tea in an empty kitchen. Despite the peripheral neuropathy that had stiffened my legs in the last two years, I was actually dancing, balancing excitedly on one foot and then the other, whistling to keep time with my private two-step. Life was good; the quest was upon me! If you waited long enough, if you had the gift of introspection, and even if you'd systematically suborned your creative imagination to achieve acceptance in polite society, sometimes the dreams and stories and answers you sought would come all at once, almost too quickly—perhaps no longer summoned by human agency, but nonetheless demanding to be seen and acknowledged by the human caught in its torrential currents.

2.

I heard the staccato of Clarissa Rowland's feet pitter-pattering up the stairs, and then pitter-pattering ever more dangerously down the same steps. She came trippingly into the kitchen—I cannot think of another word to describe her entrance—and said happily, "I knew you would be awake!"

"How?"

She was gathering up coffee and coffee-fillers for her morning ritual of making coffee in the pantry.

"Synchronicity!" she chirruped happily. "Haven't you ever read Jung?"

"Yes, yes, of course, but I don't see that synchronicity is such an original concept. Everybody knows that things can share a causal relationship without sharing a meaning."

Her hair was slightly but marvelously disheveled, and I suppressed an urge to point out how she could rearrange it, the kind of suggestion only a husband or another woman might make. No, she would catch it herself later in the day, if she stopped long enough to look in a mirror.

"Maybe we're responding to the same thing," she said, "but

in different ways!"

"That sounds more like a conflict than synchronicity."

"You're such a party pooper!" she exclaimed, and shot off in the direction of the pantry. I hoped the night counselor was wide awake—Clarissa was a little early today.

It was a Thursday, and during the 10:00 AM check-in group the consulting psychiatrist for Voyager House sat in, accompanied by a youthful female intern who took copious notes. This same intern wore jeans, as well as a sweatshirt that read, *"To keep things simple, let's just assume that I'm right about everything,"* a phrase that perfectly characterized the attitude of the consulting psychiatrist, I thought. But I doubted that he would ever suspect that it was an indirect reference to him.

I tried to stay away from this consulting psychiatrist; besides being a bit dense, he was unpredictable and hostile, and he was encumbered with by unfortunate name, Woodrow J. Frelinghuysen, which I could hardly say without suppressing laughter. Furthermore, he had the power to kick clients he didn't like out of their residential placements; and he was so hostile, and so regularly pompous, that I was fearful we might end up quarreling. So I tried to give him a wide path. It is not widely known to the general public, but a great many psychiatrists are quite mad; the psychologists are a little better.

The interns, like all interns everywhere, tended to be quite personable; and the night counselors were without question the nicest of all. The overnight counselors of residential treatment are foot soldiers, not just of the mental health nonprofits, but of the American dream as well, going to college, raising families, and often working multiple jobs only vaguely connected to the mental health racket, usually receiving deplorable wages for their efforts.

I went up to my room before lunch to lie down; and of course—without at all trying to do so—I fell into the deep sleep that had eluded me the night before. The next thing I knew, someone was knocking at the door of my room. I sprang up, still half-asleep but oddly alert, and jerked open the door.

"Well," Rowland shrieked cheerfully, "don't you want to meet your new roommate?"

I momentarily lost the powers of speech. "I thought he was coming just after lunch."

"It *is* just after lunch—you slept through the noon meal."

I shook my head. "So my roommate's here?"

"Downstairs. Come on down and meet him. You can fill him in on how the place works, but don't forget that you and I have a one-on-one in forty-five minutes!"

"A one-on-one?" I said numbly, trying to remember what that meant in her world.

"Counseling session. In forty-five minutes."

My mind felt like it was still asleep, but in reality I was as wide awake as I'd ever been. It was a reasonably good reflection of the neuropathy that dogged my legs, a condition in which I was in perfect command of my intentions but couldn't quite act them out: that is, I was seeing things clearly, but understanding them too quickly to really assimilate anything, or to put them into any broad context. In short, I was a bit manic. When the mind races, it sometimes sees everything in incredible detail, but cannot form a coherent idea of what purposes those details might be serving.

"Come on, then," she said coaxingly.

I followed her down the stairs, hanging onto the railing because my legs were stiff; when I got to the first floor I turned sharply right. It was then that I got my first look at him. He was, of course, wearing a pea jacket, which I had somehow known he would, a classic Dutch or Frisian *pijjakker*, made of heavy blue twill. It extended well below the thighs, the kind for officers on the bridge, including the ubiquitous third mate who stood watch for everybody else who wanted to sleep at night. He had what appeared to be a two-day stubble. He could have been one of the healthier-looking bums on the bowery, a graduate student or a workman or even a professional on a Friday, when everybody dressed down—truth to tell, he could have been anything or anybody.

He was handsome in an unapologetic way, tall, neat except for the stubble, and deeply tanned, a guy who had seen things and been places. He appeared to be in his early forties, and in excellent shape. A single woman of comparable age living in New York would probably have thought upon seeing him, *boyfriend material maybe, but I have to talk to him*. He could have been a criminal; he could have been a saint or a ghost; he could have been the Devil himself.

"Welcome to Voyager House," I said too loudly, my voice echoing in the hallway. "You'll be my roommate, it seems. Did you just get here?"

He did not move forward to offer his hand, but he did nod, after a long moment. I noticed a large, somewhat old-fashioned-looking seaman's bag on the floor beside him.

"I came over on the subway and the bus," he said. He looked around, and then back at Rowland and myself. "Everything I have is with me. The pharmacy at Bellevue is sending over sleep medication, but it probably won't get here until tomorrow."

The way he talked, the way he used language, was extremely interesting. I understood him clearly, but it seemed like someone else was translating each word at the moment when I heard it. No doubt it was my imagination, but it seemed like Clarissa Rowland was listening with special interest to him as well, leaning in slightly to catch every word. His way of standing very still in one place had a way of drawing one in.

It was like every one of his words was calculated, or processed, or perhaps even selected one at a time, although I suspected that—for reasons I could not begin to fathom—that he was doing it for Clarissa's benefit. I had noticed that he had no accent that I could discern, but rather he spoke with a kind of precision that was so mechanical that it came across as a form of distortion. There was something mesmerizing about the way he spoke.

"Who did you say you are?" I asked. Both Rowland and he looked at me. "I mean, what did you say your name was?"

"Bernard," he said. "Bernard is the name I like best."

Well-said, I thought to myself. He might as well have said *for the time being*.

"Have you seen the room?" I asked before Rowland could say more. "Come with me and I'll show it to you. This is a very nice program, and the food is excellent."

"Let me give you bedding," Clarissa Rowland said, rushing off to a place where the bedding was kept in a hall cupboard.

"Come with me," I said in what I hoped was a businesslike tone. "It's a nice room, usually warm at night. There's a couple of chest of drawers and a table for writing. We have a little store around the corner where they sell tobacco and newspapers, and there's a library just three blocks away. There's a Chinese restaurant not far from here."

"A library," he said.

Clarissa heaped the bedding into his receiving arms, but it was too much for him to hold all of it, so I took some of it. The three of us proceeded upstairs as an unruly group, myself staggering but clinging to the railing, Clarissa Rowland chattering happily, and the new client Bernard following at a dignified distance. Once we got into the room, she started happily making the bed that would be used by the new client.

"There!" she said triumphantly when she was finished.

I sat on my bed, and my new roommate, after regarding me for another long moment, sat down across from me on the bed that Rowland had just made.

"There's a skylight for summer," Rowland said, pointing upward. Our heads swiveled upward, and indeed, there it was. "You won't need that for another five, six months." She was still looking at Barnard. Then she glanced at me, eyebrows raised. "Don't forget our appointment!"

"I wouldn't dream of it."

Then she was rushing away, with a parting "Bye!"

Bernard and I sat on our beds across the room from each other, like cellmates in a county jail. He kept his bag close, sitting on the floor a couple of inches away from his right foot. Inside would be a small kit of toiletries, I thought, and a couple of garments . . . but no, I couldn't imagine what garments they could be. I couldn't even tell what kind of boots he was wearing, or what kind of trousers. I wondered if he carried a boot-knife. He unbuttoned the two top buttons of his pea jacket, keeping his eyes on me, but still smiling.

"Why aren't you speaking Dutch or Flemish or Low Saxon?" I asked.

"Why should I?"

"Yes, indeed, why should you . . . when we can speak in English?"

But it a kind of English I'd never heard. At first I thought it sounded like a kind of pidgin English, like the kind that people once spoke on the docks of the port cities in Europe and Northern Africa. But the usage wasn't pidgin or a Creole or anything of that kind. It sounded absolutely unique to my ear, recognizably English words, but like a radio transmission that had been enhanced in a studio. For a wild moment I entertained the lunatic idea that Bernard was about to teach me a new language, and that he had come specifically for that reason.

"I can't tell you how happy I am to finally meet you, if you really are who you say you are," I said. "There are certain things that I've waited all my life to understand, things I hope you are in a position to know about. A few weeks ago, when I began to see glimpses of you on the street, and saw you surreptitiously following me—I realized that you were ready to make contact—"

"What do you want to know about?" he asked.

"It's hard to articulate, after so much time waiting to talk about it."

"Never mind," he said, with the trace of a smile. "Just start with the important things."

"I want to know why the family's name was changed. I need to know what the treasure is, and where it's hidden. And I need to know about the curse that was supposedly put on us."

"The curse," he said thoughtfully. "That's important, no doubt about it, but a great many people haven't even heard about it."

"Some have, some haven't."

"How deeply has the curse affected you?"

"To the core," I said. "For example, despite the fact that I have an IQ of 172, and possess unusual prophetic powers, I am still homeless and mentally ill. Strong circumstantial evidence of a curse, I would say."

He smiled in a neutral way. "Has it always been like this for you?"

"Yes, more or less, in the sense that where I am now is the logical culmination of the direction I've taken all my life."

"Ah," he said, stroking his two days' growth of beard.

I cannot begin to describe the thrill I felt, now that I was at last beginning this critical conversation, one in which I had a reasonable expectation of getting answers to the questions that had long kept me awake at night. This was only the beginning, I hasten to add, but I was certain the rest would be forthcoming; and when it was, hopefully some redemption would be mine. In retrospect, I had no right to be so optimistic, but the thrill was there nonetheless. It was like opening night . . . but of what?

"First," I said, "I have to know how it was that our name was changed. Why did you and your brothers Anthony and Cornelius and Willem—all four of you—stop using the patronymics created from your father's name, and start using the name we all use now?"

"You don't know already?"

"No, all the research on that subject has been inconclusive."

"Where did you do this research?"

"The genealogy library of the Netherland Society."

"What did the genealogist there say?"

"He didn't. I tried to research the matter myself, but hit a dead end. Was there perhaps some dark or evil connotation to the name in the late seventeenth century?"

"Yes, for a great many people."

So that, I thought, would have to do with the curse, the *maldición*. But it was too early to talk about that. I had already learned a great deal, and I was not quite ready to hear more about the name's connection to evil, partly because I was frightened by it. Although I did not share it with Bernard, I had already heard the story about the name being an acronym. And I already knew it had something to do with some pivotal event that had wounded the people of that time and place; which meant it would probably have the power to wound me, even as it wounded all who were aware of its consequences.

And I felt all these things, at the very same time that I realized I couldn't say why it was happening. It seemed to be the will of God, the Goddess, the many gods, or fate itself.

"Thank you," I said. "I've been waiting for this for a long time. I have to take this in. I know there's more we have to talk about."

"Yes, I'm sure we do have a great deal to talk about." He stood up stiffly, favoring his right leg a bit. "One more question, though. I'm pretty sure you know the answer."

"Anything. Ask away."

"The toilet room?"

"End of the hall," I said.

3.

Rowland was in a fine manic state, as I had noticed earlier in the day, even before our counseling session began. She was anxious about the fact that several mental health nonprofits were about to enter into collective bargaining with the city of New York, as part of a managerial consortium that included Voyager House and two other powerful nonprofits. How did I know this? Because she excitedly shared this information with all the clients attending the morning check-in group. She presented it without editorial comment, as one more potentially distracting reality in our necessarily busy lives.

After the group she rushed about answering phones, directing clients involved in an art project in the decaying parlor, and doing her best to avoid Jeff Cohen, a counselor on her staff who was, I'd been told, the SEIU shop steward. Neil, of the night staff, had let it slip in conversation with me that night staff were the subject of some kind of disciplinary matter, and it was for that reason, I suspected, that Clarissa most likely wished to avoid talking to Jeff. In any event, it was Cohen that she spotted coming up the stairs, at the same moment that she spotted me exiting my room.

She grabbed me by the arm and pulled me into the small office across from the neon EXIT sign, then expertly hung a DO NOT DISTURB sign on the doorknob. "It's time for our session," she said breathlessly.

"Where did that DO NOT DISTURB sign come from?"

"I keep it inside the room, on a nail beside the door." She had been so quick that I hadn't seen her do that, but found myself reconstructing her movements from memory, as one does with a magician. She looked wildly about, apparently for her coffee, but it was nowhere to be found, because she had forgotten to bring it. Then she rifled through her purse, at last shrieking and looking upward. "Good Lord! How embarrassing! I forgot that I don't smoke anymore!"

"No cigarette for *you*," I said. I waited for her to sit down. "What, or who, is stressing you out?"

"Never mind. What do you think of your new roommate?"

I wanted to say something that went to the truth of the matter, as I understood it, without sounding bombastic or overly delusional. "I think he's someone I've been waiting to talk to for a long time."

Her straight face morphed into a game face, an alert face expecting surprises. "Whoa. Explain."

"Can't you guess?"

"You mean the ghost, the ghostly ancestor, the one with the treasure?"

"If you insist on putting it that way. Yes, I know that's the way people see it, the hidden treasure angle. But the net worth in dollars isn't the point."

She pouted, narrowed her eyes. "You mean there's no gold, no *gelt*?"

I wondered where she learned that last word. "There could be money—probably will be, eventually—but right now that's not what's important, as I see it."

How much to conceal, how much to talk about? But I had already decided how much I wanted her to know. I wanted her to think of me as delusional, but not dangerously so. As for myself, I was interested in her reaction to Bernard: I had seen something in the way she spoke to Barnt that made me uneasy.

"I've been waiting for Barnt a long time," I said, "because I believe he can give me more information about my family. He is the man that I've seen following me, I'm sure of it. I believe he is some essence, some representation, if you will, of a man that lived a long time ago, a man who participated in something that changed everything for me. I am separated from him by three centuries, you might well say, and I still don't know exactly what he did, and I can't say why it affects me so deeply. But whatever it was, it changed everything."

"I don't know." She sat looking at me. "It's interesting, but it just seems like too much. I think you'd be much better off if you stayed in the moment, in the here and now."

"What are you complaining about? You were singing the blues about me ever since I arrived here as a client in your program, trying to figure out whether I'm really crazy or not—and now you know. I'm not just the clever malingerer that you suspected me to be. I'm a man who has been waiting a lifetime for a visitor who either lived in another time, or knows a hell of a lot about it, who can tell me who I'm supposed to be, and *what* I'm supposed to be. He is the one who will tell me what my role will be in the story that I keep hearing in my head. Once I know my part in the story, I'll be better able to figure out the denouement, wouldn't you say?"

"How come this story—and the denouement, as you put it—has so much to do with these people in the seventeenth century?"

"I was hoping maybe you could tell me that. Or at least give me some ideas about it."

"My God," she said. Then her face lit up, which meant that a joke was coming. "Did he bring your gold? Where's the damn gold?"

I said nothing. Yet I enjoyed her high spirits, and—truth to tell—enjoyed everything about her. There was no way I could keep from laughing. "Why are you so fixated on the treasure?"

"A donation of only $580 would allow me to fix the skylight in your room before next summer. Even then, it's likely to leak."

"Oh, stop."

Now she folded her arms, and looked at me for a long time. I could see—among other things—that she enjoyed talking to me as much as I enjoyed her whacky company, which I also found somewhat mysterious, since I do not form relationships easily or often. "What a dilemma," she said. She looked again around the little room as though trying to locate something.

"Do you want me to bring you some coffee?" I asked.

"No. I should have brought a cup in the room with me."

"So you should," I said, "but I can always bring you a cup, if you need it." There was a pause. "So tell me what part of your dilemma involves dealing with me."

She looked at the ceiling, moving her fingers as though counting. "It's about how far I should go with you into this jungle of obsessive and delusional thoughts. Yes, I think you're truly delusional, I have no doubt about that now—I think you really believe the things you tell me about yourself. So you're not faking that part, far from it. But some of it sounds like elements that you are adding to the story, elements that you are making up as you go along."

"Making up?"

"The things that you study at the genealogical library—well, that probably adds to your capacity for delusional thinking. I mean, it sounds like a story you're making up, and only later come to believe in because it has a certain esthetic consistency, like a good story usually does." She took a deep breath. "And all that stuff about the shabby genteel sensibility and the landless gentry, they sound more like parts of an ideological orientation than an emotional pathology. So why should I encourage those kinds of ideas? See what I mean?"

"Absolutely," I said, "but you won't make me more delusional by hearing how my delusions work. If there's any salvation for me, it will come from understanding my delusions, not running away from them. The only way I can really be the person I want to be, is to figure out how the story in my head operates, what it is supposed to accomplish, then I'll know what's behind it. *I have to become part of that story to be saved.* I know that sounds rash to you, when I start talking about salvation, but it's something I believe. I think some higher power, what you may call God, will only survive if I participate in this extraordinary series of events, thoughts and experiences."

"And if you don't participate in this narrative you hear in your head, what happens? Do you go to hell?"

"Hell is a medieval concept. Purgatory, yes—purgatory is where we're at on our bad days. The progression from purgatory to paradise is something I don't yet understand, and it may not even exist. What matters now is that I don't have a choice—I have to participate in this story that's in my head. And in doing so, I won't commit any crimes or do anything to shock the community, because it's a private matter."

She was shaking her head. "This is really a waste of your life, and could become a big problem. You're not at all in charge of this thing that's going on in your head."

"Maybe, but trying to be a part of the story is the only way I can be saved."

"Just because you believe that doesn't mean that it's right. A sincerely held belief is just as likely to be dangerous as a hypocritical one. In fact, as any decent history of religion will show, it's likely to be *more* dangerous."

"I know," I said. "But I'm not the first to believe this kind of thing. Have you ever read Dante's *Divine Comedy*?"

"Why?"

"Dante had a delusion, a belief, a recurring obsessive belief, if you will, that the love of his life, the beautiful Beatrice, was the source of all redemption in the world. He put the blood redemption of Jesus on the cross on the same level with his beautiful girlfriend . . . of course, it was the ultimate heresy, and quite silly to say that a beautiful girl could redeem the world, but he believed it—and *that*, my dear Clarissa, is why the *Divine Comedy* is so beautiful, and so contemptuous of Christianity while using its most effective images."

"That last part took people totally by surprise," I continued. "The people of Dante's time didn't know what science fiction was, but if they had, this would have been the greatest science fiction tale ever written. So on some level *they*, all the readers of the Divine Comedy, came to believe it, somewhat, at least. They didn't know the real Beatrice, of course, but they came to believe that perhaps, if you saw and loved such a woman of completely incomparable beauty, that this same beautiful woman might be capable of saving you; and the world along with you. Readers weren't saying that she *would* save the world, necessarily, but simply that she *might* have that power."

"And that—"

"And that is like my belief, my story, my obsessive thought, my delusions, if you will. There's something in this story in my head that can save me, and might yet save the world. There's something in it that may turn the key in the lock, to let me see those things I haven't been able to see before, even how good and evil are disseminated, person to person, institution to individual. *Whatever is at the core of this story could save the world.* If there's even a *chance* that it's true, how can I not explore it?"

She took another deep breath and stared at her hands. The inhalation made me wonder how it would look if she were inhaling on a cigarette, the same phantom cigarette she had rifled through her purse looking for before, the phantom cigarette she probably still longed for but couldn't have.

"It's so predictable," Clarissa Rowland said at last. "Look, the essence of real religion is humility, imagining oneself in the small and seemingly unimportant transactions of life. Instead of that, my delusional clients—the ones that are possessed by excessive religiosity—always see themselves at the center of the universe, with everything depending on what they do next. They're never just themselves, they're always Prometheus or Christ or the Devil or whatever. They think God is testing them, like Job, or making them suffer, like Christ. They think the future of the universe depends on what they say, feel, think and do. It's all runaway grandiosity!"

I was silent. Of course, she was right—grandiosity was a big part of my own thought processes, even I could see that. Perhaps I was wrong about everything; and even if I *was* right about some things, it was quite possible that everything that happened in the next stage of my life would come to nothing. Every aspect of my vision could be mistaken. But didn't I have the right to pursue this thing that both enthralled and drove me, so that I could sort it all out, to see how much might be right, and how much might be wrong? After all, had I not already gotten information that I had long sought, about where my name had come from? I could not let that go, but must deliberate on it, and find out more about what happened during that period.

Clarissa was still talking, almost to herself. I could see that delusions—and the delusional people that had them—were things that both bothered and fascinated her. "And they all think they are perfectly positioned to save the universe, these delusional clients of mine, especially the paranoid schizo-phrenics with the really complicated delusional systems," Clarissa was saying. "They're all superheroes on a mission. All of them caught in permanent adolescence, if you ask me, thanks to the convenient balm of psychosis, which allows them to be as powerful in their delusions as they are powerless in the world."

"That's a very skillful way to formulate the problem," I said. As an intellectual and a secular prophet, I was very curious about her last sentence. "Did you just make that up, or did you write it down before, and recall it just now in conversation?"

She frowned. "It's something I've always known. Always. I've expressed it several times, in slightly different ways."

There was a very long pause.

But I couldn't resist going further, since she had opened the door. "Indeed, most delusional people *are* grandiose. It comes with the territory. In fact, *I'm* grandiose, I recognize that. But what about that one in a million client—that one in a million megalomaniacal, paranoid schizophrenic—who for some reason really *can* save the world?"

She shrieked softly and nodded several times. "There, you see? You really *are* insane!"

"Then I came to the right place," I said.

4.

Right from the beginning, Bernard occasionally used words for emphasis that sounded foreign and probably archaic, some Dutch seagoing lingo, and certain words and phrases I didn't recognize at all. How old these colloquialisms might be I could not tell. He didn't use them very often, and when he did it was almost as though he did so for my benefit, as a way of illuminating his character's back story, as they might say in the theater. Overall, he was quiet, and there was that aspect of his face — almost a kind of bluntness of affect — that made it hard to tell what he was thinking.

He was silent during the evening meal that first day, but replied politely to those people who asked questions. When asked about his life, he paused for several moments, not so much thinking about his answer, as it seemed to me, as finding the right words, words that would seem appropriate to his interlocutors. His parents were dead, and he had no wife or children. He had been a third mate, an engineer, on a series of ships sailing under a Nigerian flag, living in New York when he was on the beach. He gradually found it difficult to sleep, and his condition had gotten worse, and he began to hear voices in his furnished room in Greenwich Village — interestingly, what bothered him most about the voices was that he didn't know any of the speakers. He realized that he needed help, he said, especially because the voices wouldn't allow him to sleep, and then the nature of his dreams had become weird and somewhat morbid. Because of this, he said that he no longer wished to watch TV, and for that last reason would not join us in the parlor that evening.

After we had transported our dishes to the kitchen, Bernard and I rinsed them off and put them in our dishwasher, since that was our assigned chore. (Tonight we were lucky, and the dishwasher worked almost immediately.) By way of sharing information about the program, I mentioned to Bernard that there was an enclosed patio where smokers at Voyager House went to smoke. "Where can I buy tobacco?" he inquired.

"There's a tobacco shop around the corner," I said. I looked out the window, and it was dark. "I usually don't like to walk around here after dark, but I think we'll be okay tonight."

"Absolutely, if there's two of us," he said. I made a mental note that he did not fear random street violence, but referred to it simply as a fact of life.

I nodded. "Let's go quickly, before it gets any darker."

We went to our room, and I put on my ancient bomber jacket, and he donned his pea jacket. (I made a second mental note to buy a pea jacket after my leather bomber jacket fell apart.) We set out, accessing the sidewalk from the smoking patio, walking in what had been merely a brisk breeze earlier in the day, but was now bitterly cold. I kept my hands in my pockets, since I had no gloves.

"How many people are affected," Bernard asked, "by what I've told you about our family so far?"

"There are about five thousand people in the U.S. today that use our name."

"All descended from —"

"All descended from Thys Barentsen van Leerdam."

He has fallen into a rolling gait, a sure sign of a seaman. I could hear a metal sound from his boots, and I wondered what the soles were made from. "What are they like, these people?" he asked.

"They are mainly middle-class people, some of them vaguely aware that their immigrant ancestor came from the Netherlands in the seventeenth century."

"How many know about the *maldición*?"

"The curse?"

He looked at me sharply. "Yes, that's what I mean." We continued walking. "I have the impression that a great many modern people know nothing about it," he said. "And even back then, a great many people simply found it easier not to think or talk about it, although many people were never able to stop thinking about it." He looked at me. "Isn't that the best way for people to forget about things like that, to stop talking about it?"

"To some extent, but a curse has a power that is independent of the personality, so that remembering or forgetting may not make that much difference." We continued down the street, walking around a group of musicians off-loading their instruments from a van. "Sure, for a lot of people, it was just something they didn't want to think about all that much. After all, the colony was part of a completely new world, and people were starting to redefine themselves according to what they wanted to be in the future. But there are some things that people can't forget. My own father started to talk to me about it once, but then got cold feet. I could never get him to talk about the curse after that."

"So most of the descendants don't know about it?"

"Probably about half have heard something about a curse. But they probably don't know what part of it is folktale, what might be private family lore, and what part of it might be history."

"But *you* know about it," he said.

"Yes."

"And you are concerned about it."

"I think about it day and night," I said. I waited one beat, two beats. "Which I suspect is why you came here to talk to *me*, and not to somebody else."

We were nearing the tobacco shop, and I slowed down. Bernard staggered ever so slightly; when he walked slowly, his favoring of the right leg became more discernable. "What makes you think you can do anything about it?"

"I don't know," I said honestly. "I just think . . . something went wrong during that time. And it's a part of a story that I have to know about. And then when I'm part of it, I can figure out the end to the story."

"To help your country, yourself, or your family members?"

"All of the above. But I have to start with myself."

"And—"

"Finding out about what really happened will help me stop thinking obsessively about it. I know that it sounds crazy. But there it is."

The owner of the tobacco shop, an aging gentleman from Tunisia, had for some reason left the door of his shop propped open, despite the chill wind. He was ensconced behind a glass counter in a huge overcoat. Why he didn't simply close the door, I did not know. Middle-Eastern music came from somewhere in the rear of the store, where I imagined there would be a small apartment.

Bernard took from his pocket a loathsome, terrible-looking thing that I finally recognized as a pipe, wrapped in some kind of cloth. He held the pipe forward, and the shop owner recognized immediately the problem he was required to resolve. He poured two different kinds of tobacco in two small paper containers, handing them to Bernard.

"Try. You like, I sell more."

I did not see what Bernard gave him, but it seemed like a ten-dollar bill. It might have been more. He did not ask for change, nor did it seem to occur to the shop owner to give any. Bernard picked up two books of matches from the counter and we departed. For reasons unknown, the shop keeper had not even glanced once at me during the entire time, perhaps knowing instinctively that I could not afford tobacco.

We were silent most of the way back to our room. The street lights were coming on. There had been a little sprinkle of rain before, and the passing cars were briefly iridescent as they passed underneath the street lights. Bernard stopped every few steps to pull on his deplorable pipe, which was starting to look increasingly like it belonged on the top shelf of the evidence room in the local police precinct. The tobacco smelled ghastly, but also oddly fitting for a freezing November day.

"One question," I said.

"Uh-huh," he exclaimed, or something random like that.

"Why are you talking to me at all?"

At that point he turned slowly, and he was smiling the same fierce smile as when I spotted him in the corridor on the second floor of Voyager House. "You'll find out," he said.

"Ah."

I was somewhat relieved that he had deflected my question. I was wary of asking questions like that, partly because I was afraid of saying something that might drive him away. I opened the wrought-iron gate to the Voyager House smoking area, and Bernard and I sat down on a cold cement bench in the smoking area while he smoked his pipe. Afterward he carefully knocked out the remaining ash in a large stone ash tray supplied for such purposes.

As we came up the stairs we heard the swelling of studio strings in the parlor. (The knitting ladies were addicted to the *Lifetime* Channel.) The neuropathy in my legs was killing me, so once in the room I lay down on my bed. In a moment, my roommate came back from the bathroom.

"So . . . do you have an inheritance for me?" I asked boldly.

"What is that?"

"It's money from a family that is passed on to the children."

"So if I brought you money, it would be . . . a family inheritance?"

"I think so."

"It sounds like you're not sure," he said

"I was telling Clarissa Rowland how ambivalent I felt about money. She said that if I inherited it I wouldn't feel so self-conscious about it. But my father was disinherited, so I can't inherit his money."

There was a long silence as Barnt took off his jacket, his boots, and finally his shirt. Under the shirt he sported the upper part of some ancient long underwear, good for avoiding pneumonia in the winter months.

"Tell me about this woman Clarissa Rowland," he said, "the house manager."

He took a long time pronouncing her name, not in any salacious way, but pronouncing it as though it came from a place he was not completely familiar with.

I felt a chill. "I don't know much about her."

"Do you love this woman?"

The question caught me completely off-guard. "Damn," I said. "She's part of the story, this thing that I'm trying to figure out. I don't know where she fits in."

"Why do you want to talk to her about wanting to be rich? If you talk to her about things like that, you may be getting close to knowing *exactly* where she fits in."

"What do you mean?"

"Tell me everything you know about her."

I had one of those overwhelming moments of unwanted clairvoyance in which you suddenly feel danger coming, although you can't see exactly where it's coming from. It was like the terror I felt once while in the Midwest, right before the arrival of a tornado. It started long before the tornado touched down, or even formed, but I knew it was coming because the sky outside was turning green and the leaves hung straight down, not a bit of air moving, with the air pressure dropping so quickly one could hardly breath.

The silence was palpable and thick and overpowering, yet you could hear and see everything with perfect clarity, even as the first errant hail and wind started to rattle the windowpanes; yet all you could think about was the beast in the sky above that was growing stronger by the moment, the beast that wanted to suck you two or three miles into the roiling green thunderclouds, and break all your bones as it flung you into the next county. All of one's senses were affected in such a strange way that you felt like you were on the verge of going from one kind of time into another. It was what urban people would call a paranormal event.

"Don't," I said, not really knowing why I said it, "please — don't do anything that would hurt Clarissa, Bernard."

He was surprised. "Why would I hurt her?"

"Because you did something bad a long time ago, or at the very least you know a great deal about it — guilty knowledge, I'd call it. How do I know you won't do it again?"

"You don't, I guess," he said.

Eyes: gray. Smile: ironic but not hostile.

5.

I decided I needed the balm of dreams, even of bad ones, and went to bed early. Bernard apparently made a little reconnoiter of the parlor, because I heard the knitting ladies raise their twittering voices in greeting; later he went outside, presumably to smoke his loathly pipe. An hour or two later I heard him open the door of our room and get into his bed. At least, I thought gratefully before I drifted off to sleep, he hadn't said, *I'm going to help you, but there will be times when you will have to help me.* That would defeat my immediate goal, which was to escape from the sense of being a character in a story I didn't yet understand.

Bernard had already helped me greatly in that area; his knowledge was accurate, even when merely confirming much of what I already knew from reading in the genealogical library. His behavior would bear watching, of course; but if that was part of the deal, so be it. It was clear that where my vocation was concerned — the resolution of unacknowledged guilt and repressed aggression, the kind passed from one generation to the next — I was making progress.

As if to prove my supposition, that night I had what some call "the Actor's Dream." But I had my own version of this ghastly phantasmagoria. I dreamed that I was an actor, and that I suddenly awoke to find myself naked on a stage. In this dream it was raining outside — I could hear it. Yet the theater was jammed—a good two thousand in the audience, if not more. They sat in silence, waiting for me to get on with the show, but I couldn't remember the name of the character I was supposed to be, nor did I remember my lines, or even the name of the play. Nor could I remember what it was about. Lord Shaftsbury, God bless him, wrote that embarrassment is the test of truth, but in this dream there was, for this actor, only a dying in public, a desperate nakedness before disapproving and judgmental thousands, a misanthropic, self-hating immolation of incompetence and loathing and total failure.

Then the miracle happened. For reasons unknown, I launched into a speech of such brilliance, of such heartbreaking intensity and acuity, that the audience was lifted from their seats. No televangelist ever worked a room with such thoroughness; Jonathon Edwards himself could not have terrified them more than the world that I perceived and denounced and declaimed in my own palpable if fashionably invoked nakedness . . . it was a mad poetry that poured from my mouth, manna for the spiritually starved of New York: pure emotion it was, briefly but expertly translated into all the languages of the world. When I was finished, that awestruck audience sat transfixed and unable to move, weeping helplessly, having been confronted with, and having *seen*, the truth about themselves, each person's truth in its most egregious and personal form!

I couldn't even remember the name of the character that I played. Actually, to be completely truthful, I had *two* characters to choose from, and was capable of playing one, and then another, or both at once. Bernard—or Barnt—was there as well; it was the two of us on the stage together at the end, playing Iago and the poor Moor, but whether it was Iago that I played, or his ill-fated master Othello, I cannot remember.

Chapter 6

Barnt's first wife Neeltje, the teenage girl whom he had roughly led into sin and then married, who became both wife and best friend for many years, died unexpectedly of a fever that swept through the colony. She had been suffering for years with a series of respiratory symptoms that had weakened her greatly; but thankfully, the same fever that had taken so many young lives barely touched their healthy sons. Barnt grieved for his wife, and then grieved some more, although now the grief was for himself and his new responsibility: his two older children were already launched on the tides of marriage and apprenticeships, but he was faced with raising his youngest son, who was still at home. He started from the beginning, taking the child with him every-where he went, explaining the lay of the property and the gardens as best he could, and showing him the cattle he owned with its distinctive cattle-mark, based on his father's mark, the first in Staaten Eylandt.

He decided early to speak to his son only in English, because the boy would need that language more; but at first the lad cried because Dutch reminded him of his mother, and he missed her greatly. But Barnt took him to a Dutch Reformed Church, and for a time they gathered on Sundays with a Huguenot group where only French was spoken; in both cases, Barnt spoke only in Dutch on Sunday, and for a long time the boy answered him in Dutch. In time, however, as he used English more often with his friends, and with the men that he hired on his plantation, there came a time that he balked at speaking Dutch, even on Sundays. For reasons he did not himself fully understand, Barnt grieved all over again for himself and his lost wife, when the boy refused to speak Dutch; he and some of the younger men resumed their practice of meeting after services at the church to discuss the theological arguments of the day, which were invariably also political arguments.

Some of the older men, bemused by the enthusiasm of their sons, gathered the necessary books from the few private libraries on the island, and taught the boys whatever their elders could remember, from the days when these same elders had bravely supported the Republic of the Seven United Provinces compounded by the dream of a New Jerusalem in the New World. *Nieuw Nederland,* as they had believed, would not merely be a place of wonders where great wealth could be accumulated, but a land of dreams where new spiritual and aesthetic domains would be discovered. But through it all the older men were careful to keep intact a devout belief in the heroism of the Dutch in defeating the Spanish tyrant in the lowlands—and for that reason set about to teach the young what they understood of the liturgy and the Calvinist beliefs of the Dutch Reformed Church, since that seemed to be an important part of that victory.

For the young men it was, for some conscious and for others half-conscious, a way of challenging the rich merchants who seemed far too eager to accustom themselves to English ways, and to the Anglican church; for the older men, it was the realization that many of the earthly dreams they'd had when young were no longer capable of being realized, and that what remained was a chance to contemplate the better world waiting for them after death. Besides their loathing and fear of the Catholic monarchies, the younger men had little idea who they were, or what they wanted, even though most of them had families and worked hard to support them. Ever since 1674, and the English Re-Conquest, something had been missing, some core value relating to an overall purpose in which Dutch-speaking society could cooperate.

Nonetheless, there was always that one thing that obsessed the Protestant nations and people, and especially the Dutch: the fear that the Papacy, defeated in the lowlands, was now conspiring to gain ascendency over the English monarchy, which raised the nightmarish possibility that Dutch losses to the English navy on the high seas might be followed by an even worse religious enslavement, imposed in the New World by a Catholic king's fiat. It had all the self-serving, mindless simplicity of a modern conspiracy theory, yet there was a kernel of truth mixed in with the fashionable hatred of all things popish, real or imagined; and there was also the lingering trauma from the war with the English, the suddenness with which that war had been so unexpectedly lost, not to mention the brutal Indian wars.

Then "the Angel" happened: that was the way Barnt first thought of it, "the Angel" being his word for something unexpected, destabilizing, an attack on the personality that left him completely changed. It would be the first of two huge events that would permanently change his life. Barnt had taken to staying out all night in the Bad Woods, as the Raritan tribal people had called it, a dense place thick with trees and undergrowth. Sometimes he camped there with his son, other times he stayed out by himself. Staaten Eylandt was at that time crisscrossed by trails, all leading to Lenape trading spots, on Staaten Eylandt and East Jersey as well. Barnt had a little camp in the thick of the woods not far from the shore, and he had taken to visiting often, perhaps as often as once a month.

His son was staying with a friend and his family at New Town, the Staaten Eylandt successor to Oude Dorp. Barnt was glad for the opportunity to spend the night in the Bad Woods alone. He loved doing this because he was aware of the reputation that the Bad Woods had among the young men of the Raritan tribe—something terrible would happen to you, it was said, if you spent the night there. But it was for just that reason that certain braves *did* spend the night there, the better to strut and boast of it the next day in their dance and storytelling. There was even a name for those who had stayed there all night, although Barnt had forgotten the Raritan word for it.

What was it in those stories of Raritan braves in the Bad

Woods that compelled him to spend the night there himself?

He had made a fire in a hole in the sand, not far from a freshwater spring, despite its proximity to the salty tidal waters of Arthur Kill. It was in the morning hours, the hours when the nocturnal predators hunted; as a result, the Bad Woods seethed quietly with the soft footfall of hungry and curious animals. It was not yet summer, and as he built a fire for the night the green sticks burned reluctantly, complaining with many snaps and crackles in the heavy darkness. It may have been this that awakened him in the dead of night. He saw the dangerous light first out of the corner of his eye, and he turned and stared, transfixed. A fire burned in the Bad Woods, not burning the trees or underbrush, but burning only the air, in the way that St. Elmo's fire might dance in the sails on a ship during a storm at sea. Barnt remembered that he needed to put out his own fire with water from the spring, but it was too late. He could not pull his eyes away from the fire in the Bad Woods, because there was someone in the fire.

Standing in the middle of the fire was a beautiful woman with powerful hair that laved outward in all directions like underwater weeds in a shallow current. She had the most beautiful figure he had ever seen; and a bold, high cheek-boned face even more outrageously beautiful. Barnt knew instinctively that a man would give up his life for such a woman—this was an idea that had never occurred to him before, an idea that was nowhere to be found in either Dutch or English culture. It was at that moment that Barnt also realized, with more than a little embarrassment, how lonely he had become, because his body told him that. It also told him that this woman was perhaps of a separate world, one more perfectly formed and completely without fear.

She was a woman with the breasts and hips and legs of a goddess. If someone with authority had suggested to him at that moment that she was a creature of the Devil, he might have agreed, or at least seriously considered it. But it seemed more likely that she was an angel—that she had come to make him understand something that he had not seen clearly before. Were not the feelings that suddenly overwhelmed him trying to tell him something about his own mortality, about the death of his wife and his own longing for death?

As he watched her, the angel in the fire beckoned with both hands, motioning him forward. What did she want, and why was she not fleeing when she had the chance? What was the meaning of those beckoning hand motions, telling him to come save her? That was a big part of what he could remember of that night, or at least all he cared to talk about, remembering how he felt when he first saw her, the *brandengle*, the unearthly Angel-in-the-fire.

2.

I was starting to develop a special affection for the small room on the second floor where Clarissa Rowland and I met. I can remember it quite well now—there was a sofa shoved up against the wall, as well as three chairs and a table also shoved against the wall, and a small ancient desk with a defunct computer on it. In the closet there was what-have-you, in addition to some old clothes on hangers, and some photographs that had probably been on the wall before, but had been taken down. (I vaguely remembered a newspaper story about disputes in group homes regarding the legality of staff taking pictures of the clients. It had struck me as unnecessarily legalistic—they could have easily finessed the issue by having the photos taken by other clients, or getting people to sign releases.) Finally, in a file cabinet in the corner were what appeared to be hundreds of charts, taken out of the hardback folders and fitted into manila folders with two-prong fasteners.

"How many of these old files do you have?" I wanted to know. "And how long do you keep them?"

"Seven years," she said briskly, penning a note. "Thanks for reminding me of that. Some of these files may have been here longer. Tonight I'll get the night staff to go through them."

I hoped Neil wasn't the duty counselor tonight; he and I had become friendly, so I had an idea of how much he hated add-on night tasks, taking up time he would much rather spend studying or sleeping.

"I'm glad to see that you and Barnt are getting along," Clarissa said. "I had a feeling you might like him as a roommate. He has some ideas that I find very interesting."

"What kind?"

"About the way people remember things. About how hard it is to really remember anything in the past, and how the mind keeps changing the things that we do remember."

"Did that insight arise in your psychotherapy with him?"

She looked at me sharply. "It's rare that I do psychotherapy with clients—did you know that? I'm mainly a manager, both of staff and of clients. But I choose to do therapy with certain clients, from time to time, because I find a client particularly interesting, or particularly at risk—both qualifications apply to you, or did in the beginning. Everything you say to me is privileged, and completely confidential. Same deal with Bernard."

"Do you also find him interesting?"

"Ah," she said, "with Bernard it's a little different. He's a relatively new client, so I need to get to know him. That's not psychotherapy. There may be something I can pick up on that they didn't catch at Bellevue, or that the night staff here didn't pick up in the intake. Many people don't understand this, but the biggest part of my job is not being a clinician, but being a manager—of staff, and of clients. And because I'm so busy, I feel like I'm spending more time talking *about* the clients, than I spend talking *to* them. We reduce them to a series of clinical phrases and catchwords in the Progress Notes . . . and I end up not even knowing who they are. And the weird thing is, I want to be the first to know when they decompensate. But how can I be aware of that except by talking to them? It makes all the difference when I do."

"So with Barnard it's not psychotherapy?"

"It's information-gathering. With you it's psychotherapy." She paused. "How does having Barnard as a roommate affect you?"

"He's an interesting guy, like you said. We have many of the same interests, including history and genealogy."

"So . . . I'm wondering if you see him as being connected to the ancestor you talked about in group—the ancestor you said was coming to visit you, to explain certain matters that had happened in the past, and perhaps to bequeath an inheritance, or some other kind of treasure."

"I'm still getting to know Bernard, or Barnt, as I call him."

"So he's not the guy who's been haunting you?"

I thought about it, and answered carefully, formulating my answer in a way that I thought would appeal to her. "I've come to believe that this person from the past that I fear might be buried in the personalities—or the dreams—of several people . . . in that case, I would be influenced by several people, all of whom have proprietary knowledge of certain events in the past. In such a case, I would have to put the pieces together myself. I might even discover the truth in things that are said by people who don't even realize they are imparting it."

"And Bernard could be one of those people?"

"Could be, yes, because Barnt knows a great deal about the period in history that interests me." I wanted to make my obsession sound more like an eccentric hobby rather than a destructive pathology.

"Aren't you somewhat concerned that he might possess some proprietary knowledge that could be harmful to you?" she asked.

"I'm concerned that you are unnecessarily focused on him. He's my roommate, and we talk, and that's it."

She said nothing. She had that alert look of anticipatory pleasure in her eyes that she got whenever she was about to spring something on me. "I'm very touched that you're concerned about me," she said, "but I have to wonder . . . is it possible you're really concerned about *yourself?* I mean, is there something dangerous about Barnt that you *fear?*"

"Hmm, well." I pretended to ponder the question carefully. "No, I don't think so."

"I had to ask that question."

The pause went on for a very long time. I knew enough about her therapeutic style to guess that she wouldn't break the pause, no matter how long it went on—she would let me break the silence to see what I had to say. So I dived into the quiet in which we were both engulfed.

"Look, I don't know how to describe it," I said, "much less explain it. I just see that you're vulnerable in certain ways. I think you're vulnerable in some way to Bernard—or Barnt, as I call him—perhaps because you like to help people, but for some reason can't do so in his case."

"So?

"So be careful."

"I'm really curious to know where your fear of Barnt comes from, and your concern for me," she said. "It feels like a kind of unconscious love triangle, perhaps the kind of suppressed system that might occur in family politics. Are you afraid that in uncovering family secrets you might uncover other secrets, secrets that could harm other people you care about?"

"There's very few people I care about enough to worry about."

"Who *do* you care about?"

"I care about solving the problem of good and evil. But I have to be in control of the process if I wish to succeed. Right now I'm not."

She furrowed her brows in the manner that I always found endearing, because it so reminded me of a precocious child. "Solving the problem of good and evil? That sounds like saving the world, and all the people in it. But you don't *like* people. You don't *trust* them. So why on earth to you want to save them? Answer me *that*."

"I would like to save the world for entirely selfish reasons. It's like a math problem with emotions. Because I despise being exposed to so many forms of systemic evil, you understand, and because I have no control over it . . . and at some point it becomes tiresome and juvenile and disgusting—I end up simply wanting it to *stop*. But someday things may be different—someday humanity may grow up, and listen to my ideas. And it is for *them*, those people of the future—especially the children—that I'd like to unravel the dilemma of good and evil, even though on a day-to-day basis I struggle to do it solely for myself."

Clarissa was shaking her head sadly. "It's always the same damn megalomania with you poor people," she murmured sadly, "even the women. Delusional clients always see themselves hanging on the cross, or at the very least standing at the damn crossroads, and everything they do will either save the world, or destroy it. I feel so sorry for all of you." She was getting angry. "You put such pressure on yourselves, and put such impossible conditions on your own recovery. I wish you'd all just chill out a bit! And what's so sad about you, is that you're so damn smart, and you've been alive on this planet so long . . . and yet—"

"I never learned how to be normal, is that it?"

I could tell she was getting ready to end the session, partly by the way she shifted her body in her chair, partly by the deep sigh she would typically heave twice once we had reached the end of the road. I didn't blame her for ending the session; she already had enough to sum up my foundational dilemma, at least the way I wanted her to know it. Enough for a nice two-paragraph Progress Note, I thought.

"But wait!" she said suddenly. "What about the treasure? You're not at all interested in the Big Bucks, the Big Money? That is hardly credible. Think what you could do with your inheritance, the Old Money! It's even possible that *Barnt* knows where it's hidden, and is laughing at us as we speak."

Something along those lines had already occurred to me, but I couldn't imagine Bernard laughing at me and my money-phobia, or even at the world's greed; it was more complicated than that.

"I despise money," I insisted. "It's a private dementia. I have an obsession with being poor, a libido for poverty."

"And underlying that desire would be . . ."

"An unacknowledged attraction to the idea of being rich."

"Ha. That's why the money's a *hidden* treasure, my friend, to see how far you'll go to find it."

"You want it too," I said. "You're literally obsessed with it. I mean, all you can talk about is the money you need to make improvements at Voyager House." I sat up straight, suddenly self-righteous. "If you want money for Voyager House, stop fantasizing about my Old Money, and start putting pressure on the mayor. You'll eventually have to talk to him anyway, after the SEIU walks out of negotiations."

She emitted a soft shriek, thumping her notebook down on her thighs. "You're nuts," she said fondly. "Absolutely, stark-raving bananas."

"Then I came to the right place."

Rowland made a great show of gathering together her purse, two recalcitrant pens and one notebook, clanking keys to the med cabinet and doors, and everything else she'd brought with her into the little room. She was frowning, as though not only thinking about my concerns, but trying to sort out the objective validity of those same concerns. She had me wondering, as she exited, about the desires and the darkness that no doubt lay beneath her carefree, faux-manic exterior.

I could not rid myself of the feeling that she was at risk in some way. I suppressed the rather melodramatic thought that we were *all* at risk—because of *course* we were, regardless of our intentions. I did not particularly like social workers as a species, and the mental health racket had produced some real monstrosities; but it also occasionally produced people who were not merely trustworthy, but also worthy—for reasons I did not quite understand—of respect and affection. And I cared, however irrationally, for Clarissa Rowland, the erstwhile clinical director and LCSW of Voyager House.

3.

Barnt was surprised and somewhat piqued that his wife Neeltje predeceased him, because he had always seen her as a kind of preternatural survivor, going from house to house helping other women during times of fever, happy to serve while others died. It had taken only two days of intense sickness for her to die, and now she was gone and he was alone. He was in his middle forties; two of his three children had found niches for themselves, one working on the farm of a widow in New Dorp, preparing for an apprenticeship as a cordwainer, with the other selling furs, and then grain, in Mannahattas; his youngest son was soon to begin an apprenticeship to a joiner in East Jersey. It had finally been decided that his youngest son would be living with Barnt's brother Anthony in Mannahattas until he began his apprenticeship.

Barnt had given little or no thought of remarrying. But what now happened to Barnt was something on the order of a personal ambuscade, an emotional bushwhacking. What had happened to Barnt, quite simply, was that he fell unexpectedly and violently in love. The woman who in that manner captured his interest was wholly and completely different from any other woman Barnt had ever met.

He'd never been a romantic, and never thought much of how one dealt with powerful female beauty that demanded court, because the whole world of man-woman interactions of which he had been one part had excluded that. Men and woman married. They had children, if God was willing, and raised them together.

They helped each other, and the wife gave pleasure to the husband at regular intervals. It was simple and rather straight-forward, and at the end of earthly existence lay death, after which, if one were Christian and a member of the Elect, came eternal life in the New Earth. But his new woman was much tougher than even his wife Neeltje had been, and in fact tougher in more ways than anyone could have imagined. And she possessed an otherworldly kind of beauty that Barnt had never experienced before. He was somewhat embarrassed by his fasci-nation with her beauty, because it did not seem right, but the thoughts and emotions of lovers happen as they must, not as one wishes them to.

The colony had gradually changed, with English-speakers now exerting the main influence in commerce and the honorable professions; with the Re-Conquest of 1674, Dutch immigration had virtually come to an end. At the same time, Dutch retained liturgical and conversational pride of place in the Reformed Dutch Church, and also in the Dutch-speaking community throughout New York. Barnt embraced English at first as just another language in the teeming ports of what was now New York: there were everywhere Germans, Dutch, English, Walloons from Belgium, even Switzerland, not to mention Spanish- and Ladino-speaking Sephardic Jews; there were adult men and women who called no other country their place of origin except this wild spot in the New World. There were some Africans, some enslaved and some free, and although they kept a low profile they were there. Mannahattas and its surrounding communities probably constituted at that moment the most international spot on earth. It never occurred to Barnt, or any of the other children of Thys Barentsen van Leerdam, to return to Amsterdam—the Netherlands was a place he could hardly imagine. This place, this New York in the New World, was the only home he knew or cared to have.

This new woman with whom Barnt fell insanely in love was

of an even further and stranger world, the world of tribal people, a woman who spoke one of the Algonquin languages, a woman of the large Lenni Lenape nation, and furthermore a woman of the Raritan tribe, which happened to be the tribe that had defeated Melyn and his quixotic dream of Staaten Eylandt as a private patroonship. How could such a thing have happened to the son of Thys Barentsen, a magistrate and member of Stuyvesant's council, falling in love with a tribal woman? It had happened in the same way that all such things happen, because of feelings that could not be denied, feelings that made overwhelming sense at the time to both parties, feelings that became entwined with the most private yet most potent needs of both lovers. And truth to tell, the phenomenon of a Dutch man falling in love with a tribal woman was not all that uncommon.

Here is the story as Barnt told it to me, sitting or laying on his bed in our chilly room, his eyes burning in the near-darkness of that very cold winter. (There was a bulb hanging from the ceiling, but its light was too piercing, so our sole source of light was the red neon that came through our locked skylight.) I have to say at this point that I have no independent verification for some of the things that Barnt reported, and that further much of what he said sounded like a saga or folktale, rather like the tales told by the Lenni Lenape as they danced or stomped away their nights before hunting or war. But what came across most powerfully was the aching connection he had to the woman he fell in love with; and I have little doubt that those powerful emotions were completely authentic.

It was Barnt's honest memory of events that had changed his life; and indeed, some of it I could verify through my own historical research. But there was also much that seemed memory of past time as he wished and needed to remember it. Of course, neither of us could explain why he, in a second-story room in a house in Lower Manhattan in the early twenty-first century, would have such clear memories of things that happened over three centuries ago. But it was something I had long waited for, and it came from some deeper truth than mere historical verisimilitude, so I did not question it.

Here is what he told me about certain events of the 1680s, as we lay on our bunks, with the red neon filtering through our shadowy skylight:

Barnt had tired of his drinking companions, and after his wife's death had in fact tired of life itself, but had little idea what to do about it. He fell into the habit of wondering out to the rough thatched-roof meetinghouse where he once met his drinking companions, and pushed past it almost to the edge of the beach on Arthur Kill. What we would probably call a tidal strait today, it was a thousand feet wide, running from the place of the seals to a landing in New Jersey. It was easily traversed by canoe by the tribal people, and was the main point of passage used by them to get to the island from northern East Jersey, at the time of hostilities between the Raritan tribe and poor mad Cornelis Melyn, the would-be king of Staaten Eylandt.

Barnt had no worries of hostile encounters with tribal people, for it had been thirty years or so since Melyn had fought to make a kingdom on this island. But even if the tribes were still a clear and present danger, Barnt wouldn't have cared. He had a private store of rum, which he took with him to his camp in the Bad Woods; he planned to stay overnight at the camp, and eat the food he'd brought with him. But tonight he found—as often happened nowadays—that his appetite had disappeared. He felt alienated from the affairs of the day, and on this night especially dispirited.

He had grown weary of the raucous traders and business-people of Mannahattas, many of whom were moving into Staaten Eylandt at such a rate it was increasingly difficult to graze the cattle he owned and sold. But it was something in the people that bothered him—it seemed that money was all the Dutch could think of, and the magical process of making a profit seemed the only redemption people really cared about. All the old dreams, however corrupt and mistaken, were gone. Perhaps, he thought, it was because—although people rarely talked about it—so few had really come to terms with the English victory; wealth was now both substitute and camouflage for the traumatic loss of shared dreams.

Now that he thought about it, he had not heard recently any dream of the Netherlands winning back the thriving hive of businesses that New Amsterdam, disguised as New York, had now become. That talk had been rife for many years, right after the Re-Conquest in 1674; then it stopped, suddenly, as one stops a guilty pleasure that involves danger as well as shame. British and German and Walloon immigration boomed, but Dutch immigrants from the central Netherlands no longer found the colony an exciting destination for igniting a new life. The dream, the dream was lost, or at least misplaced—perhaps purloined by forces unknown; but what had the dream been? How could you resurrect it and tailor it to the new life, if you weren't living it on a daily basis, and couldn't remember exactly what it had been before?

Barnt had begun to feel that the new life that the colony needed, that *he* needed, was something else, something religious perhaps, but at the very least something that came from the soul, and not solely from the world's powers and principalities and the different currencies that were popular in the colony. In an odd way, the rum seemed to validate his feelings; he did not know what the new project would be, but on this night in the Bad Woods he felt something approaching on the horizon, *een Nieuw Begin,* perhaps brought by an *aerendgast,* a spirit-messenger sent on an earth-errand by the Almighty. Lately, he had been troubled by the amount of drinking he'd been doing, and wondered if God could help him stop . . . among other things, he wanted to know more about the Dutch Reformed Church, but had been inhibited by the probability that stories of his drinking had proceeded him.

For that reason, he hesitated to ask questions of the dominies—the ministers of the Dutch Reformed Churches—since he was reasonably sure they would lecture him on his behavior. (They were, after all, strict Calvinists.)

He was asleep when awakened in the middle of the night by dancing flames and the smell of wood smoke. He stumbled out into a clearing and looked up a sandy incline to see a crown of blazing fire three-quarters of the way up; and in the middle of it, a woman, whom he instinctively believed was from another world. A fire-virago, a fire-angel! And although he really had no idea what his senses were telling him, he ignored all warnings of emissaries from the Devil, and rushed up the incline toward the woman dancing in the fire.

To his great embarrassment, the first thing he noticed was her figure; if he had seen her in Mannahattas, he would have looked away, because of her voluptuous form. She was not standing in the middle of a fire, but in front of one. She was motioning with both hands for him to come forward to help her. There was a fire in a pit, but it had spread to the underbrush; and without exchanging a word, the two of them began to throw dirt and sand on it for what seemed like hours. He was aware of smiling, but continued to avert his eyes from the woman because of her beauty. When he finally looked at her, he realized she was fully clothed and not naked, as he had thought before.

She was exhausted too, but not as much as he was, because he was in his forties and she, to judge by her appearance, was in her twenties. Finally she began to speak. To Barnt's unalloyed joy, she spoke Jersey Dutch, the wild language that was spoken in Bergen Town and many other places in East Jersey, and had made its way into Staaten Eylandt, certain settlements on the outskirts of Mannahattas, and as far as Pennsylvania. Jersey Dutch was compounded of the most colorful language of Dutch and English, with a heavy infusion of the Raritan tribal dialect. Besides the Dutch in East Jersey, it was spoken by black people throughout the colony, both enslaved and free, including an especially expressive variety spoken by the tribal people at Ramapough Mountain, a mixed-race group that had long sheltered runaway slaves. Later, she told him that after one of the major defeats at the hands of the Sanhicans and their allies, she was taken by her brother to live in the Ramapough area, where they became fluent in the Jersey Dutch spoken there.

Barnt wanted to call her Engel, because of the way she sudden appeared in his life—and because of her beauty—but the Dutch word did not sound quite right; he remembered his French-speaking Huguenot mother using the word Angelique, which (without thinking about it) he translated into English, as "Angel."

She had not eaten in a long time, and had no weapons to hunt, or sacks with which to gather wild berries, subsisting on a particular kind of grass that she cooked on her fire. He fed her some of the bread he had taken to his camp. He used the rum and sulfur at his camp to rid her of head lice, also bathing with her without looking at her. Throughout his first three days with her, he was careful not to look too long at her, because of her exceptional beauty; but he greatly enjoyed simply being close to her. She was wary, but clearly grateful for the food and conversation in Jersey Dutch. Together they made a decent camp, and he used his fishing gear to catch fish for dinner.

She told him that she had a brother named Slow Turtle, who had been wounded in wars with the Sanhican, Tappan and Hackensack tribes, but would soon be coming to meet her here in the Bad Woods, either to take her away or to die near the traditional Raritan burial place on Staaten Eylandt, where he could be buried.

She said she was the daughter of a chieftain in the Raritan tribe, which Barnt and his friends sometimes called the Raritanoos, a slang expression they had picked up from the English. Barnt thought that the name of her brother, Slow Turtle, suggested that they were part of the Turtle Clan, which he thought of as belonging to another tribe in the greater Lenni Lenape world, yet she was very clear about being Raritan. At first Barnt wondered if she had said this because, during their short but violent struggle with Melyn's settlers, the Raritan had gotten a reputation as fierce warriors. Yet much that she told him rang true, especially her knowledge of the island and its many secret places.

She said that her clan within the Raritan tribe, decimated by their war with the would-be patroon Cornelis Melyn, had been in turn decimated by other tribes in a larger territorial war, and she and her brother were among the few that had been left. She gave that as the reason why she had come to the Bad Woods—she knew the area well, and had been told to wait there by her brother. The Raritan had previously displaced the tribe known as the Sanhicans, and now in their weakened state they were themselves in the process of being displaced by them. Those were the basic facts as Barnt understood them; but from the beginning there was something anomalous and rather odd about her story.

It seems that she and her brother had lived in the Ramapough Mountain area, and while there she had developed a certain liking for their way of existing at the margins of the white settlements, but without directly challenging them. But by the third day Barnt didn't care about her origins. He had discovered, in the uncanny way that men in midlife sometimes do, a new meaning to his life—a meaning that involved facing his own loneliness, but that also implied a quest for something that was at present beyond him.

The night of the third day, Barnt and Angela huddled together all night for warmth, and by the morning their bodies were on fire. Together, slowly, they made love. She was at first passive, and then exceptionally animated, clearly seeking to complete her own pleasure before his; from making love to her, he realized that she had probably been married, or at least belonged, to another man before. This is a woman who could easily bear him children, he thought—although it had never occurred to him before to have more children—but almost from the beginning, Barnt was aware that he wanted to spend the rest of his life with her. Her manner was exceptionally brave and resilient, and competent in the simple skills of woodcraft, and of the sheer animal energy necessary to surviving in the woods; but she was simultaneously a lost soul, it seemed, and at the same time an angel, by virtue of her beauty and her bold confidence in her ability to survive. Yet, he could not get over the sense that she had come to this part of the Bad Woods to die, because on some level he had wanted to do the same. Yet, she possessed a singular capacity to make him happy, an emotion he had almost completely forgotten.

The next dawn, by the gray east light, he saw that she was crying. He was overwhelmed by guilt. Had he done something terribly wrong? She had not resisted his advances, and in fact had made love to him with an amazing energy. But had he done something wrong by initiating it here in this way? He put his hand on her shoulder, and confessed his love for her. Had their seclusion from the rest of the world put an extra pressure on her to make love to him? Surely it must have, to some extent. Was she running from those survivors in her tribe who sought to punish her for some transgression? Had she shown some sign of resistance that he hadn't noticed? Most likely she simply wept because of a past husband . . . yet the sadness grew until it overwhelmed him. He prayed to God for guidance, and to be forgiven for whatever wrong he may have committed—the first time he had prayed, despite his occasional attendance at church, for a very long time. And he wept.

She was surprised and seemingly saddened by his tears. He told her what his thoughts were: "You had a husband, and you grieve for him."

"He was going to be my husband, but he was killed," she said.

"You reminded me of him, but now I belong to you. You cannot deny that, because your actions showed me what your feelings are before you even told me."

And so, the intense sadness continued for another hour, after which she left to bath herself in a nearby spring. After that, she seemed done with grieving, and free of troubling memories. They worked quietly to clean up the camp. As they did so, she subjected him to a nonstop speech in Jersey Dutch, which he found completely captivating. He was so spellbound that after a while he stopped working simply to watch her as she acted and sang out the words. Many of them were Lenape words—*maxkw, chinkwe* and *xkuk*, for bear, lion and snake; the Lenape words for *water* and *fire* he had long known; the words for head, nose and feet (*nil, hnikiyon* and *nsit*) had migrated to Jersey Dutch, as well as the words for corn and eggs and salmon, the latter of which he had caught the night before, scraps of which they ate for breakfast.

Hesitantly and a bit shyly, over a long day, the more personal phrases came, words that he recognized and knew, but had never heard expressed in the same manner, in a ripe Jersey Dutch: *beautiful moon, thank you, to eat, to sing.* Many of the words she knew already (such as *snake* and *moon*) in English, but she used them as part of the rich and irrepressible ménage that was clearly her heart's language. She also knew some English, but greatly preferred Jersey Dutch, with its unmistakable animation in the bold Ramapough manner. In so doing, he felt she was purposely inviting him into her world, the door to which had been opened by the circumstances that had brought them together.

Later that afternoon, after eating a second time, she enumerated her reason—or rather, reasons, of which there were three—for coming here. The first was simple survival. None of her tribe's enemies would look for her here, whereas she knew the island quite well and would know where to hide. The second was that there was a sacred burial ground on the island; and when the elders of the tribe left an area, they would pay a visit to the burial ground to say goodbye to the ancestors. Her parents were buried there, but she had been afraid to go alone, and was waiting for her brother, Slow Turtle, to go with him to say goodbye to her father and mother.

And there was a third reason, one that Barnt had heard of but always thought simply an agreeable tale with no basis in fact. When the Raritan knew they were in the process of being defeated by a combination of the Dutch and their tribal rivals, some tribal leaders made a last stab at getting payment for their thousand-year tenancy in the Bad Woods of Staaten Eylandt, having made note of the exotic European habit of owning, buying and selling property. Since it would function as a peace treaty as well as a bill of sale, a few whites brought trinkets, some money, and an impressive-looking paper to the Raritan braves, who in signing it would sign over ownership of Staaten Eylandt to them, the European whites.

But there weren't enough tribal adults left there to sign it, since the braves were either dead or engaged in a rear-guard defense of several Raritan villages in East Jersey that were being evacuated to Pennsylvania; so according to Angel they allowed some children that were present to sign it along with the adults. She was one of those children who did so, laboriously making a small picture of an owl with huge eyes as her signature. In her mind, it gave her certain proprietary rights regarding the Bad Woods. As long as she stayed in the Woods, and did not associate with the whites, she was able, she felt, to live there as long as she wished. The signing of the paper made it so, as long as the whites did not discover her camp.

Barnt reassured her that he would go with her to the burial ground the next day, if her brother did not come that day. From that point on her attitude toward him changed. She began to talk and interact with him as though she accepted him as her husband, and Barnt was overjoyed. She made it clear through

Jersey Dutch that she belonged to him now, and no other man. That night, Barnt noticed, Angela initiated the lovemaking. The next day they visited the burial ground on a bluff not far from their twin camps, and within sight of Barnt's own grazing land.

Angela danced and sang tribal songs at the burial site, wept, and made a loud yelling cry of grief, while stomping the ground and singing. Both her father and her mother were buried there, she said. Barnt found himself thinking of his own father, who since the triumph of the English Re-Conquest had withdrawn into his own thoughts and memories, and finally from the world itself. Thys Barentsen had died in 1682, not regretting his decision to come to the New World, yet not entirely happy since its connection with the Dutch homeland had been destroyed by historical events beyond his control.

When they returned to their camp, Barnt began to explain where the whites living on Staaten Eylandt were concentrated. The island was still crisscrossed with hunting trails used by the Raritan, and Angela knew how to traverse them, even those that were overgrown. She knew how to hide when she heard sounds of others coming. Much property on the south side had been sold, but not all was occupied and farmed; grazing land was being claimed, and those who knew how to do so would graze their cattle on unsettled or unclaimed land. Barnt drew maps in the dust, to indicate which areas she could go in, and those that contained too many whites. There was the 943-acre plantation of Christopher Billop, a reward from the British for his service in the Dutch-English War, not to mention the manorial estate of colonial governor Thomas Dongan in the northeastern hills. By 1680, Billop had built a handsome stone house, which was visible from Burial Ridge, where the Raritan burial ground was located; the Billop land by now included much of the original hunting grounds of the Raritan, despite the many tribal hunting trails that traversed it. The burial ground was not far from the Billop estate, though most white people stayed away from it, and most probably did not even know it was there.

The colonial authorities had in 1687 divided up the island into four administrative districts, the northern part of which was almost completely filled by Thomas Dongan's lush estate. But there were certain places where she could move freely without being seen, especially the peripheries of certain swampy or unclaimed lands; her present camp in the Bad Woods was in a good location, because there was a marsh bordering it on two sides, and almost impassible woods on the third. At the same time the mosquitoes were not bad, and because of the marsh, there were no wolf packs. Neither of them worried about her brother being spotted when he returned to her, because nobody would expect persons to be traversing Kill Van Kull or Arthur Kill. The tidal waters there could be treacherous, so the white settlers were careful when and how they crossed it; tribal people, on the other hand, would know when and where the waters were safest.

Barnt began to beg her to come home with him, to live in the clapboard house he inhabited, to share his food and drink and bed. He begged her to marry him; in her mind, she said, they were already married; the only person who could further legalize what already existed was a medicine man in the interior of East Jersey. Barnt did not think—refused to think—about what the Dutch-speaking community would say about her, because he did not care. His world now revolved around watching her, the miraculous fire-angel, and listening to her melodious rendering of Jersey Dutch. It was as though his drinking friends had never existed, their opinions counting for nothing in this new happiness; all he cared about was being with Angel—and because he could not imagine what living with her in the future would be like, he concentrated on living as intensely as he could with her in the present.

He told her of his two-horse wagon and his one surviving horse, which even now was probably being fed by his crippled man Deidrick, who lived in the barn. He told her of many things, especially of the convenience of living in a home, of cooking on the fire in the front room, and sleeping in a bed. He told her that although he liked the camp they had made, ultimately he preferred living in a house. Could this wild girl of the Bad Woods adjust to living under the same roof with him? If she was clever enough to survive in the woods alone, surely she was clever enough to live in a house, he told her.

But she was wilder than he was, a wildness created and formed in a unique and troubling situation. She did not trust the white people, especially the white men. Many whites had learned to live in the woods, she acknowledged, but Lenni Lenape meant "the *real* Lenape"; and the white settlers, while good warriors and passable woodsmen, did not yet qualify in the overall scheme of things as real people, perhaps because they hadn't lived on Staaten Eylandt that long. But at the same time, Angel seemed effectively separated from her own tribal roots; Barnt suspected that she was the survivor not just of tribal wars, but of internal wars or conflicts within the clan in which she'd been raised. These wars, both the final war with Melyn and the white warriors in the 1650s — and an intertribal war that occurred at the same time — might serve to explain why, even though she was a young adult, she had no husband, and insisted that she had never really belonged to any man before Barnt. He in time accepted this as her personal history. All he really cared about was sharing his life with her in the future. At the same time, it seemed that Angel was effectively separated from her own tribe and clan, because so many had been killed, and the rest driven farther into the interior of East Jersey and Pennsylvania.

The tragedy of the Raritan was but one small part of the larger tragedy of the Lenni Lenape people. The greater Lenape nation, which considered the Raritan tribe the grandfather of their tribal customs, had for some time been losing their traditional lands in East Jersey, the *Lenapehoking*. Again, she told him the story of her clan's fate: because there were not enough adults to formally abdicate all the hunting rights of the tribe—because so many warriors had been called away to fight the tribal enemies that had attacked Lenape villages in New Jersey—children had been invited to sign the 1670 treaty with the white settlers, when the Lenape formally gave up Staaten Eylandt. Angel had herself a very vivid memory of signing it, and believed that because of this, she had inherited certain rights pertaining to the land, especially the right to conduct rituals for dead family members.

As Angel again told him the saga of her clan's demise, she begun to tell him of specific instances in which family members had been killed, drawing him into the trauma of separate deaths. The rest of the tribe had been threatened with removal to some place east, which was probably Pennsylvania; most of these families had already completed the move. Only she and her brother were left; they had moved to the Ramapough area while his wounds healed, and had a few years of relative peace. Yet because of the tribal wars, it soon because dangerous for them. They had heard tribal stories of the Bad Woods, and decided that few whites would ever come there.

So she and her brother had come to Staaten Eylandt, her brother leaving to go back and fight in the intertribal wars in East Jersey and Pennsylvania. Then Barnt had suddenly come, and having been drawn together as a couple in the night, they had after three days made love as a married couple. Yet she was not yet ready to come home with him, and live as his wife under the same roof with him. Barnt had the feeling that she was waiting to ask permission of her brother, if he ever showed up. (That part rang true: the Raritans were matrilineal, and the women would be likely to obey their older brothers rather than their husbands, who after all came from a different clan.)

Here Barnt began to get emotional, and the narrative seemed to dim somewhat, so increasingly I had to guess at the story. Angel still believed that sometime before winter Slow Turtle, her brother, would be coming back; he would look for her at her camp, to take her to East Jersey before the worst of the cold weather. So she stayed in her camp in her forest not far from Arthur Kill, while Barnt returned to his plantation. He was a strong man, and did his chores all in one long day, but could not wait to get back to Angel. When he did, she was surprised, but happy to see him. They went on for many months in this manner. He brought food to her camp from time to time, and blankets and cooking utensils. He also brought a horse pistol which he thought she might use to protect herself, but she had already made a bow and arrows with distinctive arrowheads, and was somewhat frightened by the pistol.

Each time he returned to her, he could hardly wait to be with her. He used the soft caresses that she liked, proceeding slowly until sometimes she wept with pleasure. He had not understood before the satisfaction of waiting to give a woman pleasure, and the manner in which that also gave the man pleasure. They hunted together, but he warned her about lighting a fire at night to cook meat, afraid it might attract white settlers or enemy braves. They continued to speak in Jersey Dutch, but she quickly picked up many English words and phrases.

She had to leave him for the winter in East Jersey, she explained, to help surviving members of her clan to set up winter camp in a place where their enemies were unlikely to find them. With so many warriors dead or incapacitated, it would be up to her and the other women to run the camp, and to save as many people as they could. She and her brother would stay on the hunting trails, she said, and those hunting trails that had become coach roads they would use at night, sleeping in the underbrush in the woods during the day. She promised repeatedly to come back to Barnt when the weather was warm. He made her promise, once, twice, and many times; it would be almost impossible for him to let her go, he thought, but at the same time a woman like Angel would not ask for permission, but would do whatever she thought necessary.

That night, Barnt told her of a wild plan that he has conceived. This was a plan to save her, her tribe, and the marriage that he now wanted more than anything. He would, he told her, initiate a plan that would compel—or encourage—the English colonial authorities to create a new patroonship in northeastern East Jersey, where all the Lenni Lenape could live in peace, first the Raritan tribe, and then stragglers from the other Lenape tribes. Their tranquility would be guaranteed by Barnt, he explained, who would be the magistrate of the new estate; those that didn't keep the peace would be ejected by him, and in that way their tranquility would be enforced. She seemed to believe in his sincerity and his enthusiasm, but he could not tell if she really believed that this project could be accomplished. Even as he explained it to her, he felt stronger and more inspired than he had for years, which convinced him that the plan had a certain transcendent quality that he had been waiting for all his life. Was this not the reason he had been drinking himself drunk every evening for years, because he had no grand plan, no central task or worldview, around which to build a better life? For some people it was religion; for him it was being with Angel, and the Promised Land was where it would be safe for them to be together. This was his new dream, his foundational belief system, and the result of a lifelong quest that he hadn't understood until now.

In time, her brother Slow Turtle came to get her. She did not embrace him or greet him in the way Barnt thought she would; instead she built a fire slowly, and with great care, and the two of them sat next to it silently. She gave him some food and then some tobacco. During the entire period, which was an hour or two, he glanced once at Barnt, who smiled and nodded. Slow Turtle returned the nod after a pause; that was the extent of it. Slow Turtle seemed to understand Barnt's relation to his sister— indeed, he seemed grateful that someone was taking care of her, and wanted to do so in the future, especially if he did not survive the tribal war. After a time, Slow Turtle began to speak in Jersey Dutch, telling the story of the war, and the great changes that war had brought, which was also a story of the extreme dangers their clan faced. Angel listened, motionless. At the end of his stories, she nodded, a gesture both of acceptance and finality.

Barnt at first thought to give Slow Turtle some rum, but quickly thought better of it. The tribal men did not react to strong drink the way European men did. Although the night was cold, Barnt kept the fire going for a long time, and slept separately from Angel. She gave her brother two quilts, and he seemed to sleep almost immediately. After eating the next morning, Angela began to gather together the things they would need. It was the autumn of 1687, and she would not be back until the spring of 1688, she said. Barnt pushed away all thought that he might never see her again, although it was at least possible that he wouldn't. He took Angel aside and explained that since they were now married, he would think about her every day until she came home to him. He also told her that he could not go on living unless she came back to be with him.

She laughed when he told her this, either not believing him or momentarily overcome by his commitment. At the moment for parting, when she had to go with her brother, he wept. She stood watching, without moving a muscle; she had seen this before, after the night when they had first made love. It apparently seemed wondrous to her that he would react to her leaving in this way. For his part, Barnt could not believe he was allowing her to leave him, when she had brought him a happiness he had never before dreamed of; yet of course he had to, because a woman like Angel did not ask any man's permission, except her brother's. Yet the fact that she was leaving him, to return in the spring, had already begun to seem like a dream of an enormous loss.

Barnt and Angel stood somewhat apart from her brother as

they said their goodbyes. Out of respect for Slow Turtle he did not touch her. Walking toward Arthur Kill where her brother's canoe was beached, Angel walked steadily behind Slow Turtle, with Barnt bringing up the rear. He suddenly slowed his pace, and then stopped; in front of him Angel and Slow Turtle went down a slight incline. They reappeared in Barnt's sight after about two minutes, paddling in tandem in their canoe as it nosed out into the tidal currents. Slow Turtle was expertly angling sideways toward the Jersey Shore. Barnt turned quickly away, unable to think clearly.

4.

Neil, the night counselor at Voyager House who was studying at CCNY, sometimes came into work deep in thought; and on those occasions it was better not to even try to start up a conversation with him. This night, however, he was overflowing with boisterous, positive energy—just that afternoon he'd been to a concert at Central Park featuring his favorite musical group, and was still under their spell.

"But man, I'm just as good as their lead guitar player," he said plaintively, "and if I'd stayed with my band, and the other guys had stuck with it, I could have been up there today! I tell you, I could have done it, if I'd just gotten a little support!"

I knew the whole story by heart—he'd once belonged to a garage band in high school, and they'd gotten "pretty decent," as he put it; and he was completely sure, in retrospect, that if his pals had stuck with the band a couple of years after high school, they could have scored a contract and gone on the road, perhaps opening for one of the better-known bands. But ambitious millennials that they were, Neil's bandmates insisted on going to college, by way of preparing themselves for a career. I kept my mouth shut about the fact that his favorite group, the one he had enjoyed just that afternoon, was famous for writing their own material . . . and that he, according to his own report, had zero talent as a songwriter.

"Why don't you play a little guitar for the clients come Sunday?" I said. "It would be good practice, the clients would be thrilled, and I'm sure Clarissa wouldn't mind."

"Ah . . . I don't know about that, bro."

"Your relationship with Clarissa a bit strained at present?"

"Maybe." So my intuition had been right—he'd been pulled in on the carpet for some disciplinary matter. At least he'd had union representation, I thought. "That kind of stuff is all confidential, man," he said.

"What do you think of Clarissa Rowland, overall?"

"You know, she's got a good heart. But she's a little manic. She brings in staff members who are crazy. Once she told me that if there weren't interesting conflicts to handle, she'd get bored. I didn't know if she was joking, or what."

"Scary, man." So she might be bipolar, hypomanic, or perhaps ADHD. "Does she do the same thing with her clients? Accept over-the-top referrals from Bellevue because otherwise she'd get bored?"

"My lips are sealed. But it's a different story with the clients, you know? It's okay to bring in the difficult clients, the ones society wants to throw away, because those are the folks we're supposed to work with anyway."

"She works well with Barnt, it seems."

"Yeah, I've seen that. It's interesting the way she gets him to open up."

Just that afternoon Barnt had been talking a blue streak at group, which was unusual for him. He was talking about a woman he had loved, no details, just the feelings; said he couldn't stop dreaming about her, the same dream. After a while he started sounding like *me*; then he talked about wanting to ship out again, but couldn't, because there was something he had to take care of here in New York.

"What do you know about Barnt?" I asked.

"Born in the Netherlands, went through the merchant marine academy in Vallejo, California—at least he says he did. Signs up on ships flying the Liberian flag, usually as third mate. He's a quiet guy, likes to observe other people. On a ship, he'd be dependable."

"Ever thought about going to sea yourself?"

"That feels a little like running off to join the French Foreign Legion—running away from the world, you know?"

"Yes," I said, "but going to sea seems just the ticket for some people. And you always come back on the beach to collect your paycheck."

For the Dutch, a seagoing people who had lost everything, it was a good fantasy, and it could last forever, like the sea. But the actual sailing, the maintenance of a big vessel and all the worries that went with that—that could be tiresome, despite the good pay. Not to mention all the conflicts that could arise in a multinational crew, plus the piracy in the waters around North Africa.

I left the staff office and went downstairs, thinking I might sit up reading in the parlor for half an hour or so, since I'd had a cup of tea a few hours before and couldn't get my head around going to sleep. But the knitting ladies were in the parlor, knitting up a storm, fascinated by some family drama on the Lifetime Channel; it was Saturday night, and clients were allowed to stay up until 1:00 AM. I backed out quickly, before they could see me, and went upstairs.

Barnt was there, lying on his bunk and reading by the light of a tiny clip light attached to the bed stand. I didn't ask what he was reading—the guy's taste was unpredictable, ranging from Harlequin romance novels to biographies of famous people from the library, to ancient copies of *Popular Mechanics*. Although I didn't have him pegged as an intellectual, he was ravenous to understand the nuances of New York City, exactly the way I would be if I was in his situation. It seemed to require a great deal of energy for him simply to exist; when he was tired, he slept or read or walked in the neighborhood, or rested on his bunk.

I sensed that his passivity had something to do with the stories he'd been telling me, as though he were a battery-driven instrument slowly running out of current. With every story he told me, his energy level seemed to recede a little more, and took time to restore itself. So I didn't want to rush anything, because at times I suspected that the best thing I could do was simply not get in his way. Yet I was curious about him, because I had waited so long for him to come.

"I heard you opened up in group today," I couldn't resist observing.

He laughed a bit ruefully. "Clarissa asked if any of us had ever been in love. She asked everybody, but it caught me off-guard. I had the feeling that the question was aimed at me." He still seemed unsettled by it.

He started thinking about his great love, Barnt said, and then talked about his feelings toward Angel, even though he adamantly refused to mention her name. Then at some point, he teared up. "And once I got started talking about the things I felt about her, I couldn't stop. Rowland was impressed by that, I guess."

"What did she say?"

"When I was alone with her, she wanted me to tell her more about the woman involved." He looked at me, as though I could supply a reason for her behavior. "First she tells us not to use any names, then when we're alone she wants to know the name of the woman I loved."

"Did you ever say Angel's name?"

"No, no, I only talked about my feelings, just like she told us to do." He paused. "Do you know why she puts such great emphasis on emotions?"

"She's a psychotherapist. Psychotherapy is all about the emotions."

He shook his head. "In my time it seemed like emotions often got in the way of doing the right thing."

"Clarissa's probably trying to help you," I said, although I suspected it was more than that. "She thinks you're delusional, and wants to get a sense for what you've been through."

I could tell that this subject unnerved him. "She thinks you're delusional, too," he said abruptly.

"What did she say about that?"

"Nothing, specifically—but once she asked me if you'd mentioned a kind of treasure, or wealth of some kind, that you're supposed to inherit. Can't remember what it was now, but the general idea was that she seemed to think you have a rich fantasy life, and live a big part of your life in your imagination."

"I do," I said. "What did you tell her about the money?"

"I strung her along a little bit."

I had no idea what he meant by that. "What exactly did you say?"

"I told her that there had been some Old Money in your family, and that you had some money coming to you, and you'd get it when you were ready for it."

"What did she say to *that?*"

"The expression on her face was one of complete confusion."

We laughed, although I wasn't sure why. "Well," I said, "maybe she wanted to give me a chance to lock up the money in the staff office. Security, you know. We don't have much theft at Voyager House, but you never know."

"Yeah, right."

I didn't ask further about the money, because money has a way of subsuming everything else in a conversation, even if some of those other things are mainly imaginary. The way I figured it, Barnt was here to explain a few things to me, many of which might have something to do with the Old Money. Eventually he would probably be in a position to know exactly how much—and what kind—of Old Money I would inherit; I simply had to be quiet, keep my composure, and eventually, I thought, I'd discover whether I was filthy rich, dirt poor or something else.

But this other thing that I was hoping that Barnt could explain to me—that was harder. I wanted him to tell me about the curse, the *maldición*, that had changed the nature of life for people who were descended from Thys Barentsen van Leerdam. *Was there some connection between my inheritance, and the curse?* Was the curse simply a *different kind* of inheritance? Somehow they all seemed connected, although at this point I couldn't say how.

Chapter 7

In that deep New York winter, in the unforgiving month of February, a nameless fear had taken root at Voyager House, as cold and implacable as the wind outside. It had to do with money, everybody understood that much; but it was also an existential threat, having to do with the very existence of the Voyager House program. Our consulting psychiatrist, Woodrow J. Frelinghuysen, MD, had in some manner laid some exceedingly bad vibes on our program—that much we knew. But it didn't stop with the questionable psychoanalytical theories of "the Frelinghuysen," as Neil called our consulting shrink; it seems that he had said a great many disparaging words about Voyager House to people in the city's mental health system, to the extent that it had started to affect certain aspects of our budgetary outlook—what Neil referred to as "the cash-flow problem of Voyager House."

The origins of the problem lay in Frelinghuysen's fantastic and increasingly aggressive attempts to impose a neo-Freudian interpretation on everything that occurred at Voyager House, among clients and staff alike. The casual reader may find it hard to believe, but there are today still orthodox devotees of Sigmund Freud in the practice of organized psychiatry. Indeed, these ancient and mainly outdated ideologies are in an odd way refreshing, considering that the role of many psychiatrists in the early twenty-first century is solely to prescribe medications destined to be ladled into the patient's nearest orifice. (I have heard that there are psychiatrists in the mental health department of New York City who believe that it is actually *harmful* to talk to patients.)

But the main point about our befuddled psychiatric consultant, Woodrow J. Frelinghuysen, was that he was unfortunately a natural-born extremist regarding his particular form of secular Calvinism, which was orthodox Freudianism; and it was at this point in his career, and in his consultancy at this particular residential treatment facility, that his need to formulate and impose vast, schematic neo-Freudian theories on the world really went off the charts. It began with his speculations about the clients, and progressed to his florid suspicions about the staff's various plots to challenge his authority. His paranoia became, over time, a horrible pain in the ass for all concerned.

All my attempts to interest our erring psychiatric consultant Frelinghuysen in Alfred Adler, the better to wean him from the Freudian phantasmagoria, came to nothing. Of the three great foundational psychoanalysts, Adler's ideas were by far the most impressive, I have always believed, not to mention the most practical. (Of Jung we will say nothing.) Sadly, "the Frelinghuysen" aggressively deflected all my efforts, no matter how collegial and patient, to interest him in concepts that were less than completely Freudian. The problem was not merely that he analyzed every client according to his interpretation of the true meaning of Freudian thought, but that he could not re-adjust or change his analysis, once made, *nor could he acknowledge being wrong about anything.* (It was, he said, the essential, pivotal insight of Freud that one should never admit being wrong, but should on the contrary hint at the conspiratorial opposition of others.) But the real kicker was this: Woodrow Frelinghuysen, MD, became convinced that opinions that contradicted or differed from his were *based in malice*—only that, he thought, could explain why so many people arrived at different conclusions than his own!

In the meantime, I had come very close to idealizing Voyager House. If one has lived the hole-in-the-wall, catch-as-catch-can sort of marginal existence that I have endured (despite my advanced literary ideas and unusual prophetic powers), one inevitably tends to idealize the warm and friendly memories over all others; this was all the more true now because of my advanced age. I experienced this warm and fuzzy idealization of Voyager House to a ridiculous extent during that long winter, sometimes so much that I wondered if I were imagining a great deal of it. The homing instinct, I have found, arouses an intense range of emotions, one that encompasses everything from birth to death: even a dog seeks a special place to die, a place that is somehow protected and cozy, where he can lick his wounds and expire in peace. Imaginary or not, these things were affecting me on a very deep level. This included a growing sense—I am not ashamed to admit it—that for reasons unknown I loved the frantic clinical director of Voyager House, Clarissa Rowland. These feelings were buried in the deepest recesses of my personality, never to be discussed, much less confessed, but they were there.

Along with those feelings, I began to feel that it would be very much like a kind of death to lose my placement at Voyager House. Even worse was the thought, the very *thought*, that Voyager House might be closed down. The central charge made by "the Frelinghuysen" during staff meetings—which he now attended regularly, and which were becoming increasingly adversarial, not to say hysterical—was that every action of the clients inspired or triggered an opposite emotional reaction in the counselors, an uncanny symmetrical reaction that interfered with their ability to think rationally. According to him, both clients and staff were unconsciously complicit in a seamless but vivid fandango of dangerous pathology, which nobody but him could describe or even discern fully. But he, and only he, could see through it, *because he did not see the clients on a regular basis*, as we did. That was his thesis.

Staff was for obvious reasons prohibited from articulating their own interesting thesis, which was that "the Frelinghuysen" was a raving depressive with paranoid personality disorder. Furthermore, it was well-known that he despised residential programs, much preferring a hospital setting. (Much of what he said, Clarissa Rowland had been heard saying loudly in the staff office, was nothing less than an attack on the very concept of residential treatment.)

We now entered a strange period of rumor, suspicion and rampant fear at Voyager House. Clients tried to find out more about the unknown bureaucratic forces that threatened them by eavesdropping on staff whenever possible. The staff, for their part, stopped gossiping about each other's personal lives in order to totally submerge themselves in endless discussions of the crisis that threatened to take away their livelihood. Of this crisis two things were certain: the budget for Voyager House was being threatened with unacceptable cuts; and that these budget cuts had to do with recommendations made by our hostile and spectacularly unpopular consulting psychiatrist, Woodrow Frelinghuysen. To add to the spookiness of the crisis, Frelinghuysen's darting, weirdly protruding eyes had become so paranoid and intense—particularly when expounding on his favorites theses—that on Thursdays, when he visited Voyager House to sit in at the staff meetings, they began to remind me unpleasantly of some glazed accoutrement poured at the Oyster Bay Glass Works.

It was during this uncomfortable interregnum that I conceived of, and brought into being, a genius system for eaves-dropping on the staff meetings. I did this through the simple expedient of drilling a hole in the floor of our second-story closet, systematically widening the top part of it, and finally installing into it a large and ingeniously designed glass container with the mouth pointed downward, the better to trap the sounds—all this in order to better eavesdrop on the staff meetings that were being held in the parlor every Thursday afternoon. Surely a time of illumination was at hand: if we were better informed, we would be to some extent forearmed, would we not?

Eavesdropping on staff meeting was only the first part of my plan. The second was to confront Frelinghuysen at his place of maximum weakness. I had long been aware that he was using various medications, some of which were street drugs—in fact, I had several times picked up on the unmistakable aroma of crack cocaine and cannabis on his dirty tweed suits and single overcoat, which was one reason I avoided him as much as possible—and I was afraid the substance abuse would simply make him more unpredictable than he already was. His glassy eyes had gradually become little more than red slits, and they (along with his shaking hands) told me that he was not far from hitting his particular bottom. Taking him down was a little like landing a punch on an opponent who was already headed for the long count . . . on the other hand, might not this kind of intervention enable him to get a little recovery for himself?

I told Barnt of my suspicions—and what I already knew. "Damn," he said. "That puts everything on a different footing. There's no reason why we shouldn't take action, given the danger he poses to this program. How did you know what to look for?"

"I live in New York," I said. "And I've been in a fair number of programs like this one. I can point out the substance abusers on the subway. And to be absolutely frank, I was in a twelve-step program for two years—and in this town a good half of the alcoholics are poly-substance abusers as well as drunks. That's how I knew what to look for."

He paused, but only for a moment. "Do you really want to get rid of Frelinghuysen?"

"Yes, of course."

"Write a list of the words New Yorkers use to describe street drugs. Make sure that these words are authentic, but not unnecessarily vulgar . . . also any words that have anything to do with the police and the typical substance abuser. Give the list to me before the staff meeting tomorrow."

"Why?"

"You'll see."

2.

During the long winter while Angel was gone from Staaten Eylandt, the winter of 1688 to 1689, Barnt had trouble sleeping, so ravenously and constantly did his mind and body long for her in the night's small hours. He knew that whatever happened to him in the rest of his life, Angel must be a part of it, and that he would do anything to make sure she was. Many of his early drinking companions were now dead and buried—two from dissipation, one of typhoid, another from the long rattling death of consumption, others from causes unknown. Barnt's growing need for solitude over the last few years had apparently protected him from the infectious diseases that tended to manifest themselves regularly in any port area. In any case, he did not see his old drinking friends so often now, although he had first invested money in some of their ventures, including the old *Groene Draeck* tavern, now Anglicized to "Green Dragon."

He had lost his appetite for friendship, as well as for the wild drinking and adventuring comradeship of youth; and although he still loved to drink, it no longer satisfied him in the same way, and could on occasion lead him into an inappropriate belligerence and bad judgment. Still, investing in the businesses of his friends was a useful expedient for keeping those same friends close, in those troubled times when it was sometimes necessary to do so, while at other times the formalities of a business relationship helped keep them at arms' length. He went over to Mannahattas when the cold weather permitted, to drink at the Green Dragon and then sleep in one of the rooms across the alleyway in the back.

He had also invested a fair amount of money on businesses owned by Johannes, his oldest son, who—under the tutelage of Barnt's brother Anthony—had lately demonstrated an unexpected talent for business, and of banking, of all things. Barnt invested more in the *Groene Draeck* during a slow period, improving the rooms to be rented at the back, and arranging for a kitchen where food would be served. This included bread from the bakery that Barnt also had an interest in, which he was soon to own in its entirety. Bread, even more than beer and rum, was a staple of the good life in the colony. Barnt went to Mannahattas often, when the cold weather permitted, meeting at the Green Dragon with friends, sleeping it off in one of the rooms in the back, but all the time keeping a sharp eye out for powerful people from Albany who could help him.

During the 1680s, Barnt had gradually made good business contacts in both English and Dutch communities. He was aided in this by the fact that he had arrived in the colony when he was fifteen, and spoke English without an accent, and in fact had already used it regularly before he arrived, including on shipboard during the voyage from Amsterdam. He communicated well with both the Dutch- and the English-speakers, including the Jersey Dutch speakers. Many of his old drinking friends made no effort to curry relationships with the English merchants, and made little effort to interact with the English-speaking arrivals with money and connections. It was hard for Barnt to understand why they didn't. When it came down to it, the Dutch were a merchant people, and New York was a trading society. What difference did it make if your customer was English or Dutch?

But for the Dutch wealth was usually but a means to an end, not the end itself, as it was with the English. In both the Netherlands and the colony of New York, the Dutch had created the concept of a certain measured beauty that lay just under the surface of everyday life, which was expressed in the Dutch art of that time. It was an unhurried way of life in the Netherlands, based on an intense connection to the sea and the land they had reclaimed from it, acted out in the tidy beauty of their homes and domestic arrangements. It was the self-confidence of a small nation in which people knew their own worth, and therefore did not find it necessary to overcompensate, or to bully those less fortunate.

So why not, in the colony of New York, do business whenever and with whomever one can, and seek one's fortune where one found it? Of course, some went overboard in their desire to ingratiate themselves with the new colonial administration. Several members of the Livingston clan in Albany had recently and quite ostentatiously converted from the Dutch Reformed Church to Anglicanism. That kind of public acquiescence was not Barnt's way. His way was to establish himself as a steadfast and trustworthy farmer and business partner, and leave religion out of it. But he had no doubt that sooner or later, if necessary, he would not hesitate to seek help from one or more of the English-speaking gentlemen who thronged the Green Dragon tavern. The money involved did not bother him. He had been lucky in trade and farming, and required no more money than he was already making.

During this long and seemingly interminable winter while Angel was gone, Barnt reassessed his life. His plantation and cattle were doing well; he could not complain of that. Some time back, his brother Anthony and his son Johannes had served as members of the local *vroedschappen,* which started as the governing council of New Town, and then of Staaten Eylandt as a whole. Because of a Dutch tradition of participation for only two years, both young men quickly gravitated to Mannahattas, where they were soon involved in more interesting and more profitable activities. During the late 1680s, his oldest son Johannes had become a trusted employee in an English bank, his other son now apprenticing to a wheelwright.

Barnt visited the wheelwright's shop once, and saw the cheeks of the owner's daughter redden whenever she was around his son. That was good, he thought, that was the way of the world; his younger son would ask the owner of the shop for the daughter's hand, when she was fifteen or sixteen. In the way those things happened, Barnt's younger son might stand a good chance of inheriting the shop if he continued to be a hard worker, especially since the owner was in poor health. Best of all, his oldest son Johannes, having married long ago, already had three children, one of whom was a boy that he named Bernard, after him.

But Barnt was vaguely aware (although he did not want to inquire about it) that Johannes had gone out of his way not to use Dutch patronymics for his children, instead using a variety of names both for them and for himself. It was a confusing time in the period of transition between Dutch patronymics and English-style surnames. Many young men of the older Dutch families were wary of insulting their fathers by not using the patronymic based on the father's name; but at the same time patronymics were not in use by the English in New York, or indeed most people in New York generally, including many Dutch who were abandoning their use. Therefore, the same person might use many names, depending on which group he associated with.

The result was the confusion typical of people caught up in the unbidden intensity of cultural and political change, in which power was shifting from one group to another—only to be refined and defined yet again by a new group that was a synthesis of the first two. Because many Dutch people had not yet figured out whether they wanted to continue patronymics or not, a great many younger people simply invented their own surnames, and were sometimes known by three or four of them, because to do so was easier. When one of the surnames stuck, later family members would continue to use it.

Barnt often wondered why he did not resent the power the English wielded. It was, he finally realized, because he had always been a dreamer, to whom power, when it came, would not come solely in the form of incremental additions of land or money, or a little temporal power here and there. The thing Barnt longed for would be huge and inexplicable, based in part on elements in his own imagination, but with huge consequences in the real world. It would be like the treasure that his father once told him about, buried by the Dutch privateers on islands, never to be found again. (Or perhaps, in some cases, they took it to Amsterdam and turned it over to the banks to keep.) He wanted not just a better situation in the world; that was good enough for his sons and their friends. In his heart of hearts, Barnt wanted a kingdom.

He had long dreamed of some momentous, private victory of a sort over the cruel exigencies of the world, something that would set him completely apart. The English had the dream of an ever-expanding empire, whereas he had the dream of a kingdom that was intensely private. No doubt it derived from the vestigial memory of the Dutch patroonship, a private kingdom whose laws were to be defined and enforced by the owner in his manor house; but it was also animated by the fantasy of a balanced, happy middle-class existence free of social conflict. The two elements of the dream added up to a wholly impractical fantasy, he realized, yet for him had long since developed the power of an opium reverie.

Barnt spent a great deal of time in Mannahattas that winter with his brother Anthony, a grain salesman who had invested money for his father and loaned Barnt the money for the thriving bakery he now owned. Barnt was grateful that Anthony was doing well, and that his own son had found a berth in a busy shop as an apprentice. But in Barnt's mind and heart, all he could think about was Angel. He cursed himself for letting her go, fearing that he would never see her, or that she would be killed or raped or enslaved. And the more he thought about it, the more the obsession grew in him for the founding of a new estate in East Jersey that could give refuge to the remaining Raritan people, or at least those in Angel's clan, so that she would not leave him again. Somehow it had to be done. He would never spend another winter without her again, he had decided, if there were any way he could prevent it.

And as the harrowing winter went on, the dream of an estate as a safe haven became indissolubly connected to the way he loved Angel. He wanted a kingdom, but he wanted it because of Angel—that is, he wanted it because it would be safe for both of them, not least for himself, since he had grown increasingly tired of life, despite the fact that he was only in his middle forties. A growing number of physical afflictions, and the fact that rum no longer gave him the happiness it once had, had conspired to create a situation in which he could not imagine life without Angel.

That was the image, the feeling, the fantasy that he kept coming back to, even when walking in the woods or reading the Great Bible of his father by candlelight. What an excitement, what a precious feeling to have her young body next to him! The sheer happiness of a physical release in her arms! Again and again he cursed himself for letting her go to Jersey, despite being quite aware that he could not stop her, and despite the terrifying awareness that she might never return. There was a certain honor he must follow in this relationship, even if it caused him to lose her forever—and it began with acknowledging the power of his feelings for her, while acknowledging her right to leave him if she must.

He continued to immerse himself in business, singling out a few of the richest men in the colony. Despite the fact that he was mainly in Albany, Robert Livingston—one of the richest men in the colony—sometimes came to New York, and Barnt was able to offer him food and lodging at the Green Dragon without looking obsequious. After a friendly discussion lasting no more than a few minutes, he had been allowed to invest in one of Livingston's projects. Barnt also met with Livingston's brother-in-law Pieter Schuyler once or twice, even speaking to him about the foundation of a new patroonship in New Jersey. (Surprisingly, Schuyler encouraged the idea, perhaps because he knew that Livingston had his own ambitions regarding such a project, and would later found his own 180,000-acre plantation that was a patroonship in all but name.) The Van Cortlandts, Schuylers, Livingstons and Van Rensselaers were the powerful ones that lived in Albany, but came often to Manhattan on business; Barnt kept his eye on them, looking for an opportunity to get to know one of them, since it was possible they could help him.

The Schuylers and Livingstons rotated as Commissioners of Indian Affairs; and both were known to like the idea of a patroonship in Northern Jersey as a buffer both against the tribal people and the Quakers, who were also moving into the area west of East Jersey. Several people in Albany were already aware of his plan, but he needed to take the next step. Whatever was necessary to get this patroonship for himself and Angel, he would do it. He was addled beyond words—it had even occurred to him more than once that if Angel were killed, or had died of typhoid, he would spend the rest of his life living with the people of the Raritan tribe; that maybe, possibly, if all else failed, and she was dead or missing and taken from him forever, he might someday search East Jersey one end to the other, to find another woman who looked and acted exactly like her. It occurred to him that this thought was disloyal, not to mention insane. During those hard winter months of January and February of early 1689, he was a man obsessed.

3.

The first time I eavesdropped on the staff meeting in my upstairs closet, I felt like a Greek tragedian going to the Oracle at Delphi. What staggering pathologies might I encounter, what strange truths might I confront, what unimaginable challenges or inter-nalized conflicts would I be enabled to acknowledge? I might witness or overhear something that would take the study of human behavior to some new, higher level, a veritable string theory of psychology! And since it was by definition a voyage into unknown waters, I made up my mind not to enter into this secret theater burdened by prejudice; I would let the events play out as they would. Certainly I was aware that it was transgression on my part, to listen to such a staff meeting surreptitiously; residents at Voyager House would normally not be welcome at staff meetings, since it was intended for the edification of staff only. Participating in such meetings were seven or eight counselors, the clinical director Clarissa Rowland, and the consulting psychiatrist Woodrow J. Frelinghuysen, MD.

Simply to listen to people in conflict often felt to me like complicity with the conflict itself, and by necessity with one side more than the other—one reason why I have long preferred to be homeless. Who knew what hideous psychiatric grand jury I might be summoned to testify at, after eavesdropping on this staff meeting in the parlor below? Who could say what secret Star Chambers existed at Bedlam-by-the-Hudson, in the rarely visited backwards of Bellevue Hospital Center? I was already well aware that the APA, the national organization of the psychologists, had willingly participated in torture by the state after 9/11, further dragging America into depravity. What would stop the even goofier psychiatrists, then, from torturing in the most brutal manner a poor madman like me, putting aside for the moment my special prophetic powers and all it could mean for the national security of the nation?

There weren't that many people in the parlor below, but the baseline sound I heard at first was a muted milling about, like static on AM radio—the scrapping of chairs, the dull tinkle of spoons in cups of coffee, a low murmur of indistinguishable voices. I quickly got used to the way the glass in my closet transmitted sound; I could hear quite well (and in fact better) by lifting my ear a quarter inch or so above the glass poised in the hollowed-out hole. I shortly began to hear the voice of Clarissa Rowland, whose speech now seemed even more pressured than usual.

"Yes, yes, of course there's coffee in the pantry," Clarissa was saying—or rather, yelling. "And tea in the kitchen, if you want that!"

A female voice cheered. "What about cocktails?"

"Not until four o'clock. This is New York, not San Francisco." The noise abated. "*So,*" she continued as the background noise calmed down, "are there any announcements?" A pause ensued, during which she must have looked around the group. "So why don't we do reports on the clients? I think it would be a good thing to start with Paul, since he's doing well. D'Nysha, you're Paul's primary counselor . . . would you like to report on Paul's week?"

D'Nysha Williams was a tough, leather-jacketed lady born in Bed-Stuy in the 1980s (or as she put it, "the *real* Bed-Stuy"), whose buttons you would not want to push. But she could pick her battles, and was known to string fools along just to turn them out. "Paul is cool," she now opined. "Mainly he likes to draw his space weapons, and the big monster interplanetary vehicles with guns; and he keeps all these pictures in his notebook . . . actually, now he keeps his pictures and diagrams in a big *briefcase,* that he carries around with him."

"Is he willing to share his pictures?" someone asked.

"No, not so much nowadays—not if you ask him directly. You ask him *directly,* he might think you trying to *control* him. Might could be that sometime he will *volunteer* to share them, like two days ago, when he had them all over the staff office, everywhere you looked there was a space ship . . . it just hit the man that suddenly he wanted real bad for us to see what he been drawing. And you know what—the pictures were not bad, not bad at all."

I heard the scrape of a chair, and instantly knew it belonged to "The Frelinghuysen." I also knew immediately what he was going to say.

"Has he been taking his, his . . . *prescribed medication?*"

There was a long silence while the group waited for D'Nysha to answer. I could imagine in my mind's eye the quiet, expressionless look she gave to fools. There were two versions of this facial expression: one was the fixed smile, the other no smile whatsoever.

I hoped it was the latter.

"It's the law in this facility, Dr. Fre . . . Fre . . ."

"Frelinghuysen! *Frelinghuysen!*" I heard someone say, followed by a half-suppressed giggle.

There was an awkward silence.

"And if you forget to document dispensing meds to the clients, it's subject to *disciplinary action*," someone helpfully pointed out, almost surely Jack Cohen, the SEIU Shop Steward.

There was another awkward silence.

"See, appropriate use of medication, that's, that's an important part of psychosocial *rehab*," D'Nysha said. "I just want you to understand that it . . . might could be, you know, that getting them to take their meds, and documenting the exact *strength* and *dosage* every time, it's not the *only* part of the rehab, but it's a *big* part, is what I'm saying. Everybody got to know that, they want to work here." Her words were pregnant with some strong emotion, but it was impossible to tell if it was anger. "And it's, it's a big part of Clarissa's job to make sure that they get their meds, and that we sign off on them, you know, Dr. . . ."

"Frelinghuysen!"

"You always be *reminding* the clients, and then you got to check the med book, and see . . . see if they take they meds. And we don't medicate these people . . . no sir, we don't, we don't do that . . . we *remind* them, and they medicate *themselves!* And then we check *off* when they *take* the meds! And you will never see anybody, anybody who works at this Voyager House, who does not remind the client every day, *there are some prescribed meds up in that staff office,* and you better take those meds, because, you know, it's a big part of your recovery!"

There was a respectful silence after D'Nysha's speech.

"Not *my* recovery," Frelinghuysen said inexplicably, "*I* don't take psych meds."

"I don't mean *literally you*," D'Nysha said, "I was talking about the *clients*. But if you *did* take psych meds, or any *other* kind of meds, there wouldn't be, you know, anything *wrong* with that."

D'Nysha was a master of passive aggression, honed in the mother-wit of difficult centuries on American soil. Even Clarissa now seemed at a loss for words.

I heard Frelinghuysen clearing his throat, and there was an ominous rustling of some sort, perhaps of a chart.

"Now, about those graphics of Paul's," he said. I now realized that the rustling sound was of Paul's drawings and pictures of space weapons. "What do they really look like? I mean, what is the client *really telling us?*"

"That he's aggressive as hell," said someone who I thought was Eric. He was a student like Neil, but a little older and at Columbia rather than CCNY.

"And hostile!" said Jack Cohen. "Damn hostile! That's the most difficult part of counseling this client, the hostility!"

"The dude is paranoid," said Neil. "To him, people are the big-time enemy. And the enemy isn't confined to this world . . . the enemy is out there, in outer space. I asked him, one time, why anybody would need to have such monster weapons out in space, like these contraptions that he draws. He said, 'What makes you think people are going to stop being *mean* just because they fly around in *space*?'"

"Does he draw space *monsters?*" Frelinghuysen asked. "I mean, terrifying, *nightmarish* monsters?"

Several people were apparently trying to remember.

"No, not so much," a female voice said, while others agreed.

"Why don't we *see* the monsters or space creatures driving these space vehicles?" Frelinghuysen wanted to know.

The group was silent, as though apprehensive of Frelinghuysen's next insight. I myself had an uncomfortable feeling regarding where he was going with it.

"Is it the *vehicles themselves* that are the monsters? Stop and look at the vast majority of these "contraptions. . . All" of them are shaped like rockets, each of which requires maximum thrust, which means enormous powers of propulsion to escape the earth's gravitational pull!" I imagined him smiling his ghastly snaggletooth smile, a Doctor Caligari of residential treatment. "They are all, *all* shaped in the same way, to escape that same pull of gravitation! It couldn't be clearer!"

"You mean . . ." Neil said ominously.

"Are you saying that these *rockets*, or whatever they may be—" said Eric.

"Are shaped exactly like penises! Great, flying, erect penises! *That's* what the client is trying to tell us!" He was apparently shaking or rattling Paul's sketches. "I'm telling you, psychological truth is always unsettling . . . but how could it be anything else? He's a young male, you see, and his libido is frantically signaling to get out!"

There was an explosion of voices, followed by dead silence. It hit me at that moment how ugly the word "penis" could be, nothing less than a violent verbal unmasking of the male body.

"Sometimes," Neil was saying, "a rocket is just—"

"I know, I know!"—Frelinghuysen yelped in exasperation—"a rocket is just a rocket! A penis is just a penis! But no, not when he draws them that many times, over and over and *over!* He is gradually stewing, *marinating* in his own testosterone, and we have to make him aware of it, and allow him to . . . to . . . *release* these toxic anxieties!"

"Just because *we* can talk about it, doesn't mean *he* can talk about it!"

"The boy so *medicated*, he might not know what it *is!*"

I could imagine Frelinghuysen sitting bolt upright in the parlor below, the honest shaman rampant among the philistines. "I'm not saying it is easy! It's difficult! I'm the first to admit that!

But if we want him to get well, we have to push the envelope!" He rustled around with something else. "I have here a treatment plan tailored to the special needs of our client, Paul—I'll be giving each one of you a copy of it, to put in Paul's chart as you fill it out. You see, this special treatment plan has a check-off list, and two places where you can answer the questions at length in your own way. The point is to ask him *every day*, at least three times, how much sexual contact he may have had, or dreamed about, or had a fantasy about . . . and how many times he has masturbated! The importance of doing this daily, at least three times, can't be overemphasized!"

There was a long and horrified silence from the counselors.

"Dr. Fre . . . Frelinghuysen . . . I appreciate everything that you do," D'Nysha Williams of Bed-Stuy was saying firmly. "And I particularly appreciate this *check-off* list, so we can *check* off when he *whacks* off, if you see what I mean. But I am here to tell you, if I ask the boy how often he *whacks off*, how many times a day he *spanks the monkey*, I am here to tell you that this question will escalate the poor client, and my Paul will have to be hospitalized!"

"Yes, of course," Clarissa said, going at it a hundred miles an hour, "Paul is completely unable to discuss sexual issues like that, *anything* like—"

"Like *sex* and *masturbation?*" Frelinghuysen shouted. "I know what you think, and I expected your attempts to undermine me. But pray tell, how do we heal the difficult cases if not with the *truth?*" I heard the sound of Frelinghuysen scooting his chair back, followed by an awkward muffled clunk of a spoon being dropped into an empty coffee cup. "I expect everybody to use the treatment plan daily, and to ask the appropriate questions. If you don't, you'll have to answer to me. Clarissa, you are responsible for making sure that everybody in this program executes the treatment plan daily." I heard him walking to the door. "I'll be right back."

There was the ponderous clumping sound of Frelinghuysen exiting the room, apparently heading toward the first-floor restroom. Then there was a sound I didn't recognize at first, a shriek from Clarissa Rowland.

"This is a catastrophe!" Clarissa shrieked. "A catastrophe!" Her voice shot up an octave. "Poor Paul. Poor *Paul*."

Then there was a depressed silence, as the group in the room below contemplated what had transpired.

"We don't have to do what he says," someone said hopefully.

There was another silence, as counselors contemplated the likely results of a mutiny.

"I'm afraid we do," Neil said, "if we want to keep our jobs. Especially given the negative things he's been saying about Voyager House uptown."

Depressed silence reigned again.

"Paul will freak out," Eric was saying.

"Well," an unknown voice was saying, "maybe we can get him to draw pictures of the space weapons *killing* Fre . . . Fre . . . the consulting shrink . . . and that way, you know, maybe he wouldn't be so upset with the questions—"

"No, no, no," Clarissa was saying, "any talk about sex makes him completely paranoid. And to think, *each one* of us are supposed to ask him *every day* about it, three times a day, whether he's, you know, done something sexual, and then document his answers. He'll escalate, just like D'Nysha was saying, and he'll have to be hospitalized." Again her voice went up an octave. "Which is where Frelinghuysen wanted him in the first place! Everybody knows how he hates residential treatment!"

This time the silence was all-encompassing, a silence not of conversation, but of impotent fury. It went on for some time, during which I felt I was moving away from them, and from Voyager House itself, into a deep space in the galaxy where it was always cold and there was ice everywhere. But the drama was far from over; it was not to be the mute tragedy that I feared, but something that in its own way was to be even more shocking.

"Okay, everybody," I heard Clarissa say a bit shakily, "let's take a break. There's coffee in the pantry, if anybody wants it."

In my ear was the soft shuffling thunder of counselors leaving the parlor, but with voices muted now, given what appeared to be the unavoidable disaster looming ahead. There was nothing from the parlor except the sound of Clarissa crying. But I heard something else now, the sound of Frelinghuysen's doleful footfalls coming down the hall and then entering the parlor, which was apparently now empty, except for Clarissa Rowland.

"You arrogant son of a bitch," she said.

To me—listening through my special glass device in the upstairs closet—it was starting to sound like radio of the 1950s: the creaking of the door in *Inner Sanctum*, the piercing notes of *The Whistler* and his reckoning of evil in the hearts of men; the magnificent theme music of *Yours Truly, Johnny Dollar*, Jack Benny's long walk to the vault in the basement . . . it was all signals and sounds relating to the drama, but with the actual drama occurring somewhere else.

The sudden footfalls of Frelinghuysen's boots were now joined by someone else coming into the parlor, both of whom were met with a sharp exclamation of surprise from Clarissa. And then, there was the deep voice of the person animating this new persona. "You forgot something, Frelinghuysen," said the voice, which I realized was unmistakably Barnt, words that were followed up by the sharp, ominous clack of small things being dumped on the table.

There was a sharp intake of breath from Clarissa.

"You forgot your crack pipe," Barnt was saying. His voice was quite loud. "And the cannabis—I guess you take that to get to sleep. You got your works here, right in your briefcase—goddamn syringe and a damn cord and your chiva stash. And a little Crack of Dawn to wake up with."

"That's my property!" Frelinghuysen was yelling, his voice

breaking. "I mean, the briefcase! . . . I never saw these, these other things!"

"They were right there in your briefcase. And I got a couple of witnesses."

"I'm going to have you arrested."

"Call the cops. Please. I want to show them this contraband in your briefcase."

"Who will listen to you? You're a damn client!"

"No, I'm an undercover narcotics officer at the five-oh. That's a precinct in this neighborhood, but you probably wouldn't know that." Pause. "So that's it, doc. You were holding, and all this stuff goes to the evidence room at the five-oh, and we let a district attorney sort it out."

"No."

"Then walk."

"Let me have my briefcase."

"Sure, but first you understand. I make a verbal report to the captain at the five-oh, and that gives me insurance. I tell the captain at the five-oh that you're a confidential informant, but you are a junkie and the five-oh knows that you're a junkie. You step out of line and you're busted, and you lose your medical license. Remember, they can test you for drugs anytime. And I would be very surprised if they didn't."

Frelinghuysen was making a sound like the gnashing of teeth.

"*Got* it?" Barnt asked, raising his voice.

There was a stuttering, sputtering sound—then: "Yes."

"Then walk, and don't come back here!"

I heard Frelinghuysen clump out of the parlor, down the hallway, and out the front door. It was Jack Benny's long walk to the basement vault on 1950s radio, except not to the vault but to the great outdoors of total defeat.

The *ka-thump* of the front door closing echoed for some time. Nobody went to lock it.

In a moment or two, I heard a few of the counselors talking

sotto voce in the downstairs hallway. How much they had seen or heard was impossible to tell from my concealed auditory vantage point.

"Go home, everybody," I heard Clarissa saying from the parlor. I could hear her voice shaking slightly. "I've—we've had enough drama for today. Staff meeting next week. Same time."

There was the soft undifferentiated rumble of people going to the door, putting on boots and outerwear, and exiting. There was a minimum of talking, but a fair amount of whispering, which I could not understand. I could hear one group of counselors exiting the front door, then what sounded like other voices. One voice I recognized, the clearly discernable but mellifluous intonations of D'Nysha Williams, floating up from the vicinity of the front door.

"Well," she was saying, "I don't know exactly what go down here, but it looks to me like Dr. *Ferlinghuysen* got himself *Ferschnookered!*"

With this shocking pronouncement, the front door *ka-thumped* closed. Blessed peace and quiet returned.

4.

With that, I put the glass contraption away, through which I had been listening to the conversation downstairs, and sat down on my bed. How much of it was real? Had I heard something wrong, had I edited in or excised something out of my consciousness? I was overwhelmed. It was like the way one feels after an intense experience at the theater, in which one identifies certain characters as being like people one knows, but that later, in short-term memory, seem completely different. What had been real, and what were things that my fertile imagination added to the mix? I waited for Barnt to come upstairs so I could ask some questions, while I was still thinking about what I'd heard downstairs.

But then, at that moment, I had an intuitive feeling that the action wasn't quite over down in the parlor—I may even have heard some noises down there. In any case, I went back in the closet and put the glass device back into its narrow carved depression in the floor, and put my ear down close to it.

Apparently the parlor below me was empty now, except for Barnt and Clarissa Rowland. I heard their voices clearly. "Are you really a cop?" Clarissa was asking. "I mean, an undercover narcotics officer?"

The voices still came from far away, but the game—their game, anyway—was still afoot.

"No, not even close," Barnt was saying. "I'm not a cop. I'm a seaman."

"But you sounded like a cop."

"I had to, to make him believe me."

"Where did you learn to talk that way?"

"From American books. Mysteries, they call them . . . also from *Law and Order* on TV."

Another pause, then her question: "Why? Why did you do this?"

"For you."

"Why?"

"I love you. But you know that already."

Then there was nothing, nothing except the very soft, very sensual rustle of an embrace.

Even today, two years later, I don't know how much of it I imagined, especially the last part. I do think that Barnt's intervention was wonderful, even if aspects of it happened in my imagination. And it was apparently quite effective. Woodrow J. Frelinghuysen stayed away from Voyager House for weeks; and when he came back, he was careful to keep his distance from the staff. And, thankfully, there were no more lectures at staff meeting about the nature of psychological truth, and our consulting psychiatrist produced no more controversial treatment plans.

5.

"Don't you think it's about time we talked about the money?" I asked Barnt a couple of nights later.

It was well past eleven in the evening. I had a feeling that it was absolutely necessary to discuss this particular subject—now, and this particular night—partly because it was something we had avoided discussing for too long. Barnt was lying on his bunk reading a book from our nearby library, but now turned to look at me. He was growing a beard, the short stubble in the shadows giving his face a grizzled look, like a forest animal in deep winter. His bunk was his lair, his hole, his den, and when his face was in shadow, he was safe. I understood that feeling; but on this particular night, I also felt that if I went past midnight without discussing the Old Money, I would be convicted of cowardice in the court of my own imagination.

"What about the Old Money?" I asked.

"The Old Money belonging to the family?" he said, sitting up. "Yes, of course. We'll have to go outside."

That wasn't what I expected. "Why outside?"

"I don't feel comfortable discussing it in here. People have a way of listening in on other peoples' conversations." He reached for his boots. "We'll have to be quiet going out. Everybody's asleep."

I took off my slippers and started putting on my shoes, wishing I had a pair of boots like his.

He was lacing up his boots as he talked. "Don't expect any instant miracles. But you have a right to know the truth, or at least as much as I can tell you at the present time. And yes, if you get your hands on money that is rightfully yours, you should make a hefty contribution to Voyager House. Clarissa needs the money."

We put on our coats and headed down the stairs on tiptoes. There was no sound from the staff office. I let Barnt go well ahead of me, and we made our way down the stairs with many a creaking step. As we existed into the outside from the front door, I made sure it had a newspaper jammed in the lock, so it would be easy to open later from the outside. It was supposed to be locked at night from the inside, but night staff would probably not check it until later.

"Okay," Barnt said. We stood outside on the sidewalk in front of Voyager House. "All the streets in this area run true east and west, unlike the rest of Manhattan. The *Groene Draeck,* the Green Dragon, was a tavern that was located right next door to this place." He pointed to the warehouse building next door. "Of course, it was torn down. Many buildings were built on this site, and there were a couple of bad fires. But there is where the Green Dragon was located, in the beginning."

"Owned by family members?"

"Correct, including by me. Then for the next few decades owned by different family members, until most of them moved to New Jersey and Virginia."

Now I got it—the money was in the form of property! "So, the Green Dragon was there. What was here, where Voyager House is now?"

"Some rooms. A hotel, you might say. I used to get drunk and sleep here . . . it's a wonder I didn't freeze. A couple of times I got that sleepiness you get in winter, when you're going to die in the snow. But that winter when Angel was gone I was always dreaming about her, every moment I was dreaming of her, and those dreams made me get up and walk around, because I couldn't sleep." He sighed, the first time I'd ever heard him do that. "I couldn't die as long as I had those images of her in my mind."

I said nothing. What was there to say? I'd been there myself once or twice.

Now Barnt took me on a little walking tour, specifying where the different places had been located. "Here's the office of Gillis Verbrugge, part of an Amsterdam trading company. Here was the residence and brewery of Oloff Stevensen van Corlandt, the burgomaster until 1665; later on it was leased to an English firm. Here's the house of Gerrit Hendricksen and Frederick Philipse." He took me around the corner. "Here's where Frederick van den Bergh, wine and tobacco merchant, had his office and living quarters."

"And over here, here was the home of Warnaer Wessels, who bought it from Dominie Bogardus, New Amsterdam's first permanent clergyman. The office of Jacques Cortelyou, the surveyor, was over here; and here was the New Hospital, built a year before my father arrived. Next door was Anthony Jansen van Slaee, aka 'Anthony the Turk.' He liked to live close to the taverns, including the Green Dragon, and he drank in all of them."

He turned yet another corner. There was dangerous ice every-where, but by the streetlamp I could see snow falling, down through the dense layers of remembered time. Barnt had seen it all, all of this lost world; to me the pure shock of hearing the names, even though I knew about some of the people, was like wave after wave of freezing seawater in the face.

"On this corner was Dr. Hans Kierstede, the town's first doctor. Trijn Jonas, the town's first midwife lived here. And Annetje Jans Bogardus, by all accounts a strong-willed, educated woman with a powerful faith, lived next door. Jacob Steendam, Nieuw Amsterdam's first poet, lived here . . . all of his work was lost, I think. The estate of John van Beeck was located here; next door was Allert Anthony, one of the first lawyers." He paused in front of a large warehouse. "And here was van Tienhoven's house, which after his death became the property of his heirs and creditors, who could never agree on what to do with it. What a shame—it was such a big, centrally located property."

In the freezing coldness I turned halfway to look at him, to fix forever the full figure of him in my imagination. At least six foot four, he looked like nothing more or less than a seagoing man, but a little more resolute than any ordinary seaman—that fit, in a way, since he usually signed on as third mate or safety officer. (I could see him wrestling recalcitrant lifeboats and firefighting equipment during a drill on rough seas.) He was wearing four or five days of stubble, a resigned yet confident smile, and his usual pea jacket; his small pipe was wedged in the corner of his mouth, unlit, and four or five nondescript sweaters under the jacket. His pants were chinos with suspenders that came up over his shoulders under one of the sweaters. His boots made a metallic grating sound on the concrete sidewalk.

He was wearing boots that had small ridges on the bottom to prevent slippage, and to keep one's balance until the sea legs kicked in. It all fit, it was all something that I had been waiting for, and would never forget. He was a handsome man; but above all, he had a kind of authority, and a way of sizing people up: he was not an aggressor, but not a pushover either, a man who probably carried a knife in his boot, or had other ways to defend himself. Now he paused to light his pipe, and he took one long draw, looked up at me, and then took two more quick draws. All these things I saw in a light of a streetlamp shining on us from half a block down.

Having lit his pipe, he turned the corner, and started around the block, but not away from the general direction of Voyager House. "Here was Egbert van Borsum, the operator of the ferry to Breuckelen. Here was Dirk, the surgeon barber—he did pig gelding for my brother Anthony. Nicklaes Verlett was over here, the brother-in-law of Governor Stuyvesant. And next to it the 'Great House' of Pieter Stuyvesant." He stopped; we were standing in front of a huge abandoned lot filled with trash. It was hard for me to believe that there was nothing there, no marker, nothing.

"Of course, Stuyvesant built another house, a farmhouse, on the other side of the Wall after the Conquest of 1664." Barnt started walking again, with me trailing along beside him. "Not far from here was the tavern of Michiel Janse Vreeland. Next to that was the Trivial School, the Latin school that the children attended. On the corner was the little house of Pieter Pietersen, the Anabaptist, blown down and destroyed in a windstorm the winter after he died."

We had gone around the block and were now at the corner not far from where Voyager House was located. He puffed his pipe, and looked up through the falling snowflakes at the moon, the way a sailor would.

"My God," I said. "All of those people here. And nobody knows."

He turned to me suddenly. "Do you think that I'm delusional?"

"Clarissa thinks we both are, I believe. She uses that word a lot. That's not an entirely bad thing, you know—if she didn't think we were delusional, we wouldn't be at Voyager House."

Now we both looked up through the snow falling gently, the lights of the city being reflected softly from the low cloud cover.

"Aren't you afraid the Old Money is all a fantasy?" he asked suddenly.

"No," I said, "inherited wealth is real, and you have demonstrated, in a most breathtaking way, how real and how close it is to both of us. I always knew it would be something like this, something just under the surface of everyday reality, but nonetheless something of inestimable economic worth. Thanks for showing me."

My head was swimming. I couldn't get over the fact that there was no historical marker, no marker of any kind, at the place where Stuyvesant's house had been. "Why on earth is there no monument of any kind to mark the house—the Great House—of Pieter Stuyvesant?"

"You tell me. It's your country now."

We both laughed, but it was like a door opening. "Really? How much of this neighborhood belongs to me? And how do I liquidate it, when I need some ready cash?"

He glanced at my face, no more than a glance.

"It's here," he said. "It's all here."

"How will I take ownership of it? I mean, what if I want to sell some of it off?" Before he could say anything I went on: "Look, I've never had money—can you blame me if I want some now? I want to know how it feels not to be poor. Also, I want to have money in the bank if I need it to help Clarissa. You're aware of that, I know, because you want to help Clarissa yourself."

He smiled, and I had the impression that he was impressed.

"You know enough for now," he said. "We'll discuss these centrally located properties a little more when the time is right. But please be aware—it's all here, and you'll get your rightful share of it. You have every right to collect the money that is due to you—I mean, having been poor, you should enjoy some economic security before you die. And above all, you should be prepared to help Clarissa if she needs it." He paused and looked at me again. "That's one of the main reasons I'm here to help you, you know."

His speech touched on all the information I needed to know, yet there was something missing. "I thought you came to tell me what happened to our family," I said, "and how the curse, the *maldición*, came to be placed on us. The money is a separate issue, isn't it?"

"No, it's not. They're connected, the money and the curse."

So what I had long suspected was true. "How? How are they connected?"

"You'll find out. And when you do, the Old Money will be yours."

Chapter 8

In January 1689, Barnt went back to drinking rum, but quickly found that he could not become drunk. That being the case, he stopped drinking entirely—intoxication was already his, not from the cup but rather from visions of the new patroonship in East Jersey that he hoped someday to administer. (Of course, in dealing with the English colonial administration he was prepared to call it a manorial estate, unless they themselves wished to refer to it as a patroonship.) Once he was well into this particularly obsession, he began to realize that he was not the only one beset with it. With the English it was an absolute mania: apparently every ambitious middle-class English family could think of little but amassing money, building a beautiful country house, and after a period of diligent but understated public service acquiring a coat of arms, and perhaps eventually a knighthood or an even more impressive title. That was the way it was in England, and to a great extent the way of the English in the New World as well.

With the Dutch it was a little different. The idea of the patroonship came in part from the grandiosity of empire, just as did the English worship of the landed aristocracy; but most Dutch saw social elevation as a function of wealth, of success in an increasingly mercantile culture, and the leisure and the luxuries of wealth serving the ideal of homely comforts rather than imperial glory. Despite the differences between the Dutch and English ideals, the dream of success was quite similar in other ways: the capacious country house, the vast lands that could be speculated and sold in parcels for ready cash, and the power and prestige that came from being part of the land-owning elite.

Barnt was particularly fascinated by the ambition of the Livingston family of Albany, who seemed to represent the unflinching and often brutal energy necessary to get ahead in the New World. Most of his information about them came from customers in his tavern, or in various venues in New York, or from his brother Anthony, who often went to Albany. Robert Livingston's father had been driven into exile from Scotland in 1663 because he would not accept the transformation of the Presbyterian Church into an Anglican institution. The family settled in the Netherlands, and the son Robert became fluent in Dutch. In New Netherlands he became the secretary to Nicholas Van Rensselaer, because of his language and business skills; and upon the death of his employer Van Rensselaer, he quickly married his widow.

Although ethnically Scottish, he moved in Dutch circles, and nobody was particularly surprised when several Livingstons converted to Anglicanism. In the New World, ambition had brought Robert Livingston to the very church that his father had renounced in Scotland; and because of this seamless, fanatical ambition, Barnt suspected that the Livingstons might have some interest in patenting a patroonship in East Jersey, especially since Robert was Secretary of Indian Affairs, and had spoken publicly of wanting a firm buffer between Mannahattas and the tribes in the interior past the Raritan River. It had to be handled discreetly, of course, but there was little doubt in Barnt's mind that Livingston could be bribed. Barnt had a kind of open-ended appointment to talk with him in Albany, although the timing had remained a bit vague.

For Barnt, the dream of a private kingdom was different in one critical way: it was a way of ensuring safety for Angel, his *brandtengel*, his angel-in-the-fire, the passionate creature that haunted his every footstep in his house on Staaten Eylandt. Sometimes he gave up trying to stop thinking about her, gave up trying to push images and feelings of her out of his bed, in the hallucinatory hours before dawn giving up on sleep altogether, harried as he was by intensifying waves of sensation. Lust it probably was, he knew; but without any question it was also love, love complete and unremitting—that he knew, because he'd never felt anything as strong as it before, and because he was willing to do anything to help her. He ached for the day that the ice on the Raritan River would finally crack open, so that Angel could come back to him—but would that day ever come? The idea that she might not return was an eventuality he would not and could not allow himself to dwell upon.

Thus it was with a special intensity that he listened to the news and rumors afoot in the Green Dragon, going to Mannahattas two or three times a week on Staaten Eylandt's crude daily boat to the Lange Eylandt ferry house, then to Mannahattas—unless the weather was prohibitive, as it often was. At the Green Dragon there were rumors of war, and rumors of the business dealings of the Schuylers, the Van Rensselaers, the ruthless Bayards, and Governor Thomas Dongan, who was rumored to be Catholic. In the Green Dragon, and in the other taverns, the news tended to arrive with the seagoing clientele, as well as letters, newspapers and stories of the latest happenings in Britain and Amsterdam.

Recently arrived passengers brought word that a son had been born to King James II, which meant that the creation of a Catholic dynasty was virtually inevitable; but there was also word that William III of Orange-Nassau, William of Orange, was preparing to take the field against James. Finally, there was word that William had crossed the North Sea and the English Channel, and in November 1688, had landed at Devon. If William defeated James, a Protestant ascendency would be protected, which was now an issue of extreme importance to both the Dutch and the English.

One day Barnt was attending to business in the lower part of Mannahattas—or "Mannahatto," as some called it, or New York, as the English preferred to call it—and set aside his work to go to the waterfront to look at the warship *Delfland*. The *Delfland* was indeed one of the most beautiful ships ever launched, towering and majestic, and a matter of special pride for the Dutch. During the second sea war with the English it had, under Captain De Ruyter, sailed recklessly up the Thames to destroy the English fleet, one of the most amazing feats in the annals of maritime warfare. In the winter of 1688-89, of course, no Dutch person in New York would think of talking about it in front of his English friends . . . except perhaps to remark apologetically that it was hardly sporting to attack an enemy just recovering from the plague. But say what you will, and to whom you will, the *Delfland* was one proud and beautiful ship, and both the English and Dutch knew it.

The profile of the *Delfland* was extremely high, higher than he would have expected; it was beautiful, the way the ship rocked gently back and forth. As Barnt watched, a seaman or passenger from the vessel passed him, rolling slightly as he grew his land legs. Barnt grinned and gestured toward the ship.

"Beautiful, no?" he said in Dutch.

The stranger replied in good English. "Aye, and she rides the waves as hardy as a porpoise. You can see the mark of shot on the outside, but she sails without taking water."

"By the way, strangers with news from Amsterdam get a free glass at the Green Dragon, with sugar in the Kill Devil and no water."

"I like the water—as long it's mixed with enough rum to keep the sickness out. With water I can drink it longer." The stranger shifted his seaman's bag up onto his right shoulder. "Is the Green Dragon your place?"

"That's right. Down this street for four blocks, then right full rudder."

Barnt knew that the *Delfland* had just put in from Amsterdam, and wanted to hear the latest scuttlebutt, at least partly because he'd heard a militiaman from Albany saying that Francis Nicholson, the colonial administrator of New York, had lately developed a strange unwillingness to talk about recent events in London. Later that night Barnt spotted this same sailor from the *Delfland* at a table, and brought him a fresh glass. The young stranger was already holding forth with a seagoing type almost as disreputable looking as himself; the focus of the conversation was on the accommodations in Shanghai, Calais-Nord, and the Amsterdam waterfront. When the other customer left for the back rooms to retire for the night, Barnt sat down beside the newcomer.

"What's the news from Amsterdam?" he asked the young seaman.

"James II was defeated at Broad Street in the Battle of Reading. His Irish troops deserted him, or were shot dead by the people of Reading from their windows . . . it was a glorious victory against the slavery of the Papacy. James fled to France, and from there he is reputed to be going to Ireland. Those who fought popery most valiantly have declared for William and Mary."

"What is Mary to do with it?"

"She is the consort of William, and will rule with William. Both are Protestants. That way, if William dies or is killed, Mary will keep the Protestant line intact."

"Thanks be to God," Barnt said instinctively.

"Yes, indeed. It was a miraculous deliverance." The young seaman took a long pull at his drink. "I wouldn't say that all Catholics are bad. One of William's best officers killed at Reading was Catholic. He kissed the hem of the Pope's gown like any ordinary idolater, yet in his political loyalties was a valiant supporter of the Prince of Orange, and in that manner helped to save Britain from a terrible religious war. But as a king? No, if we had a Catholic king we'd lose everything we've been fighting for these last hundred years."

"Yes, yes." Barnt already knew the basic issues involved; and the more he thought about William of Orange sitting on the throne of England, the more he liked it. It solved the whole problem regarding the maintenance of a Protestant dynasty, which was the single most important issue for both English and Dutch; and it did so simply but decisively—always the best kind of solution. And William was Dutch, a Stadtholder of the Dutch Republic, to sit on the throne of England! "If we can stop the killing now it is a wonderful deliverance for us. But I say that these religious conflicts have released every kind of foul violence on all sides."

"Yes, I know," the sailor acknowledged, "but how can you refute the call of God? My brother William was a Fifth-Monarchy Man, and remains one today in his heart of hearts. He's a Baptist preacher in Boston, who says that King Jesus may still come when he's least expected . . . this is the New World—who know what Jesus has in store for us here?"

He went on for a while in this vein.

"I don't know," Barnt said. "Can the faith justify overthrowing a legally constituted government?"

"If it is Jesus himself, a Christian man can hardly hesitate to support him."

"Many say the Fifth Monarchy Men fought for power for themselves, not for Jesus."

"Only to hold in trust until Jesus comes to take the reins. How could they refuse to stand in the breach?" The stranger seemed to be enjoying the conversation, which dealt with issues that interested him. "Look at your Reformed Church. Yes, Calvin did say at first that men must not rebel, but did he not later say that when a king abandons God, the people have a duty to remove him? In such a case, it's not the agency of the people that remove the errant king, but God himself, acting through the people."

The man introduced himself as Jacob Milborne, and said he was from an English family in Leicestershire, his father being a preacher of the Anabaptist persuasion. He seemed the very living image of religious enthusiasm, unencumbered by any doubt or guilt whatsoever for his beliefs. At the same time, when he was not waxing angry about something, he had a generous and welcoming smile; and because of his height, a fair amount of authority.

"There's more," Jacob was saying. He pulled his stool closer and looked around the tavern. "I just came from Amsterdam, which is where the *Delfland* is harbored. The whole city is talking about James II—he is determined to put himself back on the English throne, and restore the Catholic dynasty! And if the clergy and the squires, the artisans and the learned men, both here and in England, don't declare for William and Mary, he will succeed! . . . and of all the places where the need is most critical, it is here—in the so-called Dominion of New England—where people must declare for William and Mary."

"I've heard nothing yet," Barnt said. "But if things have happened as you say, all must declare for the new king and queen, for William and Mary as the true sovereigns of England, because they can secure the Protestant line; but also because they now constitute legitimate government authority in both England and the colonies."

"And yet," Jacob was saying, his voice dropping an octave, "where are the merchants and the traders who should be swearing allegiance to the new king and his queen? Where are the rich families of Albany? Where are the Livingstons and the Schuylers, the ones who should be leading us to declare for William and Mary? The powerful should be the first to declare for the new sovereigns, for they are the only ones that can stop the papists from taking our freedom. If the leaders in the colony don't declare soon, it could lead to civil unrest."

"If they have declared, they are certainly keeping it a secret," Barnt murmured. "But from what you've said, they should be the first to openly support William and Mary."

Jacob Milborne repeated at length all the rumors he had heard in Amsterdam. James II had gone to France, and was reputed to be going to Ireland, to rally the Catholics there before invading England. William and Mary stood between them and their allies in France and Spain. Much of what Milborne said was unconfirmed by anything Barnt had heard, yet much of it rang true, and it was powerful news, Barnt had to admit. In the years since the Conquest—and then the Re-Conquest of 1674—anti-Catholicism had been growing among the Dutch people in and around New York. Of course, to some extent it was a kind of veiled nationalism, experienced as a bone-deep pride in the Dutch defeat of the Spanish; but it was also part of a larger struggle for a reformed Christianity against the tyranny of the Inquisition, as well as everything that was repressive in French and Spanish Catholicism. This was a pride that the Dutch were not afraid to show in the company of the English, because the more thoughtful English were now themselves being brought into that fight on their own soil, by opposing James II and supporting the Protestant William and Mary.

And all the time Barnt was listening to young Milborne, he could not stop himself from thinking, *These are dangerous things, the kinds of things men die for, yet they are things that I believe myself.* They were things he had once himself sworn obeisance to, along with many of his young friends. Yet now, at the moment when these great questions threatened to reach a tipping point in New York, he could not stop thinking about Angel. Nor could he stop himself from wondering how he could use these new dynamics as leverage to get what he now felt he had to have, the patroonship on the northeastern lands of East Jersey. Small or large, he had to have this private kingdom, the one place on earth where it would be safe for Angel, her clan and himself.

He felt that everything else would have to wait, no matter how important, he told me when recounting these events.

"I returned home the next day," Barnt told me. "I wanted to serve my ideals and my faith, but wanted to make my fortune at the same time. It was a kind of madness—I couldn't stop thinking about Angel, you see, not even for a moment. What made me think I could serve my heart and God at the same time? Yet I thought I could do it, I *had* to do it, and felt that the enthusiasm for one could clear a path for the second. There was danger in the air, and the promise of big changes. This would be my chance to secure support for a major land purchase in East Jersey."

"The weather was terrible the next day, and the boat to Staaten Eylandt almost sank. The wagon road was so frozen that I abandoned it for a Raritan hunting trail that ran nearby, breaking through the ice with my boots every ten feet or so. A mile from my house I saw smoke coming from the chimney. Of course, it was cold enough on this day that a stranger could enter the house to build a fire while awaiting the return of the owner, and in fact that was a common practice in the area, if people were caught out in the open in bad weather. But when I opened the door, I saw that it was not a stranger, but my brother Cornelius. I had written to him, and he had faithfully answered my call for help. Now he sat at my table eating the porridge I'd left on the stove."

2.

Cornelius, Barnt liked to say, was a special man, and a great lover of animals, with a kindly temperament yet still capable of dark moods and odd beliefs, not to mention an occasional outburst of temper. A handsome man, he read the Bible every day, but refused to discuss it, except once or twice when he said that Jesus would be coming soon. He stopped going to church at the age of fourteen, maintaining that the Dutch Reformed Church had taken a bad turn in 1618, in adopting the Canons of Dort and the Heidelberg Catechism, documents that denied the free will that God had given to all men.

Furthermore, Cornelius said, he himself was not of the Elect, and acknowledged freely that he was likely to spend eternity in hell as a result. Interestingly, he pronounced himself proud of that fact, because it meant so much more if he behaved as though he *were* of the Elect, and tried to live the Christian life, even as his soul was forfeit to eternal punishment. As a child and adolescent he hid in the woods whenever farm animals were slaughtered, imagining that something similar would happen to him in hell; in fact, he avoided the company of people whenever possible.

Yet you always had the feeling, Barnt thought, that there was something transcendent in his soul, some special connection to something godly and pure; or maybe he felt that simply because Cornelius was his brother. On a horse Cornelius was beautiful, in ways that weren't quite possible to explain. Maybe it was because he had a unique way of moving with a horse, leaning one way and then the other, as he guided the animal along the coach trails in early summer. It was something people loved to watch on Staaten Eylandt, including not a few young women; one swore that if he rode a wife so sweetly, she should never let him out of her sight.

"He left to go up the Hudson Valley when he finished church school," Barnt told me, "and went to a place where he could be alone. My father had a bit of land up there in the upper valley, you know, not particularly good farmland, but not that far from Albany by footpath or horse; and Cornelius built a little cabin on it. He was perfectly happy living alone, raising just enough vegetables, squash and corn to feed himself—he could never stand to kill or dress game, with his love of animals. During drought times some of the women in the neighborhood brought food to him, and he smiled when he took it, a smile sweet enough to make you give your heart away, they said."

"I wonder that he wasn't married within the first year," I said.

"You would think so, but although he would take their food and be gracious about it, he would never take the woman herself. Sometimes I wondered if he was one of those men who refused to marry because of some deep sinful problem in his nature, but he was first and foremost my brother, so it was never for me to judge him. In any case, he would never allow himself to sin if he could avoid it: his sense of the world's depravity was too strong, and for that reason he would never allow himself that kind of latitude. He just wanted to be alone, reading the Bible and the handful of books he liked, whilst talking to the squirrels and raccoons he tamed as pets. He wouldn't even go to church—he kept the Sabbath alone, on Saturday, starting at sundown Friday night, always celebrating the Seventh Day Sabbath alone."

So when Barnt opened the great door to his house on Staaten Eylandt, he was relieved to find that the person there was not a stranger. These were difficult times, and although the Bible said not to vex a stranger, it was hard to trust people one didn't know. But this visitor was as far from being a stranger as a brother could be. Barnt saw that he must have given thanks earlier, because his Dutch Bible lay open on the table as he ate his meal.

"Good day, brother Bernard," Cornelius said. He rose up halfway as though to help him. "Do you have horses with you?"

"No, I'm on foot."

On Cornelius's trencher lay cheese, bread and squash from the cooler outside, along with some salted meat for long winters and bad weather. He was drinking the weak watery beer that Barnt always drank and served to his guests. Except for a spring or two in the Bad Woods, it was dangerous and unhealthy to drink water without beer, because of the uncleanness and sicknesses that were in it.

"Hello, brother," Barnt said. "You look well. God is looking after you."

Cornelius pushed his chair back and stood up, smiling his handsome smile, and hugged him. "God looks after all his children, Bernard. It's up to us to abide by God's plan of salvation as best we can, even if we are not included in the Elect. It helps us not to want too much, and covet what others have."

"Yes, that goes without saying."

Cornelius was eating the coarse rye bread that Barnt kept in bulk all winter, in case he got too sick to go out; his evening meal was usually porridge and coarse bread, which helped him sleep a few hours on those nights when he couldn't stop thinking about Angel. From the bag Barnt carried he took a long loaf of white bread made from refined flour in his bakery. "Here you are, brother. Bread as fine as any wealthy man in Amsterdam could hope to eat, from my bakery."

"And you brought it home for your brother to eat, not even knowing I was here? Thanks be to God." Cornelius had a way of seeing God's hand in everything.

"It's a blessing that I'm here at all—the ferry almost capsized coming back. A pitiful draught of an English boy was trying to pilot her, and he almost took us to the next world. It was as though we were being held in the Lord's hands until we arrived."

Cornelius nodded. "God knows our appointed time, and will often send his angels to protect us."

Barnt went out to the cooler to get butter, and got more cheese as well, and some salted fish. "Were you doing Bible study when I came in?"

"Yes, Psalms first and then the New Testament, just like the Synod of North Holland of 1609 would have it, but without the mistakes of the Synod of Dort; also without all the bowing and scraping to the English, and the rich merchants that pay the dominies' salaries."

Barnt smiled. "I don't suppose the preachers would *ever* be paid, if the wealthy didn't do it."

Cornelius stopped eating for a moment and took a deep drink of water and beer. He sat looking at his brother for a long moment. "Well, yes," he said at last, "but the real danger would come if these dominies, with all their fine manners and their high opinion of themselves, were unwilling to stand up and fight the papists, if by chance the Pope put one of his own on the English throne. Where would the Christian go then?"

Barnt took a knife from his boot, unsheathed it, and cut off a piece of the good bakery bread, spreading butter on it. "You've been listening to the scuttlebutt, brother."

"And you, Bernard?"

"How could I not hear the latest news? I own the major interest in a seaman's tavern in Mannahattas. Of course I hear. They tell me the latest scuttlebutt whether I want to hear it or not."

There was a silence as both men enjoyed the food before them. The kitchen, where they ate, was slowly getting warm. There was nothing, Barnt thought, quite as settling and pleasant as the feeling of being in a warm home with the snow and ice outside. Except for being with a woman you loved under the quilts in that same warm house—that would be heaven.

"Where did you get the habit of worshipping on Saturday?" Barnt asked suddenly, glancing at the open Dutch Bible.

"Not because I think it will get me to heaven, but out of love for the Creator, who gave us the precious Seventh Day for rest." This belief had been reinforced, Cornelius said, by an itinerant Latin teacher who had passed through the upper Hudson Valley, tutoring the children in Latin after church school. This man called himself a Seventh-Day Baptist, and had lived in a settlement in Rhode Island where people were free to think as they wished about matters concerning religion. "Sadly, like all visionaries he didn't see the danger that was right in front of his nose, and during King Phillip's war everybody in the group was massacred by the Siwanoy tribe, except for this one man. Maybe God had a special job for him, testifying about the Seventh Day Sabbath."

Barnt was thinking, not for the first time, how much he distrusted religion. The ideas were good, as was the Almighty; but—he had seen it too many times to deny it—the leaders were often mean-spirited, or mad for power, or simply mad; and often so stupid about the real world that they couldn't tell their butts from their elbows. "Yes, I heard about this group, and about the massacre. So what happened to your one surviving visionary?"

"He came to my house, we worshipped together a few times. Then he left for East Jersey, where he said that people are freer to develop their own beliefs, free from the tyranny of the papists or the dominies of the Dutch church."

"Staaten Eylandt used to be a place such as that, a place to be free. That's why our pater settled here. For some of us, it's still free."

There was a pause.

"Do people still go to the Dutch Reformed Church?" Cornelius wanted to know.

"The women do. It's a connection to Dutch culture and language, and they appreciate the way that Dutch law calls for equal distribution of property between children, rather than everything going to the oldest son, as the English would have it. But the men—and a fair number of women, to be honest—see clearly that the pastors in New York and Albany are pandering to the English administrators and to the rich traders and merchants. It has become a Protestant form of corruption, in its own way as bad as the papists. It seems that all the Dutch pastors can think about is buying a big manorial estate, almost all of them, and living like English aristocrats, and—"

Barnt caught himself up short, realizing what he was saying. Did not he himself want to buy just such a manorial estate in the northeastern part of East Jersey? Was he not in fact ready to gamble everything to have such a private kingdom, to the point where it was no longer a matter of wanting or not wanting to do something, but a matter of having to do it, even if Gabriel himself stood at the headwaters of the Raritan River, and ordered him not to take a step farther inland?

It would be very difficult to tell Cornelius exactly what was happening to him, Barnt thought, just as it was hard for him to be objective about it. Yet he realized now that he would have to tell Cornelius about his plans, no matter what, if he expected his brother's help in Albany. He had to be completely honest about Angel and what had happened. And the truth was, he wanted to talk about the tumult he felt inside . . . so he told Cornelius that he had never needed the help of his brothers as much as he did now, addressing him first in English, then in Jersey Dutch, which had become for Barnt the language of the heart.

3.

"Forget everything you know about me," Barnt said. "Think of me as a stranger—but a stranger who is also your brother. What has happened to me is something I never would have guessed myself capable of. I am as confused and anguished as poor Job, hearing of his ruin . . . yet I'm prepared to confess this sin, and will accept the full measure of my punishment, if punishment it be. Yet there is something I must do, something that haunts me day and night, waking and sleeping."

"Only God can forgive you if you have sinned."

"It is not forgiveness that I want from you. What I want is to make what is broken whole. What I want is to mend what I have already torn apart. And I need your help."

"What is the nature of the sin that Satan has set upon you?"

"Love for a woman, love so strong that I would fight an army for her—and fight it may be, before it's all over, for these are dangerous times. But all I can think of is about this woman. And as I led her into sin, the sweetest sin I ever tasted, I can and will marry her, if she will have me."

To his great surprise, Cornelius said nothing. Nor did he look shocked. On his handsome face was an expression that Barnt found impenetrable.

"You are not surprised by this turn of events?" Barnt asked.

Cornelius stroked his chin as though thinking about a chess move. "What surprises me is that you are so much like me—perhaps all sinners are fundamentally alike . . . you are as lost as I am." He leaned back in his chair. "No, I'm not really surprised.

There was always something you wanted to keep at arm's length, some wild passion that was inside you, or perhaps out in the world waiting for you, that you were afraid of."

They were both silent.

"Is she married?"

"No," Barnt said.

Now Cornelius seemed relieved. "Thanks be to God. I would sooner kill myself than kill a man to take his wife, even for my brother."

Barnt felt a chill go through him. "There'll be no killing, brother. I so well remember how you could never stand to slaughter a hog, and would stay in the woods all night long afterward . . . I remember it well, and will say right now that I imagine it to be an endearing trait in the eyes of God. Loving animals as you do, I know you would never raise your hand to another man, no matter what manner of beast that man might be; and to be frank, you are somewhat clever to make sure that the occasion for murder will never arise, by avoiding companions entirely."

"Yes, that's the way I live my life. But what is this thing to be done, so that you can be free?"

"To marry her, first of all. I led her into sin, and will never abandon her until I can repair what I have done."

"What's keeping you from marrying her?" The silence went on too long. "Bernard, tell me the whole story, or you'll be wasting my time and yours too!"

"She is a Raritan tribal woman, the daughter of a chief. She is the most beautiful woman—the most beautiful creature, animal or human, that I have ever seen. I think about her every moment, and I will think of her every moment until I die. She is in East Jersey now, and will return in the warm months. I can't live without her, but I don't want to marry her until I can be sure I can make it safe for her to be with me."

He told him the whole story, beginning with his days and

nights in the Bad Woods, and the sudden appearance of Angel in the fire at the top of the hill, and how they put the brushfire out together. Then he told him about the days and nights of passion, how he fell more deeply in love with her every night, until the desire to be with her was a mania that controlled every aspect of his thoughts and feelings. He knew how it must sound to Cornelius, with his strong religious emotions and ideas, but his brother's face remained impassive.

Then Barnt began to weave into his narrative the second part of the dream: how Angel feared for the surviving families of the Turtle Clan, how the warriors had been culled by war with whites and with other tribes, and how she and her part of the Clan needed a safe place to settle. Then he told Cornelius how he had become obsessed with the idea of a new patroonship, or what the English would call a manorial estate, where the families of Angel's Turtle Clan could be safe; and where he could guarantee that the Raritan tribe and whatever white settlers that might come there would live in peace, because he would be the patroon, and therefore magistrate and lord of the manor.

"You would be a magistrate in such a kingdom, just as our father was." Cornelius could not suppress a smile.

Barnt nodded. "I don't expect you to approve, Cornelius," he said. "I don't care if anybody approves. She and I may die trying to make something happen that has no chance of happening, but as God is my witness, it is something I must try to do. It will drive me mad if I don't. I am already more than a little mad, thinking about it. I simply conceal it well."

Cornelius smiled and nodded. At long last Cornelius said: "You will want a manor house. They say that slaves are the best brick makers and bricklayers in Jersey, both East and West—they make bricks from the clay in the soil. Then after the mansion house is finished, they go back to their wretched hovels to live."

"I will never have the sweat of slaves on my conscience."

"Thanks be to God, brother—it's a terrible, degrading system.

It has only progressed so far in Mannahattas because of the slavers' lust for quick profits." He took another long drink, looking at Barnt out of the corner of his eye. "What if this woman has married another man during the time she is gone?"

In his heart of hearts, Barnt was thinking, *I will kill him.* But somehow he did not think that would happen—Angel had already explained that they were already married now, beginning with the time when they first made love. "Her husband was killed—in fact, almost all of the Raritan men have left or been killed. There are no young men left in her part of the Turtle Clan. It is all women, children and a few very old men."

"She may be the Devil, Satan himself, in the form of a woman."

"I don't care," Barnt said without hesitation. "I will still love her and stay with her, even if she is the Devil in the form of a woman. And I will marry her, even if it means an eternity in hell. Please understand what I am saying, and accept it."

For the first time Cornelius looked at him with something resembling shock. "Gracious father in heaven, you *are* just like me—you may not be of the Elect, after all! But look at you trying to be good, just like I do, even though we may both be destined for hell." He laughed a dark and unsettling laugh. After a time he said, "Brother, this may be your last chance—please, give her up. The Devil has powers that you can never dream of."

"There are only two places we can go after we die. But if she will have me, I will take her to my bed even if she herself is already the walking dead."

Cornelius smiled bitterly. "Cain thought that his sin was greater than God could forgive. You sound like that."

"Do you believe that a person can make a bargain with the Devil?" Barnt asked. "That if you call him forth, he will physically appear, and strike the deal and get you to sign it in your own blood?"

"Some of our own pastors believe this. Others believe that the bargain is made in the soul."

"Do you believe that all witches should be executed?"

Cornelius sighed. "I don't know. I worry about this often. I know I couldn't do it myself. If I am a sinner, what right would I have to kill one they call a witch?"

"Yes, I feel the same. I know that evil lives in this world, but it feels like it comes from inside of us, rather than sent from hell."

Cornelius smiled, looking at him intently. "Why do you ask these questions?"

"I feel a storm coming. We may have defeated the Spanish and the Pope, but I tell you there is something inside of us that is an inquisition in itself . . . it is something so horrible that it will either make this colony or leave it terribly wounded." Barnt stopped, afraid to say the words that even Cornelius might not understand. "Our leaders are corrupt and covetous. It's one reason why I can only be happy when Angel is with me, with both of us on our own estate, away from the world. Such an estate in East Jersey is what I must have. So judge me if you must, but this is my life now."

"You are my brother, and I will go to the ends of the earth to help you," Cornelius said. He closed his Bible and stood up. It was his habit to go to bed early and to rise early, using a single candle to study his Bible before sleeping. "So what help do you want of me?"

"I need you to see someone in Albany for me." Barnt went to his letterbox and took out a letter sealed with wax. As he handed it to Cornelius, he said the name of the recipient out loud, although he name was written on the front. "Give him this letter, brother. He will be expecting me, or my representative. I loaned money to a scapegrace son of one of the rich families, and the boy needs my attention to stay out of debtors' prison. This letter contains my proposal, with my promise of further service to their family in Mannahattas, if they will help me get the estate I need."

Barnt added, "The man who will receive this letter is in charge of all Indian affairs in East Jersey. I think he will be able to help me. But you must try to get a letter from him stating his intent, and any papers that I need to establish title to the East Jersey estate that I want—so bring any other letters from Albany that need to be delivered here as well. Bring the mail down by the Lange Eylandt dispatch cutter, and take the ferry at Communipaw. You can walk from there."

Chapter 9

At Voyager House, I'd long since made peace with the idea that Clarissa Rowland was in love with Barnt, and even went through a period in which I suspected that she was trying to get pregnant by him in order to hold him. Don't ask me why I suspected this— all I know is that there's a certain kind of career woman who never wants children, but who at a certain point in her life begins to talk about "the biological clock," which suddenly becomes her favorite subject of conversation; and not long afterward you see her in a much happier and more relaxed state, happily lugging a much smaller version of herself. I was pretty sure that Clarissa was—or had become—that kind of woman, although I couldn't say why.

In time, it occurred to me that Clarissa was almost surely beyond that time in her life, an important detail of the kind I am prone to overlook. In any case, every bit of my intuition told me that she and Barnt were either having an affair, or had shifted into some kind of passionate connection with each other that was beyond my comprehension. Perhaps what I thought was the desire to create an offspring was in reality simply a wish to understand the love that had suddenly come upon them, a complicated love they had not sought nor expected, but which they were now at pains to understand.

Barnt was suffering from a subtle kind of debilitation that was typical of the sudden onset of a passionate but unexpected love affair, I thought; but he was also fatigued from the stories he was telling me, because simply remembering and telling them meant to some extent reliving the events themselves. They were all very intense, these stories, but they were now reaching some kind of dangerous critical mass, both in Barnt's memory and in the emotional implications of the stories themselves.

"It's better to tell what you know about the past," I told him, "than to spend the energy necessary to repress it."

"Tell me again about that."

"The usual reason for repressing the past is to avoid re-living the pain of bad experiences recalled—feeling the bad emotions associated with the memories. But if we repress too much, we rob ourselves of the ability to learn from the unpleasant memories."

"Don't we all do it?"

"Yes, to some extent, but it's not good when you systematically repress difficult or violent memories. They become part of your personality. Talking about them helps . . . nobody knows why, but it seems to work."

"That's what Clarissa says."

We were lying in our separate bunks talking, the weak light filtering through the broken skylight of our room. For the third day in a row, the ice on the skylight was freezing. "Do you tell her about the things you've revealed to me?"

"No. She'd never believe me. You believe me, because you've done so much research about that time and place, and can confirm that my historical accounts are mainly true."

I said nothing, thinking as I had so many times before, that history, as it appeared on the printed page, was little more than a timeline without the psychological trauma. We would not want to know most history as it was really lived. Perhaps that is why, I thought, I found reading it so rewarding—that is, by reading it we could know it without the pain. Reading history on the page banished the actual effects of evil, but one ended up understanding it nonetheless.

"And then," I said, "there are people who talk about past traumas too much. They think about them so much that they have no reason to live in the present."

"That'll never happen to me. I'll only talk to you once about these things. Then they belong to you, and only to you, to retell them or to make of them what you will. I hope you will write them down for the descendants, as you say you will."

"I will."

There was a long silence. "I do have trouble getting to sleep, however," he said suddenly. "But the reason has nothing to do with bad memories. I keep thinking about the budgetary problems of Voyager House."

I understood that completely, because I worried about it too. "Why do you care one way or the other what happens to Voyager House?"

"Clarissa Rowland cares, and that makes me care. I can't help myself."

"And?"

He paused, then rushed ahead. "I didn't know I could love anybody after Angel. Is it possible that now, in my present state, I could love again?" He took a deep breath, and there was a catch in his voice. "Promise me you will give Clarissa Rowland something, however small, from your money."

"*My* money? You haven't even told me how to get my hands on it. I don't even get Social Security checks regularly anymore."

"Well, make the necessary inquiries—Social Security is your money, you earned it. Once you get your Social Security functioning again, you should start making regular contributions to Clarissa for small repairs around the house."

"I take your point," I said, intending to do exactly nothing about rectifying my Social Security situation. I found government forms too debilitating.

"Incidentally," Barnt said, sitting up on his bunk. "I think Clarissa's luck may change tomorrow."

"How? Why tomorrow?"

"You'll see," he said, exiting the room.

After that, it was even harder to get to sleep. Finally, I did.

The next day was Thursday, when the regular staff meeting was usually held. I stayed in my room until the meeting started, then got up and went into the closet without turning on the light. I fit the glass device into the hole in the closet floor, and turned it slightly one way and the other. Most of the meeting consisted of the usual house business, including a few surprising facts about clients (one of the knitting ladies had done time in prison, which I never would have guessed). I experienced a brief sensation of guilt when I heard that—the staff meeting featured information that was confidential, which I was violating by eavesdropping. But Clarissa Rowland was working the meeting slowly but surely toward new business, and I could sense something big coming. She seemed quite excited, to the point of being flustered.

"Staff, something wonderful has happened!" I went on red alert—here it came, whatever it was. "I have to tell you now, before I burst. I mean, it's about Voyager House, and our 'cash-flow problem,' as Neil calls it."

"Did some rich patron come to our rescue?" somebody asked.

"Well, I really don't know about rich or poor," Clarissa said, "but some person has made a bequest to us."

"*Who?*" demanded a firm voice that clearly belonged to D'Nysha Williams.

"I don't know, because the bequest was made anonymously," Clarissa said, "and although I've spent the morning thinking about it, I don't have the slightest idea who on earth the benefactor could be! . . . all I know is that the trust officer of the bank was waiting for me this morning. He told me that an individual, who wished to remain anonymous, has donated a fair amount of money to Voyager House, to be received in monthly installments, the money entirely for operating expenses. Then he came over here later to see me, with some papers establishing receipt of the money in our bank. We've already received the first disbursement today. We don't have to do anything, except spend the money wisely—and we'll have no trouble doing that."

Several disbelieving voices spoke at once, and then abruptly fell silent.

Clarissa's voice took on a storytelling tone, as though reciting a well-known narrative to children. *"Well,* this trust officer couldn't say whether this benefactor was living or dead . . . all he could say was that he or she had arranged at some point to donate substantial amounts of money, in monthly installments. We have already confirmed receipt of our first installment today."

Excitement got the better of her, and her voice went up an octave. "And the thing is . . . the thing *is* . . . if we keep receiving these installments each month, it will be almost *exactly* the amount needed for operating expenses for the rest of the year! And listen to this—the people at the New York City Department of Health and Mental Hygiene didn't seem surprised at all! Maybe they were just happy I wouldn't be bothering them for money for another year . . . anyway, our bank confirmed that the installment of money for this month has already been deposited in our main account."

In her voice I could hear wonder, but also something close to tears. "It's a miracle, isn't it? What did we do to receive this miracle?"

Then came the tears.

2.

Anglo-Dutch New York in the late 1680s was a place where a person could get rich quickly, if that person worked hard, made a good marriage, and had reasonably good luck. For that reason, making money and making good marriages became the main life activities of society in New York, especially among the Dutch. Because things happened so quickly, and profit could be turned so handily, it had created a society in which money felt like the most important thing under the sun, and sometimes as easy to get as God's grace. But money was never enough for the Dutch— there was also beauty and enjoyment of the moment, just as for the English there was the dream of an underlying moral order and the rule of law. So neither English nor Dutch were able to accept making money as an end in itself, although it was something you sometimes had to do. As soon as one got enough money, one would start angling for the manorial estate, and move as rapidly or as slowly as necessary to close the deal.

The beautiful manor house, and the gentle manner of the lord to that manor born, would be the culmination of the hunt. Yet both Dutch and English were to discover there was something about the hunt itself that had robbed it of its chivalric airs. Instead of inheriting their fine estate, they had grubbed for money and power, lied and gambled with others' lives, and destroyed lives along with parts of their souls. Once you did that, you could not go back to the dream of being born a Christian prince whose temperament was unfailingly charitable. The money-grubbing had a piece of you, and you had a piece of it, and you could never completely get rid of it.

For that reason, Barnt was glad he had not married into the frantic race to prosper in this New World. He had money—more than most people would have guessed—but it had accumulated slowly according to judicious decisions involving crops, cattle and investments, and he had never used the sweat of slaves to make it, or reduced to poverty anyone that got in his way. In his thirties Barnt had dreamed of someday building and owning his own flour mill on the Raritan River in East Jersey . . . the middling way, the quiet life, without ostentation or unnecessary alarums, and probably that was the way for him, without smiling in a man's face one moment and stabbing him in the back the next.

And now, in his forties, there was something new, something he could never have predicted: the shock of falling completely in love. You could look forward all day to taking such a woman as Angel into one's arms, and the feelings would never leave you. Accompanying these fantasies was now a new intoxication, the dream of a great estate, something he had never tasted before. Yet in his mind he could never rest until he could protect Angel, and the only way he could think to do that was to have an estate where his word ruled.

To complicate matters, the Dutch-speaking people around him were preparing to launch themselves into yet another crusade against religious tyranny, similar to the wars they had fought against the French and Spanish kings. The English were now also involved in that same great struggle—forced upon them, to be sure, but it was a fight they now had to engage, in one way or the other. For the Dutch, it involved feelings of national identity, for Dutch identity was felt rather than seen or intellectualized. For the English, the entire future of England now looked as though it would be determined by the outcome of what was now a civil war.

The Green Dragon was buzzing with excited news about the invasion of England by William III and Mary, brought by sailors and passengers arriving on the latest ships from Amsterdam and London. But as eagerly as each new morsel of news was devoured, the very nature of the news had created a crisis for the people of Mannahattas and the New York colony generally, a fact that Barnt went out of his way to make clear to me.

"Why were not our leaders in the colony declaring for William and Mary?" he asked me rhetorically, pausing as though for an answer. "The Netherlands was far away, receding further into memory with every day. And London—well, that was a fantasy we couldn't quite fathom, and lacked the reference points to even imagine it. But there was one thing we Dutch shared with the common people of England: a sense that the people had, after almost two centuries of struggle, defeated the corrupt monarchies of Spain and France—and by stopping the Catholic monarchs, we had given reason space to grow, along with ideas about republican government."

"In the Netherlands the battle was long since won, but in England James II seemed clearly to be moving toward the creation of a Catholic monarchy. Then came the stunning action of the Dutch stadtholder William III of Orange-Nassau and his daring invasion of Britain, as James fled to his supporters in France and Ireland. For the time being a Protestant dynasty was guaranteed, and a Catholic one defeated. But James was preparing to return to Britain at the head of an Irish army, with the French in close support. The powerful ones in Britain knew that a consensus had been reached among the people, that only a Protestant dynasty could bring peace to a warring land; so most had declared themselves as supporters of William and Mary."

"So why," I asked, "aren't the political class of New York, both Dutch and English, declaring for William and Mary, too?"

"Indeed! Why did not these jumped-up *mynheers*, these would-be 'aristocrats' of Albany and Mannahattas, immediately declare themselves as supporters of our new English monarchs William and Mary? Why were the colonial governors in Albany and Mannahattas silent? Here was to be a life and death struggle between Popish religion in its purest form, and Protestantism on the other—the order of battle could not have been clearer! If the powerful and wealthy ones did not stand against the Catholic tyrant James II, the work of two centuries would fall . . . about that there was not only consensus but enthusiastic unanimity among the common people, both English and Dutch. Yet there was silence from the so-called leaders of the colony of New York. To the people it seemed that those with power were simply waiting to swear allegiance to whosoever the lucky winners might be, without any concern for the freedom of the people, whether Dutch or English."

Even more silent than the governors and rich merchants were the dominies, the pastors of the Dutch Reformed Church. The Dutch clergy had accommodated itself far too quickly to the ascendant English after the Re-Conquest in 1674, partly because the shrewd merchants in their congregations saw no reason to pay a preacher when they could get him free. With the loss of a state sponsor, laymen refused to pay the salaries of their clergy, and the English quite sensibly refused to underwrite the preachers of what was now a foreign church. Abandoned by all, the pastors turned to the rich traders and influence peddlers of Albany, and rich Dutch businessmen in Mannahattas—and since corrupt men now became virtually the only supporters of the Dutch Reformed Church, these same religious frauds found it increasingly convenient to loudly support whatever was done by those that paid them, whether their English colonial overlords, or the compliant Dutch toadies that did their bidding.

It was a corrupt society, and sadly, no place for idealists or visionaries to criticize it—no press for pamphleteering, and only the most informal opportunities for the dissemination of opinion and news. Likewise, there was no way for people to organize themselves into intermediate institutions that could provide diversity, and give society coherence and direction. So an enormous amount of energy went into making money, and hedonistic enjoyment of the moment. The civil religion of the Dutch in the New World became the making of money, and an enjoyment of the good life. But people still lived in a deeply religious age, and a devotion to rum and pastry and beer and good bread—pleasant enough, to be sure—was never quite enough for religious people without a religious establishment worthy of the name. They despised their clergy, to be sure, but the ritualized mocking of their petulant pastors did not help them recover certain values that they felt slipping away. And they had not yet discovered something of a spiritual or transcendent nature with which to replace the corruption of the present.

"People really didn't know what to do with themselves during the 1670s and 1680s in the colony," Barnt said. "We had the idea that we had a new country, but there was no moral focus, no foundational documents or ideas around which we could weave ideas of our own destiny. The Dutch-speaking people in the New World were hardworking; but perhaps for that very reason tended to indulge themselves in every kind of pleasure one could imagine, and more than a little wildness — there was a lot of drinking, public fights, frivolous lawsuits, that sort of thing. Would you believe that at one funeral the mourners consumed almost thirty gallons of wine, eight hundred cookies, and a half-gross of tobacco pipes?"

"Imagine that," I said, thinking of certain three-day Irish wakes I'd attended.

"The Dutch didn't want to admit it to themselves," Barnt continued, "but it was enormously exhausting to adapt themselves to the English system, with its strange language and laws and byways and customs — above all it was almost impossible for the middle-aged — and even the young — to learn English well enough to use it in business. It was so much easier before, when Dutch was the language of law and business, and the English had to learn *our* language. I was lucky, of course, since I'd used English since the early 1660s, when I arrived with my father and stepmother. The worse thing about it was that after 1674 the successful Dutch merchants didn't go out of their way to help, but instead used the general ignorance of English ways as a way of keeping other Dutch people down, and in so doing creating a client class of rich Dutch whose position derived from their monopolies in certain areas, as a direct result of their collaboration with the English mercantile class."

"But the ordinary people of the colony, certainly the Dutch but also the English, did have one over-riding concern that bound them together: a vivid and deeply felt sense of the struggle against the tyrannical French and Spain monarchs. Therefore, there was enormous anxiety that the leaders of New York refused to declare for the Protestant dynasty of William and Mary, even as William prepared to meet James II and his French allies in the field of battle. What an irony — the Dutch had spent a century and a half defeating Catholicism, then were conquered by the English whose king James II proceeded to openly declare for

Catholicism! There was not one ordinary Dutch person in New York who wouldn't have risked everything, if personally asked to join the battle against James II, whether in the New World or in England. But the Dutch patroons in Albany would not say one word on behalf of William, who was potentially the savior not only of England, but of Protestantism throughout Europe."

"Therefore it was not long in New York before people began to whisper about ways to force their leaders to declare for William and Mary as their new sovereigns. But even as the people began ever more openly to discuss this, they began to feel with heavy hearts that the rich and powerful leaders of the political class of New York, both Dutch and English, were secretly poised to support the hated monarch James II. Worst of all was the Dutch Reformed Church, which would scurry to support anything the rich patroons said and did."

"The unwillingness of the rich and powerful to take sides was interpreted by the people—correctly, I am afraid—as covert support for James II because it was he who had appointed most of them to their positions. But that was a scandal that the people were called to correct. Did the people not have a duty to do something to force the hands of the rich and the politically connected in New York, to compel them to support William and Mary, and in so doing support the foundation of a Protestant dynasty under which both Anglicanism and the Dutch Reformed Church could live side by side in the New World?"

3.

Barnt knew he could never get a patent for a patroonship in East Jersey without help from one or more of the influential families in Albany; it was for this reason that, seizing an unexpected opportunity, he had negotiated an agreement with one of the most powerful of these rich clans, in return for helping one of their wayward sons. Specifically, he was engaged in renegotiating certain fines and debts of one Petrus Bayard, working with one of the magistrates who had been a close friend of his father Thys Barentsen. All parties had tentatively arrived at an agreement—partly reduced to a written contract and partly verbal—that the combined fines and debts would be paid off in installments by the Bayard family in Albany, taking funds from some property that had been previously willed to the prodigal son. There were certain aspects of the agreement to which the family in Albany had yet to agree, and there were many loose ends that had to be tied up. But they were close.

Petrus was a well-spoken but childlike man of Barnt's age, a pious individual who had fallen under the influence of the Labadists, one of the many pietistic sects that currently terrified the pastors of the Dutch Reformed Church. Its otherworldly tenets had exacerbated an essential gullibility in Petrus's character, making him easy pickings for every charlatan in the colony who sought to deliver the lamb to a thorough shearing, if not to slaughter. Petrus was one step away from debtors' prison or the poorhouse; yet like far too many religious fanatics, he had no comprehension whatsoever of the way his indiscretions harmed his own family.

In fact, he regularly acted out two personal qualities Barnt experienced as singularly irritating: the aristocratic entitlement of the very rich, and a typical visionary's disdain for his obligations under the law. But both he and Petrus knew well that his family could ultimately buy his way out of almost any trouble in which he became embroiled—and it was that knowledge that had, of course, made him so thoroughly irresponsible in the first place.

Yet Barnt found it impossible to hate him. In fact, he had decidedly mixed feelings toward religious visionaries of every stripe. He could not help but agree that the world was a brutal and difficult place, which the mystic, the prophet and the dreamer rightfully wished to escape; yet he had long ago noticed that practitioners of religious enthusiasm also had a tendency, of which they were usually unaware, to greatly magnify any social problems that already existed. They attracted violence in the form of persecution, they were usually incapable of common sense, and their spiritual insights were regularly and startlingly self-serving. Yet Barnt understood and to some extent sympathized with people who had mystical visions—his Huguenot mother had experienced prophetic dreams and visionary states shortly before she died.

Although Petrus was only too happy to accept assistance from Barnt—and from his family—he was likely, when reminded of his financial obligations, to point out that his wealth was not of this earth, but laid up in heaven, where gold could not tarnish nor could thieves break in.

"Yes, which we enjoy only by God's bounteous grace," Barnt would reply patiently. "But until you take leave of this world, please do us the favor of paying the bakers who work at my bakery for the bread you take."

"Do you not pay them enough?" Petrus inquired.

"Yes, but this is courtesy I'm talking of, the kind of courtesy required of you in this kind of situation. Charity is something that God commands of all, even those such as yourself that are predestined for heaven."

Petrus nodded, but thought immediately of something else. "How can you be sure *you're* predestined for heaven?" The question was not asked aggressively, but as though inquiring about the price of corn on market day.

"The same reason you are," Barnt answered, keeping a smile on his face and his voice soft.

Petrus planned to join his wife and children at the Labadist colony in Maryland, where they would keep all their worldly belongings—or at least as many as they had left, or were allowed to keep—in common, and eat together at a common table. First, however, Petrus had to pay off his creditors in Mannahattas, which was to be facilitated by Barnt, who was also charged with making sure that Petrus did not run up any more debt before he left in a month or two.

Barnt started out keeping Petrus at his bakery, where he mainly got in the way; then he assigned him to write letters for several of his illiterate employees, mainly in Dutch for family members back in the Netherlands. This letter-writing project gradually grew into a thriving business, with customers throughout Mannahattas, especially the apprentice boys who hadn't learned their letters. Shepherding Petrus out of debt was part of a deal Barnt had made with several members of the Bayard family, but it gradually turned into a further agreement that Barnt would be responsible for keeping keep him out of trouble until he could legally leave New York for the Labadist colony at Bohemia Manor in Maryland.

Petrus had no idea of the legal trouble he had gotten himself into; but the reality was that the authorities could seize him at any time until his debts were subjected to legally binding arrangements for repayment, arrangements to which all the principals had agreed. The key was to quickly set in place such arrangements, oversee the drawing up of papers, and get Petrus safely out of the shadow of debtors' prison and spirited onto the next schooner to Baltimore. But they could not do this until the paperwork had reached a certain level of credibility, or Petrus's departure would seem like absconding without paying his debts.

Barnt looked to his brother Anthony for help in keeping an eye on Petrus, after some time making arrangements for Petrus to stay at Anthony's house with his wife and children. Willem, Barnt's youngest brother, stayed with them as well, although he talked of leaving soon for East Jersey. The children of Anthony liked Petrus—which was not surprising, since he was quite childlike—and to Barnt's great surprise so did Anthony. Anthony had heard of Jean de Labadie's life and writing, and was grateful for the opportunity to read his book, which Petrus loaned to him.

4.

"I cannot judge him, because religion is all about a wager," Anthony said, "and poor Petrus has placed his bet. The rest of his life will be spent in hedging that bet, like a man who invests heavily on a product, then invests against it so he'll have something left if his main investment fails. Either way, the bet has been placed."

"But he is so focused on eternity that he does not notice the harm to those around him."

"Which creates an opportunity for you, unless I am mistaken," Anthony said pointedly. After a pause he continued. "Petrus has to learn of the consequences of his behavior someday. In the meantime, he must square his accounts with those he owes. And it will be your job to help him do this."

It was late afternoon in the drafty apartment above Barnt's bakery, where they were drinking watery beer and inhaling the overpowering aromatic excitement of the bread rising and pastries baking downstairs. He reflected, as he had often before, that nothing was as delicious as the smell of baking bread — which is one reason he had originally contemplated having Petrus stay in this very apartment. At least, he thought, the man would never perish of hunger, since there was such good bread baking downstairs.

Ultimately, however, Barnt was somewhat relieved to yield to Anthony's suggestion that Petrus be deposited at his house, since leaving him alone for even a short time was inadvisable. Anthony was the only one of the brothers with a pronounced gift for business; yet he was not obsessed with it, and seemed to take his opportunities when they happened, rather than manipulating events to create them. He had a knack for remembering odd bits of information, and when he had news, he had a way of waiting before sharing it.

"Who was the man that dreamed up the idea of a wager over God?" Barnt asked. "I've heard you talk about him before."

"A man named Blaise Pascal, according to the book given to me by the captain of the *Gerechtigheid.* In return I sold him enough sugared rum to keep his crew happy for a year."

"This man Pascal—was he Dutch, by chance?"

Anthony grinned. "Might as well have been—it's been said he got most of his ideas from a Dutch theologian. I've never heard of a better or more practical foundation for faith, although each man must build on it in his own way."

Anthony's approach to business was a little like his fascination with religion; he would take riches where he found them, *if* he found them. Yet despite his casual approach to the fortunes of business, he was infinitely clever about money once he had it in his sights, and was quite astute about a great many other things as well; he was probably the most educated of the brothers, having gone out of his way to study Greek and Latin, and had picked up enough French from his father to get by. In his early thirties, he was a younger man than Barnt by a good fifteen years, yet was already much richer than both he and Cornelius. And he was a loyal and caring sibling: more than once, Barnt had been forced to refuse his offers of economic assistance. But this was soon to change. He was painfully aware that he would almost surely need some help from Anthony to buy his dreamed-of estate in East Jersey, although he would never ask for loans of money directly.

"So," Barnt said, "does good fortune in business continue to pursue you?"

"I have found a way to store wheat here in Mannahattas, something you may have heard about. Mostly the merchants who export like to buy and sell the product within a few days, or even hours. But I use round brick silos, several of which I have already built in Lange Eylandt, and am about to construct several more in Staaten Eylandt. That way I am able to buy more, and wait a bit longer, in case there is a fluctuation in the price of wheat."

"How do you avoid pests accumulating in the wheat?"

"They accumulate anyway in the hold of a ship. But I have developed a method that prevents that until I'm ready to sell for export. I shovel out the wheat in smaller containers every so often, and move it to another silo. The shoveling disturbs the pests, and they leave; furthermore, I also use water, both fresh and sea, to wash out the wheat at regular intervals. That way I can keep produce in the silo as long as I need to."

"And by accumulating the wheat—"

"Or the corn, or whatever—"

"You wait for the price of the product to rise?"

"Or to go down—there are ways to make money both ways. You may not always see it." His voice grew tighter but Anthony spoke with his usual casual smile and relaxed eyes. "Remember when Sir Edmund Andros made private manufacture of beer illegal? That drove down the price of wheat overnight. It was so disastrous for the farmers growing wheat on Staaten Eylandt that all they could do was borrow on the next year's crop."

"Yes, I remember," Barnt murmured.

"And you know how that works . . . they had to borrow from Andros' Anglican friends in Mannahattas. There's about nine or ten of them, and once you're in debt to them, you're never free and clear. Andros knew it would go that way. His friends became rich overnight."

Barnt shook his head. "And all that came from Andros making private brewing illegal?"

"I didn't see it coming at first," Anthony said, "and I'm not even sure Andros did. But once it was underway, I took advantage of it."

They were silent momentarily. "But why the silos on Lange Eylandt and Staaten Eylandt both?"

Anthony leaned forward, his voice low. "Remember how Andros wanted everything exported to go through Boston? He may try it again, and soon. And if he doesn't go through Boston, there'll be stiff tariffs here. But I'm selling to exporters who go directly to the Barbados, without paying any fees here *or* at Boston. They'll load up with rum there, and bring it back here for immediate sale. If the price of wheat is low going over, we can make money on the rum coming back."

"So the exporters can load their ships at Lange Eylandt?"

"I've found a way to do it. It makes everything less complicated. And eventually I'll be able to do the same at Staaten Eylandt. If they don't like it in Albany or Boston, that's too bad, because by the time they find out, I'll quit exporting and start renting the silos out to the farmers."

Barnt laughed. That was Anthony, he thought.

While forever appearing to be drawing to an inside straight, Anthony always seemed to win the hand. In fact, he rarely gambled, as Barnt knew from observing him at the Green Dragon tavern. Instead Anthony was an inveterate maker of plans, a deviser of strategies, and a born business-warrior; he always had further plans and strategies to fall back on, one by one, if the first or second strategies didn't pan out. He refused to play chess, saying that it was impossible to imagine more than three moves in advance, yet he often seemed to out-think his competitors by several moves.

Anthony's wife Annetje—or Hannah, as everybody called her—was even more loyal to her adopted family than Anthony, if that were possible. She and Anthony had taken Willem, the youngest of the brothers, into their home; had they not done that, Barnt knew that the responsibility would have fallen on him. But he wouldn't have done nearly as well as Anthony and Hannah did, even though they still had their own children at home. If he succeeded in getting the estate in East Jersey, Barnt thought, he would invite Willem to come and help him settle it, giving him his own parcel of land as a gift.

"How is our brother Willem these days?" Barnt asked.

"I gave him a book on mapmaking, and he's made some excellent ones. He'd make a great sailor, but he's been around too many farmers and businessmen. That's the world he knows."

There was a long silence as the two men drank and ate bread from the bakery downstairs.

"So," Anthony said, "why don't you tell me why you're helping Petrus Bayard?"

Barnt was momentarily speechless.

Anthony's face remained expressionless. "You don't start helping somebody like Petrus Bayard for no reason, brother. Granted, he's a lost soul, and your natural instinct is to help—he needs all the guardian angels God could assign, just to keep his feet on the straight and narrow. But I think there's more to it than that—I think you're helping Petrus because you're getting something in return from his family. What kind of help do you want from his family and their rich friends in Albany? You'd better give me some idea, for safety's sake."

"Why do you need to know this?"

"If you get in over your head," Anthony said calmly, "you may need your family around you. To put it bluntly, you might need my help."

What Anthony had said was true. It seemed that in this chess game he was thinking more than two or three moves ahead, and it wasn't even his game.

"Thank you for thinking of that," Barnt said carefully, and took a long drink from his water and beer. "You're right, of course." He suddenly felt himself tearing up—this was a kind of brotherhood that few families would ever know. "Who taught you to think like that?"

"You did. You and Pater. If we didn't help each other on Staaten Eylandt, the family wouldn't have survived."

Barnt felt the emotion rising in his chest. He now realized he had to tell Anthony the whole truth about his current situation. But how do you talk about something so personal and so powerful, something that has changed your life so utterly, when you don't know why it happened?

"There are some things you should know," Barnt began slowly. "To begin with, this is not about business, or anything you may imagine."

Anthony nodded, waiting.

"To begin with," Barnt said, "This is about a woman. She is unlike any woman I've ever known or could dream about. She gave me more happiness than I ever knew existed. And I am completely and totally in love with her. I will do anything to be with her."

He paused, rising for a moment to pace back and forth.

"You are a man," Barnt continued, "so you know the passion that overtakes us—but this is something I think about every moment of every day, and dream about every night, and will never stop feeling, even if I lose her." He felt himself shudder slightly when he talked about losing her, because he had worked hard to keep that from his thoughts. But he thought he must say it, in order to be completely truthful. "If I do lose her, I may not wish to live afterward. I never thought I would say those words, but I am afraid they are the truth."

Anthony nodded, alternately leaning forward and backward slightly in his chair, concentrating on his brother's words. "And there is something you must do, or something you must have, to be with her . . . ?"

"I must gain a patent for a large patroonship in East Jersey, where I can guarantee that she and her people will be safe."

"Is she a Quaker?"

"No."

"A slave?"

"She is a princess of a certain Turtle Clan of the Raritan tribe of the Lenni Lenape that once lived on Staaten Eylandt. I met her when she came to go to visit the place called Burial Ridge above Raritan Bay, since her father is buried there." He paused. "She believes she has some rights to the island, since she was one of many that signed documents. But she has satisfied her obligation to her ancestors by visiting the burial ground, and will be willing to leave for East Jersey."

"Do you love her?"

"Yes."

"Will you marry her?"

"Yes, if she will have me, old as I am. I am only a few years from fifty."

"What is her name?"

"Angel."

Anthony took a deep breath, but did not hesitate. "I have four thousand acres on Lange Eylandt. You could settle there with her, and make regular payments."

"It's too thickly settled. I must have a place where the surviving members of her clan can live and hunt." Furthermore, Barnt had serious doubts that he could ever pay in full for that much land.

Anthony was silent. Barnt hated to admit it, but he cared greatly what Anthony thought of his situation, and he was deeply touched by his offer of land. "Are you surprised that something like this could happen to me?" Barnt asked finally.

Anthony took a long time answering.

"Not really," he said at last. "I could feel something like this coming. There was always something you were mulling over in your mind, drinking just enough to stay a little insulated from the world. You went along with things, but your soul was elsewhere. If you had been to university in Leiden, you could have been a good philosopher—but Pater wasn't interested in that, and neither were you. So you waited, here in this new place. You waited for something that you could throw your soul into, some storm that you could sail into just to see if you could ride it out—some great cause that would change the world, perhaps, or test your mettle. But in your case, the great cause was a crusade of the heart, something that would challenge and change you from the inside; and the prize, if what you say about her is true, is the one woman you could love more than anything else in the world."

Barnt kept his face straight, although he was deeply touched by Anthony's words, and relieved that there was no hint of judgment. Otherwise, he found it odd how similar Anthony's reaction was in certain ways to that of Cornelius. "Well," Barnt said, "there is integrity in such personal battles, especially if one asks God for guidance."

Anthony nodded sharply. "Yes, brother, and you are just the kind of man who will find integrity in such a battle, no matter what the challenge. And don't think it small—such battles have a way of opening up the world, and making it better. God understands all kinds of love, no matter to whom or where it happens. Your intention to marry her will satisfy God's sacraments, although it may be hard to find a pastor to formalize it." He stood up. "Give me time to think about this. I may be able to help with the patroonship." He continued to nod fiercely in an absent-minded way, as he considered what he had heard. "When do you plan to go back to your house on the island?"

"As soon as the Petrus matter is taken care of."

"Ah." Anthony stood, and the two men embraced.

"I'm glad you told me what course you've laid in," Anthony said. "I knew the wind was up for something, and I was getting damn tired of guessing what strange new port you were navigating for."

Chapter 10

A friend of Barnt's, a ship captain from Utrecht, paid him a visit at the Green Dragon with the latest news from England, having just arrived from London. William and Mary were now the new monarchs of England, and had declared their intention to establish a Protestant dynasty. The defeated James II would surely invade England, however, and would attempt to regain his throne; and would, if successful, establish a Catholic dynasty. For that reason, support for the embattled Protestant William III was absolutely imperative. But why weren't the leaders in Albany and New York supporting William and Mary?

When Barnt spoke of the apparent reluctance of the local leaders to support William III, a seagoing friend at his tavern—a veteran of many battles at sea—shook his head. "The people should force Albany's hand," he said. "When these religious and civil leaders see they cannot govern this colony without support from the people, they will change their tune."

"People are saying similar things throughout this colony. But our leaders are a notably selfish and bull-headed group."

"The Dutch as well as the English?"

"The Dutch leaders especially. They look around to see which king will win, and then announce themselves fervent supporters of him. But this time around they're betting on James II, who is hated by the people and is sure to be defeated."

"And the clergy?"

"The same as the merchants, who pay them."

The captain shook his head again. "I expect that from the traders, Lord knows, but this is a dangerous game for the pastors. If they're not careful, there could come a day when nobody will go to their churches. The people will read the Bible and study in groups, praying in each other's homes as the saints did in the time of the Mother Church." He upended the beer

Barnt had given him, drinking it down in a long, straight draught without swallowing as the sailors liked to do, pausing afterward to wipe his beard and eyes. "I want no revolution from the dominies, you understand—but a man of God must sometimes diverge from the magistrates, just often enough that the people know there is a difference between God and government."

"Agreed. And if the pastors cannot themselves make that distinction, they should perhaps be taught a lesson."

Barnt had long been aware that throughout the colony there were honest men and women capable of putting the good of the people before their own wealth and prestige. Many of them were young, restless, and energetic people of the yeoman free-holding class; they worked the land, owned shops and business enter-prises, and invested their money in productive local businesses. He had no doubt that, given some tutoring, they could do just as well as the established leaders were doing, and probably better. But the established leaders in Albany saw government as a business opportunity, a chance to make money through bribes, influence peddling, sharp trading and land speculation. But among the so-called ordinary people there were those capable and bold enough to argue the case against the colony's leadership, if it seemed necessary, and chart a different course.

"We have apprentices who could do better than Livingston and Schuyler and the others," Barnt said. He purposely excluded the Bayard family from his examples of unseemly corruption. "I'm not saying we should overthrow our legally constituted authorities . . . the Bible is quite clear that we must never do that. Yet one cannot help worrying about the possibility of a Catholic dynasty being established in London and Westminster, because New York would soon become a party to such an ungodly enter-prise."

"Are there murmurings among the people?"

Barnt nodded. For another free beer the sea captain shared an interesting story. "Have you heard of a man named Jacob

Milborne?" he asked.

"I believe I've heard the name," Barnt said after a moment's pause.

He decided not to mention that he had plied this same Milborne with rum for information just after he stepped off the boat from Amsterdam.

The sea captain once more drank deeply and began his story. "Jacob Milborne, who sometimes lives and works in New York, publicly challenged none other than Sir Edmund Andros, the current governor of the Dominion of New England. And he did so publicly, at the London's Guildhall. He had Andros arrested and prosecuted for falsely arresting him in 1678. Can you believe it?"

Barnt thought about it. "I've never heard of such a thing. Having a rich man arrested and publicly tried?" He poured his friend another beer. "Did he prevail in court?"

"I did not hear that. But what had the tongues wagging was that an ordinary man like Milborne would challenge a representative of the crown in such a bold and public way."

"Yes," Barnt said. "Quite impressive, I must say."

Good Lord, if only we had Dutch men so bold, he thought, and then repented of the thought. The Dutch of this colony, being a people ruled by a foreign crown, were more likely, of necessity, to be clever rather than bold. The sea captain continued. "Perhaps such public challenges as those by Milborne could make colonial officials think twice about going too far against the aspirations of the people. At the time of his trial in London, Andros himself said that such public challenges as that of Milborne were a dangerous precedent that could undermine colonial administrators throughout the empire."

Then let your colonial administrators be men of unquestioned integrity, Barnt thought, *and you need not worry about them being undermined.* After all, the people of New York, both Dutch and English, presently had no wish to take away the powers of the administrators in Albany—they only wished those powers to declare for William III against James II before the battle between the two kings was joined. But the political class refused, a great many of them, because they had been appointed by the treacherous James, and were to some extent still loyal to him because of self-interest.

Barnt said goodbye to his friend, who was staying in some rooms a few blocks away, near a whorehouse frequented by Dutch sailors. Barnt left some instructions with a serving maid who cleaned the rooms behind the Green Dragon; she was to give those instructions to a trusted man who would look after the food served in the evening. For his own part, Barnt went to the rooms above his bakery, where he usually stayed. He would sleep there tonight, he had decided, because there was too much robbery lately in the rooms behind the Green Dragon, and he wanted no part of it until the gang of thieves who were responsible were caught, convicted and hanged. He wrapped three blankets around him and lay down on a wooden bench and blew out his single candle, thinking about how nice his bed would feel back on Staaten Eylandt.

Then suddenly he could not control his thoughts about Angel. It was not a question of dreaming—it was simply a process of the dreams taking over his mind and emotions. He tried to get rest in spite of it. He had to admit that the dreams were quite pleasant, a little like a kind of poetry. His body would quickly go to a state of maximum pleasure, and the feelings would be all over his body, unbidden but not unpleasant, and unlike anything he had ever felt before.

The next morning, he packed his things, including some good bread and flour, in a large bundle that he carried down to the dock. He took the Mannahattas ferry to the Communipaw ferry boat; the tide was low and the ride uneventful. The ferry operator and his wife were happy to see him, since he was the only customer that morning. The ferryman took Barnt's large flat-bottomed skiff out of the cove where he kept it, finally handing the pole to Barnt. Using a chain and pulley arrangement set up by the ferryman, Barnt was able to pole his way along the Jersey shore until he was upriver from a freshwater opening on the other side of Arthur Kill. Then he poled rapidly across the tidal strait into the opening that the Dutch called Fresh Kill and some of the English called Karle's Neck Run. It then diverged into several small streams, one of which ended on Barnt's property.

He pulled the skiff up onto the land, and took the path that led to his clapboard house. For the entire time he had been coming home, his heart could not stop beating. His little frame house near Karle's Neck was, among other things, a refuge from the escalating political tensions one encountered everywhere in the colony. But above all, this house was not far from the second camp he and Angel had set up before she returned to East Jersey with her brother. He felt in his bones that he must go there, partly because that was the last place where he'd made love to her. He doubted that Angel would be back so soon, because it was still quite chilly, even though it was the first week of April; and in fact he could not be sure at all that she *would* be back. It was foolishness incarnate, but it felt to him as if coming home to Staaten Eylandt, to his house at Karle's Neck, and then repairing immediately to their private encampment where he'd last held her, could magically cause her to fly back to him more quickly. The truth was, he was terrified of dying without holding her in his arms again. Thinking in those terms was surely a kind of insanity, he thought, but what was insanity compared to the feelings of desire that engulfed him?

As his boots made small squishing sounds on the muddy path, his little clapboard house hove into view. The style was exquisite to him, because of its hardiness in the freezing cold of the winters, a style the Dutch called klapholt, the Germans klappholtz, and the English clapboard (although some who had been in the colony a long time referred to it simply as weatherboard). It was a way of using thin boards to protect a house from the winter winds, by putting the thick side of the boards over the thin side underneath it. The little house had been built by an expert carpenter, joiner and cabinetmaker who had been a close friend of Barnt's father, helped by an apprentice cabinetmaker under his instruction.

There was a little half-floor or attic over the first floor with a large dormer; this dormer was where he slept, and it was coziness itself, as long as he remembered not to stand up too quickly. (In that case, he was likely to hit his head on a beam that ran lengthwise for the length of the house.) The house had one quality that Barnt thought unique to the Dutch homes in the colony: they in no way suggested wealth, but were instead scaled solely to best protect a family from the winter winds. There was something beautiful about their compactness, coming partly from their lack of ostentation, and partly, in some way, from the joiners' art.

His anticipation of the pleasure of being with Angel, as he now experienced it, flowed together with the anticipation of being at last in his own house. He looked forward to the sensual process of starting the fire and warming the rooms, a languorous process not unlike the way pleasure flowed through his body when he was with Angel. Over the last night, he had become aware that he was desperate to bring her into his house to live with him. Of course, she might want to retreat to their encampment every so often, but if they were to be married, she belonged inside the house, no matter what, even if her first reaction might be to refuse. If he entreated long enough, he thought, she would eventually come around. As he came up over the last rise of the path he thought he could see as far as Billop's manor house on the little spit of land that could be seen clearly from Burial Ground Ridge. But there was nothing about the stone exterior of Billop's mansion that could compare to the beauty he imagined and anticipated in his own small wooden house.

He unlocked his Great Door with an iron key, and as the door swung slowly open, he beheld his precious small home. She had been here—he didn't know *how* he knew, but know it he did. In a moment he knew why. They had a miniature carved figure of an owl that sat on a high shelf, and it was gone. This was a Raritan trick, one the braves practiced on settlers even in the midst of war. They would steal a single, small artifact of some kind from the house, like some kind of *klopgeestpolitie,* an angry little spirit that liked to drive people crazy by misplacing or stealing familiar objects. The Raritans thought that if they surreptitiously took a small artifact, and you thought you had misplaced it, they had a power over you—as indeed they did.

"Angel!" Barnt shouted.

He turned around. She was nowhere to be seen.

The encampment they had built up on his property! That's where she would be.

He quickly pulled on a second pair of boots—his first pair had gotten water in them during the trip from Mannahattas—and set off at high speed toward the second encampment that he and Angel had set up, one located not in the Bad Woods but on Barnt's land. The foliage was still sparse, but Barnt was relieved to see that the stand of trees there would be quite adequate to cover the encampment on three sides. There were no roads here, and only a single hunting path nearby—mainly abandoned since the departure of the tribal people—and only one footpath, used by Barnt when he wanted to inspect the perimeters of his land. The encampment was close to one of the tributaries of New Spring, or Long Neck Run, so water would be no problem. Barnt hoped she had taken some food from the house.

As he approached the encampment, suddenly there she was, only partly clothed, and still wet from bathing in the nearby tributary. He could see the curve of her back, then as she turned the shock of her breasts with the black hair coming down across her body. He felt an overwhelming surge of passion; she smiled and stood up straight, and (at the moment their eyes met) straighter still. She reminded him of certain deer he had seen that would stop and eye an intruder boldly, then stiffen, the better to see and know the intruder.

He walked toward her. "Angel . . ."

She threw down the garment when she saw it was him.

"Barn-tee!" she said.

She ran to him and embraced him. She could not understand how a name could have only one syllable, so she had invented an extra one for him. It all came back, the way she spoke, the sound of her voice—

"Barn-tee!" she whispered hoarsely against his shoulder.

Without thinking he began to speak in Jersey Dutch. "*Waif . . . was it din noam?* Wife . . . whatever is your name?"

"*Ik was fernilmt nder vuer.* I was named after fire."

"Fire-angel . . ."

"*Ja,* Barn-tee," she said. "*Jdu brandengel!* Fire-angel!"

He took her in his arms, dizzy with the sweet feeling of her against his pea jacket and her cheek against his unshaven face.

"Angel. *Engel* . . ."

Without thinking they began chattering to each other in Jersey Dutch, with wild words from English and Dutch and Lenni Lenape and even French. Jersey Dutch was the *lingua franca* of the fire-born, and used therefore by those who were at home in fire, at home in the dizzying changes of a Place of Wonders, people who believed in sin and death but (perhaps because of that) were also prone to the most rapturous kinds of passion. It seemed especially invented for Angel, who spoke it in a singsong, mocking and teasing way, as though lost in private imaginings of broken frontiers and abandoned boundaries ... sometimes it was a Germanic-sounding High Dutch she had picked up somewhere, as she declared something big and unequivocal; but usually it was Jersey Dutch, which lent itself to a certain kind of playful lovers' riddles that invited a reply, the exact rhythms of which the lovers had to invent themselves, sometimes in the very act of making love.

There were many times that she spoke the Jersey Dutch in the manner she learned when she and her brother were living with the Ramapough Mountain people, blacks and tribal and whites living together on an outlaw mountain that civilization was afraid to enter, giving its denizens the freedom to create a language not of the powerful, but of the wild and the cunning. The teasing essence of what she now said to Barnt was that she had come back to him, and would stay with him, whether he wanted her or not.

"Then please listen to my heart," Barnt said to her. "I want you to come live in this house. Please, I beg you. I want you to live under my roof..."

"I am not cold," she said teasingly. "The fire keeps me warm."

"*Ik donk je know kwdit xut.* I think you know quite well why I ask this of you."

She was still smiling, but she was reaching out to touch his hand. "Barn-tee. *Je bist mein husband.* I understand that part *kwdit xut.*"

"I love you," he said emotionally.

"I love you, too," she said boldly, her chin jutting forward.

"Come, then," he said. "Help me. I must set the fire. To cook. Please." Then suddenly, inspired by God know what, he knelt down on one knee. "Every night," he said, "I thought about you . . . I dreamed . . ." He used the word in Jersey Dutch: "*Ik droomen, Ik droomen, Ik droomen . . . van min brand-engel min haus zu koomen . . .*"

She smiled broadly. "Then you must do something, you must . . ." She said an obscene word. They laughed together like naughty children.

"In our house . . . yes," he said. He started to help her gather up some of her things. For a moment she hesitated. "Over there," he said, motioning, "a short path from here, is my house. Please,

please, my dear wife—"

"*Ik koomen*," she said firmly, having now made up her mind.

Once they had gathered everything up they went to his house. She seemed impressed by it. It probably looked like a very compact woodland shelter to her, he thought, but made of the wood the Europeans made with their tools, a house secure from the elements. Once inside the Great Door, he took her in his arms again. "You'll be my wife." He liked saying the words. "*Vroux. Man en vroux.*"

"*Man en vroux.*" She knit the fingers of her hand together.

"*Ja*, yes."

He started the long labor of warming up the house. He boiled water for the bathtub, adding snow from the eaves so that it wasn't too hot. He carefully and lovingly bathed her from head to her small curled feet. He bathed her scalp in rum and camphor to make sure that no lice had survived, teaching her again a little about combing her raven hair. The Dutch dominies had not approved of mirrors, so his late wife had carefully hidden hers, and Barnt found one only after an energetic search. He wondered if his late wife had saved any rouge, then realized how stupid and irrelevant the idea was. This woman Angel needed no paint, no adornments, none of the embellishments usually associated with female beauty or status.

When he was finished he gave her porridge, which she at first found strange but quickly got used to. Bread, she had always loved; butter, when spread on the bread, she loved even more.

"We taught the English how to do that," he said, spreading the butter generously on her bread.

She laughed at the idea. "Did they say *bedank je*, 'thank you,' for teaching them?"

"No, they forgot, and *ik hak et saxon vergeten*, I've already forgotten it too. You see, I'm with my beautiful wife, and forget everything when I'm in her presence."

When she was finished, he took her gently in his arms and

took her up the wooden steps to the half-floor and his bed under the dormer. He heard a sudden intake of breath as he kissed her, which told him that she had missed him, too, although probably not as much as he had missed her. He kissed her body in every tender spot that aroused her, and then made love to her slowly, savoring the liquid shock of it. He was slow; they had not had intercourse for a long time; he was careful to move slowly. In time he came out of her, and kissed her body again.

She responded passionately to him, but his own need for a release in her arms overcame him, and he entered her again. Very quickly he felt the sharp, powerful release: *this is the way children are bred,* he thought. The release was so keen and so deep that even the part that was painful felt pleasurable. He resumed caressing her body, and she in turn also had a powerful release, after which she clung to him.

"Barn-tee," she said repeatedly, laughing.

They then lay quietly for some time, saying nothing; then he touched her again, and once again feeling the moistness stroked her body, pulling her closer to him. They kissed repeatedly on the mouth. As another release began to overtake her, she moaned softly, then loudly, as she neared a completion.

"Remember?" he whispered.

She laughed softly, putting her hand on his as he stroked her.

Even in his relentless imagination he had been incapable of recollecting such pleasure, for when she was gone from him, even memory could not replicate what it was like when they were together. It was not so much the sharp, dangerously deep sensation, but the reckless longing for that same feeling to again fire the flesh, and then enter the bones, and in that manner to stay forever. And now that it had—for it would be with him every moment—there was little else in the world that moved him as much. The feelings that winter had been an ache for something that had been missing. Now the feelings—along with the woman who caused them—had returned, and in two hours they had re-established themselves as by far the strongest thing in his world. *I will use my life to serve this*, he remembered thinking to himself.

2.

While Angel slept under a huge stack of quilts, Barnt went downstairs to check on the fire. Everything in the house felt right; it was as though a kind of benign spell had alighted on every part of it. But was it something that he embodied, a pleasure that was everywhere because it was now in his bones? Without question it was both, he decided. Just thinking about Angel created a small lurch of concern in his stomach: he needed to marry her, but it had to be soon, he thought. He could not let the situation go on any longer than it absolutely had to.

This was the house where he had spent his life with his late wife, Magdalena Jansz, raising the children, the three of them that had lived. The three that had perished caused him a pain so sharp that he had long ago decided not to think or talk about them. The dead little ones were all buried in the New Town burial ground where his father Thys Barentsen was buried, and where Magdalena herself was buried. Magdalena had been a faithful wife and good friend; and even though she was self-conscious in the later years about the weight she carried, it had never bothered him. This was the very house where they had lived together so long; yet he already felt—for reasons that he could not entirely understand—that he had also lived here forever with Angel. And most bewildering of all, it also felt like he had lived here *alone* before, the loneliness going on forever, a man with an inexplicable passion that was building every year, and a deep melancholy that at times had led him to imagine how it would be to take his own life, were it not a sin.

The reality was that he was a man who had, during Magdalena's life, grown progressively alienated from his wife, his children, and his friends; there was always something that haunted him, something that he could not put into words, or even acknowledge. Sometimes he wondered if it had something to do with the land itself, so immense it could shelter untold millions of tribal people, and therefore untold millions of ghosts of those people who had loved the land just as much as he did. He could not stop thinking about the three dead children either, so for his own protection he had cut off and permanently exiled all the positive feelings he had felt when they were still living. Something similar happened with his relationship with Magdalena, although he could never adequately understand or explain it. When people talked about love, somehow the word did not mean the same to him. The reality was, during the years before he met Angel, he was gradually withdrawing from the world, preparing himself for death. In his heart of hearts, he felt he had not hated the world enough—the world with its suffering, its brutality, and its ménage of laughable cruelties, outrages and insults.

Mixed with this growing personal alienation was a sense of a lost meaning of life, a lost purpose of life, connected—however tenuously—with the English Conquest and Re-Conquest of the colony, and the sense of the Dutch-speaking people of Nieuw Nederland as being lost in a dream, in which all purpose had been lost, a purpose that was unfortunately not that easily remembered. The great families—the Livingstons, the Bayards, the Rensselaers and the others—were nothing but criminals who used government as a way to leach money from the people, and cared nothing for those they supposedly governed. There was still something unique and good in the Dutch way of life, based to a considerable extent on the Dutch yeoman's capacity for hard work, combined with an awareness of the long struggle against the tyrants of France and Spain. But if William III was defeated, all that would be lost.

The Dutch dominies, or pastors, were unwilling to address even the most personal kind of religious question. Standing here in the kitchen of his shadow-mottled house, he remember how, not long after the death of his wife Magdalena, he had asked a pastor at the Reformed Dutch Church, *what about the man who had married more than one woman? Which woman will he be with in heaven?* This pastor, as many Dutch Reformed pastors did when asked something important, subjected him to a lecture on predestination.

Barnt asked the question again: "If a man has been married more than once, with which wife will that man live in the New Earth? Assuming of course that we all have free will in heaven."

The pastor drew himself up. "When we are with Christ through eternity, such questions will not seem important."

The answer made heaven sound like a very cold and unreal place, where reasonable questions were deflected, and celestial residents were required—or learned over time—to keep their mouths shut. The answer to Barnt's enquiry sounded like something a pastor would say when he couldn't think of an answer to a difficult question.

As the shadows deepened and the fire warmed the house, Barnt lit a single candle and poured himself a small glass of rum. It was hot and it tasted good, but quickly dissipated. He put the bottle away. The truth was, he thought, he didn't need or want the rum anymore—he no longer cared for the artificiality of chemical stimulants. He was humble enough to recognize that he might need it again someday—but not now. He hurried back up the wooden steps to the bed underneath the dormer where Angel lay sleeping. Already he could feel the warmth of her young body.

3.

Her brother had gone to Pennsylvania, Angel told him the next morning. She had gone part of the way with him and then come back with an old man who knew the trails. Her communication had become a wild mixture of many dialects, and not a few languages. One dialect she used was something the English settlers called Pidgin Delaware, a lingua franca used by traders to conduct business with the Lenni Lenape; she had also picked up some new words of Mohawk Dutch, spoken in northern New York, as well as some useful English expressions. Every so often there were a few expressions in vernacular French, which Barnt recognized because his Huguenot mother used them. He was delighted to note, however, that by far her favorite tongue was still Jersey Dutch, both the kind that was spoken around Bergen Town, and the wilder and more emotional kind spoken around Ramapough Mountain, learned during the three years when she and her brother lived there.

The current story she now told of the Raritan tribe was a tragic tale of how fast and how violently things could change in their world, particular anywhere near the frontier. The Raritan tribe had never recovered from its brilliant rear-guard defeat of Melyn; they had not returned quickly enough to the easily defensible parts of Staaten Eylandt because there were not enough young men to do so, and by the time they were ready to do so Staaten Eylandt was already irrevocably settled and defended. Other tribes had kept up their campaign to displace the Raritans, with the goal of pushing them out of East Jersey and into Pennsylvania. All that was left of the once powerful Raritan tribe, it seemed, were scattered settlements of old men, women and children.

Barnt told her of his plan to create a safe place in East Jersey, first for the Turtle Clan, and then for the entire Raritan tribe itself, those that wanted to settle there. At first Angel didn't understand; then she gradually began to see it as a kingdom, a magical place that he hoped to invent, perhaps through spells or other magic. She questioningly mimed the shooting of a gun, accompanied by the word for "war"; he shook his head "no," using the Jersey Dutch phrase for "too much blood." He wished he could aggressively mime the white way of using the law, and how the white men had gone about winning, taking or stealing land in East Jersey, but realized there was no mimicry that could encompass exactly how that worked.

He made her breakfast with good bread and cheese; now he wished he had gotten eggs at Mannahattas. The bread was exceptionally tasty; when he told Angel that he had made it in his bakery in Mannahattas she was extremely impressed. She asked three times, miming the process of making bread (which was a kind of corn bread in her clan), then pointing to him. He nodded happily, even dancing a little when he joined her in eating the bread. She continued to be fascinated with butter spread on bread; Barnt explained again that the Dutch people had shown the English how to butter their bread, something that always made her laugh. After they had finished the bread and cheese, he made porridge for them. She watched him carefully; that night she made the porridge while he watched.

He began to talk to her about marriage, and found that she had already embraced the idea without reservation. One of the reasons her brother left her to go to Pennsylvania, she told him, was that he was satisfied that Barnt would take care of her. Angel told him about a magi or witch doctor of her tribe, a man in whom she had great faith, and whom she wanted to marry the two of them. He lived in East Jersey, it seemed, and already knew of her decision to be married, and had agreed to officiate at it. (What a surprise it would be, Barnt thought, when he found that it was a white Dutchman to whom she wished to be wed!) He would have to accompany her there, of course, since this shaman could not leave the area; apparently he had many people to serve among the scattered Raritan in the interior.

The Raritan people would never recover from the hostilities associated with Cornelis Melyn's mad attempt to establish a patroonship on Staaten Eylandt. But many Raritan had elected to stay in the Bergen Town area, as close to their burial ground as they could; or further inland where there were a great many people of different tribes and races, many of which were constantly in flux, where Raritans would not attract attention. Of course, Angel would always attract attention because of her beauty, but that was a separate issue.

Both he and Angel needed a place where they could feel safe, and the mixture of races and culture in East Jersey seemed a good seedling ground. Furthermore, the omnipresence of Jersey Dutch as the preferred medium of communication there would make business and socializing easier. The higher land that was slightly inland from Bergen Town, would be a good place for a patroonship, Barnt thought. The Quakers were already streaming into West Jersey and Pennsylvania, and Barnt thought that the idea of a large estate in East Jersey would now make eminent good sense to the big families of Albany. When he went to Mannahattas he would try hard to wind up the affairs of Petrus Bayard, although he did not want to accompany him to Maryland. Getting him out of the shadow of the debtor's prison would be difficult enough.

Barnt told Angel they should think about going to East Jersey in about five or six weeks, when the mud time would be mainly over and the warmth of spring would make travel easier. Going to East Jersey would be his chance to examine the land again, to check out its amenability to crops and grazing cattle. First, of course, he had to take care of the matter of Petrus Bayard, the recalcitrant mystic, who was living with his brother Anthony in Mannahattas, but he would not go to Mannahattas for a week or so, he told Angel. He could not get enough of her, enough of her presence in his house. With great delight he showed her the accoutrement of his daily life: the great trenchers that the Dutch liked to eat from, the meat and butter cooler dug deep in the ground, the freezing privy out back (a good ten steps in the snow from the back door), the place where he kept the rum, and finally his expertly made Dutch cabinets—those, she really liked, for their neatness. She kept looking around, for what he didn't know. "What are you looking for?" he asked her.

She made the motion of a cross.

"Ah!" he said. He went into one of the cabinets. "Here," he said, "it's a small one." He took out a small cross and sat it on the mantle above the fireplace.

He asked her what she liked about the cross.

It was the white people's magic, she said.

"Yes," he said. "Shall we keep it out?"

She nodded. She trusted it, she said, to make them safe, although she also liked to display the small carved owl that brought her good luck. The two sat side-by-side on the mantle.

Barnt put on two layers of his heavy clothes, and went out to the barn to tend to his single surviving horse. He had stopped grazing cattle after the death of his father in 1684; before his death they had employed a system of grazing the cattle on each other's land, using two cattle marks that were very simple. As he was drawn into business schemes in Mannahattas, especially his bakery, he no longer had the energy and opportunity to graze cattle. His single horse had plenty of food in its stall, but needed to walk around the plantation a bit to stretch its legs; the ancient gentleman that had once taken care of the horse in exchange for food and shelter had passed away, which meant that Angel would have to feed and pasture the animal while Barnt was gone. He made a mental note to call on his neighbor Morgan, who lived half a mile away, and ask if he wanted to buy the horse.

On Sunday he went to the early service at the Dutch Reformed Church in New Dorp. Barnt did not tell Angel where he was going, but she seemed to have a vague idea. At the last moment she handed him the small carved owl she had stolen as a trick before. "The magic is yours now, when you hold the owl in your pocket," she said in Jersey Dutch. "You have the magic, but you must be careful."

"How?"

"Don't go to the Bad Woods, or you will have to trade places with the owl." She said a bit more in French, something he did not quite understand.

"I would not be a good owl," he said, and made a few faces to that effect for her, along with the predatory bird's solemn night hoot, which made her laugh.

He walked in melting snow to the Dutch Reformed Church, which was only a third full—mostly women were in attendance. A few Walloons sat in the back but the pastor did not say any prayers in French, which Barnt thought an insult, despite the Huguenot lack of enthusiasm for Calvinism. Over steaming cider that afternoon, after the service, Barnt asked about popular feeling regarding the inability of the colony's leaders to declare for William III. Everything that Barnt heard indicated that England currently had two kings—a dual monarchy, as it were, one Protestant and one Catholic.

Despite this alarming situation, the rich Dutch landowners in Albany refused to take the side of William III and the Protestant cause. Barnt had expected the general mood on Staaten Eylandt to be rebellious, but people were far angrier toward the Dutch leaders in Albany than he would have expected. The Edict of Nantes had been revoked in 1685, and travelers brought terrible stories of the persecution of Protestants in France—forced conversion, torture, people murdered in their beds.

There were rampant rumors of James II attacking the New World, using an Indian-Catholic-French alliance, masterminded by Jesuits in Canada and stretching down into the Atlantic colonies. Perhaps for this reason, in Virginia the governing secretary Nicholas Spencer quickly proclaimed for William III, by such quick and thoughtful action giving the lie to the rumors of conspiracy. Being willing to act, Spencer could not be suspected of being sympathetic to the Stuart cause. (*If only the leaders of New York had the sense to do the same*, Barnt thought.) Most of the rumors were simply runaway fears, Barnt thought, but there was a hard core of political reality to it: if William III did not get the support he needed, he would be more likely to lose on the battlefield, and both Dutch and English in New York would lose the religious liberty they held dear.

Indeed, Governor Nicholson of New York had been trying to suppress the news that James II had invaded England, calling in and threatening with leg-irons anybody who talked about the impending civil war on English soil. Perhaps most shocking of all, Nicholson had rashly tried to intercept letters on arriving ships in the harbor, the better to suppress news of the conflict between the Catholic Stuarts and the new Protestant monarchs. Inevitably, this also had the effect of making people even more suspicious, reinforcing the idea that the Albany leaders were sympathetic to James II and the Stuart—that is, the Catholic— cause.

The people Barnt talked to were adamant that the colony was in danger from the one social evil that had threatened Europe for almost two centuries, the Catholic monarchies—and if William III lost, James II would be thereby added to the list of tyrants. What was most galling of all to the ordinary Dutch citizen, according to the people Barnt listened to, was that they had traveled to this distant colony to ensure their freedom of religion; and here—of all places—that freedom was being threatened yet again by the nightmarish possibility of a Catholic monarchy ruling their colony!

After hearing these things, Barnt trudged home, disheartened somewhat but even more convinced of the importance of finding sanctuary for himself and Angel, the first step being to get married as soon as possible. She met him at the door.

He carried the small carved owl cupped in his two hands.

"I did not go to the Bad Woods," he said, "and at the present moment I am most certainly not an owl."

She laughed uproariously, asking him to bring the magic inside, and he was happy to obey. He wondered briefly if that was wrong, but quickly took her in his arms before he could think more about it: after all, they would soon be married. When he felt her trembling, he felt pure pleasure. How was it that in giving pleasure to the person one loved, it became pleasure to oneself? Was that not a miracle?

4.

He did not want to go the way of the ferry at Communipaw—it was too far away, and Barnt hated the bother of poling his flat-bottomed skiff into Fresh Kill to get home. Instead, there was a ferryman with a large family who lived in New Dorp who owned a *sloep* that would, in good weather, take people to the dock at Mannahattas. He kept irregular hours, this ferryman, but went at least once every day when the wind and tides favored him. After a last embrace of Angel, Barnt took off walking; the sun was just coming up, and he thought if he made good time in the mud he could get to the ferryman's house early enough to catch him before he left to battle the currents of New York Bay.

Alighting on the dock at Mannahattas, he went directly to the tavern of which he was half-owner. The girl who was to oversee the cleaning of the rooms at the back seemed fatigued and distracted, having just got up from a sickbed; she still had a bad cough. Barnt made an effort to stay away from her, since he had a private theory that coughing could generate disease in people in the general vicinity of the cougher. He had been careful not to share this radical idea with others, since it ran counter to the latest medical thinking in the colony, especially among New York's barber-surgeons. Actually, it had also long been Barnt's private belief that sickness in the lungs happened because of an imbalance in the four humors, or vital fluids, that could in turn release bad vapors that caused coughing.

He swept out the tavern with a broom he had bought from a captain just landed from the Spice Islands, and prepared to wash down the floor with hot soapy water before spreading straw on the floorboards. At just that moment a boy from the old Red Lion Brewery, which had changed hands many times, rather timorously put his head in the door. "Ahoy, young man, what do you want in this honest establishment?" Barnt asked.

"Rum for an honest customer, sir."

"Rum is a bad habit for a lad as young as you," Barnt said, frowning. He judged the boy to be no more than twelve or thirteen.

"An honest glass of rum for my master, *heer*. He will pay you at day's end."

"Does he not have enough to drink at his brewery?"

The boy smiled. "You would think so, *heer*. But he wants something that he is perhaps not allowed to drink at home. And between the two of us, he likes sugar in it."

Barnt smiled. "You're a saucy lad. But a glass would be good for him, then, to help him forget what he goes home to." Barnt looked around and located a half-litre German *humpen* made of pewter, closing its lid after filling half of it with rum. "Would you like to earn a bob by running an errand for me, if your master allows it?"

"Yes, if it is a legal errand, sir. Many dangerous things are afoot, and a young apprentice must be careful." That last part sounded memorized to Barnt, as though he had learned it from his master. Yet, it was without question true.

"Agreed," Barnt said, "but there's nothing of an illegal nature I would ask of you, because a tavern-owner already has enough trouble from his customers. I ask only for you to deliver a letter to my brother." He took out a letter to his brother Anthony. The address was on the cover. "Do you read addresses?"

"Whatever I cannot read I can inquire about," the boy said. "I know every street in Nieuw Am—I mean, New York." The boy was probably illiterate, but it seemed likely he could find the address by asking in his bold way.

"Good," Barnt said. He gave a shilling to the boy. "Don't betray me, boy—a betrayal means a beating, as you must know. And I may have more errands for you in the future. So go to your master and tell him this rum is free, if he will let you take this letter to my brother now. It's an important matter, you see, but even so, it is a great favor I am doing him. You must return the cup to me when he is through. If you forget, it will go badly for you."

"Thank you, sir!" said the boy. He struggled to find a place for the shilling; he had no purse, and little in the way of pockets. He finally found a pocket in his pea jacket for the shilling. He picked up the letter, looked down at the address, breathed deeply, and left to run his errand.

5.

After cleaning up at the Green Dragon tavern, Barnt went to his quarters over his bakery. He opened the wooden letterbox on his writing table; it was full of communications, contracts, bills and dunning letters regarding Petrus Bayard. As he slept beside Angel the night before, it had come to him suddenly in a dream how he was going to expedite the out-of-control world of Master Petrus Bayard; and on the rough waters of New York Bay, on the sleepy ferryman's *sloep* to Mannahattas, he had imagined the finishing touches to his plan. He needed to finish his obligation to the Bayard family, so he and Angel could be together, and leave for East Jersey to get married. Now he'd hit upon a way to do this, and quickly.

Helping Petrus was the key to his proposals for a manorial estate in East Jersey; but he had himself been in debt from time to time, and had himself been a creditor to many people in both Staaten Eylandt and Mannahattas. He knew what a toxic mess unpaid debts could become, poisoning and distorting everything they touched—and it had been for just that reason that he had gone out of his way to promptly pay his own debts. But he wanted to be with Angel, and find a place that was safe for both of them; and this Petrus Bayard problem had a bad feeling about it. What if it became a stuck anchor dragging him down in the unpredictable waters of New York Bay, keeping him here in Mannahattas, away from Angel?

He had known sailors who had lost their lives trying to pull up the rope of a stuck anchor rather than cutting loose to row for shore—it was a good way to swamp a small craft and drown in heavy seas, all to avoid the expense of buying a new anchor. He had to find a way to quickly finish the affairs of this recalcitrant Petrus, he told himself, to reconcile this prodigal son of the Bayards to his creditors, and quickly send him on to his wife and children at the Labadist paradise in Maryland.

There was only one way to do this. He could take on some of the debts himself. Not all, by any means, for he did not have access to that much money. But he could take on a significant portion of them, and with the sale of some of Petrus's property, and the family's creative use of quit-rents to raise money on Petrus's property in Albany, it could be done.

That, combined with some of the obligations the Bayard family had taken on, and some help in the form of loans (of which Petrus's brother Nicholas would be the guarantor), Petrus's various financial and personal indiscretions could be covered. Enough, at least, that Petrus could leave for Maryland to join his wife and children in the religious community that he sought. Working by a single candle, Barnt set about creating the legal and promissory premises by which this could be successfully carried out. He avoided rum and limited himself to a tankard of the weak water and beer from a barrel in the second-floor hallway.

He had fallen asleep as his single candle guttered out, but jerked awake as he heard familiar boots on the stairs. He was relighting the candle as his brother Anthony knocked sharply once on the door before he stepped gingerly into the room.

"Brother, what are you doing, sleeping while sitting up?"

"I fell tired, brother, as though taken by a spell. Yet I couldn't sleep lying down. Has that ever happened to you?"

"More than I care to admit. Rum usually helps."

"I've drunk enough rum for one lifetime, and I need to keep my wits for this." Barnt gestured roughly toward the papers spilling out of his writing box. "I need to be quit of this business with Petrus Bayard. But I also need to fulfill the promises I've made."

"You can do it." Anthony smiled ever so slightly. "Do you want me to pray for you?"

"Yes," Barnt said. "And for Angel too. For both of us."

Anthony hesitated, then said, "I will, I promise. But not in the church of the dominies, but at home, or at the Green Dragon tavern—that's where I usually pray."

He sat down on the wide bench where Barnt had slept earlier. He laid down his bag, inside of which Barnt saw cheese and bread. There was a silence. When they were both younger, Anthony would often come to him, to engage in some criticism of something their father had done, or for advice outright. But he would wait a goodly amount of time before saying what was on his mind. Barnt would usually respond in the form of pointed or humorous questions or in small talk. Now it was Barnt who had the problem.

"How is your health, brother?" Anthony asked. "Are you sleeping well?"

"I think only of getting back to Angel," Barnt said, with more than a hint of misery. "Every moment that I'm away from her I'm worried. I can't help it."

"Do you still plan to marry her?"

"Yes, of course, I will marry her in East Jersey, where her people are. They are scattered, but some members of the Turtle Clan are still there."

"How will you hold the patent for your land?"

"As a patroonship, or manorial estate, if you wish. It's the only way I can personally guarantee the safety of her people."

Anthony had tried not to hesitate too long before saying the word *patroonship*, but it was not often that one heard it nowadays, except ironically. It was not exactly an archaic word, but one that had lost its precise meaning. The English colonial administrators spoke of manorial estates rather than patroonships, but would be happy to use the Dutch nomenclature if the petitioner showed a preference for it. There was a certain pressure in the administration to get settlers for East Jersey, now that the Quakers were flocking to West Jersey and Pennsylvania.

"How will you handle your . . . problem?"

"Which one?"

"Master Petrus Bayard."

"I have decided to assume some of his debt," Barnt said briskly. "Not much, I guarantee you, but enough so that we can stretch his assets to cover his indebtedness. I am in a position, at this point, to quickly dispose of his affairs in a fair and equitable way. I will be fulfilling all of my obligations to the Bayards, but at the same time I can get quit of it. The debts will be consolidated and paid off over a period of time. And I believe I can formulate it all in a way that his creditors will accept, especially since they will be winning some favor from the Bayards in return for their involvement."

"And your assets here, such as this glorious bakery downstairs?"

"I won't need my assets here in Mannahattas if I am successful in securing a patent to the land I seek in East Jersey."

Barnt knew what it sounded like: it sounded like he was counting his chickens before they hatched. There was a kind of madness to it, to look so far into the future and expect so much from it.

"You're not afraid of betrayal by the rich families of Albany?"

"Yes, of course—they are the very image of corruption. But what choice do I have but to risk it?" Barnt put some legal documents back into his writing box, smiling. "I ask you, brother, what choice?"

"This is a crossroads. You will roll the bones and pray at the same time."

"And if I fail, the rich families and the dominies will put my head on a stake outside the Fort."

"I'm sure they would like to, brother," Anthony said, "some of them, anyway. But—"

"I'm not important enough?" Barnt asked, smiling.

"In God's eyes, I'm sure you are, but even there, I'm sure there is more than enough sin to go around."

Barnt had made a list of things that needed to be done in Staaten Eylandt, and in Mannahattas, while he was in East Jersey getting married. He went over it quickly for Anthony. As the oldest of the brothers, it was appropriate that he should assign chores and duties to the others to be done when he was gone. Barnt suggested that Anthony look in on the young woman who cleaned the rooms behind the Green Dragon, and the two cooks who made the meal in the evenings for guests and customers; they were hard workers, but benefitted from occasional supervision. Barnt said he would sell his horse on Staaten Eylandt, if he could not find someone reliable to feed her. He suggested that Anthony might tell the Morgans, his neighbors, that he would accept payment for the horse in the autumn, after the harvest was in, if they offered a reasonable price.

"Please take the money for the horse and put it to good use, if the Morgan family is able to pay you for her," Barnt suggested. "After all, brother, your family is three times larger than mine."

"Well, there is one less now, as our brother Willem has left for his apprenticeship in East Jersey. He is a hard worker, and I think he will do well." Anthony's brick house was small but well-organized, and his wife seemed to enjoy having guests and young ones underfoot, but they needed all the extra room they could manage.

There was another silence; Barnt handed a pipe to Anthony and offered him some tobacco. Anthony shook his head no to the pipe, but put a small pinch of tobacco under his lower lip.

"About those *aristocratic* families of Albany . . ." Anthony began.

Barnt waited, sensing that Anthony had news.

"I have heard," Anthony said, "that many of our rich Albany brethren are in debt to appointees of James II—as are most of the colonial officials in New York. But now I know it as a fact, having seen incontrovertible proof. Do you wonder, then, that so many of them are afraid to announce for William III against James, and the Protestant cause? They have mortgaged their souls to the followers of James II here in New York, which is why they can never declare for William III. But James will probably lose the war to William anyway."

"A nice turn of events for those in debt to James and his toadies," Barnt said, standing with some difficulty, "since if James is dead or in exile, they will never have to pay back the dept."

Anthony exploded in laughter, as he sometimes did. "Very good, brother," he said, "I hadn't quite looked at it that way before. You have clearly become the presiding *schepen* of the family regarding debts and creditors. But wouldn't it sit better for this colony if these so-called leaders simply declared for the Protestant cause now, so we could all face the same risks together?"

6.

Barnt had the contractual arrangements done in two days, and the papers signed. He saw one of the merchants, a grain specu-lator, looking at him out of the corner of his eye—it was already clear to some of the sharp dealers in New York that Barnt was putting a big part of his entire economic future into covering Petrus Bayard's debts. Now where a great many people had been indebted to him, he was indebted to just as many himself. Yet he had to find a way to get back to Angel, while discharging his obligations to Petrus's family in Albany. Indeed, one of the

Bayard family was in Mannahattas, and Barnt went out of his way to go to the house where he was staying, bringing a fresh loaf of good bread made from white flour as a present, to apprise this man that their mutual problem was on the way to being solved.

After a few words were exchanged, the representative of the Bayard family gestured for him to accompany him into a small anteroom just off the great hall, where they sat on soft benches as they conversed. The house was of stone, quarried from somewhere on the other side of Mannahattas, Barnt thought; it was cold throughout the house, and especially in the anteroom.

Barnt noticed that the Bayard emissary to New York was quite young. He accepted Barnt's gift of fresh bread without comment, and brusquely set it aside without looking at it. "Will Petrus go to Maryland, then?" he asked.

"Before the end of the month. My brother has notified the colony; they have a man who regularly plies these waters to buy supplies. He should be in the harbor in two weeks. Petrus Bayard will go back with him to Maryland, and will proceed on land accompanied by people in the Labadist colony."

"And there is no chance of further legal difficulties?"

"None, as long as everybody obeys the same laws. We have been under the English system now since the Re-Conquest in 1674, and the rule of law will be with us as long as people remember which laws to use."

"How do we know that Petrus won't, you know . . ."

"Get into more financial difficulties? He's staying at the house of my brother, who is keeping his eye on him."

"I want you to know that your efforts are appreciated." The neutral way he said this suggested that he was unaware of the extent to which Barnt was covering Petrus's debts.

"It is my honor to serve your family. As you may know, I wish to continue this relationship in East Jersey."

The man seemed interested. "How much can you tell me

about this?"

"I have already submitted my proposals to the head of your family." Barnt continued to smile, but stood up. He did not want to give this particular representative of the Bayard family the opportunity to control the interview by standing up first. "Will you convey my personal greetings to the family, and tell them that my work for them is nearing completion?"

Petrus's brother was the main mover and shaker in the family at present, and the only one of the Bayards that he had personally met in addition to Petrus. Nicholas's attitude toward outsiders was perfunctory to the point of brusqueness, but Barnt knew that he kept to his agreements. He was also the only one in the family who knew how much Barnt was extending his private resources to bail Petrus out of trouble. He would probably strive to keep that secret—the less that people knew about Barnt's help, the less they would know about the extent of Petrus's financial indiscretions.

"Of course," said the representative of the Bayards. His glance turned curious. "Do you know Petrus's brother well?"

"Only slightly, through my wish to serve his family."

The young Bayard smiled in a way that was almost leering. "So you are a servant, then?"

Barnt forced himself to smile broadly. "Yes, yes, you could put it that way. That would be accurate." This last question suggested that the youthful representative of the Bayard family was probably little more than the youngest son of a youngest son, and therefore himself a servant of his more favorably situated brothers and cousins. "After all, Christ himself tells us to serve each other, does he not?"

"There is one thing that I must bring up with you. It would be advisable," said the young man, "if Petrus would stay at a house once owned by the master carpenter from Vlissingen, a man named Jacob Hellekers, whom some called Jacob Swart."

"Also called 'black Jacob,' I believe." Barnt had heard of this man, and knew where his house was located. "He was regarded as a good and pious man, and his wife was highly regarded as a woman with knowledge of herbs and healing plants."

The young man shrugged. "Well, be that as it may, this house is where Jasper Danckaerts boards when his ship is in port here in New York. It is Captain Danckaerts who will transport Petrus to Maryland, and make sure he reaches the Lapadists and their colony safely, since he was one of the founders of that colony. It would be better if Petrus was at the house waiting for him, so there would be no last-minute mistakes."

Barnt nodded. "Yes. I will tell Petrus of the family's decision, and take him to the house you mention. My brother Anthony will check on him regularly, and take him back to his home if it seems that Petrus is falling under the influence of one of the many sharks that ply the waters in this sinful town."

The young man nodded. "Yes. It is well that you look in on him, daily if possible, until he departs."

Barnt thought he heard the shouting of a group of men on the street outside the house. It did not sound like a fight, but rather a crowd drunkenly responding to some bit of news, no doubt something about the civil war on English soil. *One of the ships has brought a newspaper,* he thought, *and the news from London is starting to make the rounds.* But he was careful not to articulate this insight, since people who were too interested in the latest events were sometimes regarded with suspicion as schemers and possible traitors — or at the very least persons engaged in thinking too much about things that didn't directly concern them.

Barnt extended his hand and his interlocutor shook it weakly, barely bothering to hide his contempt. Barnt had a brief, searing vision of landing a blow on the man's chin, even as he smiled in the relaxed, jocular manner one was forced to assume when insulted by the rich. *They call themselves supporters of the Dutch Republic,* Barnt thought, *but these would-be Dutch aristocrats of*

Albany would not know true republicanism if it bit them on the ankle.
And this young man's attitude toward the civil war between
James II and William III—well, Barnt didn't even want to think
about that. Simply inquiring about it could get a man thrown into
irons.

7.

All these things Barnt told me as we talked in the evenings in our
chilly second-story room at Voyager House. Things in late May of
1688 were starting to happen very fast, Barnt said, but not fast
enough for him, since his single recurring thought was to be
married to Angel. As a result, he took a skiff to Staaten Eylandt
from Mannahattas with a ferryman who was a stranger to him,
along with a tied, squealing pig and two older men; the lot of
them came very near to capsizing in the combination of tide and
sudden wind. Barnt decided at that moment, he told me, that he
would never again take the conveyance of a ferryman that he did
not personally know and whose seamanship he did not trust,
because it was a mean way to die, especially when one was in
love.

When he arrived home, he found that Angel had made
porridge and was anxious to see if he liked it. He had brought
fresh cheese, and bread from his bakery, and butter in a sack
lined with salt; and that evening they feasted. He talked about
the things that had to be done before they left for East Jersey.
Most pressing was to talk to his neighbor Morgan, in order to let
him have his horse, with the understanding that he could pay
whatever he owed in the autumn.

"Bad business, some would say," I said, from the vantage
point of my early twenty-first-century business sensibilities, such
as they were. I was lying on the bunk opposite his, listening to the
patter of rain outside.

"Yes, of course—with strangers I always used contracts,"
Barnt said. "People who don't like contracts are telling you they

intend to steal from you. They can use a mark instead of a signature, if they wish—that's what I did, so as not to embarrass those who didn't know their letters. But out there on my island, on Staaten Eylandt, I needed the goodwill of my neighbors, so I would not dream of using contracts for small transactions. If you went back on your word in that community, that fact would soon get around the plantations, and you would find it hard to do business."

There was also the matter of three chickens, which Barnt resolved by letting his neighbors keep their eggs in return for taking care of them, since they were good layers. There was little more to think about, except to lock the great door of the house. Yet he and Angel put off leaving for East Jersey for two weeks, because it was still cold and the roads and trails were still muddy. Every day seemed precious. "I have never felt as happy in my life as I did at that time," Barnt told me. "In fact I never knew it was possible to feel that much happiness. There were a few eggs every day from our chickens, and potatoes I had saved in the shed out back, but I was so much in love I didn't eat that much anyway."

"Once I took Angel to a hill to the south where we could see the stone house of Captain Christopher Billop, one that he called 'Bentley Manor,' after the most famous ship he'd ever commanded. He was given this land because of a famous bet, that if anyone could circumvent Staaten Eylandt within twenty-four hours, it would remain part of New York—otherwise it would go to East Jersey. Billop succeeded in sailing around the island in twenty-three hours, winning the bet. For this reason, he was given the manorial estate where he built his manor house."

"I asked Angel what she thought of Billop's house. 'It would be too cold, this house, being made of stone,' she said. "After a pause she added that Bentley Manor was not far from the ridge where her ancestors, including her parents and brother, were buried. I understood the truth of what she was saying, having been there with her before, and reassured her that we would create a much better kind of kingdom in East Jersey. She asked me how, and I told her that God would help us . . . and he would protect the other Raritan burial places in East Jersey. That would be our earnest task; and it would be this and similar tasks that would make our patroonship free of the world's corruption, because the way of this world is that the strong oppress the weak. Instead, our kingdom would be a place where the strong would protect the weak, rather than oppress them, a goal that God would surely support."

"'Will we worship your God in this new place?' she asked me."

"I told her that I would, in my own way, but everybody else that lived in our kingdom would be free to worship as they pleased, and we would try to worship God as she did too. There was only one thing I asked of her above all, I said. I told her that there was something evil in brandy and rum, especially for her people — and she agreed. Everybody drank the weak beer because water alone made them sick, but the stronger alcoholic drinks served no such healthy purpose. Rum was something that Europeans had brought to the Lenni Lenape world, I told her, but it was not a bridge between the two people, but a smooth coach road straight to hell, where people burned for eternity. I begged her to promise that she would never drink the strong alcoholic drinks, and to teach our children never to drink them, if God gave us any. And I said that if I had my way, no one in our kingdom would ever be allowed to drink it."

"She took this very seriously, and said she agreed that it was good not to allow anybody to drink the firewater in our kingdom, whether they were white or tribal."

"I put in a fair number of crops in my plantation on Staaten Eylandt, and we did the work together. Angel was a hard worker, and worked harder than myself; but how could that not be, since she was younger? We would be home soon enough to harvest at the end of autumn—if the crops were destroyed by fire or wind, we would simply have to suffer the loss. It would be worth it to be married to her."

He and Angel were in the midst of doing this, he said, when his brother Anthony came to visit. Anthony was quite respectful to Angel, although Barnt could tell that he was surprised by her beauty, as most people were when they got a good look at her. For her part, Angel went out of her way to honor him, gesturing that he should sit across from me, and refusing to sit down until she had finished serving him.

Anthony was amused and a little taken aback by the ease with which we communicated in Jersey Dutch, but Anthony knew it well, and quickly joined in the conversation. "It sounds," Anthony said, "like the Dutch the Walloons speak, with French as home language but Dutch for commerce." Barnt told him that it felt, for his part, like they were inventing a new language.

"As it should be, brother, for when people marry they should cleave to each other for the purpose of creating a new home." Anthony said nothing about the fact that in the meantime they had been living in sin, for that kind of judgment was not his way, and in any case he had seen far worse every day in Mannahattas.

Anthony told Barnt that Petrus had departed for Baltimore with Jasper Danckaerts, as they had planned. Anthony said he was there when they put sail to the wind. "I had a chance to talk to Danckaerts at his house," Anthony said. "He is both pious and intelligent, and not a little courageous. His reputation as a seaman and an officer is very high, and yet he is a Labadist like Petrus . . . but unlike Petrus, who is a dreamer, Danckaerts has much practical knowledge of the world. He sounds like nothing more or less than an ordinary seaman when you first meet him, but then you notice that he does not swear like most sailors, and will often ask to stop and ask God's guidance."

Anthony had come away from his talk with Danckaerts thinking that perhaps the Labadists were not all fools after all.

Captain Danckaerts had opened his eyes to the idea that one could be pious, he said, and yet not a toady to the pastors and their rich allies. Danckaerts had his own ideas about right and wrong, which he got directly from reading his Bible, and reading the book written by Jean de Labadie.

Indeed, Barnt told him, it was likely that their own children and grandchildren would take a similar path—not to be Labadists, but rather to read the Bible for themselves and make up their own minds how to worship. "I understand this is very common in East Jersey," Barnt said. "People can practice any kind of religion they choose."

Anthony was shaking his head. "The more I see of this world, the more I realize how evil it is, and how rancorous and full it is of the temptations to cheat, to murder, to lie for profit and power, and to steal. But is it necessary to live in communities separate from the world, as the Labadists do?"

"People must have a way to separate themselves from the world's sin, but forming communities is only one way. It is better if each man finds his own way to shield his soul from the world's corruption, without necessarily joining with others in a community. Each person could learn to be a pilgrim in their own way, through prayer and the person's own Bible study."

Anthony nodded. He continued to look on, saying nothing for a spell. Barnt knew his brother's ways well, and could tell that he had some news to share with him. He had come all the way to Staaten Eylandt to visit him—that alone suggested that perhaps his news was out of the ordinary. But it did not work to rush Anthony. Barnt got Angel to sit down at the table with them, and sat back after eating, waiting for his brother to share what he had brought.

"Just a few days ago," Anthony began. "Governor Nicholson had the temerity to order a twenty-one-gun salute to celebrate the birthday of King James's son. It is now quite clear where his sympathies lie. The people now say that to get New York to declare for William III, they would have to engage in open rebellion—but surely that would not be a crime, since William, the man they support, is now said to be the King of England." He paused for effect. "It seems a time for action. The militiamen of Abraham De Peyster's company came into the quarters of Governor Nicholson, asking him to let them post a sentry at the sally port of the fort gate, to stop some soldiers from Boston that had been spotted approaching the fort."

"What did Nicholson say?"

"Nicholson, who was naked and more than half drunk, ordered the two militiamen out of his quarters. One of the men had a cutlass, and when he did not run fast enough, the fool Nicholson pulled a pistol. 'I would rather see the town on fire,' he shrieked, 'than be commanded by mere militiamen!' There was an inquiry the next morning, of course; Nicholson said in full assembly that the people of New York, being mainly Dutch, did not deserve the rights and prerogatives of English citizens— think of it, a colonial official in New York saying that to a room full of Dutch people! And William III having been a former stadtholder of the Dutch Republic!" He paused. "When Governor Nicholson said those words, brother, it was finally too much . . . never did a colonial Governor testify more clearly under oath to the treachery of his administration, to his hatred of Dutch people, and to his own personal stupidity."

"Then what happened?"

"Some letters arrived by ship revealing that William III had defeated James II on the battlefield, and that a Protestant monarchal dynasty was now evidently assured. Governor Nicholson tried to intercept the letters, so the people would not know—but the letters were read publicly at the Waggoner Tavern, so that the people could comfort themselves with this welcome victory for the Protestant cause. But they realized that for William III to prevail, he must have the support of the colony; and for that the people of New York must take action—the treacherous fools in the colonial government will no doubt try to undermine the new king. William III, the bold young Protestant soldier-king, whom some in the colony were already calling King Billy, needed their help—it was a turning point for the colony. For that reason representatives of four of the five militias came to the house of William Merritt, where the government officials were meeting, demanding the keys to Fort James."

"And then?"

"The militiamen wrote a statement, which four hundred of them signed. It declared New York's support for William III, the Prince of Orange, and gave the reasons why they could no longer trust the colonial administration. Then they took the fort, which they vowed to call Fort William."

8.

Barnt was only too happy to leave the turmoil of New York behind, and set out with Angel for East Jersey. He could not think of a single pastor in Mannahattas or Staaten Eylandt whom he could ever ask to marry them. It seemed that the pastors were forever on the lookout for real or imagined heresies, and might well denounce the marriage of a propertied Dutch man to a tribal woman as an outrage, or even evidence of witchcraft. Barnt would never allow that—he would never subject Angel to such an insult, however temporary.

Instead it would be better, for a variety of reasons, to be married by Angel's tribal soothsayer in East Jersey whose wisdom she respected, accompanied if possible by a certificate of some kind from the tribal chief. Barnt could later find a magistrate in Mannahattas—he knew several who had been friends of his late father—who could recognize the marriage under English law after the fact. Such marriages were not unknown, although not common. Barnt had heard of at least two, one in East Jersey and one in the wilderness of the upper Hudson River Valley, not far from where Cornelius lived.

Barnt felt that he had discharged his obligation to the Bayard family well. Nicholas Bayard would be likely to be in the thick of things, he knew, putting pressure on whatever was left of the colonial administration to take steps against the impulsive militiamen that had taken Fort James. Of course, Nicholas would do better to declare his personal loyalty to the new English king, William III, and to sit down with a select committee of New York burghers to discuss their grievances. But the rich and powerful do not think rationally, Barnt had learned, the sin of pride interfering with their ability to solve problems logically. Yet, he was obligated to help the Bayard family in any way he could until he received the land in East Jersey for which he was petitioning.

He took his skiff across Arthur Kill with Angel before sunrise, when the tidal strait was at low tide and the kill slow and easy to navigate. They left his skiff in a cove with the ferryman at Communipaw, and left on foot toward Bergen Town. This ferry had happy family associations for Barnt, since his young sister Beleyte and her husband had operated the ferry for eight years during the late 1670s; the ferryman and his wife insisted that he and Angel take fresh bread with them, and would not accept payments of any kind. They were almost immediately picked up and given a ride by a farmer with a wagon and oxen.

Bergen Town was an unexpected and pleasant revelation; rather than one town, it was a series of villages, which seemed to Barnt to be six or seven in all, all of them speaking Jersey Dutch. None were far from the waters of New York, and from what Barnt saw it appeared that many of the people were fishermen. Some of the homes were located on farms; there was at least one mill located near a river. Others in Bergen Town were apparently engaged in the trades, especially carpentry: Barnt saw three homes being built, with carpenters and joiners working together, and women carrying lumber and bringing food. In all, Bergen Town seemed an untrammeled vision of what many Dutch had wanted when they set about building New Netherland: a life both simple and good, but also a life that offered the opportunity to experience God's grace in the beauty of everyday activities.

The houses were clapboard and small, but on generous lots with room for gardens, which were already growing flowers and vegetables of many kinds. He saw few children playing, and asked a farmer if they were studying in a Latin or trivial school. The farmer replied proudly that they studied the Bible in Dutch, and that they already had a Vorleezer House—a house for the reading and learning of the Holy Scripture—where children and adults would be privileged to learn their letters from the Bible, and a schoolmaster would instruct them.

Now Barnt and Angel moved inland and were once again on foot. Barnt was uncomfortable with the looks some men gave Angel on the road; he was glad that he had a knife in both boots, and a cutlass in a rough scabbard in his pack—and he knew well how to use them, especially the cutlass. They passed what seemed to Barnt to be lush farms with crops already growing, and the same clapboard houses as the kind they'd seen in Bergen Town; then a tavern hidden in some trees near a creek crossing; and finally two churches about a mile apart.

At that point, a man with a team of horses insisted on giving them a ride, and they happily accepted. It turned out that this man lived alone, having lost his wife three months before, and insisted that they stay the night in his modest house. He talked well into the night, enjoying their company, and was delighted when Barnt told them of their plan to marry. Afterward both he and Angel saw the old gentleman crying softly to himself, apparently overcome by memories of his wife. Angel and Barnt slept separately, according to their host's arrangements, and in the morning enjoyed a huge breakfast complete with fish and porridge.

Now Angel took over the navigation of their journey, as they headed into the interior of East Jersey. Their destination was to be a village of a day's journey, or perhaps two days' journey, if the weather was inclement. They were headed, she said, for the village that she'd told me about, where the people spoke mainly Jersey Dutch, made up of a great many crippled or sick Raritan people, and Dutch and French as well; it was, as Angel described it, a kind of mission run by the tribal sachem or doctor she trusted. All were welcome, she said; when her last remaining cousin died of smallpox during the last winter, and she was left alone, she had found sympathy and spiritual refreshment at this place. As we neared the place, she became noticeably excited, and in her excitement began to speak increasingly in French. That surprised Barnt greatly, as so many other things about her had.

They passed some older tribal men on the road, accompanied by a man who appeared to be engaged in a trading transaction, since he carried beaver skins and walked briskly. Angel and Barnt came to a rise or promontory in the wagon road they were using, and Angel took his arm and told him they would take a tribal hunting trail the rest of the way. Despite Angel's excitement, they stopped for a few moments to eat some bread, then continued; the path led down, then up, then down again— in the distance Barnt thought he saw a river, which he assumed was the Raritan.

They began to descend slowly, and the path widened into a cart road of a fine dusty consistency, and the trees, mainly fir, thinned out on both sides. Now they could see the small settlement that Angel said was the place for which they were headed. As they grew nearer, a group of tribal women approached them. Two of them recognized Angel, and ran toward her, embracing her as they grew abreast of them. When Angel told them that she was here to be married, they were immediately friendly and excited.

As Barnt and Angel and the women walked on together toward the settlement, Barnt noticed that she was briefly sad about something, and asked her what it was. "There are no men to engage in the games and sports that are traditional at a wedding," she explained. "So many were killed in the last war, some were pushed with their clans into Pennsylvania, and many died of *tespeheleokan,* the smallpox. It will be a wedding attended by girls and old people."

"Will you still marry me?" Barnt asked.

She looked at him with great seriousness. "Yes."

"Thank you."

The women who were walking with them smiled, hearing them speak Jersey Dutch. They were curious about Barnt, asking where she had found him.

"In a place where many people speak this language," she told them. "We must be married because it is the commandment of his God that a man must marry any woman with whom he lies, and he wants to lie with me." The women shrieked with laughter. "I will ask Our Father to marry us tomorrow. We have brought bread with us, bread made by my future husband, who has a big store in Mannahattas for making ten loaves at the same time." She waited for the other women to take this in. "We will eat it tomorrow, when The Father will marry us." She explained that the tribal soothsayer liked the people who lived in the village to refer to him as their father, rather than a sachem or sackemaker.

"Is this the man that will marry us?"

"Yes. You will meet him shortly."

As the path they had been taking now lifted up to a promontory, Barnt looked out over what appeared to be a large and somewhat rambling village. There were two long rows of thatch huts with a long row of young corn being grown in a wide band that ran parallel with the huts, and another row almost exactly half as long. The corn was divided neither into neat lots nor rows, so Barnt's guess was that it was held in common. Nestled into some nearby trees was a house, and near that was what Barnt thought to be a Voorlezer's house, which would serve as a schoolhouse and meeting place. The village wasn't as close to the river as he would have thought, but he could see the water sparkling through the treetops in the direction of the river. Some women were engaged in carrying water, although almost everything stopped when Angel came into sight—the women crowded around her, talking, mainly in Jersey Dutch or the Raritan dialect of the Lenape language.

Since Angel and Barnt were both tired to the bone, they were led to a thatch hut where there were soft animal-hide blankets piled on a long wooden conveyance that hunters might use to drag deer or larger game behind one after hunting. There were two such soft and inviting sleeping-places; Barnt and Angel took one apiece, taking care to sleep apart. It was almost evening when the people of the village called everyone to an evening meal.

They ate in a large circle, sitting on the ground or small boulders to be used as seats. They were fed copious amounts of smokefish, called *twaelft* in that country, supposedly (but mistakenly) given that name because it was reputed to be caught and served after the season for *elft*, another fish that is usually smoked. The fish was hearty and delicious, served with corn and vegetables, likewise smoked. The bright-lit, breezy weather they had enjoyed in the last two days was now turning hazy, partly because of the smoke from the fires used to cook the fish. Barnt heard a few soft drums made from hollow logs being played in the trees; they may have been to alert the settlement to the approach of visitors, judging from the restless way the people of the village stretched their legs and craned their necks to see onto a wide cart road that led from the river.

There was a group of people walking toward them. At the center of the group was a tall dark-haired man with a long black robe. To Barnt's great surprise, it appeared that he could be European, and his robe to be cut extremely well, although worn and almost threadbare. Now Barnt saw something that shocked him greatly. The black-shirted gentleman approaching them, while deeply tanned and smiling happily, wore a handsome silver cross around his neck.

He extended his hand, and Barnt took it. "I hope your travel was a good one," he said. "You are most welcome here." He spoke first in Jersey Dutch, and then French.

"This is the man we call Father," Angel said.

"I serve all the people in this district," the man said. "There is a Sanhican village a few miles from here, from which I've just returned."

So, he was clergy of some sort. But what brought him out here? With a few exceptions, Dutch Reformed pastors generally disliked leaving the town centers. And there were few that Barnt had met who cared to work with tribal people.

"I . . . I saw your Voorlezer House up the hill," Barnt remarked. "Do you read the Heidelberg Catechism for teaching purposes?"

"Not exactly."

Now Barnt, with this tall and impressive man standing before him, was beginning to get an inkling of the monumental mistake he was making. For the moment, however, he could not take his eyes from the towering but oddly unprepossessing man who stood in front of him, the man who was still smiling, in spite of Barnt's confusion.

"I am Father Marcel," said the tall man in French and then Jersey Dutch. "I am a Roman Catholic priest of the Society of Jesus, better known as the Jesuits. My Bishop is in Quebec, but I rarely visit him, because my world is here. My sole purpose is to minister to the tribal people of this area, including those that are traditional enemies, such as the Raritans and the Sanhicans. For that reason, I have made a study of Lenni Lenape and its various dialects. For that purpose, as I minister to all the people in the area, we have come together in this village." He turned to Angel and smiled broadly, saying first in French and then in Jersey Dutch: "You promised me you would bring your Dutch man back to this village so you could be married. And you did. Tomorrow we will celebrate your marriage."

Father Marcel made what Barnt assumed was the sign of the cross, smiling broadly to Angel, whose eyes were filling with tears. Father Marcel then turned back to Barnt. "I will not ask you to become a Catholic, but I do ask that your children be brought up in the Catholic faith. Other than that, you must vow before God that you will treat your wife with respect, and love her, and behave as a Christian should—do that, and I will marry you to her, whether you raise your children Catholic or not. Are you prepared to suffer the contempt and hatred of this world, or that part of it where you live, for the love of this woman?"

And from far away, beyond Angel and Father Marcel, beyond himself and the moment through which they were to be irrevocably conjoined, Barnt heard his own voice, resounding with an unexpected vehemence: "A team of wild horses could never pull me back; and if you think they could, you are very *mistaken*, sir!" He turned to Angel, whose eyes shone. "Soon, soon, you will be my wife!"

9.

And so she would. As soon as Father Marcel identified himself, Barnt realized that he had always known, deep in his bones, how different and how challenging this marriage would be. Everything about his love for Angel had taken him into unknown territory. But on another level, no matter how dangerous, no matter how unexpected, no matter how humiliating, and no matter how difficult, he would do *anything* to marry her. Whatever the burden was to be, he was ready to carry it; whatever the public embarrassment, he welcomed it; whatever the dark consequences, he would suffer them.

It even felt like God was calling him, forcing him to some new understanding of how the ways of men worked. Of course, he knew what the Calvinist dominies of the Dutch Reformed

Church would say of his being married by a Catholic priest, because they saw Jesuits as the very incarnation of the Devil, and saw them everywhere (under every bed, as his father used to say); and indeed, his love for Angel had the power to make him see the world differently than he ever had before. He was willing to even consider the possibility that Satan was taking him down by some clever ruse, and that everything he had with Angel was a snare and a delusion. But he had made his pact; and as he had told his brother Cornelius, he would cleave to Angel if she were the Devil himself in the form of a woman. And so it had come to him in the old, old way, the love of his life, a haunting and beautiful woman who stepped out of a fire, first as a stranger, then a lover, then a wife. Barnt saw that it was a miracle and embraced it joyously and completely.

The women of the settlement, who were mainly tribal women, were in a thrall of ecstasy, gathering around Angel and carrying on like so many twittering birds, dressing Angel with soft and beautiful garments and extensive garlands of flowers. These were women who at a young age had married warriors who had perished in the recurring wars of the region. In a settlement bereft of men except for memories in the hearts of women who had been married to them, there was little romance. Now there was romance—indeed, romance was the order of the day!—and soon would come the sacramental consummation of that romance, featuring a real man who was to be married to a real woman in broad daylight! The women of the settlement were transfixed.

Father Marcel gave Barnt some instruction in the sacrament of marriage, but Barnt could remember very little of it—mainly it was about the prayer book from which Father Marcel would read. But all Barnt could think of was Angel. He was not to see her before the ceremony, and he waited impatiently, unable to eat. When she appeared, she was as radiant as a sunrise. But the light did not come from her garments or the garlands of flowers around her neck. The light came solely from her face. Barnt was relieved on some deep level that she was as happy as he was—this was something as important to her as to him. Of course, he had expected that, but still … it was wonderful to see it.

The ceremony itself Barnt could not later remember, except as a kind of passionate blur while certain solemn words were said, words that seemed to bring them closer merely by the sound of them. He knew enough French to know when they were pronounced man and wife, and hugged her in sheer exultant joy . . . then looked into her face (which had never looked so beautiful as today), afterward kissing her softly on the forehead, then kissing her lips once, and then again. A deep sigh emanated from the women. It was as though they were unable to turn away from the lovers, now married in the eyes of God and the world . . . yet slowly they did so, slowly they turned away to help set out the food, still smiling with the warmth of what they had seen. Angel turned at last from Barnt to smile through tears at Father Marcel. And Barnt shook Father Marcel's hand solemnly.

Barnt had a good talk with Father Marcel later, as they all sat eating the wedding feast. The conversation was a dreamlike thing, something he never would have imagined having—yet he thought it important to try to explain to Marcel his feelings about war and religion. So much stood between them—and although words were not enough to erase the historical events that haunted them, some talk was necessary, thought Barnt, at least so Father Marcel wouldn't think of him as a man who hated all Catholics. The man had been decent to him—he had given him the greatest gift of all, he had married him to the woman he loved. And something about him suggested to Barnt that all in all he was a good man, beyond just his willingness to perform a particular marriage ceremony.

"I want to thank you," Barnt said to him. The two of them sat at the end of a slightly raised table, sitting on mats before heaping servings of food. "I will always be grateful for what you have done, and I will always be obligated to you. I want you to know that. I don't believe that all Catholics are evil . . . but you must understand that we, the Dutch, fought the Catholic kings for a hundred years. And I will be honest with you—I fear the Catholic kings of Spain and France, and fear that they long to impose their religion on us. The long struggle against the Catholic kings were what created the Dutch people. Yet I see the evil that religious wars do, the suffering it causes." He paused. "I wished we could have more moments like this, when we could see each other as people, rather than as part of an opposing army."

Father Marcel nodded, smiling slightly. "You have been honest with me, and I will speak honestly with you. I fear the English—they want an empire, and not just for trade. I believe that a French empire would be better for America. We are better for the tribal people, because we convert them to our faith without insisting that they change their culture completely—we let them live as they did before, and our priests live with them. But be that as it may, I too see the madness of religious war. It is the women and the children who are hurt most."

"And what Christians we become, to kill and torture each other as we do on the field of battle!"

Father Marcel shook his head, in the way men do when they confront thoughts that are deeply felt, but long suppressed. "If more people could read, perhaps they could choose the religion that is right for them. I'll be honest—I think most people would choose my faith. But shouldn't all people have the right to choose?"

"That's exactly the direction toward which the Dutch are moving. We believe that each man should choose his religion based on his own lights."

Father Marcel gestured at the wedding party that surrounded them. "Why not leave it to each of these tribes what religion they could practice? Would that not be a simple way to solve this dilemma?"

Barnt knew that few Dutch—or English either—would acknowledge that tribal people had the right to choose their own faith, or had any rights at all, for that matter. He looked at Father Marcel. He was older than Barnt, and his skin was both wrinkled and darkened by the sun; even his hair had been darkened, and with his dark skin and hair, he was beginning to look like a tribal man himself. Father Marcel was becoming one of the people he served.

"I am aware of the injustices inflicted on the tribal people," Barnt said. "There are even white people that give blankets infected with the smallpox to tribal people, because they know that God has not given their bodies the wherewithal to withstand the disease. It kills them by the thousands. And the white people rejoice."

Father Marcel's eyes filled with tears. "Yes. I know. And I'm afraid that now that they have discovered this new form of murder they will use it more often." He turned to Barnt. "What do they want to accomplish by doing this? What do they want from a land with no people, when they do not even hunt for game themselves?"

"They want to own the land. When you own land, you can sell it to others and receive money for it. This can be good as well as evil. I have decided that I want to buy a large parcel of land in East Jersey, to turn it into a place where Angel's people, the surviving members of the Turtle Clan, can be safe—and so can any other tribe that abides by my rules. No slavery will be allowed, and no war. I can personally guarantee the safety of everybody who lives on my estate."

Father Marcel smiled, his eyes softening. "I would like to visit such a place."

"You can live there, if you wish."

"Will you protect me from those who might want to kill me for my faith?" He raised his eyebrows mischievously, as though playing a game.

"Yes, as long as you give everybody the right that you claim for yourself—the right to follow their own religion, or no religion at all." Barnt was moved by their conversation, but was starting to feel that the subjects they were discussing were too hot, and required the cooling-off that could only come from contemplating them at leisure—and perhaps dreaming about them. "I know that I will always be in your debt for what you've done for me," Barnt said finally in a businesslike manner, "always." He paused for a very long time, considering his words carefully. "Thank you for your hospitality, and your honesty. I will think about these things when I return to Staaten Eylandt with Angel." He paused again. "How can I be in touch with you, if that becomes necessary?"

"There is an elderly man of the Raritan tribe named Talley, who lives close to the ferryman's house at Communipaw. If you give him a letter, he will deliver it to me."

Chapter 11

Barnt stayed a few days to help Father Marcel with certain jobs that were too heavy for the women. There were no more conversations between Barnt and Father Marcel of the kind they had enjoyed on the day of the wedding — there was too much bloody history in the subject matter of those conversations, and far too much pain. The most insurmountable part of the history, Barnt thought, was not the wars fought by Protestant against Catholic, but the fact that these wars, which had once seemed to Barnt to be simply good against evil, were at the heart of the nationalist saga that created the Dutch as a nation — giving identity to Dutch men and women, even those in Staaten Eylandt and Mannahattas. Someday, Barnt thought, his descendants would inherit a different kind of identity, an identity forged solely in the New World. Today, however, what was foremost in Dutch minds and hearts was the century-long wars against France and Spain on behalf of the Protestant cause.

What the identity of his children would be in the New World, and what tasks would create and formalize it, he could not guess, except that it lay in the future. And yet, he had personally sat and broken bread and chatted politely with a Jesuit priest who was clearly educated, a man of goodwill, and as decent a Christian as any Barnt could imagine. But Catholic and Protestant were still at war. It was an unknowable conundrum that was incapable of resolution, it seemed to Barnt — one could only pray for strength to resist its worst and most corrosive effects, until future generations could find a better way.

Angel wept when they left the settlement, and made several of the women promise to contact her if they needed her. Barnt sensed a deep sadness among the tribal women — Angel had cast her lot with a strange Dutch-speaking man, and as a result she no longer belonged to the tribes and clans to which she had nominally belonged in the past, however broken and scattered they may have been. In the beginning she had been the daughter of a Raritan chief, however different and rebellious she may have seemed. Now she was the wife of a Dutch man living on Staaten Eylandt. As Barnt and Angel said their final goodbyes and started their journey back home, the tribal women reached out to touch her hair, her dress, and her hands, as if she was being gently borne away by an invisible current; and both she and they wept openly.

As soon as they got home, Barnt did an assessment of his crops, especially the special corn he had planted. It was in surprisingly good shape, except for some plants that had been eaten by raccoons or other creatures. Once home, Barnt spent much time reading his Bible, and talking to Angel; they had reached the point where they understood each other almost before they spoke. But Barnt wanted to understand, in detail and in context, everything she said—her thoughts and feelings had become a matter of great importance to him, almost as though he feared that they might be separated so roughly that he could rely only on memories of her. But Barnt also knew that he would have to go to Mannahattas soon, since it was necessary for him to reassert his willingness to help the Bayard family, and if possible to receive instructions for how to do it. It would be hard to leave her alone, but it seemed he would have to do so to win his estate in East Jersey.

In the end, Barnt decided to stay with his small plantation of crops right up to harvest time, working a few hours a day and spending every free hour with Angel. She had started to tell him supernatural stories from the Turtle Clan, bizarre although oddly familiar, many of them, as though coming out of a time before history; some of them felt like ghost tales he had himself dreamed in his camp at the Bad Woods—in fact, was that not why he once so often spent the nights in that fearful locale, to plumb the depths of the horrific, and to experience directly the melancholia involved in embracing death? Yes, he had, only to find the most beautiful wife of which any man could dream, stepping out of the fire to take his hand. Her stories of supernatural beings and earth spirits now seemed no more than a way of closing the circle that had begun in the fire of the Bad Woods, with the woman at the center of it, the *engelbrandt*.

In return, Barnt tried his best to tell Angel of the longing for death that had arisen in his soul these last few years, his loathing for the world's cruelties that had long tormented him. (It was not something he could discuss easily with another person, even his brothers.) About his love for her, he could no longer adequately speak. At times he prayed with her, however, and his prayer was always the same . . . *Lord, keep my wife in health, and protect her from the dangers of this world.* He continued to read his Bible almost every day, which often seemed like slow sailing, because he had not read the Bible that often since the days when he learned his letters. But reading the Bible was no longer a chore; like his love for Angel, it took him to a new world, a different world. Yet like his love for her, the stories in the Bible felt strangely familiar: war, love, violence, dreams, and desperate attempts to know the will of God.

They harvested the good corn together, with the help of a lad from a neighboring farm. Angel learned quickly, and had a way of shucking the corn that he'd never seen before—quick as lightning, with a way of firmly grasping the husks and pulling them off with a single jerk, dropping them, and leaving the denuded ears in a pile. She asked him to save the husks for some special cookery of her own, and a weaving of blankets and pottery done in the tribal way. The boy who was helping them with the farm work was good once he got started, but he spent most of his time in the mornings ogling Angel. Barnt watched her himself out of the corner of his eye, as she worked beside him. He wondered if there was anything in the Bible that prohibited making love to one's wife in the morning, as well as at night. It seemed as natural as swimming, or riding a horse, or playing a musical instrument. It simply happened. After they made love in the morning, it was as though the Love Medicine had given him the strength of ten men.

Finally, they were finished putting his corn in his brick silo. He rested a day, and the next day awoke early, his things ready for a quick visit to Mannahattas. They ate porridge and salted fish in silence in candlelight before dawn. Barnt showed her again how to lock the great door, and how to use a cutlass if attacked; he made her promise not to answer the door unless it was one of his brothers.

"You could use this for planting squash," Angel said, laughing and grasping the cutlass firmly.

"This is an edge tool. I sharpened it just two days ago, so be careful with it." He quoted a phase he'd heard the Raritan women using: "If you are attacked, do not shame your ancestors, but kill your enemies, as they would kill you!"

After embracing her one last time, he hiked to his skiff in the early light, and pushed off into the low waters of Fresh Kill, and from there on Arthur Kill and Kull van Kill to the ferry at Communipaw, and from there to Mannahattas. The wind was not strong, but steady, and carried them easily to their destination without difficulty.

He made his way to the Green Dragon tavern. Barnt was happy that one of the two boys that worked for him was there early, doing what was necessary to open the place. On the other hand, the boy harbored some bad tidings: the girl Barnt had lately hired to clean out the rooms in back had succumbed to a fever and lung ailment, dying in New Hospital a few blocks away. As he drank a watery beer and ate a slice of bread, Barnt realized that he knew nothing about the girl, and nothing about her family; most sinful of all, he couldn't even remember her name.

"Do you know what she was called?" he asked Joost, the

young lad who was preparing for the business that day.

"She would never tell me her name," he replied sharply, "and her parents are dead. I understand she had an uncle, but she hadn't seen him for several years. She may be one for the potters' field *lang de waal*, on the far side of the wall."

"When did the young woman pass away?"

"Three days ago she could no longer stand, and two nights ago she died."

"Do you know the state of her soul?"

"No, I don't, sir. But God extends his grace to all his creatures who ask for it." His voice quavered slightly. "Is that not true, *heer*?"

"Yes, yes, of course. That is one thing about which we can be sure." The boy went back to sweeping. As Barnt fired up his oven in his small lean-to kitchen, he heard the lad crying.

Fate was such a brutal and fickle thing, Barnt thought, to bear away a young woman without notice or warning, to take her gentle mind and body away from the earth so quickly that she hadn't even had time for a day or two in bed, and probably spent her last hours being bled for bad humors. Not all the sermons in the world would ever convince him that there was anything good or Christian in such an early death. Barnt had been around death since infancy—including the deaths of his own children—but there was something about this that especially unnerved him. If a young girl like her could be taken so quickly, he thought, so could his wife Angel, as young and spirited and healthy as she was.

From now on, Barnt thought, he would have to be vigilant, and be aware of anything that could make Angel ill—he had taught her to drink weak beer mixed with water, and she did so daily, since water from Staaten Eylandt's springs made people sickly. He made a mental note to give his young male employee bread for his mother and sisters at home, and to inquire about a grave for the recently departed servant girl.

Afterward he went to his small apartment above the ovens in his bakery, and was delighted to feel the heat rising up through the floor, as well as the rich smell of baking bread. Whatever else happened, the smell of baking bread always generated feelings of hope and anticipation. Life went on! No matter what happened, the living needed bread . . . for a moment he felt joy for the privilege of making bread that others could enjoy.

He wished he was at home eating fresh bread with his young wife. When she ate alone, she attacked her food with a certain ferocity, as though she feared it might be snatched away from her; but when she ate with Barnt, she watched him carefully and sought to imitate the sensuous, slow way he liked to eat, pausing often to speak, laugh and drink.

Barnt decided to inquire from the local stonemason about a modest gravestone, ultimately rejecting the ghastly anonymity of "Beloved of God" and "Child of God," determined now to ferret out the correct name and spelling of his late employee's name. On the street he was joined by Anthony, who was evidently headed toward his second-story rooms. As they walked rapidly down the street, Barnt noticed that Anthony was smiling to himself, as he always did when he had news of some sort.

"Why are we walking so fast?" Barnt asked. "True, you are younger than me, but you walk as though the bailiff was two steps behind you."

"There are things going on here that you must know about. I'll tell you more when we get into your rooms."

"You talk as thought you are afraid of being overheard."

"That is exactly what I'm afraid of," Anthony said.

Once they were settled in the apartment above the bakery, Barnt got two half-liter *humpen* of beer and water, dipping them in the barrel in the hallway. "So what exciting news do you have for me today, brother?" Barnt asked.

Anthony smiled. "You have heard, have you not, that the militias in Mannahattas took the fort from Andros and the so-called New England Dominion?"

"Fort James?"

"Fort William now, brother. These are tricky times, when getting the name right might save you a fair amount of trouble."

"I have heard a little gossip on the ferry coming over. I heard the militia captain Jacob Leisler is the main leader of these remarkable events."

"He is the main leader, but there are many that agree with him. Four of the five militias threw in their lot with Leisler when he took the fort. There were many rumors about an invasion from the New France Jesuits in Canada, when our defenses were down and government disorganized and unable to function."

Barnt thought immediately of Father Marcel in East Jersey, but pushed the thought away. "Is there some truth in it, that we might be attacked?"

"Since August last, England and France have been at war."

"Does anybody know what France's intentions are for Mannahattas?"

"In September there were rumors of imminent attack from Canada. But the usual so-called leaders did nothing to assuage the fears of the people. In fact, the rich landowners did nothing, except to make their usual crude jokes directed at the honest Dutch-speaking people they are supposed to be leading. They grovel before the English aristocrats, and seek to curry favor with them by making obscene jokes about Dutch backwardness!" He paused to drink. "If they think that by defaming their own people they can win the favor of the English, they are sorely mistaken. Neither the English nor the Dutch admire a traitor to his own people. That leads to nothing but contempt."

"Yet the English give the rich ones power."

"So far they have, to be sure. But if the English wish to have an empire, they must pick rulers with more discretion. Government should have some thought and consideration for the people governed, shouldn't it? Do these so-called leaders like

Livingston and Bayard and Van Courtland and Schuler really think that insulting the common people makes them better administrators?"

"No, of course it doesn't. It creates disgust in both ruled and ruler."

Anthony breathed deeply. "We know we must learn to live under English rule, and to adapt to the English language and law and customs—and it is perhaps easier for people like ourselves, especially you, since you have spoken the English language before the Conquest of 1664 and the Re-Conquest of 1674. But for many people it is close to impossible, to learn a new language and a new system of law at this point in life. And it simply makes everything harder, when corrupt and brutal people like Livingston and Bayard openly disparage their own people."

"Nothing in the world will change the fact that we are conquered," Barnt said. "We must learn to live under English rule, and to make our fortunes and our fate in this New World in spite of their incompetence and their distrust of our ways. But I agree with much that you say. Treat people with scorn, as both Dutch and English leaders like to do, and sooner or later the people will revolt." He drank deeply and sat his cup down on the table. "So what kind of an administrator is Leisler turning out to be?"

Anthony sighed. "Ay, there's the problem. He is stopping people on the street, intercepting and inspecting all the letters coming into Mannahattas, and breaking into people's houses to ask about their religion and their loyalties. He had a couple of set-tos with the place-men of the Albany patroons, but gave as good as he got. He's strengthening his hand, putting his people into positions of power around Mannahattas, and even in neighboring states. In that way he is quite clever. The brave pultroons—excuse me, patroons—are laying low for the time being; but they are sending their representatives to London to plead their case directly to King William."

"Did Leisler send his own representatives to plead *his* case?"

"Yes, but he has no understanding of the English court. Leisler and his band have connections in Amsterdam, and he can be very shrewd in using his Dutch connections here in the colony, but it is the connections in London that matter most now. Poor Leisler doesn't understand English law, and doesn't even speak or write the English language very well."

"Then he will lose in the end, I'm afraid," Barnt said.

"But his secretary and lieutenant is English-born, a man named Jacob Milborne. Have you heard of him?"

Barnt hesitated, wondering how much he should say. But he could not justify keeping important information from Anthony. "Jacob Milborne came into the Green Dragon while he was still getting his land legs, having just put in from London. He brought news of that place, for which I was grateful. He is quite bold, and knows the coffee-house society in London."

"He is a strong Anabaptist, I understand."

"Like his father, who is a preacher in Boston and a leader of those demanding that the colony declare for William and Mary. His brother is a Fifth-Monarchy Man there."

"Yes," Anthony said thoughtfully, "and Milborne knows the English system; but whatever that may gain him he squanders with his foolish and overbearing enthusiasms. I believe that all such enthusiasm has its origins in melancholy and morbid thoughts on death, or unfounded fears of damnation in spite of God's freely given grace, which produces a kind of distemper. Some enthusiasm may be divine inspiration or diabolical possession, but I think much is simply a kind of sickness, like the plague victims that dance before they perish."

Barnt shivered slightly, thinking again of the late servant girl. "And Leisler?"

"His enthusiasm for the Protestant cause is sincere, but like Milborne he has no gift for discretion. You see him and his men at all hours on the streets, checking for papists in disguise, dragonnading people on the street, just as the French do to the poor Huguenots. He sees papists and Jesuits everywhere, or those that he says are 'popishly affected.' That kind of fear is a great detriment, brother, because it creates suspicion that is passed from one person to the next like the plague. But it also creates a feeling among fearful and neglected people that somebody is looking after their interests. I would say Leisler will have power in Mannahattas for the next year or so, at least."

"And after that?"

"King William will send troops to take back the fort. They will put Leisler and the other ringleaders in prison for a few months, no more. It was a time of civil war, after all, a political emergency, during which the Albany patroons did absolutely nothing to prepare us for attack. The powder in the fort wasn't even usable until Leisler made sure it was dry. And Leisler declared for William and Mary, with the whole colony behind him . . . that, and that alone, forced the patroons in Albany to declare for William, and give up their support for James and the Stuarts."

"That was a good day's work when the colony declared for King William," Barnt said, nodding. He drank his watery beer, then asked, "What does Leisler stand to gain from all this?"

"Revenge, perhaps, at least in part."

"For what?"

"That's an interesting little story." Anthony drank a little more, pausing for effect. "You see, Leisler and his sons were on the high seas on one of his ships, along with a shipment of wine, tobacco, and furs, heading to Amsterdam to sell his goods. But they were besieged by Algerine pirates who took Leisler and his sons hostage; and as is the practice among the Turks, they demanded a ransom to release Leisler, his ship, and his sons. Leisler's church determined to pay the ransom, and collected money from people near and far, giving the full amount of 2,500 sterling to Governor Andros to ransom the Leisler family."

"But Governor Andros set aside—that is, he stole—much of

the money intended for Leisler's ransom, and used it to build a new church. Leisler was forced to pay a great deal of his own ransom, even though his church had collected more than enough to free him and his sons. Of course, responsibility for this contemptible theft lay with the church pastors, who can never wait to shout 'three cheers' for any corrupt action by the English administrators, and the Dutch leaders as well. Imagine—despite the fact that several lives depended on the ransom being paid in full to the pirates, Andros stole the money." He paused. "Leisler never again attended the Dutch Reformed Church, although he stayed on the membership rolls. Nor do most Dutch men attend these days, because of the church's great corruption, although many of the woman still attend."

Barnt thought about what he'd heard, shaking his head slowly. What was happening to the world, when the church was a sink of corruption? "Does Leisler have any other reason for acting as he has, in addition to his contempt for a corrupt colonial administration and a corrupt church?"

"The same as every other man—he thinks he's doing the right thing, even when it hurts him, or hurts others. And there's something else . . . as a Dutch merchant under English law, he has lost a fair amount of power and money. He may see this as his last chance for greatness."

Barnt sighed. "I wish I knew what the Albany patroons are planning, especially the Bayard family. I wish Cornelius was back, and could give me some idea what they're up to."

"He *is* back," Anthony said calmly. He paused before continuing, chuckling at Barnt's amazement. "Our elusive brother Cornelius just came in on the dispatch cutter from Albany, after stopping at Lange Eylandt. He's resting at the house of Captain Danckaerts, a short walk from here, waiting to meet with us."

2.

Barnt walked rapidly with Anthony in the direction of the Danckaerts house. It was just like Anthony, he thought, to hold back on delivering good news, or news of any kind. "Damn you and your craziness," he yelled into the wind at Anthony. "Why didn't you tell me right away that Cornelius was here?"

"It's more interesting the way I do it," came the answer.

Anthony continued to walk very quickly, glancing around behind him once or twice. They were soon at the house of Jasper Danckaerts, the house where Petrus Bayard had stayed before going to the Maryland colony of Jean de Labadie. Cornelius sleepily answered the door, but instantly came awake upon seeing Barnt. He motioned for them to come inside. The three of them sat down in the small parlor room of the house; Barnt kept his pea jacket on, as did Anthony: no fire had been laid in the fireplace, and it was now too late to do so. Building a fire in such a house was best done in the morning, with warmth at night coming from nine or ten quilts on one's bed.

"I have letters for you," Cornelius said to Barnt, "and it will be my pleasure to deliver them to you by hand. But first let me tell you what happened, before I get them from my trunk."

"It couldn't have been easy to get the letters through," Barnt said. "I heard from Anthony that all letters were being intercepted by Leisler's militiamen."

"You heard right."

"Tells us what magic you performed to get them through."

"Not magic," Cornelius said, "that is the Devil's art. I used the arts of deception . . . and a little faith." He settled himself in his chair, smiling first at Anthony and then at Barnt. "It was not a single letter, but a packet of them. They were in a letter pouch with a single word on the outside—the people who sent these communications were enemies of Leisler and his militia, and assumed we were as well; so the markings on the outside of the pouch were in the form of a concealed message, consisting of the letters *S W A I M.* And those letters, in turn, stood for Society for the Withholding of Aid and Information from the Militia."

"The militia lad sent to intercept all letters from Albany boarded the cutter immediately after the captain docked. He was no more than an apprentice boy, and perhaps had not learned all his letters. I produced the packet of letters and he took one look at the writing on the outside, and began to bluster and march about. 'What is the meaning of this, these letters?' he demanded. "Don't pretend that it isn't a code—we deal harshly with papists here. If you value your life, you'd better just tell me. What exactly to these letters stand for?'"

"'*Stand* for?' I asked, as innocent as could be. 'Why, those letters don't *stand* for anything.'"

The boy was fit to be tied. "Well, what are they then, if they don't stand for anything?"

"They're a name."

"A *name?*"

"Yes, *my* name. Swaim is the name of my ancestors for many generations—there's nothing I can do about it, even if I wanted to. And I wouldn't want to, since it's quite a beautiful name. Swaim—it's unusual but quite distinctive, don't you think?"

By now we were starting to laugh. Cornelius, despite his eccentricities, sometimes had a way of making difficult encounters sound hilarious.

"It doesn't sound very Dutch, this name," the militia lad said suspiciously.

"I'm as Dutch as the day is long," Cornelius said, finishing with an obscene Dutch expression.

"But is it based on your father's name? Is it a patronymic?"

"It might as well be. It memorializes not only my father, but the male line of his family going back six generations. It refers to a castle belonging to my father deep in the Utrecht region, by the largest lake there, the name of which means 'Place of the Swans.' Swaim—well, you couldn't find a more Dutch name, if you are from Utrecht, and especially Leerdam; a name that not only honors my father, like most patronymics, but the male ancestors going back ten generations."

"I thought you said 'six generations,'" the lad complained.

"Six, ten—it all depends on how you calculate a generation."

The young militiaman was getting tired of the game, but wasn't quite ready to give it up. "'Do your brothers use the same name?'" he said. "It sounds English to me.'"

"Then let us not insult the colonial administration of the English for no reason." Cornelius tossed the packet of papers into his trunk, which sat beside him on the deck of the cutter. "If you give me your name, I'll put in a good word for you with Captain Leisler when I see him."

At last aware that he was being teased, the lad snorted and turned away sharply.

Cornelius smiled broadly as he finished the story. "You are a cool one," Anthony said admiringly. "Thanks to this vivid illustration, I can now see the advantage of having a surname in addition to a patronymic."

"Actually, it has become a fashion nowadays," Barnt said. "The men of the second generation continue to use the patronymic in the Dutch community, but have a provisional surname to use with the English-speakers. And after this story no one could doubt the usefulness of it."

The brothers were silent for a moment.

"Honestly," Cornelius said, "I think it was the work of the Holy Spirit to make me think of it as a name, at the very moment when I was tempted to forget my wits."

"So," Barnt said, "having given ourselves this name, we must answer to it. It will become my name as well, Cornelius, or at least one of them. I am known on Staaten Eylandt as Barnard Thysen, the son of Thys Barentsen; but now I will also go by this new name, when the time is right to use it. Bernard Swaim—it has a nice sound, although it will take some time to get used to it."

"It was the Holy Spirit that put this name into my mind," Cornelius reiterated. "I'm sure of it," he said, shaking his head. "But it does have a bit of an English sound to it, doesn't it?"

"Not if we pronounce it like 'place of the swan' — remember how Pater talked about the big house in the Old Country, how people there were called 'dwellers at the place of the swan?' And the way we say it, it could be either English or Dutch. It will all depend on how we pronounce it."

"I knew the story about this big house," Cornelius said, "and God be thanked that I remember it. I remember Pater talking about it. But honestly, brothers, I thought it was simply a tale like those told by old people on winter nights by the fire."

"No," Barnt said, "there was more to it than that." He remembered the long trip across the ocean, remembered the things their father had told him during that ghastly dangerous voyage. Barnt had been fifteen when they arrived in New Netherland, and even then had sensed how important the old family stories were to his father. "Pater told me the story on the high seas, during the two months that it took to sail from Amsterdam to Nieuw Nederland. I was just a fifteen-year-old boy, but I remember it well. 'Dwellers at the Place of the Swan' refers to a big house owned by our father's grandfather. The reference to the swans was a kind of code."

"During the worst of the troubles in France, the Protestants were given refuge at the 'Place of the Swan'; our father and my mother first met there as children. The French Protestants that took refuge in that area learned to speak Dutch like native speakers, and for all intents and purposes *became* Dutch. As a result of these experiences our pater had a vision, about how the world would be if everybody was allowed to practice religion as they wished without interference, and to claim allegiance to whatever faith they chose. This vision was one of the reasons Pater decided to leave Europe and come to the New World."

"Such a vision could possibly be a burden to anyone who experienced it," Anthony said thoughtfully. "Or at least a responsibility. To say the least, it would change one's life."

Barnt couldn't help but think of Father Marcel in East Jersey. "But our pater had the vision, nonetheless, and he went to the trouble of telling me about it," he said. "I have always suspected that perhaps my mother, who after all was a Huguenot, may have influenced him. So let us cherish and honor Pater's vision." He paused. "Who knows, maybe someday Protestant and Catholic can live together in the same country, and sit at the same table."

The brothers were silent.

They were briefly interrupted by the drunken shouts of two men arguing on the street outside, but the voices of the disputants gradually faded. "In any case," Anthony said, "if we pronounce Swaim in the English manner, it is an English name. If we pronounce it in the Dutch way, it will be a reference to Pater's 'Place of the Swans.' Only the family will know the difference."

"Could there be some spiritual danger in assuming a family name that was first used to deceive?" Cornelius asked anxiously. "It was a necessary lie to use it in that manner, but a lie nonetheless. I gladly assume the risk, but I would not willingly impose it on my brothers."

"You said yourself that the Holy Spirit must have put the idea into your mind," Barnt said. "If it was put there by God, how can we question it?" *Poor Cornelius,* he thought—*always striving to avoid sin even while assuming his soul was already lost for eternity.* "As I see it, it came to you in a way that was truly providential. If we can share in this good providence, we are simply doing God's will."

Anthony nodded; and after a moment's hesitation, Cornelius did as well. "Yes, I must agree. Coming in that way, it was a gift from God, and it would be a sin to refuse it."

But deep in his bones, Barnt privately wondered if there might not indeed be some danger in having an English-sounding name.

Not physical danger or even danger to the soul, but danger involving the immutability of a name in an English-speaking world. Under the English, a surname was always the same, generation after generation, nipping at a man's heels like a dog chasing a rabbit, unlike the Dutch patronymic that lasted a generation and then discreetly faded into the mists of time. The name Swaim, on the other hand, had come to them in the midst of enormous social upheaval and hate, something unlike anything this place had ever see before; and sooner or later all the people that lived in this world—Dutch, English, tribal people alike—would be affected by these upheavals. *Was the immutability of the name a harbinger of the immutability of evil?* Was an English or English-sounding surname like a curse, one that plodded relentlessly in the very midst of a family from one generation to the next?

"Well," Anthony said, "are you ready to open the packet, so we can see what secrets this new name holds?" His question was asked in a teasing tone of voice; Barnt was reasonably satisfied that neither he nor Anthony had any particular desire to see the inside of the pouch; yet Anthony's joking query was not completely free from a certain curiosity.

"I'm so tired I can hardly see," Barnt said. "I'll look at these important communications tomorrow."

Anthony sighed. "I doubt that you will receive a communication from Nicholas Bayard," he said, "since Captain Leisler just put him in irons at the fort."

That came as a surprise to Barnt, since he had not heard of it yet. Nonetheless, Barnt expected some communication from Nicholas's brother, or perhaps from another family member in Albany; above all he hoped to hear some word on his application for a land patent in East Jersey. It would be wrong of him, he thought, to assume that his proprietary relationship with the Bayard family would be common knowledge in Albany—but it was likely that Nicholas would have shared Barnt's prayer for land with his brother, perhaps many other family members, or perhaps with another powerful Dutch family. Barnt simply wanted to save his brothers from any danger associated with his dealings with the Albany patroons.

But there was also something on a deeper level, something that had to do with how they saw themselves in the small world of Anglo-Dutch New York in 1688. Barnt was now in a game of risk and deception occurring in a milieu they'd always despised. The sons of Thys Barentsen were smart and hardworking and likeable; whatever else could be said of them, they thought of themselves as being above the petty money-grubbing and influence-peddling of the Bayards, the Van Cortlandts, the Philipses, the Livingstons and Van Rensselaers, not to mention the Schuylers with their perennial attempts to corner the beaver fur market. The Dutch patroons of Albany were always to some extent living a lie, because it would be a very long time before they were the landed aristocrats they fancied themselves becoming. The sons of Thys Barentsen van Leerdam, on the other hand, made their money honestly, and could tell the world to kiss their bums if they felt like it.

But just as Barnt had entered the Bad Woods of Staaten Eylandt, and therein lost his heart to a fire angel, Barnt was now entering another kind of Bad Woods, a place of intense corruption, where he must find his way until he raised up his private kingdom in East Jersey; it was simply the way of the world that he would be forced to live by its corrupt standards for as long as he was lost in it. His brothers knew, or thought they knew, exactly the obsession that drove him, the obsession to make a safe kingdom for Angel; and they could both understand how such a wild love could happen—what person, man or woman, could not understand how such a thing happened?

Yet, they were also fearful of the dangers that Barnt now lived with, and not merely dangers to life and limb. You entered the world of corruption and exploitation and lying, and thought you could leave when you were ready; but the quicksand could pull you down when you least expected it, no matter how virtuous your cause. But whatever else he was, or would become, Barnt was above all the oldest brother; and it was to that brotherhood he would be loyal. The younger brothers knew that, but could not help but be worried about him.

Barnt stood up, buttoning up the top button of his pea jacket over his thick scarf. The November wind would be cold, he realized, and he didn't want to make the sore throat he was getting any worse. He picked up the mail pouch with the word S W A I M on the outside, as both Cornelius and Anthony watched him without getting up. "Can you stay here in this house for a few days?" he asked Cornelius. "It probably won't be too bad when a fire is laid."

"I'm afraid to do that until the chimney sweep does his work here," Cornelius said. "There is so much tar and soot in the chimney that it could easily catch fire, and the neighbors would not appreciate that, I vow. I can have the boy here by tomorrow or the next day."

"Good," Barnt said. That was Cornelius, he thought—conscientious to a fault, and perennially alert to all potential dangers.

"Will we see you before you go back to Staaten Eylandt?" Anthony asked.

"Come by the bakery, both of you—I'll have fresh bread for you tomorrow in the late afternoon." It occurred to Barnt in passing that he would almost surely need Cornelius's help again, if only to take another message to Albany. But Cornelius lived a simple life, and Barnt wanted to find a way to give Cornelius a small income. When Cornelius came by on the morrow for his bread, Barnt would give him some money and ask him to stock the house of Captain Danckaerts with food, give some money to the chimney sweep, and keep the rest for expenses that would arise if he had to go to Albany again.

3.

Barnt went to his rooms above his bakery. He opened the mail pouch by a single candle, and sat down at his writing desk with his hands and face held close to the candle. There was but a single letter in the pouch. He had been hoping for a packet, perhaps with the hoped-for patent for land accompanied by a letter congratulating him on his new estate. But they would want more from him before fulfilling their end of the bargain, he knew, and even then there were no guarantees regarding their behavior—as was well-known, the rich and powerful Dutch patroons around Albany had an astonishing tendency to break their word, as well as a huge array of justifications for their inability to keep their promises.

The letter had a seal of the Bayard family on it, which he broke gently. Inside was a short letter from someone who was apparently Nicholas Bayard's brother Balthazar Bayard, which caused Barnt to think back to a recent encounter with a youthful family member of the Bayard family. He wondered if that had been Balthazar—but that was not likely, that individual representing the Bayard family had been far too young. And Balthazar would never speak personally to someone asking a favor; since the granting of favors was the main source of both his power and his income, he would want to limit such interactions to letters, contracts and various kinds of proxy relationships.

The letter read:

Estimable Friend,
Thank you for most helpful information received post last.
My dear brother Nicholas has lately been imprisoned by the
impertinent Leisler king of the rabble. Pls utmost importance
to discover the plan for Leisler's criminal confederate Jacob
Milborne, we have heard he will attack Albany, we are
concerned about the safety of our families. The vile usurpers
fired at my brother's slave John and missed, think how the

fiends would murder and torture our poor little ones.
Advise please earliest

Het was goed om van u te horen.

Met vriendelijke groeten

B. B.

And not one mention of Barnt's application for a land patent!
Typical behavior of the Albany crowd, Barnt thought. You were
supposed to do what they asked, when they asked it, no matter
how dangerous it might be to you personally; and maybe,
maybe, in the fullness of time, your request might be considered.
Or maybe not. It was a deliberate strategy to keep people off
balance, to keep various supplicants unsure of exactly where
they stood, yet implying just enough largesse to keep financial
loyalties intact. It was also intended to remind people,
consciously and unconsciously, of exactly who had the power
and exactly how arbitrary the use of that power might be.

On the other hand, Barnt was not surprised that the Bayard
family—not to mention the other rich Dutch families—were
worried about the next move in the game of chess unleashed by
Leisler's takeover of the fort. Any thought of compromise with
elements of Leisler's followers would naturally be unlikely to
occur to the patroons of Albany. Nor did it occur to Balthazar
Bayard, who mentioned in his note the near-lethal attack on
Nicholas Bayard's slave, that slavery was itself a form of torture
and death. The rich in Albany lived in a fantasy world in which
they were always right, and therefore suffered from a kind of
moral insanity, in which nothing mattered, culturally or morally,
except their own wealth and prestige. That was their biggest
weakness in the face of such social uprisings as Leisler's—they
could not begin to imagine how other people might feel, and

therefore could not predict their behavior. For those reasons they could not imagine the compromises that could save them in the short run, and lay the groundwork for future cooperation.

So how would he respond to this unilateral demand for services from "B.B.," with no mention of recompense? Would he send Cornelius all the way up the Hudson River bearing a reply? No, *no*, most certainly not. Let Balthazar or Balthus — or whatever his real name might be — stew in his own juices for a bit. He would write no answer to his letter; perhaps his silence might make the Bayard family make some acknowledgement, however slight, of the payment he would eventually receive. Of course, the payment he sought was land in East Jersey, as he had made perfectly clear to them; and he had already received some fleeting interest from Nicholas, based on his longstanding notion of a buffer between the new Dutch-speaking settlers and the English Quakers to the west, and between the settlers and the Sanhicans and other tribes being pushed farther into the interior. But Nicholas Bayard, according to this latest communication, was now in the dungeon ensconced deep in the bowels of Fort William.

In the meantime, he thought, he might have something for Cornelius to do in Mannahattas. Following Dutch custom, the brothers would never directly pay or loan money to each other for their help; they would always find indirect ways to give money to each other, so that it did not look or feel like money paid for services rendered, and could always be given back at a later date. But Barnt was grateful for Cornelius's help, since he did not have much money at any given time. He suspected Anthony had already given him funds to live on; but it would now be up to Barnt also to provide enough for him to survive comfortably. In addition, he had a vague sense that it would be good for the brothers to stay in frequent contact with each other during this period of upheaval under Leisler and his English lieutenant Milborne.

In the meantime, Barnt wanted to get back to Staaten Eylandt. His cold was getting worse, and he wanted to be with Angel in a warm house with a store of food, water and beer before the chilly winds of autumn set in. When Cornelius and Anthony came over in the afternoon, he would give them as much bread as they could carry, and offer Cornelius work at the Green Dragon, which was short a person after the death of the serving girl.

If Cornelius accepted, he could stay at the rooms above the bakery, and he would never go hungry as long as the people of Mannahattas continued to patronize the bakery's fine bread. If there were further communications for Barnt from Albany, Cornelius could receive them at the Green Dragon or the bakery; and in that case, or if there were rumors of trouble that required Barnt's attention, it was but a short ferry-trip to Staaten Eylandt. It also crossed Barnt's mind to offer Cornelius a job of harvesting his crops in autumn, as well as tending the new crops during the spring of 1690. If that worked out, it might be comfortable for Cornelius to build some kind of small house or shack on Barnt's property not far from Fresh Kill, at least during the warm weather, whereas in the cold weather he could live in the main house with Barnt and Angel.

When the crisis in Mannahattas was over, Barnt suspected that Cornelius would probably go his separate way again, somewhere in the wilderness land up the Hudson River. Until then, he thought, the brothers should stay close to each other when the hard winds blew. They all sensed that 1690 and 1691 would be crisis years—of what kind, they were not entirely sure. But whatever the storm brought, it was something they must prepare themselves to ride out, by helping each other in any way that presented itself.

4.

The next afternoon Cornelius and Anthony arrived at different times, but the three of them were able to share an hour. Cornelius accepted the offer of a job at the Green Dragon tavern, and agreed to stay nights at the rooms above the bakery; Barnt had already apprised his two bakers of the guest who would shortly live in the rooms above. Barnt's cold was getting worse, so the two brothers left for the evening, Cornelius having decided to spend two more nights at the Danckaert house. The next morning Barnt left after eating nothing but bread, anxious to get home to Angel.

At the ferryman's hut a small and indescribably ugly pup had somehow gotten on board, and now growled at anyone who tried to put him back on dry land. Barnt took some bread from his pack and crumbled it in his hand, and fed it in small handfuls to the little dog, which whined its appreciation. The ferryman explained that a wharf dog had whelped a litter, and this pup had left the comfort of its mother—and the familiarity of its litter—before any of the others. Now he seemed to have chosen Barnt's company, sitting at his feet and watching him closely. When they reached Communipaw, and the dog prepared to follow him, Barnt glanced at the ferryman, then at the dog. The ferryman motioned for Barnt to take the pup with him, if he chose; and the two of them departed together.

The dog, having been born on a wharf, was not startled when Barnt pulled his skiff out of its hiding place, but instead jumped onboard. The current had gotten stronger, and Barnt saw the little creature looking at the shore on both sides, preparing to swim if necessary. But when the mouth to Fresh Kill hove into view, Barnt poled the skiff cleanly into it, where there was little current. A few moments later they were on Barnt's property, and he hid the skiff, giving a few more crumbs to the little canine rider.

He felt a rush of desire for Angel as he saw the outline of his house against the still-dimmed dawn; at the same time, the headache and lung sickness that had been dogging him got worse. It was as though a friendly fate was holding the tide of sickness and disability back until he reached the sanctuary of his bed, and Angel's arms. As he approached his great door, he made the call of the owl, a prearranged signal they had devised so Angel would know who approached. But Angel had already heard something, some sound of someone approaching, and had exited through the back door.

He saw her come around the side of the house. She carried the cutlass he had given her.

Seeing who it was, she laughed and also made the call of the owl, the mysterious "who" of the night predator, even though it was far too late and too light in the morning for hunting.

"Is that husband?" she called loudly, although she was already smiling, for there he was for all the world to see.

"A happy husband," he replied in Jersey Dutch, "home with his wife."

The wife is happy, she replied—and placing the cutlass carefully on a windowsill, ran to embrace him.

"Precious," he said, using their favorite word.

"Precious."

The little dog growled, and then wagged its tail, unsure what these events signified.

"This is my new friend," Barnt said, pointing at the dog.

Angel laughed, although Barnt had a moment's uncertainty whether she would let the animal in the house. Indeed, Barnt suspected that the puppy, being born on a wharf, might not have the instincts of a house dog. But the little mutt surprised him by going into the house, after respectfully letting the humans go first. Angel glanced once at Barnt's face, and let him stay inside. The dog looked around, but found a spot not far from the fire, in a place well out of the way of the humans, where he lay alertly watching them.

Angel immediately sensed his sickness—or did he tell her? Later he couldn't remember whether he had mentioned it to her, or if she simply felt the fever that was encroaching on him. She put him to bed, and immediately began to fix various concoctions; but he called out to her, sensing that within minutes she would go outside and gather whatever herbs she was familiar with. (And there would be many, since she of necessity was familiar with all the medicinal herbs on the island.) But he called out to her, and even staggered partway out of the eve of the dormer where they slept together, because, as he told her, more than anything he wanted to hold her.

She immediately embraced him. He felt the sickness gaining momentum inside himself, but gave himself over to the love-making, letting it lift him up. Later, once launched into the maelstrom of feverish days into which he was entering, he would remember these moments of sheer sensuality as a particular kind of fever few people were likely to experience. He could already feel himself hanging or standing in the portal between life and death, the life he had lived before, and the feverish wasteland he was about to enter. But this moment was, mysteriously enough, the one experience he would always remember in all its aching richness. How was it that a man could feel death so close, and yet feel more alive than ever before?

5.

The next few months were the most bizarre and challenging of Barnt's life. He never knew the exact name of the fever that gripped him—only that it was nearly impossible for him to stand and to walk. He had a good day every so often, when he could get up and help Angel, but most days he was completely bedridden. Angel continued to make love to him daily, but in a few weeks he was too weak for the physical effort involved. The bizarre little pup he had picked up ensconced himself on his bed, and would not leave except to go outside twice a day to do his business; when Angel tried to take him off the bed, he growled, then wagged his tail, so Angel let him be. Barnt dubbed the little animal Drupt, for mongrel, whereas Angel preferred Espan, the Raritan word for raccoon; the dog was delighted to get a steady diet of breadcrumbs and other scraps.

Barnt ate nothing but porridge, because he had no energy for anything else. Many of the herb medicines Angel made for him seemed to help, but above all what Barnt felt was a monumental weariness. Could death be far behind such a devastating illness? And yet he had never felt such joy before, to be with Angel in this little house, while the snow and ice and wind laid waste to the land outside. His intuition told him that death would come for him this winter, but that God had given him the extraordinary comfort of a brave and beautiful wife, to make the dying easier.

Then came a time when he could no longer walk or even stand very well; he simply lay in the same place, waiting for her meals of porridge, and thankful that he could still had breath enough to survive. He needed Angel's help to get down the plank ladder, in order to go to the outhouse in back. Above all each day he waited for Angel to nestle beside him. He had a fleeting fear that something about the sickness could pass to her, but he no longer knew how he could send her away. Her way was to suddenly be beside him under the quilts, snuggling with him, before he knew what was happening.

He enjoyed talking to her as he faded in and out of consciousness, and the successive waves of fever that washed over him. "Why did you marry such an old man like myself?" he once asked her, half expecting her to tell him a story about the braves that were killed in war.

Instead she said she would tell him a story about an old woman, one that her mother often told. "Once upon a time, a strong young man approached a wise woman in the tribe. This was a very old woman, but people who knew her said that she had the answers to many of the questions people asked."

"What does a man do when he wants to marry a woman?" the man asked.

"Well, it is very important that a young man should first marry an older woman," she said. "That is, in that way he could get used to being married. It is well known that an old woman is wiser than a giddy young thing. The old woman will soon die, after teaching the young man all that he should know about being married. When the old woman dies, the young man can always marry a younger woman."

"Is this the truth, auntie?"

"I have no reason to lie. It is in your best interests to follow the ways of the elders."

"If that is the case, will you marry me?"

She appeared to think it over. "Well, why not?"

And that is how an old woman got a very young man to marry her.

According to the story, Angel said, the old woman lived for another thirty years. Then Angel would do her stomp-dance, and the whole house would shake. But it couldn't have made Barnt happier, as weak and as transported into sickness as he was. When she was finished dancing, she would slip into the bed beside him.

"Aren't you afraid?"

"Of what?"

He coughed to show her what he meant.

She laughed at this inquiry, or perhaps at the manner in which he expressed it, but pointedly did not reply one way or the other. What he felt from this encounter was that she was more prepared to die that he was. Not just by the events in her life, but by temperament; she had never been afraid of death, she told him, but was always prepared for it. Even if she wasn't, she nonetheless felt that her place was with him, beside him in the bed.

As Christmas approached, they experienced an unexpected visit from a neighbor. Mr. Morgan, who lived in the farm between their house and Ould Dorp, still had Barnt's horse but had never gotten around to buying it. He was assured by Barnt that he now owned the animal, because the expense of boarding it had been more than anything either had discussed as a possible sale price. Still he seemed to feel some obligation to Barnt. When he called,

Barnt warily made his way down the ladder from the sleeping room, realizing that he was quite unshaven and perhaps smelled bad in the bargain. The neighbor had brought brandy with him, something that Barnt had not drunk since his youthful carousing days. The neighbor's wife had not come with him; the old man did not hide his appreciation of Angel and expressed his admiration by speaking to her in English, Dutch and French.

When Barnt had consumed two drinks, Angel escorted him firmly back to his sick bed. Barnt noticed that throughout the visit she had kept the cutlass in easy reach, but he was happy that the old man had visited. A week later he and Angel were gratified by another visit, in which the old man and his three daughters came to sing from the wagon path in front of their house. Christmas was a contentious issue in the colony, because so many of the Anabaptists—and those influenced by English Puritanism—disapproved of any Yuletide celebration, so each family kept their celebrating, if any, to themselves. Very rarely did anyone sing Christmas music—but here in the country on Staaten Eylandt, where there were so many Dutch, who would know and who would care? If there was anything that the Dutch loved, it was Christmas music.

Suddenly they were there outside the house, a family singing beautiful Christmas music in the deep snow. One of the girls carried a lantern, although it was still light. With a rush of nostalgic emotion Barnt recognized "Nu Zijt wellekome" and "O Herders al soetjens" immediately, the latter being his favorite Christmas song, as well as the tune to "Ons is gheboren een kindekijn." The sound of voices singing in Dutch in the starry night, and the four of them standing in the snow in this strange place, was unnervingly lovely.

Angel invited them in, but the daughters seemed hesitant to enter, especially as Barnt was not strong enough to greet them. He was far too weak at this point to get out of bed, although when he sat up and leaned forward he could see them with aching clarity through the dormer window. He felt his eyes filling with tears. How sweet life felt, he thought, when accompanied by the consciousness of death!

In February, Cornelius brought news of business at the tavern, along with fragrant bread and fish and weak beer; he reported strong sales of rum and brandy at the Green Dragon. The receipts were so good, in fact, that Barnt wondered if perhaps the man who previously worked at the tavern had been stealing. Cornelius also spoke of his visit to Anthony's farm. Although Anthony lived mainly at his house at Mannahattas, he also owned the father's old stone house on the other side of Staaten Eylandt, which one of Anthony's young sons planned to fix up in order to move there in warm weather and plant crops. Cornelius had stopped at this farmhouse to visit for a night, and was welcomed by his cousin, as well as his wife.

Both wife and cousin were religious enthusiasts, having gone through a conversion experience shortly after marrying; they spent the evening reading, by candlelight, from a gorgeous new Dutch Bible and a packet of Anabaptist writings printed in Amsterdam. They asked Cornelius's opinion regarding certain fine points of the Canon of the Synod of Dort; this at first flattered him, but he soon pronounced himself theologically incompetent. Cornelius knew his beliefs were likely to shock those that had never heard them, and the last thing he wanted was a theological argument.

From Anthony's farm Cornelius came directly to Barnt's house. After greeting Angel, Cornelius called upstairs to see if Barnt was awake. "Come on up, brother, if you have the strength to climb the ladder," Barnt said. "Otherwise, I'll have to carry you up on my back."

Cornelius came up the plank ladder. He observed Barnt closely, probably noticing his pale complexion and a certain gauntness of the face. Cornelius sat on a flat sea chest in the crowded loft; the two brothers chatted as Angel cooked downstairs.

"I visited our father's grave," he told Barnt after a long silence.

"How is it?"

"The graves are all on Anthony's Staaten Eylandt land, and are in fine shape at present. I cleared out the brush and straightened the iron fence. This time around I noticed a small mistake by the stonecutter that I hadn't noticed before—Pater was born in 1621, not 1619. Anthony says he will get the mistake corrected when the stonecutter comes back to Staaten Eylandt. Otherwise the place is well-tended, lying as it does by a slight grove of trees. I cleaned the area all around Pater's grave, and the graves of your three little ones."

"Does it look like the right place for a family graveyard?"

"Yes." They had discussed this before.

"Will you bury me there?"

"If you go first," Cornelius said without hesitation.

"Of course—that's what I meant."

"Of course," Cornelius said.

There was a silence. Barnt had a good idea what was coming.

"You must prepare Angel for the possibility that you may die," Cornelius said softly.

"Will you take care of her, if I go?"

"This house," Cornelius said firmly, "should go to her. You should write a will immediately. Once you do it, it will be out of the way."

"I—"

"I know. You're very tired. Still. Everybody is tired when they write a will. Your condition is not the point, but your respect for those still living."

"Did you talk with Anthony about this?"

"Yes, and he's of the same mind, exactly. He even said something about writing his own will soon."

"I'm surprised he hasn't done so already. These are violent

times; everybody should write a will and be done with it." Barnt was already getting tired, just thinking about it. "God will take care of the rest," he said weakly.

Barnt spent most of the winter and spring sleeping, with Drupt sitting on his legs or under his arm, and Angel nearby, singing or talking or dancing. She spent a great deal of time sleeping beside him; Barnt tried to read his Bible, but could not make the letters stop moving. That year spring came late. Angel could not stand up completely under the low roof of the second story, but she had a way of dancing bent over, singing, talking, chanting and dancing, that over time became extremely comforting. It was life, a young tribal woman's life, with all the animal energies of youth ... it caused Barnt to wonder at the distance he had come in his life, and the roads he had taken. There had been a time when he would have considered the chanting of a woman in the Raritan tribe at best passing strange beyond the telling of it, and in the worst case frightening. When he looked at things in that way, he sometimes felt as though he had lived the life of a stranger; but in another way, considering his love for Angel, it made sense now more than it ever had.

After the long winter, in March, April and the first week of May, he thought he felt life coming back into his bones and muscles. Trees were budding and flowers had begun to bloom. He knew that the soil would soon be dry enough to plow, so he had to stand. He found that if he forced himself to stand, he could feel his legs loosen a bit, and his back stretch, although the pain made him feel faint. He still tottered about when he walked, but forced himself to walk using a crutch, since it was the best way to keep the juices flowing. Once he fainted, but for reasons unknown to them, both he and Angel responded by laughing uproariously, as though it were a joke. When he once more lay down, the stiffness would overtake him; but despite the stiffness, his breathing was a little less labored, and with his crutch he could walk. After one terrible attack in May during which he could not move, his progress toward health returned. He told Angel of his plan to plant corn again this season, and that he had already arranged for Cornelius to help with the planting.

He was just learning how to walk again, in May, when he gathered together his most precious metals, including gold, and put them in a small trunk, as the Dutch often did when they thought death near, and buried them near a fine stand of yellow poplar trees not far from the house. He made Angel memorize the exact location where it was buried, then set to work on his will. He took out a moldering copy of his father's will, which his father had copied in his own hand in the Dutch language; the English version was for the magistrates. Copying this will, he replicated the language used by his father, first in Dutch and then in English. He left the house to Angel, and part of his land to his son Johannes, along with his Great Bible, and another portion of the land to his son Matthys, currently living in East Jersey. When he was finished, he slept for several hours, and when he awoke again he explained the will to Angel. When these things were finished, he felt at peace.

The sickness lingered, however. It took all his energy just to get up for two or three hours every day. Still—Barnt was glad there were no doctors treating him. Barnt had experienced some terrible hours with doctors in the past, as had a great many other people—which was one reason, he thought, why so many people preferred the home remedies and folk medicine of the maiden aunts and the tribal practitioners, rather than being bled by surly male doctors and surgeon-barbers who thought their patients would do better to keep their mouths shut in the presence of their betters. The concoctions made from herbs by Angel did not stop the fever, but made the pain easier to bear. Oddly, he felt no compulsion to drink rum or brandy.

The next time Cornelius came to visit, he told him about the buried trunk. Using a crutch, Barnt was strong enough to walk to the yellow poplars with his younger brother. "How many people know the location of the trunk?" Cornelius asked as they walked.

Barnt hesitated and then spoke. "I couldn't remember at first—my mind is still cloudy. But Angel's the main one, of course—she's the person that I made the will for. She gets the house, and whatever money I've got. I've willed my Great Bible, the one that belonged to Pater, to my son Johannes; the land will be divided up between my three sons, and some for Angel. That is, if they want to stay in Staaten Eylandt. Otherwise they can sell it for homestead money elsewhere."

"Good."

"I'll show Anthony where the valuables are buried when he comes. But the trust we have for each other is more valuable than the precious metals, Cornelius. You and Anthony, and brother Willem, when he is old enough to understand—you are the only ones that will know, and the only ones, beside Angel, that I care for."

"You should show Anthony as soon as possible." The words *before you die* remained unsaid, but resonated in the air between them. It reminded Barnt that he was losing weight, sometimes shocking people who had known him before his current sickness. Above all, people did not have discussions about wills unless there was some tangible evidence that death might not be far off.

"Show Anthony the location of the treasure if I die," Barnt said. "I happily give you my permission to do that. My will you will find among my papers."

That night Cornelius slept on a shakedown bed on the floor, what some people called a kermis bed, in the corner near the fire. He was a good addition to the house, since he kept building the fire until after midnight, so that the embers still glowed come morning. Barnt also liked the way he behaved around Angel—he was clearly aware of her beauty, but didn't look at her the way most men did. She sensed this, and treated him like a brother, but with the same subtle but discernable deference with which she'd treated Anthony. The next day Cornelius got up early to make porridge, but quickly abandoned that to Angel, since she saw it as her job. Instead he created a path that led to the place where they would plant the corn, a good seed he had bought from the Niyak tribe in Lange Eylandt. Cornelius laid down wooden planks over the wet and marshy areas, to make access easier, only once glancing at the yellow poplars, which were the main reference points regarding the place where Barnt's valuables were buried.

He realized that he would soon have to force himself to go to Mannahattas, and was oppressively aware that he had to help Balthazar Bayard in some way, since Balthazar had, after all, communicated directly with him asking for his help. (And he had originally asked Nicholas for his help; and now, if he didn't do something fairly dramatic, his dream of a manorial estate would lose its urgency.) What he could do he didn't know. He generally thought that the situation at Fort William was reaching a climax, which was important to him because he might be able to do something important for the Bayard family.

"Cornelius," he said softly after dinner.

Angel was upstairs fetching bedding for Cornelius, for his shakedown bed on the floor near the fire. Cornelius had already placed fresh-hewn wood in a neat pile near the fireplace, as he usually did before sleeping. Just now he was reading his Bible at the table.

"Yes, brother," he said, carefully closing the Bible on a cloth bookmark.

Barnt noticed that Cornelius was using English rather than Dutch. "The patroon that wrote to me is fearful of an invasion of Albany by Leisler," he said. "At least he was when he wrote this letter."

"Many of the patroons of Albany are similarly fearful."

"On February 8 the French and their tribal allies fell upon the people of Schenectady, killing sixty innocent people and taking thirty prisoners. There is more feeling now that perhaps people should unite to protect themselves, and many are looking to Leisler to help them. Indeed, Leisler sent Milborne to Albany with two men, and they assumed command of the fort, turning the English troops out." He paused. "Leisler will call a conference of all states in the colony, to form an army to invade Canada—or New France, as they call it—and defeat the enemy."

"Who was to be the leader?"

"Leisler wanted Milborne, but Connecticut is insisting on Major Fitz-John Winthrop, an old friend of Livingston. Winthrop is staying at Livingston's Albany mansion, so there is little doubt that Winthrop is under Livingston's influence."

Barnt rolled his eyes heavenward. "Good Lord, this is a set-piece, not for battle but for obstruction. Winthrop will halt marching and declare defeat!"

"That has already happened. The troops reached Wood Creek near Lake Champlain, and turned around to return to Albany, complaining that they had no canoes and provisions. Smallpox has ravaged some of the Indian warriors with them, they say."

"Is Leisler being blamed for the fiasco?"

"Completely. A large group of about twelve led by Nicholas Bayard's wife attacked Leisler on the street in an attempt to kill him. He threw the lot of them in jail, and pardoned them shortly afterward."

"Balthazar Bayard," Barnt said thoughtfully. "Was he among the attackers?"

"Yes. Or Balthus, as some call him."

So Balthazar was in town, although probably in hiding. Barnt shook his head. "This is a strange revolution—Leisler arrests those who try to kill him, and then pardons them."

"Well," Cornelius said, "you have to consider Leisler's background as a soldier. Perhaps he interpreted it as a simple street brawl, and not an assassination attempt."

Barnt laughed, and ended up coughing. He saw Angel start down the plank ladder from the sleeping quarters above. "I'll have to go to Mannahattas," he said softly to Cornelius. "I would appreciate it if you could stay here."

"Of course," Cornelius said. He hesitated, but only slightly. "Do you want me to start the planting?"

Barnt was relieved. He was about to mention that himself, but was glad that Cornelius had brought it up. "Thank you. I'm hoping that I will be home when it's time. But if I'm not, you can start without me. Please plant but a little space, and leave it alone—then another, after a short time. That way a bad windstorm might not destroy it all."

Cornelius nodded. "I am happy to do so. But—"

"Yes?"

"Are you well enough to go?"

"No."

"But you're going anyway."

"Yes," he said. "I'm afraid I have to, no matter how sick I am."

The brothers were silent. Barnt figured that if there was more that he ought to know, Cornelius would tell him before he left. But Anthony would be the one he should see, if he wanted to know more about what was really going on, in that farrago of greed, power-mummery and misrule known as Mannahattas, also New Amsterdam, and now the city of New York.

"Get some sleep," Cornelius said.

"I've been sleeping off and on all day. But just now I will lay down. I'll be up before dawn, and we'll sit down for breakfast before I leave."

The next morning Angel gave him a large packet to carry on his back, loaded with salted *twaelft* fish, which tasted like salmon and could last up to nine months on the trail. She proudly counted out exactly the correct amount of money to give to the ferryman, in both half-cents and wampum. Barnt was too weak to pole his skiff to the Communipaw ferry, so he caught a ride with a sloep that had gone aground in Fresh Kill, waiting two hours for the tide to carry it off the mud.

When Barnt got to Communipaw, he paid the ferryman a stuiver in *zeewan*, the Dutch half-cent, and six white beads of wampum, which when taken together equaled the ferry's going rate. In Staaten Eylandt the people had continued to use Dutch currency, often in tandem with wampum, which was also still being widely used. Angel loved using wampum in tandem with Dutch and English currency, loved adding them together, as though that were proof that the two worlds—tribal and white—could co-exist, and were both important.

Barnt was weary to his bones, and dreading the expedition to New York; yet the dread was also making him angry, which energized him in spite of his fatigue. He prayed briefly, to get his soul right with God just in case the ferry capsized, as it regularly threatened to do. On the dock at Mannahattas the ferryman let his passengers off, and Barnt headed for his bakery. When he entered, he was surprised to find Anthony up to his elbows in dough, working away with the two bakers and his helpers.

"Bernard!" Anthony said. He took off his baker's skirt and shook the flour off his hands. "My God! You need pastry—you're skin and bones." Barnt looked for a place to sit down, realizing finally that they'd have to go upstairs for that. "Yes, yes, let's go upstairs," Anthony murmured, noticing his weariness. "You can rest there."

They made their way up the stairway. Anthony followed him, poised to catch him if he fainted or slipped. Once upstairs, Barnt sat gingerly on the wide bench where he often slept.

"I'm sorry," Barnt said. "I've been very sick, and I need rest."

"I can see that," Anthony said, but Barnt could see that he was holding back some important news. He waited a long moment before joyously sharing his good news. "Barnt, I've discovered a new way to make koekjes. You put them on a long tray and cook a hundred of them like small cakes! The English love them, and so does everybody else. The English like them so much that they want me to change their name."

"To what?"

"My bakers spend all day baking small apple-filled cakes, which we call appell koeken, but the English want to take out the apple and change the name to koekjes . . . same thing, pronounced almost the same way." He paused in triumph, the eternal entrepreneur. "That's what the English-speakers want to call them, and believe me, I'm only too happy to oblige!"

Barnt realized his head was too clouded to retain anything that was being said. "By all means," he said softly, stretching out on his side and putting his feet up. "If the English want to give our appell koeken a different name, who are we to deny them that pleasure? Anyway, it sounds kind of festive, if you know what I mean."

"Like Christmas."

Barnt was about to tell Anthony about writing his will, but fell into a deep sleep. It was not until the next morning that he awakened, covered with quilts, which somebody—apparently Anthony—had put over him. He was stiffer that he could remember being for many weeks, and it was freezing, despite the baked goods being prepared down below. His stiffness was, he knew, the result of all the walking he had done the day before. If only he had some magic cure that would absolve him of this affliction, if only for a month or two, until he had done what he had to do ... he reached for his half-hidden bottle of rum, drinking directly from it. He waited before drinking again. He hated to start drinking again, but it was only way he could move.

He had been sick for too many months; Staaten Eylandt was a place where you could lose track of time. Events in Mannahattas were spinning out of control, it seemed—he had even heard some men referring to the town as "the Mannahattans," whereas others had started calling it by its English name, New York, for the Duke of York. Things that others here already knew a great deal about he hardly comprehended.

What to do?

First, he had to see if he could make contact with Balthazar Bayard. If that was impossible, he decided he would try to make contact with Livingston. Livingston was a slaver and a criminal, but he knew everybody, he was capable of telling lies of astonishing virtuosity, and he would stop at nothing; most importantly, he could vouch for whatever Barnt did on behalf of Albany, if it involved getting land in East Jersey. For a man with all his money, he was surprisingly stingy, and would never pass up an opportunity to cheat someone out of a service or a payment, or to engage in any of the other sharp practices for which he was widely known. That being the case, his efforts to gentrify himself and his patroonship struck Barnt as pathetic. He was now, and always would be, a man in hopeless thrall to the guilder, not in the sense of taking satisfaction in money earned honestly, but of squeezing it out of associates in any way he could think of. For him money was not a means to an end, but the end itself.

But who was he to judge? After all, he was helping people like Livingston, no matter how temporary that help might be. Good people he knew throughout the colony were supporters of Jacob Leisler, and there was no doubting the sincerity of Milborne, although he was clearly a fanatic. So why, Barnt asked himself, was he helping the Albany crowd? Because he was himself in thrall to the dream of a patroonship for himself and Angel, one that would provide safety to all in her circle, including—this alone would make him a traitor to many people—safety for Father Marcel, and any other Jesuits that might be lurking in the woods. He would make his manor a place of safety from the smallpox, the killing of people because of their religion, drunken settlers, and surviving tribal warriors that sought revenge on the Raritan tribe.

Nor did he believe that to be a Devil's bargain. What comforted him was Anthony's certainty that there would be no punishment of Leisler and Milborne greater than a year or two in prison. Anthony knew the people in this city and their beliefs, and he would be able to make a realistic assessment. If only a year or two was the price of Leisler's rebellion, it would not be too much for men like Leisler and Milborne to pay, and in the end they would still be heroes to many, perhaps most. In the end, it was Anthony's certainty on this point that made the whole thing, the dream of winning an estate as the result of service to the Bayard family, possible for him.

Anthony came early in the morning to be with him, as Barnt knew he would. Barnt had eaten nothing but a little of the salted fish in his pack, fish that reminded him of the wedding feast in East Jersey. He hadn't bathed or cut his beard in some time; yet in a port town full of sailors and former sailors he didn't look that unusual, until you saw the extreme thinness of his arms and the shakiness of his step.

Anthony joined him in drinking rum, and ate the fish happily. "You must come to my house now," Anthony said.

"No," Barnt said firmly. "I have a theory about this illness. I think the bad humors in the body turn into vapors—I can smell the vapors on my own breath sometimes. And when someone with these vapors breathes on someone else, I believe that the healthy person is affected, which can cause him to be sick. Luckily, the vapors are not active today." He shrugged. "I know that's not the latest medical thinking, but it's what I believe."

"Did you get this idea partly from Angel?"

"No, she has her own beliefs, about spirits and the spirit world, and the way sickness comes to people. Honestly, I don't know what to believe, brother. But the vapors I believe in." *Partly because of the arrogance of doctors and surgeon-barbers*, he thought. *They had their ideas about everything, and scorned as uneducated anybody who saw things in a different light than themselves.* "What's important is that I will never give these vapors to anyone in your house, and the only way I can be sure is to stay away."

"Perhaps you're right," Anthony said. "Clearly you've given

the matter some study. We've been lucky, staying indoors when rumors of the plague are heard." Barnt was shocked, and it must have shown on his face. "Yes, plague, I've heard it talked about, and the smallpox too."

"I will miss being there with you," Barnt said, immediately regretting it. He didn't want Anthony to talk him out of staying away. "I will never be able to thank you enough for taking care of Willem after Pater's death. Willem takes after you in many good ways."

He had stayed at Anthony's house many times, and loved the dear coziness of it. It was small, but everybody in it learned to make room for others when they moved about, simply to keep from colliding. Anthony and his wife Neeltje—or Hannah, as she liked to be called—had a way of lovingly touching each other in the course of household work; their children Johannes, Cornelius, Matthys, Jacobus and Elizabeth were respectful and religious, but they also had a way of teasing each other that kept things from getting too solemn. Neeltje was a round little woman whose life was her family, but who often shared strange but interesting stories of the supernatural she claimed to have experienced, or heard growing up in a village in Utrecht. Even in town she would wear wooden shoes instead of leather ones; and like many Dutch women was most comfortable of all with no footwear at all, except when it snowed. She was proud of Anthony's business acumen, and often talked about it to others, seeing it as a kind of spiritual gift. She had a taste for pastry and sweets of every kind, and Barnt did his best to keep her well supplied with treats from his three big ovens.

And Willem . . . Willem, the youngest of the four sons of Thys Barentsen, especially loved living in Anthony's house. He had, from the time he first started living with them, helped with the activities and raising of the children, as naturally as if he were a sibling rather than an uncle. He was currently finishing his apprenticeship as a cordwainer, or cobbler, on Lange Eylandt;

when his apprenticeship was fulfilled, it would give him a highly marketable skill if he chose to leave Staaten Eylandt and travel south to East Jersey, as he had often talked of doing. He had an idea that he could wander among the frontier settlements, repairing shoes as he went. Willem was special, the one of the four brothers who was bound to achieve something amazing, Barnt thought. Anthony's high energy and good habits and fundamental business sense had greatly influenced Willem, and many a buxom young girl followed him with covetous looks; but he seemed in no hurry to choose a wife.

"Do you still pray regularly?" Anthony asked.

"More than you might imagine, brother."

"Well," Anthony said, "you know what I think about our vaunted Dutch clergy—they're a group of treacherous scoundrels out only for themselves, a nest of scorpions if I ever saw one. But to speak plainly, the deplorable state of our clergy aside, you are at a point to be thankful to God Almighty. Do you pray about your situation? No one is too wise or too foolish not to benefit from prayer when you are close to the last steps of the journey. Brother, I say that only because I love you."

Barnt smiled and nodded. "Angel and I pray every morning and every night. We use her word for God, which is *Kishelemienk*—that is the way we start the prayers, to prayerfully beg his help on this earth. We pray in Jersey Dutch, because it is Angel's heart language, and has become mine. To tell you the truth, I've never felt closer to God than I do now. Of course, the main reason I feel such hope is because of Angel, whose presence gives me constant sustenance—there is something about her that chases away the death in my bones. And besides, when death is riding close, you cannot help but feel God's closeness."

"I am glad Angel prays with you. Who is to say whose prayers are most sincere, the Turk or the Christian? Both have their infidels, and both seek to slaughter all who disagree with them."

"To tell the truth, I had lost all faith whatsoever before," Barnt said. "It was only when I heard Angel's word for God, and heard her saying that word in prayer, that I got some of it back. I had to hear the word in another language, a language completely different from mine. Only then did I understand that the word was for everybody, and could work for me."

Anthony laughed, but his eyes glistened. "Passing strange, passing strange," he said, speaking slowly. He wiped his eyes. "But yet I understand it. It is going to the strange lands, hearing the strange languages, that we discover the yearnings of our own hearts. It's the same thing on the high seas. The Almighty has a way of using strange words to explain what is familiar to us."

"Truly, that is what is happening to me." Barnt motioned for Anthony to take another drink of rum. "Even Cornelius understands this. He lives in fear of the Synod of Dort, fearing that he is doomed by a predestined fate to eternal suffering in hell. Yet when I spoke to him about the prayers I say with Angel, he understood completely."

The conversation turned to family matters. Barnt mentioned that he had invited Cornelius to stay with them through the harvest. If they could bring in even the smallest harvest, they would get through the autumn and the next winter without help. The conversation gradually turned to the delicate matter of what Barnt would do in Mannahattas in the present moment; it was Barnt's idea that he now needed to make personal contact with representatives of the families he thought could help him in East Jersey. First, he would try to make contact with someone in the Bayard family, and then perhaps the Livingston family, the latter of which he knew mainly by reputation. But soon he must return home, that much he knew. He was simply too weak not to do so.

"I'm not sure that you could make contact with either family here," Anthony said thoughtfully. "They've all left, or are in hiding because of Leisler's taking of Fort William. I've heard that Stephanus Van Cortlandt, one of the most important of the

Albany crowd, is in East Jersey."

'What on earth is he doing there?"

"Hiding out from Leisler's militiamen. He left Mannahattas, went to Albany, then to Boston and New England, then East Jersey." He paused, as though mentally reviewing the sequence of events. "He's with friends near Elizabethtown. One might be able to talk to him there, although one can never predict how someone like Van Cortlandt will respond to one's efforts to help him."

Barnt was thinking of something far more basic. "I don't know if I have the strength to get there."

Anthony nodded as though he had already considered that. "Yes, yes, I know." He paused. "The thing is, talking to the Albany leaders is tricky. You have to have your wits about you. As a group, they're too insecure to talk normally about anything having to do with their own power."

"What do you mean?"

"They're all playing out a charade, a game, you see, and that makes them skittish as cats. When people in this colony call them 'aristocrats,' polite people do so with raised eyebrows, others with a sneer. Philip Schuler's father was a baker, Stephanus Van Cortlandt's father was an enlisted soldier and his mother the sister of a cook's mate. They all come from poor peasant stock, the children and grandchildren of butchers and whores and chimney sweeps and cobblers, no more aristocratic than you and I—in fact, far poorer stock, most of them, than the freeholder yeoman that Pater believed to be the true backbone of a free nation. These Albany people know the truth about themselves, but they're obsessed with the idea of being a landed aristocrat in the English style, and all they can think about is somehow buying a title in England to give to their oldest sons. To do that, they have to live a lie, to pretend to be better than they are. That makes them dangerous, because they're always taking out their poor estimate of themselves on everybody else."

"Is there any way out of this wretched business?"

"With Leisler? A negotiated settlement between the parties. That should be advocated to Van Cortlandt, although I don't think he'll entertain the idea for a moment."

"Why not?"

"The rich people in Albany are very unforgiving in that way. That's how they are."

"And my proposal for East Jersey?"

"I think there's a good chance they'll accept it. Especially when you tell them the latest gossip from inside Leisler's circle. It will be very persuasive."

Barnt felt a leaden weariness entering his body and mind. "I don't know," Barnt said. "I don't know if I can do that."

"You don't have to," said Anthony, smiling.

"Why not?"

"I'll do it for you," he said.

6.

Had not Anthony stepped forward to help him, Barnt realized, he would have embarked to East Jersey in a doomed effort to find Van Cortlandt himself, sick as he was; and most likely he would have died in a day or so on the road. The Leisler conflict appeared to be nearing a resolution sometime in 1691, since royal troops would be arriving around that time; and since the patroons would have no need of information then, the window of opportunity for Barnt be fast closing. For his part, Anthony had — in addition to everything else — some personal business interests that he knew would be of interest to Van Cortlandt. They had spoken two or three times before, although Van Cortlandt had no doubt forgotten him.

Barnt was relieved he did not have to meet personally with Van Cortlandt, whom he knew to be driven solely by greed, and a consummate liar. So Barnt concentrated on getting home to Angel, while Anthony acted on their audacious plan; based on some privileged information he had received, he would seek out Van Cortlandt in his East Jersey hiding place, and talk to him on behalf of Barnt, and also on behalf of his own business interests.

Anthony believed that a simple bribe might be the best and simplest way to elicit action by Van Cortlandt on Barnt's proposal; the bribe could come in the form of a loan, it could stand free, or it could be combined with other business. Both Van Cortlandt and Livingston wanted a buffer zone in the form of a manorial estate between Dutch settlers in East Jersey and everybody else. Meanwhile Anthony had information about the latest disagreements in Leisler's circle, ensconced as they were behind the walls of Fort William. This information would be of great interest to Van Cortlandt and the other patroons, many of whom—like Van Cortlandt himself—had presumably gone to ground.

Anthony did not have much difficulty finding Van Cortlandt. He was on the other side of Elizabethtown, staying with the permission of friends in an abandoned farmhouse—"in seclusion," as he might have put it (or "hiding," as most people would say). "He was nervous and contemptuous," Anthony told Barnt later, "as though fearing ambuscade or betrayal; but he listened intently to what I had to say."

'What did he say?" Barnt asked.

"Van Cortlandt asked me at one point what I thought of Leisler. 'He reminds me of a waterfront dog I saw once,' I told him. 'The dog was focused on nothing but the cargo he was told to guard. The cargo was a barrel of butter that melted in the sun. Everybody on the waterfront tried to get the dog away, so the butter could be saved, one man even firing a horse pistol to frighten him away. Nothing worked—the dog wouldn't move, but sat there growling ferociously. The dog remained utterly faithful to his job, as he understood it. Yet the larger goal, the uncontaminated delivery of perishable cargo, was not served.'"

"Van Cortlandt kept pacing and glancing at me nervously, as

though wondering if I was on an assassin's mission. 'I should say not!' he said.'"

"'Like the waterfront dog, Leisler is not always aware of the effect of his actions,'" I said. "'He is loyal only to the task at hand, and cannot see the larger effects of it.'"

"'If a wharf dog commits capital offenses, he must be shot down in the street,' Van Cortlandt insisted. 'Did not Leisler commit such offenses?'"

"'Yes, mercy is no answer in such a situation. But it may be precisely the right time for discretion.'"

"'Explain yourself!'"

"'The return of stability is all the people yearn for today. There is little doubt that this colony now supports William and Mary. War with the French in Canada is not an immediate problem at this time, since even the strongest defenders of the Protestant cause have no appetite for war until these other problems are resolved. And since the original complaints that caused Leisler to take the fort are no longer of critical importance, the fort must be returned to the authorities that have declared for William and Mary.'"

"'So how, then, can you argue for mercy?'"

"'Look at the people who support Leisler,' I told him. 'They are not criminals, but hardworking people, vulnerable to fear in times of war and crisis, especially if their leaders do not act. At one time their fear of an invasion by the French was quite credible. And many of the colony leaders dragged their feet instead of immediately declaring for William and Mary—and you cannot blame the people for thinking that these same leaders supported James because he had appointed them to their positions. If you had declared for William and Mary in the beginning, Leisler never would have happened. In short, you lost the confidence of the people.'"

"'The confidence of the *people!*' roared Van Cortlandt. 'Their confidence, or lack of same, is of no consequence! They should worry about *our* confidence in *them*, or we will give them some reason to worry! It is their duty to do everything in their power to ensure that we are not discomfited!'"

"'You must look to the future. There are thousands of people who are willing to help in the betterment of this colony. They want to become just as wealthy as you have become. But there is a perception among them that the rich patroons exist not to encourage the people of this colony to flourish, but to keep them down so that they, the rich ones, can grow richer.'"

"'This is despicable incitement,' Van Cortlandt said."

"'Someday, sir, there may be people who think that leaders must govern only with the consent of the governed,' I told him."

"Van Cortlandt's face had been getting redder by the minute. At this point, it was everything he could do to speak. 'Why do you say these treasonous things?' he spluttered."

"Because I'm here to help you, and I can only do so by speaking plainly."

At that point, Anthony shared with Van Cortlandt all the intelligence he had obtained, and made a few recommendations. Jacob Milborne could not be bribed, because he was a fanatic, forever driven by his brand of religious enthusiasm. But there were some men who were amenable to working for a solution to the problem, for finding some way to allow Leisler to hand over the fort to King William's representation in such a way that both parties—Leislerians and anti-Leislerians—could claim some victory. Central to this was the idea that Leisler and the other conspirators should suffer prison, but short terms only. They had too much support among the townspeople to lock them up for a long period.

"What did Van Cortlandt think of this idea?" Barnt asked.

"He said nothing about my plan for peace, but it was clear that he didn't like it. Seeking compromise is not the way of the patroons. But your plan for a patroonship in East Jersey, as a buffer between the Dutch settlers and the tribal people, especially the French and their tribal allies, he liked very much. In the end, he appeared to complete disregard my advice about the Leisler problem, but liked your proposal for a manorial estate. For that reason I suppose I would call the interview a success."

"More than that," Barnt said. "Any day you can speak such truth to a rich Dutch landowner from Albany and not end up in irons, God's grace is with you."

7.

Cornelius had taken in the corn harvest, as well as some squash, and although it was a small harvest it was enough for the winter. Cornelius had also brought vegetables and eggs from the Morgan family a mile away, and was staying on to make sure that Barnt could survive the winter months. It would be his second winter of sickness. Barnt took to his bed at the first chilly winds and didn't get up for days; somehow the eight quilts, although welcome, were not enough to make him warm. He heard Cornelius talking to Angel about him downstairs in Jersey Dutch, speaking in low, concerned voices, talking about his illness. After sleeping for four days, Barnt awoke weak but ravenously hungry, which he thought a good sign. He pulled himself up and came very slowly down the wide plank stair to the first floor. What he saw was a shock. Standing there was Angel, wearing a dress that belonged to Magdalena Jansz, his first wife.

"Magly!" he said softly. "Magly . . ."

Who was he talking to? Was he talking to his wife Angel, or was he talking to his former wife Magdalena? It was like talking to both wives at the same time: he wondered how that could be possible. Angel usually wore a motley of tribal garments alternated with typical Dutch garb made of patches of this and that; but they were patches that his first wife had set aside, probably for making quilts, linsey-woolsey and other homespun materials. And to top it off, Angel was walking around barefoot, just as

Magdalena had done in the winter, trusting to the straw on the floor for warmth.

She smiled at this astonishment. "I found these cloths in the kas," she said. The kas was a large armory for keeping clothes and other personal things.

As soon as Magdalena died, he had given away her clothes almost immediately, partly because it was the custom on Staaten Eylandt, and partly because the presence and sight of them plunged him into deep melancholy. But Magly had left some dresses in a rough trunk on the floor of the kas. Angel must have found them there, he realized.

"Does it bother you?" she asked.

"No," he said. "It just surprised me. But you are . . . beautiful."

In reality, Banrt found it exciting: it was like seeing both wives at once. But it was also disturbing, and he was unfortunately too deranged with illness to think it all through. What he was seeing with his eyes loosed a flood of memories, both of Magdalena and of Angel. They more he looked at her, the more he saw only Angel, and the feelings that he had for her; but somehow the dress also reminded him, because Angel was wearing it, how special Magdalena had been. How on earth could such disparate thoughts and feelings be in one man's head at the same time?

"I'm glad," he said weakly.

She helped him sit down at the table, murmuring endearments in Jersey Dutch. *"Brot en boter? Hett porridge?* Can husband want hot porridge?"

"Porridge nourishes the sickly hen," Brandt said absently, before remembering that this had been one of Magdalena's favorite sayings.

Angel took bread from the box and prepared to get butter from the cooler outside, excited and happy. Barnt smiled, remembering how they had laughed together about the Dutch teaching the English to spread butter on their bread. "Now you make it possible to give thanks—you're making a feast," he said jokingly. "*Nau zale waif en je zankbar tait habbe—nau makt je en fist.*"

"*Ak ban dankbar dat main man e az taus,*" she said. "I'm thankful that my husband is in the house."

The endearments in Jersey Dutch, the happy, singsong way she said them, all became part of the moment. "*Dankbar, Ja, goode vrouw,*" he said—yet this wild young woman, so quick to laugh, was the very opposite of the *goode vrouw,* the portly hausfrau of a certain age.

"*Ja, goode vrouw!*" she parroted happily.

She ladled out a bowl of porridge from the pot in the fireplace, and put it in front of him. It was warm and nourishing, and he ate it slowly. Yet as welcome as the food was to him, Barnt could not stop thinking about the two women with whom he had shared his life and dreams. What was this magical thing called marriage, anyway? A sacrament from God, he believed, but was it not also a world of dreams? His feelings for Angel somehow made him see Magdalena in a different light—and he had put so much effort into forgetting Maggie, because he thought he would be alone forever; but now he had a new wife, and memories of Magdalena in the bargain.

In truth, on some level he had been very angry at Magdalena for leaving him. Now that he could see it wasn't her fault, it occurred to him how beautiful both women were. Magdalena had a temper, but she had been the kindest person he knew. And Angel . . . there was no way he could explain or describe her. She was just Angel. And this was his house, the place where they would live forever as long as he was alive.

The porridge warmed his stomach in the same way that alcohol could. But he didn't want brandy or rum, especially if death came to him suddenly and without warning. He wanted to have a clear mind to thank God for the gifts he'd been given.

"I know I won't die," he muttered suddenly, apropos of nothing.

"How do you know?"

"I couldn't see you if I was dead. So I can't die." As he stood, her breast brushed against his arm. She was naked inside the dress. She gave a startled cry that turned into a sigh of desire. "Don't leave me!" he said without thinking, his voice shaking.

"Na, I won't leave you," she said. She was looking up into his face, her brown eyes wide. "Do you want me to lie down with you?"

"Yes, Angel. Please, please lie down with me."

And she did. Afterward, he went to sleep again for another two days.

Through his blurry sleep he sensed the rhythm of the house. Drupt often went with Cornelius to keep him company as he built his shack; when he came home with Cornelius he came up the plank stairs like a small meteor, jumping on Barnt and burying himself happily in his quilts. The dog had also bonded with Angel, going downstairs each morning to watch Angel prepare breakfast; when Cornelius left in the morning, Drupt felt free to leave with him. According to Angel, Cornelius was building a small hut made of planks he had previously used to lay down a dry walk to the tilling area.

Knowing Cornelius, Barnt knew that this little hut would be extremely small and cozy, but he asked Angel to insist that Cornelius eat with them—he had a tendency to isolate himself, and might drift away. Cornelius had already spread a thick layer of straw from the barn on the floor in the main house, and Angel had adopted the habit of going barefoot, just as most of the young Dutch women did also; but outside, she wore the wooden shoes, although sometimes she wore a pair of Barnt's boots. Seeing her like that, she continued to remind him of Magdalena, and something about it continued to take his breath away.

Waking up later that month, he heard heavenly music in the night outside the dormer where he slept. He awkwardly lit a candle from the flint that he kept in a shelf next to his bed. The ground outside the dormer was white, layered with snow; but there was something else, Christmas music being sung by several people, and it came from outside, on the trail that led to the house. They were singing his favorite Christmas songs, as though it came from a place beyond the earth, beyond the snow, beyond the night.

He pulled himself up to the window. It was his neighbor Thomas Morgan, and his three chubby, unmarriageable daughters, standing in the snow and singing as though their hearts would break in the beauty of the diffused moonlight. Morgan was as English as a man could be, but he had a Dutch wife, and she had taught the daughters well. But had they not already come, once before, to sing for him and Angel? Or was this perhaps for Twelfth Night? Was he not indeed close to death, Barnt wondered, that they were making this special effort to come again and sing for him? No, it was probable that the unmarried and seemingly unmarriageable Morgan girls wanted to get a better look at Cornelius. Yes, it was probably the latter reason, Barnt decided, but whatever the cause, the night and the people in it was precious to him. This night needed no candles, because the moon lit everything from its hiding place behind the low clouds.

Oh Shepherds, all sweet and without noise,
The Messiah is resting here.
Na na na little Child
Na na Emmanuel
Sleep flower of Jesse's tribe
Now sleep innocent lamb.
Sleep little King,
Sleep Emmanuel.

Goe liekens van buyten O stillekens al
Die comt in desen stal

Na na na Kintjen kleyn . . .

He still weeps, he still cries from bitter grief
In this deep cold.
The straw is too hard,
It hurts his tender limbs
Come rather into our hearts
So you may warm yourself.
Come, Little King, and rest in our hearts . . .

Could it be his neighbor Thomas Morgan singing, Old Man Morgan, or was it some previously unknown family member? Morgan's perennially unmarriageable daughters Barnt thought he knew well, for he had often bought eggs and squash from them. But had they not grown up? Perhaps the young ladies he heard singing so sweetly were *their* daughters, perhaps the daughters he remembered had gotten married after all, and had daughters of their own? Above all, why had they come over here to *sing* for them? What an act of charity! And what unaccountable thoughts, what instinct caused them to pick his favorite Christmas songs? As they sang a second time, Barnt clumsily sought to rub his eyes, and found that the tears were streaming. Was God here with him? Was God calling him home, or blessing *this* home?

He heard the great door open and saw Cornelius going out to talk with their Christmas visitors. Barnt saw Cornelius ask something of Old Man Morgan—or whoever it was—and the old man nodded, while the young ladies laughed knowingly. Cornelius handed him the brandy, and the old man took a modest drink. Angel stood quietly in front of the great door, while Cornelius talked with the neighbors; little Drupt sat happily beside Angel, wagging his tail and watching his humans. In his bed, Barnt looked through the window at the dark but beautiful tableau outside, thanking God for the moment, and all that the moment contained. If there were no more moments, he would be satisfied with this one, the Advent of the Messiah who came as a helpless infant. *Yes*, he thought, *come rather into our hearts, so you may warm yourself. Come, little King, come and rest in my heart . . .*

8.

What Barnt learned during this winter was that he wouldn't mind being sick forever, if only Angel was with him. She seemed supremely happy in this small house, often dozing off beside him, waking at irregular hours to prepare food and dance about in her bare feet while singing tribal chants and songs that she was particularly concerned to remember. She told him she was grateful for having a place to be during the cold winter, a sturdy house where the banked snow did not drift in through the eaves, a house with a husband in it. He made love to her as often as he had the strength to do so, although because of his weakness she had to help him. Then there were the long languorous afternoons when he also made love to her with stroking and caresses, in slow ways that did not require much effort. The fevers that swept over him and through his body did not detract from the deep pleasure he felt, but rather added to it; when he told Angel this, she told him in all seriousness that if he could die at the height of love-making, it would cause his soul to speed to its destination like an arrow. A similar scenario had occurred to him spontaneously, during a period of lucidity, but he was glad she put it into words first.

Yet there was something that perplexed him. How was it that he could be so sick, so close to death, and yet feel satisfaction so deeply and fully? It was as though his otherworldly rejoicing had taken him to a place of such intensity that only death could follow, as though to exult as deeply as he did was a sin to be punished. If this was right—and from what Barnt knew of the world, it could be—he was ready to go.

In the morning, or whenever he woke up, he and Angel both prayed together. They used her word *Kishelemienk* to call God, or that part of God that might hear them. It made Barnt happy to use that word, because he knew that if he'd never known Angel, never known anyone who used a different and completely foreign word for God, he might have despaired of God at all. Learning that melodious word—and even more, using it—somehow freed him to experience the hatred he felt toward the Dutch Reformed dominies and the Calvinism they espoused, not to mention their greed and self-serving duplicity. His recurring fevers made him even more certain that there was a God out there, a being who loved his human creatures and listened to them when they prayed. The delusions of established churches could hide that reality momentarily, because the dishonorable behavior of the preachers and theologians got in one's way; but praying with Angel reminded him that God was independent of the established churches, and was different from what they said he was. The pastors tried to control him with their theologies and sacraments and intrigues, but God was part of a different world.

The first time it snowed them in, Cornelius spent the day inside with them, since he had not yet finished building a small fireplace in his hut. So he stayed with Barnt and Angel, spending his days reading his Dutch bible, and reading it aloud. For a time they tried to play a game of cards and sticks he's learned while working as a seaman before the mast, playing endless hours with his shipmates when the wind failed them. They sat upstairs near Barnt's bed and played; but Angel had difficulty understanding the rules, and Barnt could no longer remember the cards. Still, it was a rich pleasure being together like that, using a single candle on dark days and nights. When they lost track of the playing cards, and could no longer tell who was winning or who was losing, they exchanged stories. Cornelius had an odd but palpable gift for telling stories, especially on those occasions when he could lose himself in the narrative.

Cornelius busied himself on several tasks outside when the snowfall let up, and it was not long until one of the Morgan sisters showed up, offering him a job at their house refitting the barn for their livestock.

"Be careful of the Morgan girls," Barnt said, to Angel's titters. "When a woman wants a husband, she is like a ferocious animal. And three at once could be dangerous to one's health, as they might all come at you from different directions."

Cornelius was not amused. "Work is work," he said firmly.

He left early the next morning. According to Cornelius's arrangement with Barnt, he would board at the Morgan place every two days, then come home to Barnt's house. He did so for a week, but then suddenly started returning to Barnt's house every night. Angel was greatly amused by this, wondering aloud to Barnt if perhaps the ferocious animals had finally attacked; but Barnt decided that this particular joke was already a bit too shopworn, and stopped referring or elaborating on it when Cornelius sat down to eat with them.

"Do the Morgans feed you enough?" Barnt asked innocently.

"Yes, they are all great eaters. Mrs. Morgan is very friendly, and she has taught her daughters to speak Dutch in the East Jersey way. She was raised near Bergen Town, and speaks Jersey Dutch well."

Over time Cornelius once again began to stay over at the Morgan place, coming back home every two or three days, and on the weekends. It was too hard, and too dangerous, to come back every night. The winter grew darker, the deserted paths and wagon roads thicker with snow in the air and on the ground. Angel helped Cornelius make the special webbed footwear used by the Raritan tribe, as well as other Lenape clans, to walk on the deep drifts without falling through. Some nights the wind blew straight off the sea, although there were two and a half miles of forest that should have stopped the whistling frigidity of it; but it blew right through the tallest trees, to the point that even inside their house there was a slight but discernable draft, sometimes so great that it blew out their candles so many times that they stopped using them, depending on the fireplace for light.

The ground had gotten so cold that going out to the privy required one to be quick, so as to avoid frostbite. Yet there was something endlessly cozy about where they were, being in this small house in the dark wilderness. It reminded Barnt of the Bad Woods, before he saw Angel in them, except that now he had taken part of that wildness into his bed. Now he was in a winter just as dark, or possibly darker, than the Bad Woods; but replacing the bad spirit was instead an irrational joy. The three humans and their small dog were a clan unto themselves. They had the Bible, not to mention the stories they told each other, so the world was there with them. Over the weeks the pleasure of it deepened, and Barnt's conviction that he was dying intensified; but he felt blessed beyond words that such inner peace was paving the way for it. What a wonderful thing, that God would help him come home to Jesus in this precious way, causing him to actually long for the darkest of the dark winter nights!

And yet, there was something about it that bothered him. He was as sick as any person could be, yet he did not die. What did it mean? In this colony in the New World, people got sick, and they were taken away by the advent of fever and shortness of breath, and they died and their remains were buried, and they were mourned. Many of them refused to be bled, preferring the anonymity of death at home to the kind ministrations of the surgeon-barbers. He was ready to go; death was part of what they did in this colony, part of who they were. But although prepared as never before to die, Barnt continued to live; what was the matter with his part of this story, that the familiar fable did not end as it was supposed to? He had lost so much weight that he looked like a skeleton, Angel said. Yet he did not die.

In March the winds were so strong that they blew the snow sideways, horizontally; at nights the three of them sat downstairs with quilts over them, huddling near the fire or the fire's embers, lighting and relighting a single candle. Cornelius had an oilcloth with a chessboard printed on it, and they whittled enough pieces to play. Barnt had never been good at chess, because he could not coordinate the taking of a single piece with any overall strategy; Angel, on the other hand, understood the moves but had not mastered the checkmate: she wanted to take the king off the board, rather than put him in check. To Barnt's surprise, Cornelius did not play well, but Barnt suspected that he was losing to him on purpose.

Barnt could only stay downstairs for an hour or two, before returning to his bed. One night in late March, after Angel had gone upstairs to find some cloth for sewing, Cornelius told Barnt that he would be going to check on his cabin on the upper Hudson River. "I'll go when the weather gets warm enough to travel. I just want to check on things there—I'll only be gone a week or two. I'll be back in plenty of time for planting the corn."

"Are you missing your wild animals?"

"They know how to survive the winter. Like us, they burrow into their holes or nests, and sleep most of the time. But I want to see if my cabin is still standing."

"Will you continue to work on your cabin here, by Fresh Kill?"

"Yes. It would be good to have a cabin here. I may have some help in building it when the warm weather is here." He paused. "Mr. Morgan may help me as I finish up. He is a carpenter, before farming and raising cattle."

Cornelius stared steadily into the fire, as though he saw his future there. In the robust emotional ecology that had grown up between the brothers over many years, each knew when the other had something on his mind. As always, Barnt knew not to ask. Even so, he could never have guessed the tidings that Cornelius was about to share.

"I will be marrying the oldest daughter of the Morgan family, Gertruyd, sometime this summer," Cornelius said. "We can stay at Fresh Kill, and she can help me while I put in the crops. When you are well, she has agreed to go with me to the Hudson wilderness."

It was as though one of the shooting stars they sometimes saw in the summer had just crashed through the roof and exploded in the fireplace, and at that moment struck them deaf and blind.

"*You?*" Barnt inquired in astonishment. "Married?"

"She wants this."

"Well—" he said. "What about you?"

Cornelius continued to look into the fire. "It's hard to say, but you deserve to hear the truth from me, since you have been so honest with me," he began, but immediately afterward was silent for a moment. He tried again, and now the words came. "She told me she has always wanted to marry a man who will live as a brother to her, with whom she can live as a sister. It was the only kind of marriage she could countenance. She tried to talk to her mother about this, but the mother would not hear of it." Cornelius paused. "And so, with the other daughters unmarried and not likely to get married anytime soon, Gertruyd's status had become—"

"A problem."

"Exactly."

"What does her mother say?"

"I don't think she knows yet that we're planning to get married."

"You cannot keep *that* from a Dutch mother." A long silence ensued, as Cornelius continued to look into the fire. Angel started down the plank stairs, but Barnt gave his head an abrupt shake. "Mrs. Morgan will be extremely happy that her oldest daughter is—well, getting married."

"Yes," Cornelius said.

"But are *you* sure about this?" Barnt asked. There was a particular danger in this situation that he had to touch on, however briefly, as Cornelius's older brother. "I am concerned that the mother might be involved in some scheme for marrying off her daughter, a scheme that might hurt everybody later on. If it turns out that Gertruyd wants something different, once you are married—"

"No. No. She's sure about that part—and so am I. She is very grateful to have found me." For the first time he looked at Barnt. "She's a good person. Like me, she's just—different."

"And you're sure she can live without—"

"Yes. And so can I. That's the way I've always lived."

"Indeed." It was starting to make sense now to Barnt.

This Gertruyd, the oldest daughter of the Morgan daughters, was mannish and thickset, and nobody's idea of a beauty; but Barnt knew from watching her that she was an extremely good worker. And he could imagine the pressures she must have felt to get married, in order to clear the way for the two younger daughters. It was the last thing in the world Barnt would have expected for Cornelius, but it was after all Cornelius's choice, as well as Gertruyd's, and maybe the arrangement would work out after all. There was peril in it, Barnt thought, but was there not peril in every marriage?

"And are you asking my blessing for this union?"

"I am."

"Then let me be the first to congratulate you," said Barnt.

The two men stood and embraced.

It was not the healthiest of lives that Cornelius had been living, to live alone in the deep woods, particularly since there were credible rumors of war with the French and Iroquois in that neighborhood. In addition, that area was close enough for Gertruyd to visit her parents and sisters at Staaten Eylandt. If he died of his illness, Barnt thought, they could stay in the shack Cornelius was building at Fresh Kill until the crops were brought in, and they could keep an eye on Angel, who would inherit Barnt's house.

That night, he told Angel about the impending marriage as

they shivered under the quilts, listening to the winds outside. Angel was happy; but she professed not to understand when he mentioned that Cornelius did not want children—or perhaps she had always understood that part, in the intuitive way that women had, and was only pretending not to. Sometimes, Barnt thought, a woman with a striking figure could tell a great deal simply by the way people looked at her—the men openly or covertly lustful, the women jealous but trying to hide their jealousy. She had known a great deal by the way Cornelius looked at her, or rather didn't look. But she thought it well that Cornelius would have a wife to help him in the wilderness. If Barnt continued to fight off his illness, they would welcome Gertruyd as a new member to their family.

He began to have dreams, extremely lucid and simple ones, but dreams that seemed to be telling him that it was, after all, permissible to die. Or perhaps the dreams were really his way of saying goodbye to the life he had enjoyed. In one recurring dream, he was in the house with both Magdalena and Angel: in the dream they all moved very slowly, doing chores, completely oblivious to each other. There was no sexual tension. They ate dinner without looking at each other, and afterward the two women packed food and bid him adieu, and he began his long journey to the New Jerusalem where Jesus was waiting.

That was his dream.

How much clearer could a dream be? And yet, in the real daily world where he and Angel and Cornelius lived, his body refused to die. He was even starting to gain a little weight, and he could stay out of his bed for longer periods every day. How could his soul be so thirsty for heaven, yet his body so inured in the mortal offices of daily life? How could lying in bed give him so much pleasure, when he was headed toward heaven? Were these pleasures just an illusion created by the sickness that was killing him, or were these contradictions real? He had survived deep winter, yet was moving toward something more troubling than death.

One day Cornelius came home from the Morgan farm a few hours early, and came upstairs immediately to see Barnt. "I have news from Mannahattas," he said. "I am not sure if this matter concerns you, but this is something you must know about. Colonel Henry Sloughter has arrived, supposedly representing King William in England, and ordered Lieutenant-Governor Jacob Leisler to hand over the fort to Major Ingoldsby. When he did so, he and his secretary and son-in-law Milborne were promptly arrested."

"Arrested?"

"A trial is being prepared."

"What is the current opinion here on Staaten Eylandt?"

"People are strongly supporting Leisler. People say he always acted for the safety of the colony, and for the Protestant cause. There is great fear that the trial will not be fair."

"Have the people here planned anything?"

"Some will meet at the estate of Thomas Dongan to present a petition to spare the life of Leisler, although it is well known that Dongan fled for his own safety some time ago."

Barnt had heard Dongan was a papist—*just as well he's not here*, he thought. "But the people will go to Dongan's estate anyway to petition the court?"

"That's what I've heard. They will present the petition if Dongan or his representative is at home, and if he is not present, or the petition is refused, nobody seems to know what the next step will be. Old Man Morgan is helping to write the petition, although I wasn't even aware that he could write. Like most people on this island, Morgan believes fervently that Leisler was good for us, economically and in other ways as well . . . and that he was doing his best at a time when our so-called leaders refused to act."

"Well, Leisler will not remain in prison long. These Albany patroons are stupid, but not stupid enough to make a martyr out of Leisler by giving him a long prison term."

Cornelius was silent, a silence in which Barnt felt a fair amount of apprehension. Barnt felt misgivings himself. The thing about dealing with patroons was their unpredictability—if they decided that they could get away with cheating you in some manner, they would always be tempted to do it. When you dealt with people like that, you lost all control over events. They simply did not see you as a person to be taken seriously, with interests, opinions and obligations of your own. In fact, the whole of their social duty consisted of keeping everybody powerless except those families in their own class. *And it is with these people and their fortunes,* he thought, *that I have hitched my own destiny.*

He shuddered briefly. "Brother, are you all right?" Cornelius asked.

They were upstairs, where there was enough room to stand up in the middle of the long room. Barnt swayed and felt like fainting, but firmly grasped the beam where the two sides of the roof joined. "I'll be alright," Barnt said.

"I thought you were losing your balance."

"I was," Barnt said, "but that's nowhere near as bad as those afflicted with the plague in Europe. They danced before dying, and spoke in tongues."

Cornelius shuddered. "Perhaps they were already feeling the punishment of eternal fire." He took a deep breath. "I'm almost afraid to ask, brother, but—do you plan to leave for Mannahattas?"

"Yes, at the end of the week. Warmer weather should be coming."

"You are not well enough to do this."

"I know, but it must be done. Let us have a good meal together with Angel."

Later, after they had eaten and Cornelius was busy stacking wood in a neat pile next to the fireplace, Barnt told Angel that he'd be going to Mannahattas.

"*Das boddert me*, Barn-tee," she said after a pause.

"Me too, but I must do it."

"*Wareum*, Barn-tee?"

"To build our kingdom where you and I and your people will be safe."

She gestured toward the cutlass that sat on a shelf near the door. "With this, Barn-tee?" she asked.

He shook his head. "That is for you, for protection. What I must do now, I must do with cleverness and luck."

9.

That night the dreams returned: Barnt could hear the soft boiling of thunder in the background of the dreams, and felt the sharp undercurrent of sadness and foreboding. If he was honest with himself, the sadness came from the fact that he had not died. To die in the middle of deep winter, with your wife in your arms and your brother sleeping by the fire, that would be a gift from God. What had he done not to deserve the New Jerusalem, the shining city that Jesus had won with his suffering? Barnt had been willing to go, but the illness that had dogged him for two winters would not let him go, it would not kill him and get it over with.

He had been suffused with joy at Christmas and the Twelfth Night, because of the Advent of the Child. It was at that time that he had declared himself ready to die, and still thought it had been the right time. Truth to tell, if he could not go to the New Earth, he simply wanted to live in his small house in the deep winter woods with his wife, to celebrate her whims and share her jokes, in such a way that the world would pass them by. But as Jesus had not taken him at the height of his sickness, it was now painfully clear that there was something here for him to do. He would have to create his own kingdom in the broken world he and Angel had inherited.

Chapter 12

The *stadt huys*, the town hall, was located just outside the fort at the tip of Mannahattas. This is where the trial would be held. The dungeon where the prisoners were being held was in the depths of the fort. The fort had been built with quarried stone, although the parapet was of packed clay and earth. The Anglican Church was located inside the fort, although Barnt had heard that this same church had been used from time to time by the Dutch Reformed clergy. (Which was only just, since the name of Dutch Governor-General Willem Kieft had been inscribed, in 1642, on the front of it.) There were four batteries of cannon guarding the fort from God alone knew what, and a double row of palisades. The cannon were for the most part iron, although there were also some fine brass pieces, some still showing the mark or coat of arms of the Dutch commanders who had once owned and fired them.

The fort had once been called Fort Amsterdam, when defending New Amsterdam until 1664. Under the English it became Fort James, until King James was overthrown during the Glorious Revolution by King William III, when it suddenly became Fort William. For those unaware of its provenance, or those cautious souls unsure of the latest political developments, it remained simply "the fort." Running in a fast tidal channel— almost a tidal strait—was the East River, between Mannahattas and Lange Eylandt, whose strong currents made it necessary for sailing vessels to pass between Noten Island and the point of the fort, where all vessels were commanded by several batteries of cannon.

There were but a few main streets suitable for wagons in Mannahattas, although Barnt noticed that some side streets had been improved. First was the bouwerij, or Bowery, which led to the outlying farms and homes, of which there were many. The second meandered by the water, and was called by some Pearl Street. And then there was Bowling Green, which was an open space where people could gather to socialize. There had once been fairs held here, and a sturdy brick tavern had been built to accommodate all the visitors. This brick building eventually became the *stadt huys*, the town hall. The *stadt huys* was inside the long wall on the eastern side of town, its roof built in the stair-step patterns favored by builders back in Amsterdam.

Under the Dutch, the fort had boasted two gates. The English had bricked up the gate on the waterside, making it a false gate; the fort now had only one functioning gate, opening onto a wide street or plain, called Broadway (or Beaver-way, by some of the older trappers). Over this gate was prominently displayed the coat of arms of the Duke of York. *Most impressive*, thought Barnt as he walked by a battery of cannon, *although God knows what external enemy the colony is protecting itself from, since the real danger comes from within.*

Barnt went immediately to his rooms above his bakery, got some watery beer from the keg in the hallway, and lay down on his wide bench. He could hear the sounds of the people working and smell the pastries and rising bread in the ovens below. An otherworldly smell, he thought—and in a moment he had slipped into a deep sleep. He became aware of someone entering the door only after he was in the room. Looking up sleepily, he saw it was Anthony.

"Good morning, brother," Anthony said, whispering in the comical manner of people who had already awakened a sleeper, and were at pains to show that they were sorry. "Did I wake you?"

"Of course you did," Barnt said, "and I'm grateful you did." He sat up with effort. "There's an extra cup on the shelf by the door. How did you know I was here?"

"Someone at the Green Dragon saw you on the street. I go there almost every day to make sure that everything is all right."

"How are your wife and children today?"

"Everyone is well, thanks be to God."

"And business?"

"People are drinking more, but eating less, and they are driven by a bad temper, which sometimes causes them to fight. Everybody fears that the trial of Leisler and Milborne will not be fair."

"Do you have enough help to get by?"

"Toby is good, but I have constant turnover for helpers and housekeepers. One of the helpers may be stealing, I think, but I must be sure before I act."

Anthony took the cup on the shelf near the door and disappeared into the hallway with it, returning with a full cup of watery beer. Barnt took up his own cup, which still had beer in it. He momentarily felt like apologizing to Anthony for his sickness, because of the work it was causing him. But Barnt didn't want to dwell on how weak he was: it was quite obvious, in any case. His hand shook, he had trouble getting up, and his balance was not good. Above all was the shroud of fatigue that covered everything, making it difficult to think. He went to a shelf on the far wall, took down a bottle of rum, finished the beer, and chased it with rum.

"Where will you stay?" Anthony wanted to know.

"I still have the key for Black Jacob's house, the house used by the Lapadists, and will stay there some nights if it isn't in use. I'll alternate between here and there."

"A good plan."

He wondered if he should mention Cornelius's wedding plans, but decided against it, since Cornelius might not want the news to get around just yet.

Barnt poured some more rum in his cup and drank it; Anthony noticed this, but said nothing. Barnt was aware that Anthony was observing him, and in the short term found it discomfiting; at the same time, he thought it good that Anthony saw how weak the sickness had left him, and how close to death he had come. "Anthony, give me the news," he said. "I understand I must do something to help my patrons in order to win my estate in East Jersey, but at this point I'm not sure what the next move should be."

"There are certain things I can do, that you can't," Anthony said, finishing his beer. "There are rumors of bribes. It will work for many, I think. To spare the leaders who currently face trial— Leisler and Milborne—it will be difficult, although possible. But that would not be the main purpose of the bribe you wish to place. Getting your estate will be the chief goal."

"Yes."

"So, that being the case, do we also want to argue the case for Leisler and Milborne?"

"Yes. If they are too harshly punished, it will divide the colony."

Anthony walked restlessly back and forth in the small upstairs quarters. "Our friends in Albany have set a task for us," he said, grimacing slightly. "They are intent on 'borrowing' some money from one of Leisler's in-laws. I'll handle that part of it. The money will come from a Leisler in-law, and will be given to the patroons through one of his in-laws. It's better that you don't know which ones."

"What will this accomplish?"

"It will make the rich and powerful people in this colony more disposed to your prayer for an estate in East Jersey. It will help them see you as their agent there."

Barnt nodded. "Just as you say, brother. Take as much as you need out of my accounts." Anthony would know how to do that, since he now had close to complete control over Barnt's business affairs. Barnt also knew that he was close to selling one or both of his two businesses, and that this gambit might use up his remaining resources. "I suspect that I am being watched, but I don't feel that I'm in danger. The question is, will you be in danger for helping me?"

"No, because I have already done business with many of the principals involved. I have on several occasions engaged the power of the patroons, without threatening them or their position in the colony. They already know what I'm capable of, and I know what *they're* capable of, and they see me as potentially helpful, but not yet a competitor."

"In addition to arguing the case for my estate in East Jersey, have you expressed the idea that one aspect of the bribe would be to help Leisler?"

"Others are active in that area."

Something about that didn't ring true. "Why would the 'aristocrats' of Albany want to help Leisler?"

"It has nothing to do with helping anybody, brother. For them, it's just a chance to make money, with far less risk than tobacco or beaver furs."

Barnt sighed. "And after a bribe is negotiated, according to the way the game is played, they must forget that you exist, or at most refer to you with loathing as a criminal."

"I don't think they will forget that *I* exist," Anthony said, "and I don't care how they refer to me. I know a few of their secrets, just enough to protect me."

Barnt was finding it harder to fight off the weariness that afflicted him, and after a certain point lay back on the bench. "Sorry, brother," he said weakly, but could not rouse himself to sit up. He wondered what Sloughter, the new English governor, was up to. "What is Governor Sloughter preparing by way of a trial?"

"He has created a council to advise him, made up entirely of men who hate Leisler. Then he appointed a special Court of Oyer and Terminar, and from it a committee to examine the case and bring charges against Leisler and Milborne. All the men on this committee were either enemies of Leisler, or English officials. The speaker of the New York assembly was bribed, and has already recommended death for Leisler and Milborne, but that is strictly for show. Leisler and Milborne, on the other hand, have refused to plead guilty or not guilty."

"Is it possible that they really intend to kill Leisler and Milborne?"

Anthony energetically shook his head. "No, no, that would be too much. It would make Leisler and Milborne martyrs. Some of the older patroon class may lust for revenge, but reasonable people in their right minds will keep them from going too far."

Barnt thought he detected some doubt in Anthony's voice. "Have bribes had any effect so far?"

"Samuel Edsall and Peter Delenoy were loyal followers of Leisler, both were charged with treason, but soon acquitted and released. I believe that bribes were made in both cases, although extortion would be a better word for it."

"Wasn't Delenoy the mayor of New York under Leisler?"

"Yes," Anthony said, "and the leaders in Albany probably took that into account, that and the fact that he was elected by a popular vote—but it must have pained them greatly to recognize that fact, since colonial officials and their toadies in Albany believe democracy is treason." The tone of Anthony's voice changed; became deeper, less speculative, more focused. "Barnt, remember that until this trial is over, that you and I are operating as representatives of the Albany families—that is, if you want to receive an estate in East Jersey. Just remember that. Once you have the patent for land in East Jersey, you can navigate a fresh course away from these charlatans."

Barnt thought immediately of Angel, and wondered why he hadn't been thinking of her all along. Maybe, he thought, it was because she was in a different world than the world of treachery and corruption that he was in. But now that he'd thought of her, love for her swept over mind and body, pushing away all appre-hensions.

"Yes, Anthony," he murmured, almost too softly to be heard,

"I won't forget why I'm here."

"Good. By the way, Cornelius had the chimneys cleaned at the house of Black Jacob."

"I'll go there tomorrow, and stay a day or two," Barnt said.

2.

The next day Barnt felt stronger, so after imbibing some black bread and beer, Barnt went to the two places of business where he had a personal interest, the Green Dragon tavern and the bakery downstairs from where he'd just slept. He asked everybody what had been going on since he was gone, assuming the air of one who knew absolutely nothing, and to whom political events were as impersonal and an inconsequential as the weather. Barnt got a great conglomeration of answers in response, but he was gratified to discover that people seemed to have little fear of speaking openly.

One thing that all people appeared to agree on was that Leisler had gone too far, but that even on those occasions when he did, was doing his best, after his own fashion; and that therefore this somewhat inexperienced militia captain deserved minimal punishment. One recurring complaint was the tendency of both Leisler and Milborne to assume that everyone who disagreed with them was necessarily papists or "popishly affected," or in league with the French, who still threatened to attack from Canada. It was a peculiarity of reasoning that seemed coterminous with the various forms of religious enthusiasm that gripped the colony.

At the same time, even those who thought Leisler heavy-handed and intrusive were enthusiastic supporters of his economic policies directed against the colony's oligarchy; particularly popular were those reforms that made it easier for small farmers to sell to markets directly, without receiving permission from the English colonial administration.

"They want you to go through the government warehouses at

the waterfront," one of bakers at his bakery had told him. "But half the time the rats get fat eating your produce, and those that are allowed to sell first are usually the English traders."

"Some things never change," Barnt said.

"Right you are, sir, but all the same I'd rather not have the corruption in my laws, if you know what I mean."

Governor Sloughter had arrived on March 19. On Saturday, March 21, Sloughter announced that convening of his council would occur in early May, and that an examination of the evidence against Leisler would immediately commence. Then on Sunday, March 22, Rev. Henricus Selyns preached a fawning sermon from the Dutch Reformed pulpit, thanking Sloughter for delivering New York from Leisler and his murderous rebels. Governor Sloughter was there, but few others were, causing Selyns's paean to colonial power to echo embarrassingly in the almost-empty sanctuary.

Barnt was appalled but not surprised that those appointed to examine the evidence against Leisler were without exception Leisler's political enemies. Thus, they almost immediately decided that Leisler and Milborne were to be tried in civil court for treason and murder. Strategic bribes had gotten Samuel Edsall and Peter Delenoy released; still to be tried were Abraham Gouverneur, Dr. Gerardus Beekman, Thomas Williams of Westchester, Mindert Coerten of New Utrecht, Johannes Vermilye of New Harlem, and Abraham Brasier. All these people, Barnt knew, had been simply local leaders who were trying to keep their people safe in an unsettled time, and were, in effect, simply following Leisler's orders, since he was the man in charge. Balthazar Bayard and Van Cortlandt were preparing the evidence; whereas all of the king's counsel were likewise confirmed anti-Leislerians. It would be a flagrantly unfair trial.

There were rumors that Governor Sloughter wished to appeal directly to King William III for a ruling on the Leisler case. William had a habit of sending people to the London Tower for real or imagined transgressions, and then letting them out as part of a mass pardoning of criminals; it was an extremely astute political gesture, since it established the monarch as strong, on the one hand, and compassionate on the other. Sloughter was probably angling for such a compromise, a few years in prison and then a release. But the rich patroons could see that Sloughter was in uncharted waters. Barnt had heard that Sloughter had a tendency to drink, although so far he'd heard no stories of public drunkenness on Sloughter's part. Virtually everybody complained about Sloughter, most of all those who sought to manipulate and control him. Overall, Barnt had an uncomfortable impression of him as a man who devoutly wished to discharge his responsibility well, but was too weak and too flawed to do so.

So far, the only encouraging note discernable to Barnt was that both Leisler and Milborne had been assigned counsel, despite the fact that they had not asked for any. It was still possible, Barnt knew, for someone charged with treason to arrive in court and know nothing about the charge until the moment he was sentenced. At least they had counsel with which to discuss the specifics of the treason with which they were charged.

After chatting with the customers at the Green Dragon for an hour or so, Barnt retired to Black Jacob's house. Cornelius, having stayed there before, had given him the key; Barnt let himself in carefully, wondering if there was anybody home. The Labadists owned the house, and had used it before embarking to their new colony in Maryland, and Barnt half-expected them to show up sooner or later. Once inside, he sneezed from the mustiness of the house before noticing that there was fresh wood; he used his remaining strength to build a fire, muttering a prayer of thanksgiving that Cornelius had gotten the chimney cleaned. Barnt put a single candle on the table in case he would need it later.

Like so many rooms in Mannahattas, this room—which

would be called the parlor by the English—consisted of an interesting clutter of furniture and influences. Besides the Dutch hinged window and half-door, there was a gateless table with high-back chairs of walnut and yew, a leather chair, a walnut rocker, various oak and pine chests, not to mention an over-size long case clock. Also, to Barnt's relief and delight, parked in the corner was a press bed with bed-hangings. Strangely, he had not seen it before—or maybe he had sat on it without realizing fully what it was. It was quite often that people of this colony used the parlor as a sleeping room; the bedroom directly above it would usually be referred to as the parlor bedroom. Barnt shucked off his pea jacket, tore off his boots and sat briefly on the bed, praying.

Once he had closed his eyes, however, he fell asleep in mid-prayer. Although it was still light outside, he fell into a sleep that he knew would last until the next morning. In his dreams were several of the people he'd seen during his long day. They were all dancing, slowly and with great concentration, exercising enormous care not to collide with others in the same dance. He started awake at one point, in the transition of one incubus to another, and found himself wondering why characters in a dream could not waken themselves, when they grew tired of the dream in which they were entrapped. But of course that would be the responsibility of the dreamer. Only the master of revels could set the dancers free, by ending the revels.

3.

The trial began on March 31 and lasted until April 17. On trial were Jacob Leisler and Jacob Milborne, and six others charged with murder and treason. Breaking his promise of a general amnesty, Sloughter arrested some twenty-nine men, suspected of aiding and abetting Jacob Leisler in the commission of the high crimes of which he was charged. One thing had changed, however, something Barnt had not previously been aware of.

Jacob Milborne had married Mary Leisler, the daughter of Jacob Leisler himself, three months before, so Milborne was now Leisler's son-in-law. That explained reports of Leisler addressing Jacob Milborne as "son" in court. It made sense, Barnt thought, that the radical Anabaptist Jacob Milborne, who believed Jesus might return at any time to dispense judgment and punishment, would marry into the Leisler clan.

He ran into Mary, Milborne's wife and Leisler's daughter, a few times in the vicinity of the *stadt huys*, the town hall. She was no more than fifteen or sixteen years old, and was growing increasingly panicky and distraught as the news from the trial got progressively worse. Barnt felt like comforting her somewhat, but quickly caught himself. It would be beyond bad taste, and beyond any imaginable moral propriety, given what he was engaged in doing, to talk with her at all, he thought, much less comfort her. But he could not get the look of extreme panic on her face out of his mind. She was a plump but not unattractive girl, a very young person—a child almost—seemingly caught up in something she could never have predicted nor understood, but desperately trying to make an adjustment to the things that were transpiring. There was no doubt that she was trying to play out her role as bravely as she knew how.

A few of the burghers, those who knew Leisler and many who sympathized with him, tried to comfort Mary as they passed her in the street. "Good girl, Mary," said one as she wept unashamedly, "we are doing everything we can. God hears the prayers of the faithful, and certainly you are that. You must pray both for your husband and your father."

"Yes, yes, I am," she said, trying to mask both tears and despair with whatever adult bravado she could muster.

Barnt had heard that observers were not allowed within the *stadt huys* during the trial, but in practice it was quite easy to get in, especially when the three grand juries were coming or going. What he saw was disgusting, mainly because everybody—

including the juries picked for various pleadings—all seemed to be coached, if not as to the desired verdict, at least on what they were supposed to believe. Of the three juries of twelve each—forty-eight men in all—it seemed that all were English except for two men. On the other hand, Barnt suspected, the preponderance of English might have happened not because of a deliberate English strategy, but because of a reluctance of the Dutch to participate in such a farce. Either way, it didn't matter. The court met when and how often as they felt like, sometimes adjourning for a day or two, but meeting quickly to pass judgment on questions that had likely been decided by pre-arrangement.

The handpicked jurors promptly proceeded to denounce those arraigned in court as guilty of treason and felony, since being "false traitors, rebels and enemies," they were "seduced by the instigation of the Devil." The intent of those charged was "to depose and cast down the king's power, title and government," the grand jurists said; and to levy war against the king, to the great terror, ruin and destruction of the king's loyal subjects. Abraham Gouverneur was charged with murder, and others that had been rounded up were charged with being accomplices to murder, apparently because they were friends of Leisler. Later Gouverneur would testify under oath that this court had offered to spare him if he would say that Leisler, in the role of a colonial Mephistopheles, had led him into a mad career of murder, treason and bloody revolution.

A skinny young lad was told he was accused of a "riot," but could not understand the indictment, because he did not understand English well.

"*Mynheers,* I need an interpreter," he said. "I cannot understand!"

"Riot!" yelled Van Cortlandt. Others in the courtroom took up the chant, stamping their feet and yelling. "Riot! Riot! Riot!"

The lad stood his ground. "Translator!"

Stephanus Van Cortlandt advanced on the young man and

shoved his hawk-like features in the boy's face. "You are charged with riot," he said, "and all that is required of you is to plead guilty or not guilty!"

"Guilty or not guilty!" cried the king's counsel, and the cry was taken up by jurors and spectators. "How do you plead, boy? Shut up and enter your plea! Guilty or not guilty!"

The young man looked around the room and stoutly replied: "I will be damned and in my grave before I will accuse myself in a case where I may already have been found innocent by the King of England!"

The crowd gasped, and there was a moment of shocked silence. A second later a howl arose from the court, the grand jurors, and the spectators. "Speak English! Speak English!" They screamed, knowing full well that he could not comfortably do so.

"To whom would I give my plea?" said the young man in perfect Dutch. "You should be ashamed, all of you, for making a mockery of your own court!"

"Speak English!"

"You think it sport to try a man for his life, or kill him before he can reply!"

The infuriated Van Cortlandt, who understood the boy's Dutch quite well, now lost all composure, and rose up on his tiptoes and began to shriek and writhe, pretending to translate for the accused but doing so in a deliberately mischievous, malevolent and clownish manner, again shoving his ugly countenance in the face of the accused.

The boy again stood his ground. "If you expect me to ask for mercy, you will be disappointed—I know I cannot get it here. Here, in this court today, it is only 'crucify him, crucify him!'"

The clerk of the court leaped up from the table at which he sat, to the roar of the spectators and jurors, and drew his cutlass, seizing the young man by the neck. "You will die today, if you do not repent this wicked democratical impudence!"

The rapt crowd fell silent to see the boy's response. He quietly unbuttoned his jacket and shirt and bared his chest. "If murder is your goal today, use your cutlass . . . but I say you are a coward, and lack the courage!"

The clerk hesitated; the king's counsel gaveled for order; and the abashed clerk went back to his seat.

Leisler was brought out to face his accusers, but again refused to plead. Instead, he said, the Sloughter government, while it now had power, did not have the power to pass judgment on *his* government. Unless the present government could explain how it could judge the behavior of a previous government, he was under no obligation to plead either guilty or innocent. This seemed in part a broad hint to Governor Sloughter to put the matter before King William III, before a judgment in New York was made or carried out. In fact, both Leisler and Milborne had sent written communications to King William III asking to be tried in England.

It was at this point that Leisler's enemies undertook a major campaign to manipulate Sloughter into signing a death warrant before the matter could be considered by King William. The court knew well that the king would greatly reduce the sentence of Leisler and Milborne, and might even exonerate them entirely. That would defeat the barbarities that the court wished to visit upon Leisler, Milborne and their families.

Exactly what the court had in mind for the guilty was revealed on April 17. Leisler and Milborne were asked if they had anything to say, and they again cited their reasons for not entering a plea. They were again charged with high treason; and only then did the court reveal what it had in store for them:

"They will be carried to the place from whence they came and from thence to the place of execution, that they be severally hanged by the neck and, being alive, their bodies cut down to the earth, that their bowels be taken out and, they being alive, burnt before their faces, that their heads should be severed from their bodies and their bodies be cut into four parts which shall be disposed of as their Majesties shall

assign."

They would first be hanged until half-dead, in other words, and then publicly disemboweled, after which their internal organs would be burned before their eyes; and then, and only then, would their agony be ended through beheading. It came across to Barnt as more of a ghastly form of public torture than any kind of punishment. After hearing the court's verdict, Barnt's failing stomach rebelled, and it was all he could do to get outside, before promptly vomiting into a nearby drainage ditch.

4.

Barnt went directly to Black Jacob's house, avoiding both his tavern and his bakery. He lay down on the press bed in the parlor and began immediately to pray. *What have I done? What am I doing?* He felt the tears cascading down his cheeks, and after praying made no effort to stop them. He wanted to ask God for mercy, and he did so; but knew that things would never be the same, and wasn't sure how exactly one asked for mercy for some evil affiliation, if one was still caught up in it. The problem was, he still couldn't believe what he had heard and seen. Surely good sense would prevail and a lesser sentence imposed on Leisler and Milborne.

Anthony knocked twice on the door, his usual knock, and Barnt let him in. Anthony went directly for a bottle of rum on a shelf that Barnt hadn't seen before. "You'll never believe what has transpired today," Barnt said.

"I was at the back. I saw most of it."

Barnt was surprised that Anthony had been there, since he hadn't seen him. "Were you a witness to the court's malevolence, when it refused a translator to the Dutch lad?"

"Yes, I saw that."

"Out of three dozen grand jurors, only two are Dutch. All the rest are English."

He offered the bottle to Barnt, who took it and drank deeply.

"Yes, it was outrageous. They made no effort to hide their corruption. They want to humiliate, terrify, torture and kill as many of their perceived enemies as possible, and this trial is simply the first step to that end."

"Yes, yes, that's clear now."

Anthony fell into a high-back rocker near the table, and sighed. "Look, we can't blame it entirely on English hatred of the Dutch, even though we have been a conquered people since 1674. The outrages we are seeing today are committed not by the English, but by the big Dutch landowners. Bayard, Van Cortlandt, Schuyler and others in the Dutch cabal are using English law and English institutions to murder Dutch men and women who threaten their position."

"That is convenient for the colonial administration," Barnt said.

"Yes. But even more convenient for the so-called Dutch 'aristocracy'—although there is precious little that is aristocratic about them." He paused, shaking his head. "They don't seek merely to kill Leisler and Milborne, but to torture them in public, so that the people that once supported them will be compelled to witness their agony."

There was a long silence, during which Anthony drank again.

"Did you hear Leisler's sentence?" Barnt asked. "All of it?"

"Yes. It was ghastly. And there is more to come."

"What do you mean?"

"They are making out bills of attainder against all of the accused. Not only will they all be hanged, the money and property of their families will be taken by the court, so the families will be reduced to poverty."

Anthony got up and built a small fire in the fireplace, his hands shaking. Barnt felt tears of anger, and then shame, stinging his eyes.

"I never thought it would come to this, brother," Anthony was saying softly, not looking at Barnt. "I just didn't see this coming.

If I had, I would have advised you against your present course of action. I was so sure, but—"

"I didn't see it coming either. Not this."

"I'm sorry," Anthony growled harshly. "I thought I understood the situation, but I didn't."

"Do you know where the sentence is to be carried out?"

"The sentence is to be carried out in the street in front of Leisler's own house on the Strand. Imagine, Leisler and Milborne are to be hanged until half dead, then disemboweled in full view of their family, and only then beheaded. Then their remains are to be buried under the gallows, in the street in front of their house, so their family will be forced to walk over their remains. Then, of course, the families are to be reduced to poverty."

Barnt sighed and rubbed his eyes with his hand. "How many people have these so-called aristocrats sentenced to death already? Not for one moment did I think they would go this far, especially to engage in the depravity of such public torture. It is nothing less than a crucifixion . . . and I am complicit in it, because I have served and encouraged the Albany criminals."

Anthony said in a low voice, "Brother, I am sorry—"

"Please, let us understand one thing," Barnt said gruffly, almost shouting, "nobody forced me to do this, to help these tyrants!" It was time to sound like an older brother, no matter how sick he was, and not sound like an unknowing victim. "This was something *I* wanted, and it was *I* who asked for help from *you*, because of the manorial estate that I craved for myself and Angel in East Jersey. Once the idea took hold in my mind, I could not stop thinking about it . . . it became my life's-dream—became *my life*, and it still is. *I* chose this way. And now—well, I am trapped."

"You did it for Angel."

"Did I?" He paused, thinking. "Yes, it was for her, and a better life for both of us, that was what it was in the beginning. And I still want that. But—" He fell silent for moment. "What is the next step?"

"I will help in the placing of another bribe, specifically for Leisler and Milborne. I don't know how much good it will do. We don't want to come across as Leislerian partisans." Anthony sighed and continued, "Leisler and Milborne will surely die, under the most horrible circumstances, circumstances we heard recounted by the court earlier today. And there are at least eight more convicted of treason and murder, and all of them will be likely to die just as horribly. If you allow me to give the right persons in Albany some money, there is a good chance we can save some of the eight who have been condemned. At the very least we can stop them from being tortured to death in public. What this court is doing will bring this colony to ruin, and we must try to stop it."

"But . . . must I continue in the employ of the Albany oligarchs?"

"I do not see that you have a choice. If you do not serve the oligarchs now, after having promised to do so, you will forfeit all chance of the estate you wish to have in East Jersey. And your money is already at risk, because it has already been promised. You have risked more than I—in a way, you've risked everything. This gamble has become your life."

There was a long silence between the two brothers.

"Think of Angel," Anthony said, "and all your dreams of safety for her people and a better way of life for the two of you. And think what it will mean to this colony if we can stop the rank murder of the eight condemned men, who are now charged with treason and murder."

"Yes, to stop the murder of men who do not deserve it—that would be a good thing. But I have never seen the rank corruption of the patroons so clearly as I do now."

"Think of Angel."

"Of course I think of Angel every moment," Barnt said as though talking to himself, "and in truth you will never know how much I think of her. And of the poor people of this colony. But I wonder if we have willingly stepped into a trap of the Devil."

"I understand how you feel. But I am already committed. I have raised the money from your business interests . . . and if I don't make sure it is brought to the right people in Albany day after tomorrow, I will be in a very dangerous position."

"How dangerous?"

Anthony hesitated, but only momentarily. "If I don't fulfill my obligation to the oligarchs in Albany, I will have no more future than a dead man in the East River," he said.

So that was it. If Barnt did not continue to play the game of corruption, and play to win, it would put other people at risk, including his brother. He would lose everything if he did not do as he had promised—and the dream of the East Jersey estate would be forfeit forever. If he got cold feet now, it would be as if all the effect he had made before was being wasted and thrown away—yet he was also aware that this was the way honest men became corrupted, and trapped in a cycle of sin and lies. If he did not continue to play this game of death, everything he had done before would go for naught; it was winner-take-all, the players had to play all their chips to stay in the game. Every move was one step deeper into the Devil's debt, one step closer to the endgame.

"Don't worry about me," Barnt said firmly, "I will see this through. And I want to thank you for all that you've done for me." He wiped the tears roughly from his eyes. "It is a terrible thing we're in. But we must see it through."

"We have no choice."

"We have no choice."

Was it not, Barnt thought, like the corrupt Calvinist dominies said it was, that you could never really be sure you were truly saved, and could never act as though you were, even though you wanted to be, and thought you were? In the end they were all in a kind of living death, as sinful as those possessed by the Devil were thought to be, but with no way out of the path predestined to them. All they could do was to bear up and play out their part with as much integrity as they could manage.

5.

Barnt slept most of the next three days, drinking perhaps more than he should, but also quite sick, with considerable inflammation in one ear and with an ugly cough and the same stiffness in his limbs that had plagued him for the last eighteen months. He had been praying regularly for illumination—for some signs that what he was doing was right—but he abruptly stopped doing that; instead he simply thanked God that Black Jacob's house was free, so that he had a place to rest, thanking God also for Angel. Each day he went to his bakery and to the Green Dragon tavern, to hear the latest news and to breathe the fresh and warming sea air, which he hoped might improve his health. Anthony came, bringing his own news.

"Have you been to Albany on business?" Barnt asked him the second time he came.

"I didn't have to go that far afield to take care of my business. The right person was here in Mannahattas. He received a gift."

"Who was that?"

Anthony paused a long moment, sitting on the high-back chair at the table. Barnt waited patiently. "None other than that old hyena Robert Livingston. He has been in litigation for ten years with Jacob Milborne over the Thomas Delavall estate. The money Livingston received yesterday could give him a clear title. For Milborne, it's a chance at survival. To anybody outside the transaction, the gift will look like a loan."

"Will the bribe be . . . effective?"

"That depends on what you hope it will accomplish. I made the case for mercy for all ten of the prisoners charged with treason, as boldly as I could, especially Leisler and Milborne. I made sure to remind him of your hope for a manorial estate in

East Jersey, and your sincere hope that you could serve the Livingston family in East Jersey. This will surely help you in the esteem of the Livingston family, and that is really all you can expect."

At the Green Dragon, Barnt was happy to discover that the dependable lad who had been working at his tavern was still there, directing the two serving girls and supervising the rooms rented across the alley. The boy was happy to see Barnt, but his eyes went to Barnt's wizened face, thin arms and shaking hands. "You are still sick," he said. "*Heer*, what is this thing that afflicts you?"

"There are no names for the pains that afflict the old," Barnt said. He estimated the age of the lad at about fourteen. *To him, I must look as though I'm at death's door—and maybe he's right.* "What is your name, young man?"

"Nick Roosevelt, sir." He sensed Barnt's curiosity, and said, "You wouldn't know my family. My parents have left this world, and only my two uncles are left. They raise pigs and sheep on Lange Eylandt."

"You have done a good job here, it seems to me," Barnt said, with some difficulty extracting a shilling from his purse with shaking hands. "Please continue to help me, and perhaps you will inherit one of these businesses someday."

The boy grinned in a way that was just short of impudence, but likeable. "I would do a good job even if I inherited nothing."

Barnt laughed. "That is a refreshing attitude, lad," he said. For a moment he envied the young man. Not for this youngster was there a suffocating sense of an irrevocable or predetermined fate: he was too young for such thoughts; soon he would be looking for a pretty wife, and lose himself in the pleasures and torments of marriage. "I have something to ask of you, however," Barnt said.

"Anything, *heer*."

Barnt led the way out into the alley. Once there, after looking both ways, he explained to the boy that many things were happening in the colony at this time, and that he would be grateful if the lad would keep him informed of the latest gossip.

The boy seemed to understand, and even seemed a bit impressed. "But of course, *myn heer*. I can be your eyes and ears, as much as I can." He grinned. "But if there is no news, or I am working too steadily to hear it, I will not make any up for you."

Barnt was impressed. "I wouldn't have it any other way," he said.

Barnt soon heard news about Governor Sloughter that was far from reassuring. Apparently the governor drank every day, and was not drunk just in the evening as most "gentlemen" were, but in the morning as well. Leisler and Milborne were confined to the casement of the fort at this point, not far below the office were Sloughter reigned. No doubt the prisoners had become aware, from various sounds and exclamations, that Sloughter was drunk every night.

Barnt heard that at one point Sloughter had staggered down the stairs to the cell where his two prisoners languished. Kneeling before them in the most melodramatic way, the drunken governor wept, and promised no harm would come their way. "*I promise you,*" he sobbed to the heavens, "*as God is my witness, that not a hair of your head will be harmed!*" His drunken caterwauling was not calculated to reassure the prisoners, Barnt thought; he came across not as a figure of compassion but one of pathos and selfishness, a silly and oafish and immature man, precisely the kind of man who would not be remotely capable of standing up to the pressures of the organized corruption that now oppressed the colony.

From a journeyman bricklayer in the Green Dragon, Barnt learned that there had been riots in Staaten Eylandt, where Leisler was quite popular. The actual offense was the "subscribing of papers," in which people were petitioning the colony's government on behalf of the accused, asking simply that their lives be spared. The government had ordered the sheriff to arrest the ringleaders, and in particular was concerned to arrest a particular minister who had been circulating the petition.

"It was none other than the Huguenot minister, Reverend Daille," Anthony said when he and Brandt talked later at Black Jacob's house. "He is very actively advocating mercy for Leisler and Milborne. Amazing, isn't it? Previously, Reverend Daille always opposed the measures taken by Leisler as excessive, but now, he appears to be the only man who sees what a disaster to the colony it would be if the court's sentence is carried out. So he took a public position for mercy, and was encouraging others to do so as well."

"Yes, amazing," said Barnt softly. "Trust the Huguenots to act like Christians when Christian behavior is called for. They are the only confessing Christians in this colony that do so, apparently—it makes me proud that my ancestors are French Huguenots as well as Dutch. What will the court do to Daille?"

"Well, first he spent some very uncomfortable time in the prison. And then, when he refused to tell the court anything, he was remanded to the bailiff . . . no doubt he was not treated gently while in the bailiff's company. Anyway, when he was brought back to court, he responded to the court's questions by saying that his wife had destroyed all the petitions—destroyed the evidence, in other words."

"Good man!" Barnt said.

He was briefly jealous of the Huguenot minister. According to Anthony's account, Reverend Daille had acted with complete integrity at every point—criticizing Leisler's excesses when he was in power, yet petitioning for mercy when he was sentenced to death. And then, when closely examined by a corrupt court, he managed to protect himself with testimony that exonerated him, while defeating the court's intent. Unable to examine evidence, the court was forced to let him go. "That was good day's work for Reverend Daille, I have to say."

"He wrote a letter to the king on Leisler's behalf, I have heard. It was sent to good people in the Netherlands, who are forwarding it to King William in England."

Which was why, they both knew, Bayard and Schuyler and their friends were moving so quickly. They wanted to kill Leisler and his son-in-law before the King could intervene.

Sloughter was already calling his new legislative council together, mainly to reinforce the death sentence against Leisler and Milborne. At the same time, the assembly voted to support most of the previsions of the Charter of Liberties of 1683 . . . the same charter that Leisler and Milborne had used to justify their own regime! At least one of Leisler's supporters had been elected to this council, but was not permitted to take his seat by Bayard and Schuyler. This assembly, despite its undemocratic makeup— or perhaps because of it—agitated for the speedy carrying out of the death sentences against Leisler and Milborne.

This vote was on the 14th of May. Of course the entire assembly was not consulted, perhaps for fear it might lead to substantive discussion of the matter. Bayard and the others were very careful to have only five people to represent the assembly, barely a quorum, rather than the entire assembly: Bayard, Nicolls, Van Cortlandt, Philipse, and the ambitious Minvielle, the latter being the only one of the militia captains who had declined to follow Leisler.

But the death warrant still had not been signed by the governor. The legislative council could disport itself in any way it wished, it could pass any resolutions that it cared to . . . but until the royal governor appointed by the king signed off on the motions passed by the legislature, they had the status of opinions only. That meant that until the governor signed off on the death warrant, there could be no execution. The rich oligarchs immediately launched a frantic campaign to get Governor Sloughter to sign the death warrant. One way or the other, by hook or by crook, they had to get him to sign it—they could not wait even a day, *it must be signed that night.*

Accordingly, a great dinner was planned for Governor Sloughter. Since the governor was already staying at the house of Bayard, the feast would happen there. Sloughter was already drunk by the time the food was served; and the dinner gradually turned into a kind of dreadful bacchanal of corruption, as all the rich men of the colony somehow found their way to the Bayard house, the better to shriek imprecations in the ear of the distraught Sloughter. As this witches Sabbath reached its inglorious climax, Sloughter seemed only half-conscious. What a loathsome portrait of corruption it was . . . an empty bottle of Madeira tipped over but unnoticed at the table; Sloughter childlike and insane with alcohol; standing around him, like feeding hyenas, the unseemly oligarchs of New York, shouting, begging, screaming, ordering the half-conscious Sloughter to do their murderous bidding; ordering him, again and again, to sign the death warrant to execute Leisler and Milborne—

Which of course he did.

6.

The next day, Friday May 15, Barnt could not drag himself out of the little press bed at Black Jacob's house. He had been prostrate since the night before; luckily, the weather was warm, so there was no need for a fire to heat the parlor. All night he thought about the dilemma in which he was caught. He wished forgiveness already for something that was still to happen, which meant that the forces with which he had been complicit had not yet done their worst. There were ten men sentenced to death on the 16th, early Saturday morning; the first and most important of them, Leisler and Milborne, would be killed tomorrow, early in the morning. And it would not be just a killing, but a public demonstration of medieval sadism. First, the men would be hanged, but not enough to quite kill them; then they would be disemboweled publicly and forced to watch as their entrails were burned; and then, and only then, they would be beheaded, killing them and ending their torment.

It was all too horrible. Yet he was caught in the middle of it.

Would the two bribes help? There were two objectives, of course. First, they were intended to solidify his appeal to the Livingston family, and to the other rich families of Albany, that he stood ready and willing to assume the responsibility of a great estate in East Jersey. If he received the patent for such an estate, needless to say, he would be on permanent standby to help the Albany patriarchs in Jersey, depending on whatever kind of help they needed there. The second bribe, on the other hand, was intended to give the oligarchy some reason not to subject Leisler and Milborne—and the others charged with treason—to the most odious kind of public torture.

Anthony stopped by with the latest news. "Someone in Sloughter's council has received a letter from London pardoning Leisler and Milborne," he said, "but some legal excuse has been created to seal the letter, so it will never be seen."

"My God, have they no shame? But I'm not surprised."

"Furthermore, a scaffold is already being built in front of Leisler's house. They need a ladder so the doomed men can mount the scaffold . . . but no carpenter will make them one. Given the circumstances, to do so would be a flagrant invitation for the laying of a curse . . . no sensible man in the colony would make such a death-ladder. But it is said that Rev. Henricus Selyns made such a ladder with his own hands, the better to demonstrate his groveling loyalty to the English administration and the corrupt patroons of Albany."

"Judas himself could not have advertised his treachery more brazenly."

Anthony left, but returned after nightfall. Barnt still sat on the bed, very close to where he had been sitting that morning, a single candle flickering on the table. Anthony was even more shaken than he'd been earlier. He walked back and forth in the parlor a few times before he could speak. "Is there no brutality that ambitious Christians will not engage in?" he murmured.

"You'd better tell me what you're referring to," Barnt said, "although I have a bad feeling neither of us are going to like it."

Anthony sighed and sat in the high-top rocker. After a moment he got up and poured a glass of brandy; afterward he resumed his seat, then sat drinking and looking into a middle distance. Barnt knew well not to interrupt his reverie.

He would tell all, when he was ready.

"Leisler and Milborne were preparing to eat supper," Anthony began. "They had waited, hoping that some family member could join them, but that was not to happen. In any case, they finally asked for food for sustenance through the long night's death-watch . . . Dominie Selyns was lurking about, they say, waiting for an opportunity to impress the administration. He volunteered to tell the convicted men that they would die the next day. He waited until both had started eating and then rushed in to give them the horrible news. Their appetite disappeared, and they could eat no more."

"As he knew would happen," Barnt said.

"That's not all. Can you imagine how he broke the news?"

"No."

"He said, 'Gentlemen, I have good news. Only two of you will die tomorrow.'"

Yes, Barnt thought, that was the way they acted, those who had power. There was no harm they would not inflict, if they had the chance. But why had he not seen this all more clearly? Sloughter, according to what Barnt had heard, was already drunk—and was likely to remain so for days—so he would not be impressed by Selyns's desperate attempt to ingratiate himself. Nor would the oligarchs gathered in New York to witness the death of Leisler and Milborne be impressed—if the English governor and the Dutch oligarchs shared anything, it was contempt for Selyns's toadying behavior. The Dutch oligarchy were focused solely on revenge, served up cold for the entire colony to witness in all its depravity.

7.

No one got to sleep that night. The streets of Mannahattas cleared well before sundown. As the night progressed, it rained intermittently. Depression weighted down upon the town, as though the Black Dog itself had entered the slumbering minds of the colony's people. In their dreams the faces of the doomed men shone like wraiths, the apparitions of men about to be violently taken from the world—and yet to Barnt, it seemed like he had never seen them so closely or so clearly as now, in his mind's eye. Nor had he ever seen his own guilt so clearly. Barnt did not bother to light a candle, but simply lay unmoved in the little bed in the corner of the parlor at Black Jacob's house. This was the way it started, the curse that divulged itself to Barnt in the fullness of the violent events the next day.

For Barnt this same curse began with an exquisite awareness of everything that was happening around him, beginning with his own breathing, which was accompanied by a kind of paralysis. It was as though he were an observer rendered helpless by dread of the thing soon to be observed, rendering the observer bereft of the powers of speech or action.

Because he could not sleep, he knew exactly when to rise up from the bed. He got up a little after 5:00 AM, although he knew he was getting up early—indeed, he sat bolt upright in his bed. He didn't bother to shave his face or wash himself—he would go to see the condemned die in a condemned state himself, he thought; and for that reason he did not bother to change his clothes. He arose with the wrinkled garments in which he had slept, and put on his pea coat and his boots. He did not eat anything. Instead he opened the door and started walking. It was not far from the place called "the Strand," in front of Leisler's house, where the two men would be publicly tortured and murdered.

He saw the crowd beginning to build up well before he reached the place of execution. They were walking silently, like the walking dead. Not a person spoke; there was the occasional sob, but nothing more. He saw the gallows, and a shudder passed through him; he stopped walking, and stood looking up at it. The two nooses hung at the top, swaying ever so slightly in the breeze. The square was filling up, and he had to move slightly to the side to let a woman pass—afterward it took him a full minute to start walking again toward the gallows. There were already what looked to be three or four hundred in the street. And the most chilling thing, as Barnt saw, was that this gaggle of normally garrulous New Yorkers was completely silent. On the faces of the people was a terrible recognition that they were about to witness the death throes of men with whom they had interacted many times before, some on a daily basis.

As Barnt sought a place near the scaffold—but not too near— he thought he recognized a few of the faces around him. One he had difficulty recognizing at first. Standing about a hundred yards away, on the other side of the scaffold, was none other than Robert Livingston, of the Albany elite—and the one to whom one of his bribes had been aimed. Barnt shuddered, looking up at the scaffold: he had made up his mind that he would stand here, no matter what. If he could not stop the grisly proceedings, at the very least he would not turn away from the damned. That was what he would have done at the crucifixion of Jesus, he thought (watch but not too closely, nor stand too closely either); and he felt a strange force—perhaps the Holy Spirit, he thought— leading him to do the same today. His connection to the oligarchs meant he must now force himself to see exactly what they had wrought.

People were starting to talk to each other in whispers. Barnt felt someone at his left, and turned to see his brother Anthony. Like himself, his brother was unshaven and unkempt. Anthony moved closer to him. "I have news," he whispered. "There will be no disemboweling. We will at least be spared that."

Barnt felt a shudder of disgust at the very idea of disemboweling, followed by relief. So at the very least they would not be forced to watch *that* particular exercise in barbarity. "Was that the effect of our—contribution?" he asked.

"I don't really know. But I made the case against disemboweling."

"At the same time that money changed hands?"

"Yes."

"But our commission was not enough to save their lives?"

"No. They made that clear the very moment I brought the subject up. They thought they were being incredibly merciful not to disembowel the men in front of every man, woman and child in the colony."

But hanging a man until half-dead, and then beheading him, was barbarous enough, Barnt thought, wondering again at the minds that would conceive of such things. "I just saw none other than Robert Livingston at the edge of the crowd," he said.

Anthony nodded. "I talked to him. He's overjoyed he will never have to pay a guilder to Leisler on the Thomas Delavall estate. He had been in litigation with Leisler for at least a decade over it. No doubt Livingston owes Leisler a great deal of money; but by the terms of our agreement, he has already received a commission of payment at least as much as the amount he owed Leisler."

As they stood there talking, a light rain began to fall. It was more mist than rain, although some men put on hats, and several women donned scarves. Thank God, Barnt thought, there was not a cold wind—that would be too much, too much. Somewhere, in the dungeon of Fort Williams where prisoners were held, were two men who were living their last few minutes of life, before the sharp disjuncture that would deliver them to death. Knowing that they were religious men, Barnt suspected that they were praying, either together or separately.

There were streaks of light in the darkened sky. Dawn was preparing to break. Barnt could not take his eyes away from Robert Livingston, who—having seen him—started walking toward him in a deliberate way. Barnt had met him once or twice in Mannahattas, and supposed that perhaps Livingston recognized him. When he was abreast of Barnt, on the other side of Anthony, Livingston's cold lips broke into a smile. "Your contribution was greatly appreciated," he said in a practiced and very confident undertone to Barn, as if to underscore his complicity in the day's business.

"*Heer*, I am your sure servant in these matters," Barnt said. "But I am surprised and saddened that my poor charity was not enough to purchase the lives of these misguided men. It would have been better for the colony if—"

Livingston shook his head roughly. "You must think first of what is best for yourself and your family," he said in perfect Dutch. "Then you can think of the colony." He looked intently at Barnt. "I am hopeful that it is something one can learn."

Barnt felt his stomach knot up. "Of course, one learns," he said heartily, forcing himself to grin knowingly. "That's the way of the world, is it not?"

The words were true, but burned like lye. Was such a lesson learned in the mind, Barnt wondered, or did it arise full-blown from the depravity of the soul when summoned by the world's temptations? He momentarily felt like vomiting, and was grateful he hadn't eaten that morning.

Livingston moved away to a place that was only a step or two behind Barnt and Anthony. Glancing backward, Barnt took in the pale, anxious faces in the crowd behind them. It was precisely then, at that moment, that he heard the slight but discernable ripple of gasps and soft exclamations go through the crowd, as spectators responded to their first sight of the prisoners moving slowly toward them from afar, with their morbid retinue of death-providers. When the crowd saw the condemned men, there were cries that slowly gathered volume and reached a tumultuous climax of shrieks as they came closer.

Then, just as suddenly, the cries faded out into nothingness. Silence reigned as the crowd looked on in fascination as the small group made its way toward the gallows. At some distance behind the party of death were four guards carrying two black coffins.

Jacob Leisler and his son-in-law Jacob Milborne made their way toward the gallows with steady eyes and unfaltering steps. They moved slowly, and quite noisily, because they were in irons. The people accompanying them were government officials of various kinds, two pastors, several prison guards, the hangman with his black bag of murderous accoutrement (the blindfolds, ropes to tie wrists and feet); and the guards carrying the terrible black coffins in which the bodies would be placed.

Governor Sloughter was nowhere to be seen. Glancing upward at the scaffold, Barnt became aware again of the two nooses, fixed and ready. By themselves, they registered nothing in the mind; it was only later, when one realized what they were required to do, that the stomach felt the violence. It was still beyond his ability to conceive, or to picture in his mind, the fact that the two men were to be hanged, and taken down while still alive, and then finally beheaded. He was vaguely aware that straw had been scattered over the scaffold, and assumed that was why it was there, to soak up the blood.

As the prisoners continued toward the scaffold, there was a rising murmur of prayers from the spectators. There was not a man or a woman among them that had not had some kind of interaction with Leisler when he was Lieutenant-Governor of the colony, or his assistant Jacob Milborne. Both men were extremely active around the colony, and people were used to seeing them. It was well-understood by most that Leisler had gone too far in a number of instances, specifically due to his habit of seeing Jesuits everywhere, and of accusing people of being "popishly affected," whatever that meant.

On the other hand, Leisler had been an enthusiastic supporter of King William III at a time when the Albany oligarch still supported James; Leisler had gotten the fort into fighting shape, as it had fallen into disrepair under the patroons; and he had sent troops to attack New France after French troops and their tribal allies had massacred sixty-two people in the Schenectady massacre. People saw him as decisive; his economic policies were well-meant and widely supported, and favored the up-and-coming yeoman class over the rich.

The popular belief among the people was that there should be nominal prison sentences for Leisler and Milborne, but not executions—certainly not hanging and beheading. Now that the grisly show was under way, the people of New York were depressingly aware that the dreadful performance was in large part aimed directly at them. It was a warning to anyone who might be tempted to challenge the greed of the Dutch oligarchs and the English monarchy that supported them.

Barnt glanced at Leisler's house, which was just to the right of the scaffold. It was still and dark; the family members must have absented themselves, or had been taken away by friends who wished to protect them from the worst. (Indeed, Barnt had heard that Mary Leisler had been spirited away to New Rochelle, the Huguenot refuge.) Watching the horror to transpire would surely be too much for the young Mary, who would lose both father and husband in one day to the executioners. And then the remains of Leisler and Milborne would be buried in the road, in front of the house, where the very family members must pass over them every day!

The prisoners had now reached the gallows. Barnt now heard the unmistakable sound of sobs and weeping behind him, quiet but steady. Suddenly he saw two things his eyes had difficulty believing. The first was the flutter of a curtain at the second-story window of Leisler's home. Was that—could it be—a family member? Or was it just his dreadful imaginings? Or was it a servant, beset by sudden curiosity regarding the events below? The idea that it could conceivably be a family member was deeply disturbing.

Equally disturbing was something Barnt saw next: the tiny figure of the Reverend Henricus Selyns, the Dutch Reformed pastor, suddenly appearing out of nowhere, trotting on his stubby legs up to the scaffold, awkwardly carrying a wooden plank ladder on his back. As the condemned—and the people in general—watched in amazement, Selyns placed the ladder against the scaffold, aided by an apprentice, and fit the ladder to the scaffold; and there it was!—the ladder Banrt had heard so much about!—the ladder to death that the government had wanted, but that no carpenter in the colony would prepare . . . the ladder that Selyns had been so anxious to supply—

Selyns must have feared that if he left it overnight it might be stolen, Barnt thought, thereby slowing down the approaching death of Leisler and Milborne; so he not only made the precious death-ladder with his own hands, he had kept it at his house, where nobody could steal or misplace it. Now, when it was needed for the death-ritual, the pathetic Selyns had obsequiously trotted it out. His fanatical desire to see Leisler and Milborne executed could not have been more obvious to the assembled spectators, as well as his compulsive need to appear compliant— indeed subservient—to the representatives of the English admin- istration. Like all attempts to pander and ingratiate oneself to power, it was a disgusting performance. Leisler and Milborne stood looking at the show, first with surprise, then with a grim amusement.

Then, with the help of two sturdy guards, Leisler and Milborne awkwardly mounted the scaffold where the men were to face their Golgotha, first by hanging, and only afterward, while still alive, beheading. Once firmly on the scaffold, they stood up straight, despite the irons they were in, and looked at the crowd boldly. In response the crowd's crying escalated to wailing, as though the execution was already under way. Leisler lifted a hand, briefly placating the crowd. "Listen to me, my friends. Allow me this final opportunity—give me leave to make my final representation to God and the members of this community!"

He continued his oration in a beautiful, German-inflected Dutch. The crowd listened raptly. "Although I am standing before you as a man you all know, in a few moments I will be before God, listening to the angels rejoice. I am far from perfect, and have made many mistakes. I took power to pilot the ship of state when the colony was at risk, but I was often not equal to the storms we had to face. But know you, all of you, that in the commission of every mistake, and every sin, I was striving to help the colony. I did my duty as I saw it, asking God for help at every step. But even with God's help, I made many mistakes, some that hurt good people. For that I ask God's forgiveness, and the forgiveness of all the people here assembled."

There was a spontaneous outburst of murmuring, as though in response to a liturgy. Leisler turned to Jacob Milborne, who stood beside him on the scaffold. "Son, what have you done to merit this treatment? Nothing, nothing except to follow my orders, and execute my government's recommendations and policies! You have done nothing to deserve that fate to which you have been sentenced . . . before God, I say that you are innocent of any wrongdoing—and of anything except your Godly zeal to serve the people of this colony!"

Jacob Milborne nodded. "Thank you, father, for your prayers at this moment." There was a sob or two in response to the tableau of the younger man addressing his father-in-law so affectionately on the scaffold. There was now a light misting drizzle besprinkling the crowd and the two men staunchly awaiting their painful death. "Today we have rain in our eyes," said Jacob Milborne, "but shortly we will see with the vision of eternity, as our heavenly Father admits us to the company of the angels."

Scanning the crowd intently, Leisler spotted the smirking countenance of Robert Livingston, who stood several rows behind Barnt and Anthony. Livingston had a look of indescribable pleasure on his face, which he did not bother to hide. "Die, usurper," Livingston yelled suddenly, "so we will be rid of you forever, and can walk over your bones each day!"

"You have cheated me of the money you owe me," roared Leisler, pointing a shaking finger at Livingston, "and you have caused the king to kill us, but you will give a full accounting before God's tribunal, and you will pay your bill with your eternal soul! . . . above all, you will face God's justice for your greed! Make no mistake, you are cursed, cursed all the days that you have left, for the pain that you are needlessly bringing to two innocent families!"

"Cursed!" echoed a woman from the back of the crowd, "but he was not the only one! They that brought Leisler and Milborne to the hangman's noose know who they are!"

The crowd roared its approval.

"Yes, cursed," said Leisler, "but even those that are cursed are not beyond God's forgiveness. All it takes is a single word, and God will restore them to their rightful place among those destined to heaven from time's beginning! . . . I pray today that this colony will forgive those who do this to me, because they know not what they do. I pray that there will be no retaliation against them, and that peace will take the place of strife. And I pray that those in the governance of this colony not direct their hate against those innocent ones that worked with me for the welfare of this colony at the height of its danger."

Barnt felt as though he was bleeding inside, starting in his chest and stomach. He felt, in other words, as though death was entering his body even as he watched the two men above him prepare for it. As dreadful as it all was, Barnt noticed that nobody in the crown was leaving. *Nor will I,* he thought.

Leisler again surveyed the crowd. "I am ready to die," he announced at last. He turned to the hangman. "I am ready. Are you?"

Since there had never yet been an execution in this colony, the executioner had no costume or mask; Barnt did not recognize him, and imagined that perhaps he came from Boston, since there was something in his drab clothing that suggested the influence of English Puritanism. The hangman fumbled clumsily in his black bag, at last withdrawing a black cloth blindfold. After a moment's hesitation he offered the blindfold to Leisler.

"Away with your blindfold!" shouted Leisler, gesturing sharply with his hand, his irons clanking.

"Yes, sire," said the executioner. "As you wish, sire." He turned toward Milborne, who also waved away the blindfold.

Leisler turned slowly to his son-in-law, standing beside him on the scaffold. "Son, we are about to die," he said sadly. He spoke in the abashed voice of a child, for whom the threatening game had suddenly reached its end, and become too real.

And now, when it seemed that there could be no greater pathos, Leisler suddenly pointed directly down at Barnt, standing in the fourth row. He shouted in Dutch as though possessed. "You!" he yelled at Barnt, "behold yourself if you can, standing next to the monster Livingston, chatting with him in the manner of old friends! Don't think for a moment that you are innocent because he does your sin with his money and power! God knows your secrets! You are cursed forever, because you brazenly helped Livingston in his despoliation of the people!"

Horrified, Barnt took a step backward. To be publicly cursed in this manner by Jacob Leisler was the last thing he would have expected, for he was only one of hundreds in this crowd, and did not even wish to see Leisler die. Yet in an odd way, his own feelings of complicity had caused him to fear something like this.

Leisler's voice boomed out, pointing with shaking hand at Barnt. "Yours is the worst," he said contemptuously, pointing a second time at Barnt, "the murderer who allows another man to do his killing! For that cowardice you will be cursed today and forever—and your descendants as well." His voice flattened into a declamation, as though reading a lesson at church. He leaned down toward Barnt, the better to rasp out the terrible secret. "Listen to me! Listen!"

The crowd grew quiet. "Today I place a curse on you and your house, and all your children, and your children's children—may all of your descendants suffer under it, to the tenth generation . . . it is a curse that will cause many to die, and many to sin, and they will suffer the torment of hellfire. Although today I place this curse standing on the governor's scaffold at the moment of my death, let this curse be executed throughout eternity by the will of Almighty God, who knows the black hearts of men!"

He suddenly stood up straight, looking directly ahead. Barnt felt like fainting. The people in the crowd sighed; some moaned uneasily, fearful of what was coming, and perhaps wishing desperately for it to be over. But the curse they heard Leisler place on Barnt and his family, the cause and provenance of which they did not comprehend, frightened them and caused many to believe that what they were experiencing had already passed human understanding—and that they had already been borne to the place of nightmares.

The executioner slowly tied together the ankles of the condemned men, then their hands. As someone in the crowd wept softly, the executioner placed the noose over the head of Leisler, then of Milborne. The drizzle was turning into a light rain, but nobody in the crowd moved. There was a very long pause. Barnt was seized by a wild fantasy that perhaps nobody in the colonial administration knew how to operate a scaffold. But someone did, because a moment after this thought occurred to him, a guard at the back of the scaffold moved, and the double trap doors leapt open and the two figures fell downward three or four inches, jerking to a sudden stop, leaping upward a few inches, then stabilizing, as the men squirmed in asphyxiation. They had not fallen far enough for their necks to break, so they were still alive.

There was a distant murmur of thunder as the crowd watched, awed and horrified. The moment of agony seemed to go on forever; in the midst of that long moment, Barnt thought he heard a bell tolling. Without warning, the executioner moved to cut the men down. As Leisler hit the ground, he emitted a sudden exhalation of air, then a wrenching gasp as he struggled for air, his contorted face a terrible purple. He continued to gasp as two of the guards tried to drag the dying man to the top of the scaffold, but the plank stairs could not support their weight. Instead, then, the executioner dragged Leisler to the street facing the crown and made him kneel. He untied Leisler's hands so he could support himself.

The guards helping him did the same with Milborne.

Leisler crumpled and fell repeatedly sideways, each time the guard lifting the shaking and dying man back to his knees. As he began to fall backward, his eyes flew open in his purple face and his trembling hand lifted upward, pointing. He once again pointed at Barnt. It seemed as though he was seeing him for the first time.

With a whistling child's voice, Leisler said: *"Cursed!"* Then his airways opened up enough for him to shriek.

"Cursed! . . . *Cursed!"*

Then Leisler could say no more, his eyes fluttering and his mouth spewing vomit.

A woman standing behind Barnt fell backward, twisting in convulsions as she lay on the ground. Her hips ground as she screamed. Barnt thought he had entered a place where horror was beyond comprehension; but Anthony, standing next to him, immediately understood. "She's giving birth—she shouldn't be here, watching this. It can make the child insane."

Anthony sprang to the side of the woman and held her hand,

but was soon encircled by women. There was a harsh prattling of Low Dutch, as the women gathered around the fallen woman like magpies around a fledgling, pushing the men aside and scolding them for being too close. There were other cries of people fainting toward the rear of the crowd, the reactions of the people standing or kneeling in half-circles around them like tableau of the half-dead and dying, even as Leisler and Milborne were, as they knelt asphyxiating on the street before the scaffold.

Now, however, the executioner sprang into action. He took a thick sword from the scaffold, where it had been concealed under the straw. He approached the men, positioning himself behind Leisler, who knelt before him, balancing on his knees. The executioner raised his sword above his head, as Leisler lifted his head briefly, looking directly at Barnt. Making a slight adjustment, the executioner swung the thick sword directly on the nape of Leisler's neck, and two spurting fountains of blood shot at least six feet from the condemned man's neck, as his body slowly crumpled on its side.

The front rows of the crowd screamed and jumped backward, tripping over each other to get away from the foaming blood, which now ran profusely on the street. And then, the executioner did the same to Milborne. The cut was not quite as clean, but clean enough to kill: again the two fountains of blood exploded from the severed neck. A single wail of horror and despair rose above the houses of New York, coalescing in the sky. The wail lasted six, seven, perhaps ten seconds, before splintering into individual sobbing and cries of disgust.

Meanwhile, the executioner had stopped to rest, the sword still in his hands with the tip resting on the ground. When he had gotten his breath he took the sword to a bucket brought by the guards, and washed it off with a wooden-handled ladle. He went to one of the two black caskets carried by the guards, and opened it. Barnt felt very close to fainting as he realized that the coffins were not only for the headless victims, but also for the heads themselves, laying in oceans of blood on the street.

As soon as the executioner knelt beside one of the dead men, a door suddenly opened in Leisler's house, and two furious servants ran outside, a man and a woman, both of them beside themselves with rage. They pushed the executioner aside. "We will sew the head back onto the body for the funeral," screamed the male servant. "You can kill him here on the street, and you can bury him here, too, underneath the blood you have spilled! But you cannot stop us from having a funeral according to the rites of the Heidelberg Catechism, damn you! Move aside or you die!"

Without a moment's hesitation, the female servant swept up the head of Jacob Leisler into one of the caskets, the male servant likewise retrieving the head of Jacob Milborne and placing it in the second casket. A few people from the crowd helped them lift the two bloodied headless bodies into the caskets, and arrange the heads at the narrow ends of the long black coffins. Other people spontaneously helped them take the caskets up the stairs, first one and then the second after it; once inside, the servants slammed the door of the house behind them. Nothing more could be heard from the interior of the house. Then came screams from the house's interior, and the fierce sobbing of grief.

From far away came the first fearful roiling of thunder, but the crowd stood motionless until at long last the rain came. It was accompanied by fresh gusts of wind off New York Bay, which blew the rain into the faces of the spectators—still, many did not move. One of the guards was already splashing water from his bucket on the foamy ocean of blood in the street. Barnt glanced at Anthony, whose face was stoic but extremely pale; and the two of them drifted slowly away from the scene of the execution toward the house of Black Jacob. Anthony stumbled once before vomiting into the street.

At the house of Black Jacob, both men sat, unable to speak for several moments. Anthony drank rum; the disgust that Barnt felt was too pure, too omnipresent, to address with brandy or rum. He let it flow through his limbs like a poison eating its way to his heart. He had enough experience to know that sooner or later—in a matter of months, perhaps—the physical disgust would dissipate, partially or wholly. But there were things—especially the rasping voice of the asphyxiating man—that he would never forget. He knew then that it would visit him in his dreams. That was the price you paid, and the stupidest thing you could do was try to ignore it.

"Did you hear him?" Barnt asked finally.

"Yes," Anthony said.

"He accused me. He pointed directly at me."

Anthony said nothing. Then added: "Perhaps he was pointing at both of us."

"In a way I'm sure he was," Barnt said. "But I saw it all very clearly. He knew, at that point, that I was working for Livingston and the other vultures of Albany. I don't know how he knew, but he did. When he looked at me, he saw all the other climbers of this colony, willing to use the English administration to line their pockets and climb up over the backs of their friends and families and step on their necks of their neighbors in the pursuit of power and wealth."

He stopped, wondering again if he should drink something, and deciding again not to; it could not suppress his feeling of complicity in the sins of the powerful Albany elite, sins that alcohol and opium would only transform into the most terrible kind of recurring dream. "He saw the truth about us, or at least about me. And he wanted to tell me the price that I would pay. I can feel it already."

"What are you saying?"

"He placed a curse on me," Barnt said, "and my whole body is on fire with it."

"Even the Synod of Dort would not agree that a human alone has that power," Anthony said, but did not seem completely sure of that assertion.

"But God does," Barnt said. "God allowed his first family to enter a world of depravity and sin. That was their curse."

"Because his children choose to disobey."

"As we have done."

"We're forgetting God's grace," Anthony said softly. "After the Fall, God's children entered a world of sin, but God Almighty has promised to deliver us from that sin, and take us to the safety of the New Earth. All we have to do is to believe in His suffering on the cross, which he endured for us."

"Does poor Leisler's suffering save us from sin?"

"Brother," Anthony said in a low voice, "don't say such things. You know better than to ask that. You have been wounded by the things you have seen."

"I have failed. And I have lost everything. My love for Angel caused me to be blinded. How could that have happened?"

"I have lost something too," Anthony said, his voice still soft. "I won't deny it. But maybe our grandchildren will be better people than us."

"Maybe."

"After all," Anthony said, "they have a whole continent in which to redeem our mistakes, as well as their own."

Yes, Barnt thought, *that's what I'm afraid of.*

8.

At a certain point Barnt laid down on the parlor bed at Black Jacob's house, and fell instantly asleep. His dreams raced, filled with storms of death. Death was entering his limbs and body; at a certain point, he woke up in the afternoon to discover that the thunder he heard in his dreams was real—the house rocked with rain and wind. Barnt also discovered that Anthony had left without saying goodbye, leaving him alone. It was just as well, Barnt thought; he decided to continue to sleep, however intermittently, until dawn the next day. He knew he should visit

Anthony at his house the next day, but knew he wouldn't—he was too tired, and simply being in Anthony's presence created a certain sense of shame, because Anthony knew the full extent of his collaboration with the rich men of Albany, and had helped him in that endeavor; he suspected that Anthony felt the same guilt about it as he did. He felt a powerful desire to leave, to go back to Staaten Eylandt. Physically, however, he wasn't ready.

He fell asleep intermittently throughout the afternoon, and then through the night. The dreams were different each time, but always returned to the images, sounds and sensations of Leisler singling him out to place his curse. Gradually the roiling waters of his intermittent dreams calmed; the night outside the house became a still black night in his mind's eye; gradually he slept soundly, in the early hours of the morning.

Well before dawn he awoke again. Desire for Angel had suddenly overwhelmed him. For several days the machinations of death had pushed her visage out of his mind, something that had not happened before. Now she came roaring back, her beauty more compelling than ever, clear sounds of her bell-like laughter and her teasing, singsong greetings. He considered the fact that if he took the ferry early enough, he could almost be assured to be home by evening. He would spend the night with her. He arose with alacrity, hurriedly putting on his boots and his pea coat, despite the enormous weariness of his illness. He needed to go home, and to do that he had to start the journey before images of her faded.

Although he couldn't quiet remember, it seemed to him that today was Sunday. Or was it Monday? But even if it was Sunday, if he got to the ferryman's shack on the waterfront soon enough, before anyone was likely to see him, the fare would be his. He checked his leather purse. He had enough. He shouldered the bag Angel had given him, munching on the cheese she had enclosed. He opened the door. The freshness of the black night was refreshing and unexpected.

He closed and locked the great door. As he walked down the deserted street, he continued to eat the cheese from his bag. It was slightly old, although not quite moldy; yet the fact that she had packed it for him made it all the better.

The ferryman's shack was warm from the foot-stove he used as he sat waiting for his fares. Barnt politely tapped on his door, even though the door stood open; the ferryman jerked awake. "Ferryman," Barnt said with what he hoped was a jovial tone, "take me away from this melancholy town."

"Where do you head?"

"Staaten Eylandt."

"Yes, yes. I will take you to Communipaw."

"Here is the fare I paid last time," Barnt said. He gave the combined guilders and wampum to the ferryman.

Out on the river the currents ran strong against them, although this ferryman was skillful in tacking his small craft toward its destination. Suddenly the currents changed; they sailed smoothly toward their destination as though they sped home on clouds wet with pig's grease, as though the little boat knew the destination itself and was in a hurry to get there.

At Communipaw, the ferryman hailed him as he stepped out of the boat onto *terra firma*. "I saw you," he said. "You were there, when they hanged Leisler and young Milborne."

"Yes," Barnt said.

"A terrible thing," said the ferryman.

Barnt noticed that the ferryman was quite old, which surprised him; he sailed with the strength and vigor and skill of a much younger man.

"It was terrible," Barnt said.

"But they are with God now."

Barnt thought, *I hope so.* "Yes, yes, thanks be to God, they are safe from the cruelties and injustices of this world."

Barnt got a number of rides, including across to Fresh Kill and one on a wagon not far from the Knarl's Neck. The day passed slowly. Barnt was excited, because he was soon to be with Angel. Like Leisler and Milborne, he would soon be safe. He said goodbye to the family that had taken him as far as Knarl's Neck, and walked carefully on a trail, avoiding the muddy wagon road. When he felt his foot sinking down in the muck, he quickly pulled it up before the boot would get stuck. *Soon,* he thought, *in a month, no more, this will be ready for planting. The mud time will be a thing of the past.* Whether he would be strong enough to be part of it was a separate question.

About a half mile from his house he noticed two things. First, there were no wisps of smoke coming from the chimney—but that made sense, he thought quickly, because it was only late afternoon on a warm spring day. But would not Angel be cooking? Second, he noticed his brother Cornelius walking toward him from the area where he had built his little shack. As soon as he saw him, and the purposeful but slow way that he walked—and the fact that he did not wave—Barnt had a bad feeling.

Barnt stopped walking, to let Cornelius catch up with him. "Brother!" he called out.

But Cornelius did not answer, until at last he came abreast. His face was serious.

"Brother," he answered, nodding.

"Where is Angel?" Barnt asked.

"Angel is not here," Cornelius answered. "Talley, the old Raritan man who lives near the ferry at Communipaw, came here with the news. I was with her when he talked to her. Father Marcel is deathly ill with the smallpox, he said, and probably would not survive the night. Angel left immediately to help him."

"Did she leave word for me to follow?"

"As he is sick, she may fall sick as well. You must go to her. I will help you."

"No," Barnt said suddenly. A powerful strength poured

through his limbs. "No," he said again. He placed his hand on Cornelius's shoulder. "I know what you're thinking, that I have been sick, and may need your help. You must let me handle this thing."

Cornelius pulled out guilders, shillings, and wampum. "Go then," he said, "but if you are not back in four days, I will come after you. The Raritan man at the Communipaw ferry knows the settlement where she is going, and if necessary he will take me there."

Thinking of Angel, he remembered the small dog that gave both of them so much pleasure. "Where's Drupt?" he yelled, turning back toward Cornelius.

"Sleeping by your bed, waiting for you to return. I'll look after him."

The brothers embraced, but Barnt pulled away roughly before the embrace was over. He was desperate to find Angel.

"Barnt," Cornelius whispered, "please, be careful."

But all Barnt could think about now was Angel. He realized with a combination of fear and anger that everything was suddenly changing; indeed, in place of the miasma of fatigue was now an insane energy. He was now ready to engage in extreme measures to save himself and Angel. In some distant quadrant of his mind he was also aware that he needed to be careful, because East Jersey was a volatile place. But whatever extreme or dangerous thing was required of him, he had to act.

Barnt continued on his way, deliberately walking off-trail in the marsh, so that Drupt couldn't smell his trail and follow.

He used his old skiff to get to Communipaw, wondering at every turn what he was going to say to Talley, the Raritan elder who lived a few hundred feet from the ferry house. According to Cornelius, he was the one who had come to Fresh Kill at Staaten Eylandt, to tell Angel about Father Marcel's sickness. The tides were with him, there was no wind, and he was quickly there. Barnt parked his skiff about a hundred yards from the ferry shack, pulling it roughly up on the land. He walked swiftly toward the small house where the Raritan man lived.

He was waiting just inside the door, and saw him through the open half-door. He was standing at though expecting him. He nodded gravely when he saw Barnt. "Angel went to take care of Father Marcel," he said. "She told me she was going to him. Father Marcel is very sick."

"When did she come here?"

The old gentleman counted slowly on his fingers. "Four days. Five."

"How sick is Father Marcel?"

"*Tespehele,*" the old man said, "he is *tespeheleokan.* He has the smallpox. I have heard that from many people."

Barnt shuddered involuntarily. If the old Indian understood his fear, or shared it, he did not show his emotions. But he seemed aware of Barnt's anxiety.

"I'm going there now," Barnt said. "I'm also sick, and very weak. I may need help getting there."

The old man opened his door and stepped outside, as though wanting to get a better look at Barnt's face. "Yes, yes, you'll have to go there." He turned to go back inside his door, "Sit down and eat before you leave," he said over his shoulder.

Barnt followed him inside and sat at his table, saying a quick grace under his breath. The old man served him salted *hespaen,* or raccoon, very fat. The taste of meat was welcome, because he would need the energy later. He drank water and beer with the food, and some squash on the side.

When he was finished, he stood and offered the old man money. He was clearly tempted by the wampum, but he refused. Barnt left a fair amount of wampum under his plate, and an English shilling. Although the ancient tribal man saw him, he pretended that he didn't.

"I will remember your kindness," Barnt said. "And now, may I ask you to accompany me part of the way? If you are sick, or too tired, it is not necessary."

Thankfully, the old man appeared to be pleased to be asked. "I will come part of the way with you," he said. He did not seem surprised at be asked, indicating that he still worked as a guide. "I know the way, but if I am too tired I will rest, or come back to my house."

"Good. You know the settlement where Father Marcel lives?"

"Yes, of course. All the Raritan and Lenape people know where it is."

He turned and put on a fringed deerskin jacket, as well as a sturdy pair of the white man's shoes. And he packed some food.

"We are ready," he said.

The next two days Barnt remembered as a kind of blur. They set out on a dirt road in good condition; apparently, it had not rained so hard here as it had in Mannahattas. There was little mud, and what there was proved passable. At a short distance was a kill with many salt marshes, bays and inlets. Beside the kill was a good wagon road that they turned off on, which took them past a tavern near a slightly swollen but fordable river; the tavern seemed to be doing good business now, with several carts left outside. After they forded the river they began to gain elevation. They got a ride with a man driving a cart with several sheep, and another ride from a man with produce for the market day on the other side of Bergen Town.

At nightfall they slept on a ground-cover for a few hours, and were up when they heard the trundling of a wagon in the night. A married couple gave them a ride, as they explained that they were headed for a river in the vicinity of Father Marcel's settlement. The couple immediately asked, "Father Marcel?" It turned out that both were Catholics, but without a church to attend, and as such had heard of Father Marcel from travelers. They were immediately friendly.

They penetrated into the interior of East Jersey, crossing Millstone River, which was often mistaken for the Raritan Kill, the couple told them; it was quite dry, despite the recent rain, which was a good thing, because it was necessary to cross it three times before they got to their destination. At the end of the third day, they rested by an abandoned mill on the Millstone River, the wheelhouse of the mill leaning over, as thought about to fall. As they were nearing their destination, Barnt asked the family to accept two ducoons, which was equal to thirty-two guilders in *zeewant*, or money for fare.

The family was at first reluctant to accept the money, but Barnt could see that they were poor, and insisted that they take it. The thought crossed his mind that he might offer them twice as much to transport them to Father Marcel's settlement, and then back to Communipaw; but the dangers of being in a settlement afflicted by smallpox would be too great for any payment to cover.

Barnt and Talley, his tribal companion, were finally only a few miles away from their final destination. They bid goodbye to the young couple, and began their trek on one of the side trails. It was only noon; Barnt and Talley made quick time, eating as they walked. As they neared the settlement, they were surprised to see two or three people on the trails. On some level Barnt had expected everybody to either be dead, or to have fled. But of course some would be left, he thought. There were two people, a man and a woman, standing in the middle of the huts; they saw Barnt coming, and stood waiting for him and his companion to come up and speak with them.

As he approached, Barnt saw that the two people recognized him.

"Where is Angel?" he inquired, aware of the brusqueness in his voice.

They motioned toward a path that led to a grove of evergreen at the top of a slight incline, in the center of which were more huts. Barnt noticed that the people to whom he was speaking looked at him as though he was a ghost. Not an unnatural assumption, he concluded, since the people to whom he spoke had no doubt been around a great deal of death.

"Do you come for her?" the woman asked.

"Yes—I come to take her home."

"Come," she said.

She led Barnt to the hut closest to him. "Where is Father Marcel?" he asked.

"We buried him two days ago, using the book he gave us."

"And Angel?"

The woman looked at him pityingly, and then gestured toward the inside of the hut. "There," she said.

Barnt could feel his heart pounding. There was nothing he wanted more now than to see her face, and to hold her in his arms. He pushed into the doorway, brushing aside the animal skins that obscured what was inside. The hut flooded with light, and his eyes were momentarily blinded by it. But his eyes also made out the form that he was hungry to see above everything in the world, the sleeping figure of Angel. He knelt beside her, grasping both hands with his.

Her eyes flew open.

"Husband," she said. Her smile was beautiful. "Barn-tee." She seemed to think for a moment. "Why are you here?" she asked anxiously.

"I'm here to take you to your home. Our home."

He could see that she was covered with the pustules of smallpox. It occurred to him that he could save her, if he could just get her home. Then it occurred to him that she might be beyond help. But he wouldn't know one way or the other until they were home.

"*Tespeheleokan*," she said weakly, "I have the smallpox."

"All the more reason why I must take you home," he said, "but first, we rest."

He lay down beside her and took her in his arms. He slept for several hours before awakening to go outside; Talley was nowhere to be seen, and nobody was stirring. He went back and again lay down beside Angel. When he awoke, it was night. He could feel her breathing against him. *Thank you, God,* he prayed, *to have given us this time together.* Then he went back to sleep. As terrible as he felt, having gone several days without bathing, eating regularly, or drinking good water, he felt complete holding her, and sleeping at her side. It occurred to him that if she lived through the night, they might both have a chance. But the fatigue he felt was pulling at his spirits like a tide going out.

He awoke in the morning hoping she could walk, but she couldn't sit up. Her body was ravaged by the sickness that was attacking her. He would have to carry her, he realized. He found Talley, the old man who had been accompanying him, and told him of their dilemma. "Perhaps the two of us can carry her," Barnt told him.

The old man thought about it. "We need another man."

"Yes," Barnt said. "We won't make it without one."

The old man nodded. "Then rest some more, and perhaps one will come." Barnt suspected that the old man was hoping he would decide to stay here with her.

He walked down the path they had come up, stopping at a pool fed by a spring. He saw that it had a sand bottom. He took off his clothes and sank down in the delicious cool water, his feet being bathed by the cold water coming up from the sand and pushing through his toes. It was wonderful, but it immediately occurred to him that it meant nothing unless he could transform it into energy to get Angel home. He staggered to the side of the pool and fell instantly into sleep. In an hour or two he awakened and made his way back to the hut on the other side of the settlement. Angel still couldn't sit, and could hardly talk; he lay down beside her again, and went back to sleep.

The next morning he awoke well before dawn. He started gathering his things together, planning a way they could travel. He got two poles and prepared to lash them to Angel's ground cover, and broke short branches to put cross-ways to support her body. At the same time that he pondered how to lash the branches, something caught his eye: walking in the middle of the settlement was his brother Cornelius. Barnt stepped out of the door of the hut, and Cornelius saw him.

He came up to Barnt, anxiety showing on his face.

"What are you doing here?" Barnt said. "I thought you said you'd wait for several days before coming after me."

"Yes, that I did, but I learned just enough letters to read the Bible, and never did learn my numbers."

"Praise be to God!" Barnt muttered.

It was as though the four gates of the New Jerusalem had opened at once. Barnt had never been so happy to see anyone—with the help of Cornelius, the three of them could manage the job of transporting themselves, and Angel with them, back to Staaten Eylandt. God had answered his prayers, Barnt thought; but he had answered them not through theology, but through the kindness of a brother.

Barnt would remember the return trip as a half-forgotten dream. It took three days for the three of them—Barnt, Cornelius and Talley, the old tribal gentleman—to get Angel home. They traveled day and night, stopping only to sleep for a few hours. The rivers they forded were dry enough to walk across, and there were good paths and wagon roads to follow; but they did not try to ask for rides. One man insisted they get in the back of his wagon, and did not look too closely at Angel, whom they had swaddled with blankets like a baby, even covering her face. By the time they got into the vicinity of Bergen Town they were all half-crazed from lack of food, rest and decent water. Cornelius, however, did not utter a word of protest. When they reached the ferry Barnt insisted that the old Indian gentleman take a large payment in guilders and wampum, along with some good fishhooks that Barnt knew he could use in barter.

Talley said nothing, but watched as the small party got onto Barnt's skiff, and set off poling across the tidal strait that separated Communipaw from Staaten Eylandt. The tide was strong, but Barnt paid it no mind; at the proper point, he peeled off the current with a strong shove of the pole, sending the skiff spinning close to the shore, then into French Kill, which would take them to his property. They beached the skiff near his house, and walked the last two miles or so with Angel dragging comatose behind them.

9.

Drupt was barking excitedly inside the house. The two men got the great door open, and carried Angel inside. Barnt went straight upstairs using the plank ladder, and Cornelius half-handed, half-carried Angel up to Barnt, who put her into their bed under the eave. Barnt helped tuck her into the bed. *Thank God we're home*, Barnt thought.

"Whatever she may need, I will find for her," Barnt said.

"Will I be in the way if I stay here, in my bed by the fireplace?"

"You'll stay here as long as you need to, brother," Barnt said firmly. "The house is a better place with you in it." Barnt made porridge, and the two men ate like starving men, and then rested. Angel was too weak to eat.

Barnt did everything he could for Angel, but she had trouble keeping anything down. He prayed for the effects of the sickness to pass. The days began to fly past like the flocks of birds that were flying north, flying low over the marchlands and alighting in the small stands of trees that were near them. It was not anything that Barnt could control. Angel could get up to use the privy outside, when she needed it, but could do little else; soon she was too weak to do that, and refused all food. Barnt was not thinking clearly, but had a vague sense that Angel was losing weight, and perhaps losing her battle with the disease that had taken so many of the Lenni Lenape and Raritan people, reducing their numbers so that the clans were a shadow of what they had been before.

After a few days Barnt heard a muffled conversation downstairs. It was the Morgan girl that Cornelius would soon marry, talking in whispers to Cornelius. From their muffled conversation Barnt understood that she had brought him food. "It's really not necessary," he heard Cornelius say.

Listening upstairs, Barnt winced. Would Cornelius drive this girl off, too?

"Do you not read the Bible?" the girl demanded aggressively in her harsh voice.

"Yes, but—"

"Then you must know that a wife does certain things. If there are things that she cannot do, she won't do them. But if it is preparing food for her husband, and she can cook, not doing it would be against the will of God. It happens that I—"

"I know very well," Cornelius interrupted. "There was never any doubt, and no doubt now, that you can cook well."

"Then sit down when you eat. Give thanks first."

This girl would not be scared off easily, Barnt thought. Such an irony, he thought, that she and Cornelius were shaking out the contours of a relationship they both believed was God's plan for them—however amended it might be by personal limitations and preferences—at the exact moment that Barnt's wife and greatest love Angel was dying in the bed upstairs. Barnt felt a surge of envy, which he immediately pushed down. Cornelius and Gertruyd had a right to whatever happiness they could have with each other; personally, Barnt felt blessed to have had the happiness he had already experienced. And in any case, wasn't this the path they had all chosen in this new world?—to live, to survive as long as one could, while knowing that death and sin visited all? They were all making it up as they went along, here in this colony of lost and found souls.

Cornelius prayed for Angel and Barnt, then left to work with Gertruyd, who was helping him finish building his small shack near Fresh Kill; Barnt suspected that she had probably asked him to enlarge it, a reasonable request. Now he and Angel were alone in the house. Barnt could tell that Angel was declining, despite the remedies and soup that he gave her daily. Yet he loved the fact that he could lay snuggled next to her day and night. There came a time when he stayed in bed, getting up only to make food for Angel and fetch the beer and water that Barnt was convinced was the healthiest thing that sick people could drink.

The rest of the time he stayed in bed with her, singing and telling stories that he thought she might enjoy. While she smiled and giggled in response, he was frightened by the sound of his voice echoing in the little house, since it reminded him of how it felt when he had only himself to talk to. It was getting harder for her to talk now.

Drupt had become skilled at running up and down the rough plank stairs. Most of the time he would lay beside the bed, looking up at the two of them; but when Barnt left, the dog would jump up on the bed and lay near Angel. As Angel's breathing became more congested, Barnt let the little dog lay on the bed with the both of them. Barnt had a special quilt that he put down for Drupt, which the dog recognized, and would run toward it with a kind of frenzy when Barnt spread it over the bed. Once on the bed, however, the dog quickly went to sleep.

Barnt prayed for Angel every two hours or so, with Drupt looking up at him curiously, as though unsure whom Barnt was talking to. Barnt wanted more than anything to talk to Angel, and did so as regularly after he prayed. But usually Angel was too weak to answer him; after some time, he talked loudly to Drupt, hoping that then perforce Angel's eyes would at last flutter open, her lips part in laughter, and join them in whatever precious joke was current in her feverish dreams.

Her skin was covered with blisters bursting with an opaque fluid, and covering every inch of her body, although the large blisters seemed to be receding somewhat. Her skin was hot to his hands that touched her. Barnt was hoping that the smallpox wasn't injuring her eyes—he kept lukewarm water to splash into her eyes while he bent over a washbasin, but now her fever was extremely high. When she could speak, she told him that her muscles felt like they were on fire, and her head pounded; she was unable to get up. Nausea and vomiting were ongoing. Lesions had appeared on her mouth, tongue and throat, bursting and disseminating more toxic fluid.

The blisters were less aggressive now, however, causing Barnt to wonder if the worst was past. Then he saw the bleeding under the skin: he had seen this before. It was the Black Pox, a kind of smallpox in which the skin turned black. It was always fatal.

Barnt now knew what awaited them, and knew also that it was all the more important to speak to her one last time, since death was to be her portion. Speaking to each other was what they most needed to do, he thought, just one more time . . . not that it was possible to say everything in such a short time, or even much at all, but simply to communicate the words that lovers and spouses had used forever in these circumstances. *I love you. Don't leave me. I'll see you in heaven.* In any case, they had little time. Barnt knew what the Black Pox did to the body. It got into the soft tissue, everywhere the body was soft, and caused it to disintegrate, and the person would bleed until dead.

He began to pace back and forth in the small attic bedroom, with hardly enough room for his head under the long central beam. He thought of the brandy and rum downstairs, and—half falling—quickly went down the plank stairs to get the rum. He came back up the stairs very slowly, and as he reached the top stepped off onto the second-story floor. What he saw almost made him faint.

Angel was sitting up in bed looking at him. She was entirely black. The sight of her took away his breath.

"Bury me on Burial Ridge," she said.

"*Angel—*"

"Bury me at the Raritan Burial Ground. You know where. On

Burial Ridge."

"I want to bury you at our family burial plot," he said, "on the land where my father built his first house at Old Dorpe. It is the job of the sons to see to that, in a place like this where there is plenty of land—"

But of course she knew all about that, all of his reasons.

"Bury me on Burial Ridge," she said, "you know where . . ."

"Angel . . ."

". . . with my ancestors at the Raritan burial place . . . promise me."

"Angel . . . you're my wife . . . you belong in my family place."

"If you don't bury me with my ancestors, I will wander without sleeping. Don't make me suffer that way."

Now the tears were coming. "I'll be there with you," he said desperately, and could no longer speak.

"My bones will lie with my ancestors."

He hesitated, but only momentarily. "Yes, I see that now. I'll bury you on Burial Ridge."

He had heard her talk of this before. But, when they were both alive and well, it hadn't seemed real. The very idea of burial had escaped him then, and had perhaps been little more than a passing fancy to her as well. But the place was very real in her thinking. It was central. He recalled the circumstances of their meeting; it was all coming back to him: she had gone to the burial ground to sing the traditional songs, and dance the traditional dances for her father and other family members, who were buried there.

"Promise me," she said.

"I promise." He breathed heavily, wondering how many minutes they had. "Do you want me to do the stomp dance afterward?"

She laughed. "I'm here," she said in Jersey Dutch. "Come and lay down with me. Aren't you tired standing there looking at me? Lay down with me."

It was the singsong, idiomatic Jersey Dutch, heavy on the slang and the Ramapough rhythms and filled with Raritan words and references. He sat down beside her, wondering at the miracle that they had found each other, but that she must leave so soon.

"Was Father Marcel sick when you got there?" he asked.

"Yes, very sick. He was happy to see me, but worried too. He asked me where you were."

"What did you tell him?"

"That I didn't want you to get sick," she said. She paused a few moments. "I gave him the medicines that I knew how to make. In the end there was no hope for him."

Barnt heard a whisper of thunder not unlike the thunder he'd heard after the execution of Leisler and Milborne, and shivered. The wind was seductive, calling to him, rustling the still-dry grass, but telling him that the rain was coming. Thunder at night was a judgment—or sounded like it—but it was a soft judgment, a loving judgment. Best of all was the spring wind that caused the limbs on the trees to scrape, the wind that bespoke both love and judgment, invoking a complicated world in which to act out one's responsibilities—or to renounce them entirely.

"I want to tell you something," he said. "I'm proud of you for trying to help Father Marcel. I love you for that."

"But look at me, husband. I'm dying."

He choked up. "Yes, yes, we didn't get to our kingdom in East Jersey." Now he was crying helplessly. He had done a great deal of thinking about this, and wanted to tell her about the Other Kingdom, the spiritual kingdom. "There's another Kingdom, in the Otherworld—"

"Will you come?"

"I promise I will."

"To live there forever?"

She was starting to fade. He thought he couldn't answer, but then did so. "Yes, my darling," said, "forever."

He lay down beside her, as she had asked him. He held her as tightly as he could.

"You can go, if you have to," he murmured to her. He wanted her to know that she could let go, if she was ready. And she *was* ready. She was bleeding out. He couldn't stop it—she was going. He had known this would happen . . . yet he hadn't known then that lying right next to her, there was nothing he could do to save her, and how helpless that would make him feel. How could you love someone so much, and be completely unable to help them?

As the breathing became more labored, and then more shallow, he held his own breath.

She breathed out.

There was a pause.

She drew breath in sharply . . . and then—out.

In.

And then out—a very long breath—

Then nothing.

8.

Barnt and Cornelius took her to the Raritan Burial Ground. It was easy getting her there. They did not have to imagine her suffering, because she was already dead. Still they transported her gently, carefully; they took the two stout limbs they had used before to transport her home from East Jersey when she was still alive, and lashed a few fresh saplings across them. Then they placed her on the rough sled they'd made for her, lashing her body to it, and swaddled her with all the cloth and coverings they could find, including an old canvas sail that Barnt had once tried to use on his skiff. They securely covered her blackened face. Then they set out without speaking and eating. They did not have far to go, but it would take an hour or two. They used the old hunting trails and then an abandoned and barely discernable wagon road going in the general direction of Burial Ridge.

As they neared the burying ground they saw Billop Manor, far to the south, the prize of Captain Christopher Billop for his loyal service to the British Navy. They went out of their way to avoid being seen, which was relatively easy since the manor house was at a lower elevation, on a spit of land that jutted out into Raritan Bay. Cornelius and Barnt kept to a higher wooded elevation that led to Burial Ridge, wherein was located the Raritan burial ground. The approach to the burial ground was partially sheltered, but afforded a clear view to the south. The trails they took were completely abandoned.

They slowed down as they approached the burial place. Barnt was wheezing; he gently lay down Angel's remainds. He was completely exhausted, and sat down on a rock to look over the area, with Cornelius not far away. Once he'd seen a few bones, he began to see many more. For reasons that Barnt did not understand, most of the graves were quite shallow—two to three feet deep. But it was just deep enough to keep animals away; the bones that he saw looked as though they had worked their way up to the surface over the centuries.

Barnt glanced at Cornelius, who was clearly exhausted, but seemed anxious to give his older brother the opportunity to lay the remains of his wife to rest in whatever way he saw best. "Did you ask her about the family burying place on Ould Dorp?" Cornelius asked.

"Yes. She insisted on the burial ground." Barnt looked out at the gleaming ocean of Raritan Bay, past Billop's manor house, toward the Jersey shore, which was shrouded in fog. "I suspect that perhaps some of her nephews and cousins might like to come here to perform the traditional dances and songs, if there are any left. They will know where to come. They could never find their way to our family plot, even if we gave them directions."

"I hadn't thought of that," Cornelius said.

"Well," said Barnt, "let's start." He needed all his energy to stand up. "We need to get back well in advance of sundown. As warm as it is, a storm could still come up out of the northeast."

"Of course, brother."

They picked a spot that was near the center of the burial ground, but at the same time separate from the other graves. Barnt used the shovel he had brought; then Cornelius took it from him, bade him sit down, and finished the digging. *She will need a deep grave,* Barnt thought.

"You will see, brother," Barnt said, "that many of the bodies are buried with the knees drawn up to the chest. I want her to be laid out, like the daughter of a chief." Besides, her limbs had already started to stiffen.

"Yes, of course."

When Cornelius was finishing digging, he sat down on a boulder and waited for Barnt to speak.

"Help me bring her down," Barnt said finally.

The two of them laid her down flat in the grave. It was cool there, and long enough to accommodate her full length. They left in the grave the old sail and the other clothes with which they had swaddled her remains as they transported her. Cornelius stepped into the grave to arrange the things they'd left, and then stepped out nimbly as they finished.

Barnt sat down, in a place where he could just see his wife's swaddled remains at the bottom of the grave.

"Angel . . ." he said.

There was so much he wanted to say to her now, but he knew it was either too late, or not the right time. He could come back someday and say some of it, or even more of it than he could imagine now — he could come back as often as he needed to — and he already knew he would be compelled to do that; he would probably bring Drupt with him too, if the little dog was able to stay on the path and not get lost in the woods. Now, however, what was important was finishing the task of putting Angel to sleep in the earth. He reached into his pea coat and took out the precious little carved owl he'd brought with him.

"What's that?" Cornelius asked.

"A wooden owl," Barnt said, "a carved wooden owl."

"Beautiful," Cornelius said. "Can you tell me what it means?"

"Well, not entirely," Barnt said, "I can't tell you exactly what it means, or how it works. But I can tell you it is something of great power. She and I used it to signal whether we were home or not . . . so, you see, I want it to be with her as long as she sleeps here. I think her soul is already somewhere else, in the Otherworld. But even there, she will have a connection to this place, and to this grave. She knows what the owl means. When she knows the owl is here, she will know that I'm here too—that I'll be with her in the fullness of time."

He knelt, pushed the owl through the swaddled cloth, past the old sail, to a place next to Angel's cheek, and left it there. As he did this, he took a last look at her still beautiful but blackened face, and leaned to kiss the top of her forehead at the place where her black hair began. It was just too much, he thought, to leave her here, even knowing that she was dead, even knowing that he could come and visit this place. It seemed to him that she should be exactly where he was, and the presence of the owl would guarantee that he would always be with her, even if she was in her grave. He rose unsteadily. Cornelius gently shoveled the first soft load of soil onto Angel's form at the bottom of the grave; and as Barnt turned away, the wracking sobs welled up in him like a storm from the northeast.

11.

He asked Cornelius and Anthony to give him a month alone, so he could rest and sort things out. They were worried, and said so; and they made it clear they would check on him every so often, making porridge for him when they did; but they made it clear, also, that he didn't need to get out of bed when they were there. So he went to sleep, his little dog Drupt sleeping on the bed with him, and both stayed that way for a month. For the first week Cornelius visited every day, not so much after that. Barnt bathed every three days or so, and shaved some facial hair, simply because it was comfortable for him to do so. Then he went back to bed. The illness didn't go away, but he was getting better at managing it. Barnt had a vague memory of Cornelias cutting his hair.

About three weeks into the month of rest, there was a strange knock on the door. Barnt knew it wasn't family, because the knock was tentative, like that of a visitor.

Barnt opened the door. Outside stood a bent-over African man with a dispatch mail pouch like those transported by the Albany express cutter. In one hand was a walking stick, and he leaned heavily on it.

"Mist' Barn'?" said the visitor.

Drupt barked until Barnt scolded him. Barnt now recognized his visitor as John, the slave of Balthazar Bayard. "Come in," he said. "You are Balthazar Bayard's . . . servant, are you not?"

"Sah, John belong sa Balthus Bayard man, yah. Him rich plenty." With people he didn't know well, John would typically break into the pidgin English used by the Spanish and Portuguese slavers.

"Come in, please," Barnt said. He glanced at the mail pouch. "What's this?"

"Mr. Bayard gift, sah."

John entered Barnt's house cautiously, smiling and bowing and looking around apprehensively. "Him give'm jah thing," he said, handing Barnt the mail dispatch pouch. "You take'm sah, yes sah."

"Very well," Barnt said as though he was expecting it, which he wasn't. Inside the pouch was something that looked official. "Would you like to sit down?"

"Thank'em, sah," he said, but made no move to sit.

"Want some brandy?"

John laughed nervously. "Na sah. Make des jah man lose'm

mind."

Barnt was getting quite unsteady on his feet, so he sat down. Looking up at the old black man, he said, "John, why don't you use the Jersey Dutch when you talk to me?"

Barnt had heard John speaking various forms of Dutch (and English) in the past when delivering cooper's staves from Albany to various businesses in Mannahattas. John spoke Jersey Dutch like the people in the Ramapough area, in communities where there were many free blacks and runaway slaves. It would remind him of Angel to hear it spoken that way again.

John laughed nervously. "Yah, sah, John speaks'em."

Barnt sat down and looked in the pouch. He pulled the enclosed papers out. It was the patent for a large estate in East Jersey, he saw; it was the patroonship he had been angling for—fifteen thousand morgan, which would probably be around thirty thousand acres. That would be a huge spread, truly a manorial estate. But with an excruciating pang Barnt remembered that Angel was gone, no longer his wife, and with her was gone also the dream of a private kingdom of their own, a kingdom where her clan could be safe. What meant the manorial estate now? And what connection could he possibly have with the Albany elite now? For a wild moment Banrt experienced an overwhelming compulsion to throw the papers into his open fire, but overcame the impulse.

Instead he smiled at John. "Thank you," Barnt said, his voice breaking slightly. "That'll be all."

But John made no move to leave. "Sah, Mista Bayard give'm something. You write'em now?"

Suddenly Barnt realized what John was waiting for: a note acknowledging receipt of the valuable papers and thanking his benefactors, specifying some details about the content to show that he'd truly received them.

"No," Barnt said firmly. "I'm sorry. I can't. Not now."

His illness and weariness overtaking him, Barnt began to cry, heedless of the old man watching him. If he wrote a note of thanks to Bayard, he would still be in their game. He was glad to have the patent in his possession, because that would force him to make sense of the events that had overtaken him. But this was the great turning point in whatever was left of his life, a watershed that would influence everything he was and everything he could be; but the terms of the deal were completely different now. What was required of him, of course, was to write an ecstatic letter of thanks—one pleading his lifelong gratitude and obeisance—but there was no way he could do that now.

He wiped his eyes, gesturing toward a chair across the table. "John," he said presently, "please be seated. I hate to see you standing there while I'm sitting. You're my guest, even if only for a moment."

John grudgingly sat in a chair. "John th-th-th-thank'em sit down, sah." Like a lot of slaves, he stuttered when power relations became confused or indistinct.

"I won't write a letter just yet for Mr. Bayard, John. Because . . . I have to just think about the words I want to use. You tell him that, won't you?"

The two men were silent for a long period. Barnt wasn't sure that John believed him, or even knew what he was talking about; but for now this excuse would have to do.

"I think I should go now," John said in perfect Jersey Dutch. "You can send a letter later, in a few days, to acknowledge receipt of the papers."

"Yes."

John stood, using his hand on the table to push himself up. "I'll tell them that . . . that . . ."

"That I received the patent for the land in East Jersey . . ."

"And that you . . ."

"Wept when I saw what it was. Don't forget that."

"No, sir, I won't forget that."

John exited, walking stiffly and leaning heavily on his walking stick.

In fact, he *had* wept when he saw what it was, and John *had* seen that. And he would almost surely report it. But John, and the Bayards who owned him, couldn't possibly know what the tears meant. At this point, neither could he, at least not completely. The last few months had turned his world completely upside down, but it was his responsibility to sort it out—because if he didn't do it, who would? He was gradually getting closer to understanding how he was going to play the cards he'd been dealt, both the good ones and the bad ones.

But he needed a little more rest, Barnt thought, a little more time to pray, and a few more days to ponder what lay ahead. With great weariness he made his way back upstairs again; Drupt bounded up excitedly behind him, to lie beside him on his bed. Barnt lay there sleeping for the next two weeks, getting up only to take care of the necessities. He was eating nothing but porridge, but for the first time in a long time was starting to enjoy the taste of it.

In another ten days, Barnt was well on his way to sorting things out. He took to bathing and shaving his facial hair every other day. He cut out alcohol completely. Although the ground was still frozen outside in a few places, spring was clearly on the land, and the warm days were upon them. Drupt seemed thrilled that his human had survived the winter, and followed him everywhere. June would be a good month, perhaps a good month for planting, if he had the strength to do some; at present Barnt doubted it. Above all he missed Angel, missed her presence, and still couldn't admit, in his heart of hearts, that she was gone forever. In an odd way, that feeling of loss made every-thing else easier, because the normal exigencies of life no longer seemed that important, at least not in comparison to the way he missed Angel.

Cornelius was getting married to his betrothed at the Morgan farm soon. Barnt knew he wasn't strong enough to make it to the wedding, and was briefly uneasy regarding his brother's reaction, but Cornelius put him at his ease. "It's not necessary, brother, for you to attend the wedding," he said, "but as long as we're discussing the future I hope we can live for a time in the little house I have built by Fresh Kill."

"Of course, of course, that's a very good plan. I'll visit when I have more strength," Barnt said. "I'm glad you will be here for a while, to be honest. I'm mending, but God knows it's slow."

"Furthermore, if I live at Fresh Kill for a while longer, I can help you lay in a few crops when the planting season is here."

"Thank you," Barnt said. "I appreciate your kind thoughts. I'll do as much work as I can, but I'll definitely need your help." He wanted to ask about Cornelius's cabin north of Albany, but decided not to.

"Have you heard from Anthony?" he asked casually.

"He'll be coming to visit you soon, perhaps as early as tomorrow," Cornelius said. "Word is you have received a large proprietorship of land in East Jersey. It's a subject of much conversation at the Green Dragon tavern."

So Cornelius knew about that, and had probably discussed it with Anthony. And if it was common knowledge at the Green Dragon, most of New York must also know. Barnt was silent for a long moment. "Yes, I can understand how people would be curious. This is a time of many changes."

Clearly Cornelius was also curious about what Barnt was about to do, but he did not ask about it. He left after eating some bread and porridge, and Barnt went back to his bed, where Drupt was waiting happily.

12.

The next morning, after a long and restful sleep, Barnt made his way carefully down his plank ladder. He was in the kitchen when he heard an encouraging knock on the great door. "Come in, brother," he shouted.

It was Anthony, who was surprised at Barnt's salutation, but clearly happy with it. "How did you know it was me?"

"I didn't," Barnt said, "but I was hoping it was."

Anthony got inside and took a good look at Barnt. "Good Lord, brother. You're still a shadow of yourself."

"I'm just starting to gain a little weight. I still need to rest most of every day. But I'm determined to get better, so that I can assist in whatever plantation is undertaken on this land. I make porridge in the way Angel used to make it, and eat at least twice a day, sometimes three times. If you bring me bread from my bakery before you sell it, and a little butter, I will eat as much as you bring."

"I'm glad to hear that, and I'm glad to see you have regained your old resolve. I think it was badly shaken these last months, but clearly you still have it. I'm concerned, though . . . surely we must, with God's help, take things at a proper pace."

"We will. But before we discuss that, please have a seat."

He offered Anthony rum, which he accepted. He had one swallow, but didn't finish the drink, which Barnt was glad to see. "What about you?" Anthony asked.

"None for me."

Anthony sat down across from his brother. "What is this I hear about your receiving a patent for the estate in East Jersey?"

Barnt sighed and leaned back in his chair. "I've been waiting to talk to you about that."

He paused to collect his thoughts, looking out the far window. A family of blue jays had built a nest deep in the crook of the tree outside, and the mother was busy feeding the fledglings. Barnt was always amazed at how silent the blue jay fledglings were—most baby birds created an unholy racket demanding food, but blue jay fledglings were quiet as the grave, crouching at the bottom of the nest waiting patiently for the food to arrive.

"I have given much thought about this subject this past

month," Barnt said. "The so-called great families in Albany are nothing more than criminals. I feel no obligation to them whatsoever at this juncture. They expect us to do what they say, and they try to terrorize us with as little consideration for our common humanity or our rights as they can get away with. Sadly, we do not have the same rights as the ordinary citizen in Amsterdam, in the Dutch Republic—and that is a tragedy, because Pater was a strong supporter of the Republic, and believed we could create another republic here in the New World. Instead, as we've all seen, a few rich Dutch families seized land and power, by hook or by crook, taking it all in order to tyrannize over their Dutch brothers and sisters."

"Yes, sadly."

"Their treatment of Leisler and Milborne was atrocious. There was no necessity for it. A year in prison would have been enough."

Anthony shuddered. "Yes, yes, we agree on that," he said. "But the point is, I never saw it coming. I never believed they would do such a thing. Such public sadism does not terrify the people, it enrages them. It has divided the colony. And I feel responsible for your involvement, because I advised you that the colonial administration would never execute Leisler and Milborne . . . and as we have both seen, I was terribly wrong. But you, on the other hand, cannot consider yourself guilty of the administration's cruelty, because nobody could have predicted what happened."

"Of course I'm guilty," Barnt said. "Think about it, brother. If I had not been in Mannahattas trying to place bribes for my own self-interest, I would have been at home in Staaten Eylandt. And I would never have let Angel go off alone to take care of Father Marcel—instead, I would have accompanied her. My being with her would have made a difference. Perhaps I could have made the difference that kept her from catching the smallpox that killed her in the end."

Anthony said nothing, but simply shook his head sadly, as though repenting in his own mind for whatever part he had played. "I encouraged you," he said simply.

"Look, you cannot blame yourself in any way for my decision to work with the Bayards and other families of Albany. It was entirely my idea. I asked for your help and you gave it. You were in no way responsible for what happened. You became involved, but only to help me, because you saw that my love for Angel had driven me to gamble with fate."

The two men were silent. Anthony waited but was clearly impressed by what Barnt had said.

"Still—" Anthony said.

"There is nothing more to be said about it. I had an obsession, and you helped me, after I asked you for your help."

"But your intent was a good one," Anthony said. "You wanted to create a refuge for Angel and her people."

"Yes, of course the creation of a refuge was a good idea . . . but I asked evil people to help me achieve it. Such people cannot create anything good. They corrupt everybody with whom they come in contact. To deal with them, you must lie constantly, and pretend to love them, knowing all the time that they are not worthy of your respect. And once you have hitched your wagon to their corrupt enterprises, they will take you straight down, first to their own level of cheating and intimidation, and then straight to hell. Accepting a gift from them is the kiss of death. They will use your obligation to them as an opening to create evil wherever they go."

"Perhaps—once you are on your own land in East Jersey, you could go your own way, and not do their—"

"Do you really think that is the way they operate? You know better. Once you accept a gift of that size, you are their servant. You mean nothing to them except what they can get from you, and from your service. From their point of view, I am now their property—otherwise, they wouldn't have even considered giving me the estate."

The two brothers sat silent for a moment. "Have you received notice of the land patent?"

Barnt got up and retrieved the mail pouch. He handed it to Anthony, who opened it and examined its contents. He clucked softly when he examined one of the papers. "Fifteen thousand morgan," he said. "At least thirty thousand acres; or—"

"Or more."

Anthony carefully put the papers back in the pouch. He looked steadily at Barnt. "I know that the love of money is the root of all evil," he said carefully, "but I have always believed that the proper antidote to it is not to run away from that kind of power, but to learn to use it responsibly."

"That is not my way at this point. I am not strong enough to take on that kind of inner struggle. Even with God's help I am not strong enough spiritually and in body."

"So what will you do?"

Barnt replaced the mail pouch in the canvas-wrapped hole in the kitchen wall where he kept important papers. "The only way for me is to detach myself totally and completely from the activities of these jumped-up sons of whores that call themselves 'aristocrats' in Albany. I will be here, on this little place, for the rest of my life. I have some plans. They are all modest ones, but they all involve my family."

"Tell me what you will do with the estate in East Jersey."

"Ah, well," said Barnt as he sat down, "that's the truly interesting part. Are you ready to hear it?"

Anthony nodded.

"We belong to a relatively prolific family, wouldn't you agree?" Barnt began. "Our grandchildren will have even more children than Pater did. Many of them will be moving into East Jersey, because they are disgusted with events in this part of the colony. In East Jersey, there are now preachers who don't give the sacraments, but simply preach about how one should live one's life with God's help. They are tired of John Calvin, and more interested in how one can raise good children. These new preachers speak of being directly in touch with God every day, without having to hide in a theology written long ago, or somebody else's holiness. There are a plethora of churches and groups there, all preaching different doctrines . . . but one can choose one that is good for oneself, and let the others alone. I think that is by itself something of a revolution, and a revenge on the Dutch Reformed pastors in this colony who have played such a wretched role in the lives of the people."

"Yes, I follow that."

"Most of our grandchildren will want land. Many will practice the trades in places like Bergen Town, of course, but I suspect the majority will keep one foot on the farm, while practicing business in the towns or in Mannahattas. The majority will want to raise crops and farm the land and perhaps raise cattle, just as Pater did from the first time he arrived here. They will all benefit from the ownership of property."

"You will give them your estate?"

"No, not exactly. Here's the way I want to do it. I will not answer any letters or inquiries from the Albany family that provided me with this land patent. As far as I am concerned, they are dead to me. But my children and grandchildren will want land in East Jersey. We will study the land patent, and see where it applies. Family members will be encouraged to buy land in the area specified by the official patent, without making contact with the Albany 'aristocrats'—but if they have any problems with claim-jumpers or others, we will use the patent to enforce their ownership. Our family members will claim only those lands they can personally farm. In fact, those family members that don't have the money to purchase plots can work the plots that have not already been claimed, and in time claim them as their own, as long as they are not too big. If any family members have trouble, we can argue their case for them in Bergen Town, using the patent as best evidence of their right to ownership."

Anthony was nodding. "Very good," he said. "You will not live on the estate, but will encourage family members to live in its confines. Any legal trouble they have can be argued successfully on the basis of the estate."

"And all descendants can expect my help, or your help, only if they are careful to only claim land they can personally look after, even if all they use it for is to graze cattle. Otherwise I will withdraw my help. I would ban contact with the Albany crowd under any circumstances. That rule will not be compromised."

The two men sat quietly for a moment.

Anthony nodded. "Yes," he said, "I see how that could be done. Two of my boys could benefit directly from that, as could your two sons. And certainly our young brother Willem would be a natural candidate for it."

"And I will continue to live here," Barnt said.

"How will you exist?"

"As Pater did. I will raise cattle, and probably also some oxen, which are becoming popular for pulling carts in these muddy roads. And each year I will raise a small crop, perhaps enlarging it every year somewhat, depending on my health. I know my combined holdings in Mannahattas are only a fraction of what they once were. I know I will never be rich—and I don't want to be rich. I want nothing more than to live in this small house with my memories, my dog Drupt, and as much goodwill toward the world as I can muster."

Anthony nodded, clearly impressed. "You will have my help, as well as my prayers and appreciation."

"Thank you." Barnt breathed deeply a few times, struggling a bit for air, working to get his breathing back to the shallow rhythm that worked best for him. "What are your plans, brother?"

Anthony had been smiling, as though to himself, as he listened to the last part of Barnt's explanation. "Not that different from yours, brother," he said.

Barnt was surprised. "How so?"

"I am also selling my business interest in Mannahattas and moving back to Staaten Eylandt. I plan to live in Pater's old house, over near Ould Dorp. I think I can make a brick addition to it that will be quite seemly. It will take a great deal of work, of course. I will plant some crops every year, just as you plan to do, and see if I can survive on it. It is not too far from here—there are no good wagon roads, but good trails, which will someday take wagons, and even coaches. Riding a mule, I could be here in an hour. And hearing you talk, I too am beginning to wonder if grazing cattle might not be good for at least another twenty years or so on this island. In fact, I hope you'll let me use a variation on Pater's cattle mark—it was the first one on Staaten Eylandt."

"We'll both use Pater's mark, with slight variations," Barnt said. He suspected there was more, but didn't know how much to probe. "Did the disaster that befell us influence you that much?"

"How's that?"

"Something has happened to you. You've changed."

Anthony laughed, a little uneasily. "I've been reading a book about the Labadists—you know, the same group that have their own colony in Maryland—"

Barnt was careful not to laugh, or even smile. "Go on."

"I'm not going to live in a state of extreme religious enthu-siasm," Anthony said firmly, "or live with people that do. That's not my path. I've just been thinking, and praying a great deal about the state of the world, and of my own soul. And I think a simple life on a farm on Staaten Eylandt might be just right for me, with plenty of time to read and pray. In any case, I've had enough of Mannahattas." He smiled. "It's so crazy there now that decent Dutch people don't even call it by its right name, but call it things like 'Mannahatto' or 'the Mannahattans' or just 'Manhattan,' and so many other strange things I can't remember them all."

There was something so serious in Anthony's voice that Barnt burst out laughing. "Indeed, it is a place that barely knows its own name these days. It is all very well to call the colony New York in its entirety, but each city must have a name, and Mannahattas is a city separate from all the others. Even the people that call it home are often likewise confused."

"So I intend to sell many or all of my holdings there," Anthony said, "and turn over the house there to my sons and stay there only when I'm there on business. My wife will move with me; living here, she will be closer to some of the children and grandchildren in East Jersey. In time, I think, my sons will all go to East Jersey. People are disgusted by the Dutch Reformed pastors, and disgusted by the Albany crowd and their hateful games. They want to get away from them, without necessarily losing all connection to their families in Mannahattas, Lang Eylandt and Staaten Eylandt. Almost all of them take pleasure in speaking Dutch, or Jersey Dutch, or even High Dutch on Sundays."

"We must all sit down and discuss the boundaries specified by the patent," Barnt said. "I will not be living there, so the children and grandchildren can live anywhere in its precincts that they choose. If necessary, we can hire our own surveyors and chain-carriers to measure it, but we will be honest in measuring it, which most land speculators usually aren't."

"I will do it, if nobody else will."

"The important point is this: I refuse to profit from it in any way."

"That is understood. I feel the same way. I have plenty to live on, and like you, I do not wish to profit from any of those powers and principalities associated with Albany."

There was a very long pause.

Anthony cleared his throat. "What about the curse that was made on that day?" Anthony asked, his voice breaking slightly.

"One does not forget such a thing easily, and the people of Mannahattas have not forgotten it, although most hesitate to talk about it publicly."

"No, most will not talk about it openly," Barnt said, in a way that indicated that he'd given it some thought, "but are likely to talk about it in small groups. It will become a subject of gossip in the colony, there's no way around that. The people who were there will especially want to talk about it, and the story will circulate among family members, especially the children and grandchildren. But in our family, we will not talk about it unless the children and grandchildren want to hear about it." Barnt's voice was firm. "Until then we must live with it—you and I must each find a way to loosen its hold on us. But in the immediate future, we cannot deny that it happened, and accept that it has changed our lives forever."

Anthony nodded. "But would not talking about it help the children avoid the dangers that brought it into being? Would it not be a kind of cautionary tale they could benefit from?"

"It might," Barnt said, nodding. "I think that living in this country will not be as easy as we once thought. There are many temptations, and much sin, that we cannot see now. Knowing about it could help them. But it is up to every generation to decide whether to talk about this curse or not. Some of the children are too sensitive, and it could burden them."

Anthony was nodding, and placed his hand over his eyes, then wiped away tears.

The two brothers stood and embraced. "We'll all be closer now," Barnt said. "Cornelius and his new wife, you and your wife near Ould Dorp. And the children and grandchildren in East Jersey, or moving there soon—"

It's like we're all starting over, Barnt thought, *except that we're all different now.*

Anthony finished his rum, and turned toward the door, then turned back for a moment.

"Brother . . . you still drink water and beer, but you no longer drink strong spirits. Is there a reason why you don't?"

"Yes."

"Could you share the reason why you don't?"

Barnt opened the great door, and a soft blast of warm spring air entered the house. "Some men drown their memories with alcohol. But I *want* my memories. I want them here with me. They will be my companions."

"They must be beautiful memories," Anthony said.

"The terrible ones are also part of the puzzle. I do not need to know why certain things happened to me, but I will need a long time to understand how they are changing me, how they brought me here, and how they made me what I am. This curse that has befallen us will not go away by itself—it is something I must answer to before God. That will be my work in the time left to me."

"I don't think it is an accident that it happened," Anthony said. "There is a warning in it, and something to teach us. I can't yet put most of it into words. I pray to God that in time we'll see what those things are."

Chapter 13

Every immigrant to a New World is given a puzzle to solve. It is a logistical and aesthetic puzzle, but most of all a moral puzzle. The way the voyager solves the puzzle is the way he lives his life, the things he learns, and the changes he makes. For each generation the puzzle is slightly different, although the problem at its core is always about the same thing, the search for truth, justice, and beauty in a strange land. For the immigrant generation, the generation of Thys Barentsen van Leerdam, the problem was to reach the New World, to procreate children there, and to raise those of one's offspring—those that didn't die, that is—in the values one believed in.

For the second generation—that is, the sons of Thys Barentsen—the problem was personal integrity, or identity. What would they call themselves? Some abandoned the use of patronymics immediately, adopting English-sounding last names that their sons could use in an English-speaking world. Some clung to the patronymics, calling themselves after their fathers, out of respect for what those fathers had endured. Some had new surnames handed to them by fate, and they accepted these new names with varying degrees of equanimity, seeing them as part of a new American reality, sometimes alternating or combining the new surname with the patronymic out of respect for the past. Over time, the changes were made. The brothers Swaim were lucky to have a turning point that seemed clearly marked, so that they could use a surname that seemed special to them alone.

In that manner Barnt, Anthony, Cornelius and then finally Willem, the youngest of Thys Barentsen's sons, alternated the new surname Swaim with the older use of patronymics. It was in a document in 1707 that we first encounter Anthony referring to himself as "Tysen alias Swaim," using both surname and patronymic in the same legal transaction. Afterward, the two were often alternated, with Swaim increasingly gaining favor, and finally winning out. A few retained the patronymic Thysen—son of Thys—but with their success in business the patronymic itself became frozen in common usage, and the spelling Anglicized to Tysen. The Tysens stayed in Staten Island, thriving in business and politics. The Swaims went to Jersey, and a great many hit the immigrant trail.

But with the puzzle of the name resolved, for the third and fourth generations the greater riddle remained. That greater riddle was what to love, and how to love. The presence of the curse emanating from the death of Leisler and Milborne made it especially important that they solve their own personal, over-arching riddle. Why were they here, what were they searching for in the wilds of America?

Thys Barentsen van Leerdam, the immigrant ancestor, brought with him a spiritual hunger typical of the Dutch during the seventeenth century, the Golden Age of the Netherlands. This hunger can be seen in its purest state in the great paintings of that time, in Rembrandt and Vermeer especially, in different ways and to different degrees. It is an idea of a simple moment in a simple but elegant place, accompanied by pleasure that in some way keeps that simple but perfect moment resonating in the memory. It was memorialized in the architecture and the canals that Amsterdam was building, punctuated by small but tidy living spaces that were also designed to create a sense of profound domestic pleasure.

The homes in the most famous Dutch paintings were clean even when cluttered, and full of domestic life that was fulfilling, capable of realizing itself in each new moment. It was tempting to say that it was about a kind of domesticity, but it was more than that. It was a moment of deep happiness, very often connected to one's family or civic group, but also about affection that goes beyond civic groups and familial love. It is above all a paradoxical sense of simplicity as heroic, recognized and experienced in lush moments of satisfaction, around things that are fundamentally simple and familiar.

The Dutch immigrants to Nieuw Nederland sought nothing less than to democratize this feeling, this experience, so that everybody could explore it. One sees this in their profound love of bread and fruit and beer, of work that ironically becomes pleasure, of children and domestic animals, and of simple things experienced in such a way that they inexplicably become part of the viewer's personality. It is a miracle that people living under a Calvinist church could invent such a sensuous understanding of the individual and his world. The entire history of Dutch-speaking culture after the Synod of Dort in 1619 is one long struggle between liberal sensibilities and Calvinism; and liberalism won, as the Netherlands became the most liberal country in the world. The Dutch in America took these sensibilities and fused them with the English love of the rule of law, which together became the American Dream.

God alone knows why Thys Barentsen took his vision with him to Nieuw Nederland, rather than simply reveling in it back in Utrecht. It may be because he had internalized a certain heroism that had arisen in the military struggle against the Hapsburgs of France and Spain, and it had become commingled in his personality with a love of unexceptional but beautiful moments, topped off with an ecstatic love of religious liberty typical of the Huguenots with whom his family had intermarried. According to this theory, Thys Barentsen loved above all the moments of deep domestic happiness that happen in simple but beautiful circumstances. That is why Thys Barentsen stood before Pieter Stuyvesant in the summer of 1661 and asked for land on Staaten Eylandt not merely to grow crops, but land for gardens.

Gardens . . . who thinks first of gardens? This immigrant did. His children and grandchildren took that puzzle and struggled to solve it in their own way, changing it slightly in each case according to the sensibilities of their own generations. We know they loved their families with a passion that would exhaust modern sensibilities. Perhaps the invention of a surname was itself quite exhausting for them, experienced as it was at the same time that they began to reject the Dutch Reformed Church, and its mediocrity, sin and corruption. The memory of the public suffering of Leisler and Milborne, which finally ended up being a crucifixion in the memories of those that experienced it, would haunt everyone in those first four generations on American soil, alienating them from public power and convincing many of them that happiness could only be found in small things, in a private faith.

Why, then, were these first four generations in America at all? What were the first four generations looking for, what were they here to accomplish?

It was a certain Anthony Swaim, a great-grandson of Thys Barentsen and grandson of Barnt's brother Anthony, who most proficiently solved his part of the puzzle. He did it by building a house in 1744, showing in the building of this house exactly what the Dutch imagination in America had been so assiduously seeking. Like many good things, it was in violent reaction to a style that invited pandering and prejudice. It was in flagrant reaction to the idea of the manor house that had so powerfully entered the Dutch-American imagination. Anthony built a house that was simplicity itself, but beautifully so. Anthony built a house that was not large, but not small either, a simple clapboard house, which he built with his own hands—he was a joiner as well as a carpenter, and a joiner is above all a craftsman who joins wood together to make new structures.

He built a house that was neither castle nor mansion, nor an imitation of either. In fact, he built a house that was the exact opposite of the manor house and the castle. It was, instead, a masterpiece of vernacular Dutch architecture, an insanely personal idea of a kind of power that one felt at home, rather than in the world. This was a clapboard house for life, death and love of one's family.

Not one slave sweated to build this house—it was a house designed and built by the man that lived in it. It was here that Anthony Swaim and his wife Abigail had their children. There are remembrances of Anthony and Abigail around the house, including a beautiful wooden carving in one wall. This was a different kind of beauty, combining the functional with the elegant, which it achieved through radical simplicity. Anthony Swaim understood with astonishing acuity what the Dutch immigrants really sought in America—deep satisfaction in things of a simple or domestic nature, but which all people, of whatever class, could enjoy. Anthony Swaim found, in the fourth generation, and in a single stroke, the key to the puzzle the Dutch had been struggling to solve for a century. And for whatever reasons, he, in his brief time on earth, expressed the perfect truth not in Utrecht but in the wilderness of the New World.

That vision was in no way an artistic or spiritual panacea. Death, sin and tragedy was part of this house, because they were a big part of life then, something that people in those days recognized, accepted, and did not try to deny. Anthony Swaim the joiner died in 1758, at the age of 40; Abigail died in 1764. Their underage children were raised by guardians. The achingly beautiful and perfectly constructed house sheltered many more families, including members of the Swaim family, defying wind and rain and winter's chill, with children being born—some dying and some living—as old families moved on and new families moved in, living in what became known as "the Old Swaim House," in what eventually became Springfield, Union County, New Jersey, bearing witness to a powerful but often misunderstood or overlooked vision.

It is still there, nearly three hundred years later. It still bespeaks the same uncomplicated but lovely vision, of beauty not in imperial grandeur, but joyously discovered in the vernacular world of the family and the familiar. Its beauty could not forestall the pall of death, nor could it defeat the curse of evil, and the perfidious misrule that accompanies evil. But it could exist in counterpoise to them. Ensconced in the seductive world of the familiar, the imagination of a just society in the New World could not be far behind.

2.

"And so we resumed our lives," Barnt said. He was telling me about the aftermath of the Leisler tragedy, and the death of his wife Angel. "We knew we could never go back to the way everything was before, but we also knew that there is integrity in facing the questions that life raises. I was still sick, and as far as I knew I might remain that way forever. During the planting time I recovered enough that I could work a good four hours a day, before having to go back to bed. I got used to living mainly on porridge, although people constantly brought other kinds of food for me. The worst part of it was missing Angel. Sometimes I couldn't sleep for many nights in a row, knowing that she would never be with me again. It was the *physical* memories that haunted me most. But after a time I got used to the pain and the piercing desire."

"At first, as we all got into the rhythms of our new lives, we stayed away from serious discussion of the curse placed by Leisler in his last awful moments. But gradually we began to discuss it. I had very clearly seen Leisler point at me while still alive, and cry out 'curse, curse, damned!' while pointing at me . . . and all the other things he said. I was there, it happened. It could not be denied—everybody in Mannahattas had seen it. It was useless to pretend it didn't happen. And Anthony, who had seen the ghastly business himself, did not try to talk me out of it. We decided between us that indeed it was a curse, and one that had been willfully placed on us, but that also there was no curse that could not over time be dealt with or deconstructed, with God's help, and in that manner defeated. Anthony and I would have to each decide how we would live with ours . . . but we would have been fools not to look for a chance to work it off, to live it down, and in that way to get rid of it forever."

"Did you discuss the fact that this curse could be passed down from one generation to the next?" I asked.

"In those days all curses were thought to operate that way."

"So could each new generation attempt to lift the curse in its own way?"

"Exactly!" Barnt said. He sat up excitedly on his bunk. "We came to that conclusion almost immediately. Anthony and I could work off our part of the curse in our own time . . . but for others, those family members that came later, each generation would have to deal with it in its own way. Every individual would probably approach it differently—presumably some would find a solution earlier than others. Knowledge of the curse would be transmitted by word of mouth. But after our time we knew nothing of how the curse affected family members."

"Well," I said, "Others must have heard about it. I am acutely aware of the existence of such a curse, after all those centuries. My father knew of it, although he chose not to talk of it."

"I hope the things I've told you, and everything we've discussed, has helped."

"More than you realize. Simply knowing how it came about means everything to me. It's not the hideous, supernatural thing I feared, but simply the result of the evil that exists in the human character."

He was delighted. "Do you think that there's a chance that you might—"

"I think there is a very good chance that I will dissolve the curse in my time. Knowing about it gives me power."

He seemed awed. "Imagine that," he said.

But I was curious about something else. "What kind of redemption did you and Anthony seek in your own time?"

"Redemption through simple tasks, things that hurt no one and were hardly noticed by our contemporaries in Staaten Eylandt, but which were nonetheless accompanied by much humble prayer."

"Give me an example, if you can."

Barnt smiled. "We had never had a Vorleezer House in Staaten Eylandt, although we heard that Bergen Town had one, or was building one. A Vorleezer House is a place for reading scripture. It was an especially attractive idea for a community that was sick of the pastors sent from Amsterdam. Any lay leader who knew his letters could read the Bible in a loud voice—he would need no theological training, since he was simply a reader; but it was a perfect arrangement for the people who were in open rebellion against the Dutch Reformed pastors, having seen the harm they could do."

"It sounds like a rebellion of pietism against the established church."

"Yes, I read a book just the other day that put it that way," Barnt said. "But Anthony and I also built the Vorleezer House as a family project, as a form of penance. There were planks left over from Cornelius's house, and he arranged to bring more planks over from Mannahattas. Then a man on another part of the island opened a crude sawmill, and we bought planks from him. It took a long time, and most of the money that we had left, but we built a very sturdy little structure facing a well-used path. People started to come on Sundays, and I was the Vorleezer. I had always signed my name with an "X" so as not to embarrass those of my contemporaries who hadn't learned their letters, but I was always able to read, albeit slowly . . . at first I had to study hard to get back to the place where I could read the word of God easily. But with God's help there came a time when the words came quickly."

"Once we had built the structure, we turned it over to the community as a gift. We initiated the practice of asking the children in that part of Staaten Eylandt to recite everything they had learned the week before in school. It was heartwarming to see the adoring parents watching their children perform on Saturday and Sunday, but it was serious business, as there were also strict consequences for the child who had not worked hard in school."

"After the children I would read the scripture, sometimes well into the afternoon. It was our way of acknowledging the importance of God and God's work in our lives, but without the influence of the preachers that we felt had betrayed us. After we had finished with the reading, we would break bread together. These were joyous meals, truly love feasts. That was one small way we worked against the curse laid upon us. When we had finished constructing the Voorlezer House, we turned it over to the community to govern its use. It was our gift."

I greatly enjoyed hearing his story, which I knew from independent sources was true. "Would you believe that this Voorlezer House that you and your brother built is still in existence?"

"Good Lord," he said. "Imagine that."

"Of course, they moved it. They moved it to Richmondtown, not far from St. Andrew's Church."

"Why? Why would they do that?"

"For the tourists," I said.

3.

"Tell me about those in our family that came afterward," Barnt said.

Barnt and I were lying on our bunks in the chilly bedroom that we shared on the second floor of Voyager House. Spring was in the offing, but winter winds continued defiantly to blow. Snow had fallen two days before, but was just starting to melt.

The clouds were low; but as is often the case, the moon shone stubbornly through them, the diffused yellow light just strong enough to light the streets outside in the late afternoon. As I lay thinking of how to answer Barnt's query, a loud report that sounded like a gunshot—two blocks away, maybe three—echoed in the street. It was closer than I would have liked, but it was not close enough to go outside and investigate. Gunshots are not welcome in New York, but neither are they an anomaly.

"Those of our family that stayed in Staaten Eylandt mainly took up with the Anglicans, and many are buried at St. Andrew's Church," I told him. "But a great many moved into East Jersey, just as you anticipated. It was a good starting point for them. Then they spread into Pennsylvania, and Virginia and North Carolina, having many adventures along the way." I told him the saga of Matthias Swaim, and how he secretly courted Abigail Hedges, the daughter of Judge Josiah Hedges in Virginia, and how she crawled out of an upstairs window of the judge's manor house to elope with him. I told him about Michael Swaim, who bought land in Virginia, and while measuring it hired the young George Washington to be one of the chain-bearers.

I told him of John Swaim, a young lieutenant from New Jersey in Captain Curyea's Company, 1st Battalion State Troops, in the Revolutionary War, and how he got caught in a fence while retreating, while a British soldier shot successive holes through his coat. Jack got loose, and turned to fire on his tormenter, bringing his man down with a single shot. John took the British soldier's gear, not for booty but to give to his comrades that were unarmed. It was war. John fought at Brooklyn, White Plains, West Point, Vannest's Mills, Staten Island, Monmouth, Princeton, Germantown, Brandywine and the Battle of Trenton.

I told him of Albert Swaim, who became a loyalist, moved to New York, and almost immediately died; he is buried at Trinity Church. I told him of a certain William Swaim who became an elder in the Episcopalian Church in the wilds of North Carolina, and then astonished his church by marrying a Cherokee woman; she astonished him in turn by leaving him and taking their three children to live with her tribal family. Later on he married one of the Tryon women.

I told him of Moses, Benjamin and William Swaim who together founded the Manumission Society of North Carolina, an anti-slavery group that operated in the Piedmont, and who with the Coffin and Mendenhall families established a major terminus of the Underground Railroad. William Swaim also founded the Greensboro Patriot in 1827, an anti-slavery newspaper, and in 1830 wrote and published *An Address to the People of North Carolina on the Evils of Slavery.*

"Good Lord!" said Barnt in wonderment. He was very impressed by the work of William Swaim, and wanted to hear more. He couldn't get over the idea of someone publishing an anti-slavery pamphlet in the 1830s. "From what I've read of American history, it doesn't seem possible that anyone could publish such a thing in the south in 1830 and survive."

"He didn't. In 1835 he died of a mysterious wound that was never explained."

"Had dueling become popular there at that time?"

"Yes, the barbarous practice had become common throughout the entire south, and the men were very careful to keep it secret from their womenfolk."

I told him of Cicero Demosthenes Swaim, a Kansas legislator who fought the eastern banks on behalf of the farmers, but whose son committed suicide. There was more to the story of the family in America, but I didn't want to overwhelm him.

Barnt was quiet for several minutes.

"Did the story of the curse survive?" he asked suddenly. "How did they handle that knowledge, those that may have heard of it? How do they handle it today?"

"It did survive, in various forms. Many saw it as something similar to original sin. People are born with a consciousness of sin, and each man or woman must devise a way to redeem themselves from the sin itself, to the extent to which they are complicit in it. Before the twenty-first century, almost everybody thought that meant redemption through Jesus, who was crucified in our place. Modern people often interpret it a bit differently, of course. I personally believe it means changing one's behavior in the future, rather than redeeming oneself of past sins. The point is, you must address the curse as it presents itself, both in yourself and in the world around you. Whatever evil is there, you must fight it, and in so doing strive to be among the just men and women of all times and places."

"Did William Swaim, the anti-slavery newspaper editor, feel that he had redeemed himself of the evil as it confronted him in his day?"

"Well," I said, "I believe he did everything he could to redeem himself, at tremendous risk to himself. Of course he failed, in worldly terms, because William Swaim—as well as Moses Swaim and Benjamin Swaim and the others in the Manumission Society—failed to stop slavery. But the willingness to be publicly ridiculed is the test of truth in all worlds, because men abhor ridicule more than death. The truth is, we have still not defeated the evil they fought. But from the struggle against that evil we have the literature, music and moral complexity that are America."

Barnt looked at me steadily. "And the treasure that I buried by the yellow poplars on Staten Island? Did that story survive?"

"I cannot say how it happened, but it survived in a different form, as the myth of overnight wealth, get-rich-quick schemes, and instant riches. For a hundred years, from 1820 to 1920, some family members enriched themselves from the sale of Swaim's Panacea, a horrible patent medicine that probably contained mercury, and perhaps opium. They were ashamed of what they had to do to get the money they craved . . . so they postured themselves as inheritors of old money—some ancient aristocratic fortune—just as the patroons of Anglo-Dutch New York had done. Of course, their money was all spanking new. Some people handled it well, but many more used their new money to cheat others and keep others down, so they could have more for themselves. Today, Americans struggle under new Lords of Greed—they struggle under billionaires that corrupt our elections, and seek to undermine those Americans whose hard work creates the wealth of the upper classes. Some things never change."

"Are there Americans willing to oppose these new Lords of Greed?"

"Yes, yes, of course." There was another long silence. There was something else I needed to ask him. "What was in the chest that you buried near the yellow poplars?"

"That? Well, I fully expected to die," Barnt said, "so I buried a few things that I wanted my brothers to have. Then, after Angel died, I was too melancholy and too tired to dig it up, and had no reason to do so."

"There is no money in this treasure?"

"Just everyday things, but they would be worth a great deal today. One or two things in particular would be worth millions. But they had importance in my life alone."

"Did you put your Great Bible in it?"

"No, no, no," he said, shaking his head sharply, "I gave it to my brother Anthony, and he gave it his son, and it went down the immigrant trail with the grandchildren. Most likely it was washed away while fording some rising stream, or burned in a house fire, or stolen."

"Do you still know where the chest is buried?"

"I could find it."

"What if it was caught in some land reclamation project, and washed out to sea?"

"That's quite possible."

There was a very long silence. I was hoping that there would be no more gunshots from the street outside, and that if there were, they would be moving farther away from us, rather than closer. But there were no more, although I caught a glimpse of flashing blue-and-red lights from a police car going in the direction where the shots had been fired.

Barnt took a deep breath. "And what about the Dutch Reformed Church? Did any of Thys Barentsen's descendants stay in it?"

"The Dutch Reformed Church in New York was completely discredited by its shameless toadying to the Albany elite, and the fact that it then supported the public torture and murder of Leisler in 1691. In the Netherlands, the next three hundred years were an exhausting struggle between the Calvinism of the church, and the instinctive liberalism of the Dutch people. Today, the Dutch are the most liberal people in the world, perhaps at times too liberal. That's how the Dutch solved the problem. The New York Dutch solved the problem by becoming Americans. They moved to Jersey, Virginia, Pennsylvania and North Carolina, and chose to attend other kinds of church, or no church at all."

"No Dutch Reformed?"

"Some of the women stayed with it for generations," I said, "but the Dutch men usually didn't care to attend."

I saw that Barnt had inadvertently given me an opportunity to tell a family story that was likely to amuse him. "There is a small town in North Carolina," I told him, "that has a mural at the town hall. The mural depicts four Swaim men on mules, horses and foot. Each one is a preacher, each one is going to a difference place, each one to preach a different sermon, and believe it or not, each one is a hundred years old or more. The mural, which is famous in North Carolina, is called *March of the Patriarchs.*"

"How many Dutch Reformed among them?"

"Not one."

He took out his pipe and clamped it in his teeth. "Thank

God!" he muttered.

4.

A couple of days after this I suggested to Barnt that we walk to the grave of Albert Swaim at Trinity Church. Barnt became slightly uncomfortable when I told Albert's story, as though he was afraid of becoming involved in a family quarrel from a time in which he was not directly involved. Indeed, I was starting to notice a change in Barnt: his voice was becoming less distinct, his strong seaman's face a bit blurry, and his interests now seemed to center around things he could not discuss with me. I was ever more convinced that he was in love with Clarissa Rowland, the manager and clinical director of Voyager House; in fact, there was an enormous energy about them when they spoke to each other, although they rarely said much. Above all, there was an overwhelming sense that they were planning something together, something that required them to be secretive.

Above all I felt that Barnt's mission in New York, and his work with me, was nearing completion. Some power in his personality was fading, or being transformed for purposes of a new challenge. The same day he declined to accompany me to the grave of Albert Swaim at Trinity Church, he agreed to accompany me to a slightly disreputable bar and grill in the neighborhood, a place where he could buy rum by the glass over the counter.

"Barnt," I said, "I am at a turning point in our relationship. I'm curious to know what your plans are. And there are still a couple of other things that I'd like to know."

We were surrounded by the human flotsam of the shipwreck that is lower Manhattan: two retired men that arrived each morning when the bar opened; a would-be pimp who talked to himself; a warehouseman who had once worked in the neighborhood; and a wretched homeless man who washed out the wooden flats behind the bar with boiling water to pay for his whiskey. "What do you want to know, specifically?" he said, after tasting his rum.

"I understand that you needed to talk to one of your ancestors, to explain what happened. And for reasons unknown you chose me. The truth is that I expected it, I had been waiting a long time for it to happen, and it changed my life. I hope it was a blessing to you as well. But why, from your point of view, did you choose to tell me the story of your life?"

Barnt looked at me sideways, sitting there beside me.

"You are an intelligent and thoughtful man," Barnt said, after a long pause. "That's why I came to you—that's one big reason. But there's also the fact that you are so well-informed about New York in the late seventeenth century. And you were aware of me personally—you knew many details of my life, and the lives of my brothers, because of your interest in genealogy. That made it easier for me to tell you about what happened, and about how Anthony and I were cursed on the day Leisler was executed. I didn't have to explain much—you knew a lot about it from your own research."

"Thank you," I said. But I had the feeling there was more.

Customers were coming into the bar where we were sitting. During lunchtime a surprising number of desperately poor people came to eat the management's special chili, which never seemed to vary but which could qualify as a hot meal, and could be eaten at the bar. Above all, a bowl was only two dollars. We were surrounded by these very special customers now. I could almost taste their hunger even as they assuaged it.

"I'm going to be leaving soon," Barnt continued in the same conversational tone. "I guess you know that. You are very intuitive."

"Are you leaving New York?"

"Yes."

The way he announced it was a bit too casual, although that part didn't surprise me; everything was starting to have a dreamlike ambiance connected to it, as though it was both real and unreal at the same time. Barnt didn't look the same as he had when I first got to know him, or even five or six days ago. "Okay," I said, "you're leaving, that's your decision. But why are you leaving now?"

"I'm going back to Amsterdam. I signed up as second mate on a freighter under the Liberian flag. It will dock in Amsterdam five weeks from now. I usually sign on as a third mate, as you know, but this is a special case—they're short-handed, and most of the crew will jump ship in Lisbon, where we're making port before Amsterdam. Furthermore, this company's ships sail down the pirate's road in North Africa, so they're having difficulty getting a full crew."

"You're not afraid of the pirates?"

"Hell no," he said, taking a big gulp from his rum. "Since I'll soon be going, do you mind if I make a critical observation? I think you should do something to improve your appearance. You're flesh of my flesh and blood of my blood, so I know you're a good person. But you come across as a little unkempt—and even scary to some people."

It had occurred to me that I might not see him again, and that made it important to be honest. "It expresses my attitude," I said. "There's a reason for it. There's something seriously wrong with the American people, and I'm disgusted with everything that's happening."

Barnt nodded. "You're right, what is happening to America now is dangerous in the extreme, but it is also an opportunity. Don't you see that America has been at war with itself since its beginning? Surely my life illustrates that point. You must do your part, and not simply complain, nor try to frighten people by looking like the craziest bum on the street. You must try to disabuse the people of their shallow worship of money and power. They believe that manipulating money is the way to redemption . . . as though it were a sacrament, almost. You're half in love with the idea yourself—look at the way you asked me repeatedly about the treasure I supposedly brought with me—"

"I'm afraid of money. Maybe that's just a different way of worshiping it."

"Not only that—you saw the treasure as connected to the curse, as though Old Money could help you buy your way out of it." He paused and turned halfway to put his hand on my shoulder. "Look, you're a good writer. I know, because I looked up something you wrote in a little magazine at the library. So use your talent and your gift for prophecy. Americans think that money is the True Church, and they will start wars for it. Use your skills to challenge the worship of the billionaires amongst the people. Warn the people of the danger they are to themselves, and to the country."

"I will. I'll tell them."

He finished his rum, stood up, and prepared to go.

"Why," I asked him, "why are you telling me these things?"

He stood there looking at me. "It's been exactly ten generations since the Curse was placed. I needed to tell my story to someone in the family, about how the curse came to be. You were that person."

"Why me?"

He stood there buttoning up his pea coat, smiling. "You're so intuitive, yet you still haven't figured that part out?"

"No, I haven't."

"Only a delusional man would accept my existence. You were that man."

5.

I can't remember exactly when it was when he left, but I think it was early the next day. I started to notice that some of Barnt's belongings were disappearing, being put away in his big seaman's bag, or given away, or simply disappearing. In a neighborhood with many second-hand shops, it was easy to dispose of unneeded belongings, especially the many books Barnt had accumulated. The day after we went to the restaurant-bar where Barnt drank the rum, he put on his pea coat, had some coffee in the kitchen, and left. His seaman's bag left at the same time, of course, although I never saw exactly when he left the premises. I saw Clarissa Rowland talking to Barnt outside on the sidewalk, and there was a desperate radiance in her face, and also a kind of fear. I couldn't get a good look at Barnt's face, but it was clear that he was leaving, and that this was a kind of leave-taking. I wondered if Barnt would go directly to his ship. Maybe he had drawn a watch while the ship was still in harbor.

The other clients did not have a going-away party, because they were not aware of his going. One of the clients mentioned it, but Clarissa quickly changed the subject. Barnt really hadn't been at Voyager House very long, and in any case the clients seemed to understand that his going was hard for Clarissa, although they may not have understood why. For her part, Clarissa became unusually focused, bypassing many opportunities for conversation. Everything was at the same turning point, it seemed—therefore it was not a surprise when Clarissa announced she was leaving. On some level, everybody had expected that.

I did not wish to attend the going-away party for Clarissa—it turned out to be rather elaborate, with many people from the mental health bureaucracy stopping by, as well as old friends she had worked with in other programs. There was a lot of shouting and tears; the clients appreciated the party atmosphere, but were not active participants in the partying. I waited until the party was over. I assumed that Clarissa might be back the next day, perhaps to take away her things. But there was no way to be sure about it.

I waited in the smoking area. When she came out of the door she was weighted down with a cardboard box worth of personal items. "Here, let me help you with that," I yelled. I walked over and took the box from her hands. "Is your car in the parking lot?"

"On the street," she said.

I noticed she was tearing up. *Emotional, all these changes,* I thought.

"I didn't get a chance to ask you about it," I said, as I carried the box to her car, "but I assume you have another job somewhere."

"You assume wrong," she said.

"Where are you going?"

"Amsterdam. I—I've always wanted to visit there. I really have."

"I don't doubt that," I said. "Amsterdam is on the short list for many people. And I have an idea why you're going there."

We reached her car, and she put the cardboard box in the trunk. She had that distracted air of the person who is leaving everything familiar, and for just that reason can hardly wait for the departure to be under way. "You know very well why I'm going," she said. "Bernard is going to meet me over there."

I paused. There was a long moment as we stood on our dangerous street in lower Manhattan. "I know you're going there to meet him. But what if he gets—stuck? What if he doesn't make it?"

"I'll take that chance," she said. "What I know is that I love Bernard, and I will do anything to be with him. If he makes it, we'll have a life together."

That was simple enough.

"He gave me something to give you," she said. She took an envelope out of her purse. In it was a letter, two shillings, two guilders and some wampum. "He said it was the *zeewant* for the ferry to Staten Island. Just in case you feel like going home."

"Doesn't he know the ferry is free these days?"

She probably didn't hear the question. She was going through her keys, separating her car keys from some old keys that once belonged to Voyager House, but apparently no longer fit.

"I have something for you to give to Barnt," I said.

It was a typewritten quotation from William Swaim, the anti-slavery editor that Barnt had found so intriguing. It was quite a quotation, and very typical of William.

The ignorant and degraded of every nation or clime must be enlightened, before our earth can have honor in the universe.

"What does it mean?" she asked.

"It means the best is still to come. It's a message of hope."

"For me?"

"For all of us."

She opened her door, sat down, and fired up the engine of her car. She was ready to go. "I love you too," I was saying, "in my own way—"

But she was already gone.

Chapter 14

I have ridden the Staten Island ferry twenty or thirty times since then, but never disembarked on Staten Island. I love the skyline of Staten Island as the ferry approaches it; and the even more impressive skyline of Manhattan going back. But actually disembarking would seem like a huge anticlimax. It is in the emotions aroused by the ferry that I come closest to what I know about my ancestors. Their world was so different one cannot in a single lifetime bridge the difference—only a small craft going back and forth can suggest what it was like. Riding the ferry, I feel the spectral tension between past and the present, between which there is no real tangible connection except in the emotions of the traveler, not in intimations of place but in simply traveling from one place to somewhere else. You could do worse than to get stuck on the Staten Island ferry. There are a lot of children, and they are all beautiful.

After Clarissa left Voyager House, Neil got her job on a temporary basis. It became common knowledge that Clarissa was going to fulfill a lifelong fantasy to live in Amsterdam, but the others did not know why. I examined the letter from Barnt that Clarissa had given me—it was written in very small script on a single sheet of paper; it looked like Dutch, but I could read it, so it must have been in English.

"Your finances were in a constant state of chaos because you failed to complete some simple forms for the Social Security Administration," Barnt wrote. "I brought your Social Security claim up to speed by completing some paperwork you've been neglecting to do. Thanks to my intervention, from now on you will receive your payments regularly each month, going directly into your bank account where you won't be able to screw it up. And there will be a large lump sum consisting of all the payments you missed. That is my gift of Old Money to you."

In Barnt's letter was an intricate Coat of Arms from the Swaim family featuring a lake of swans, and an icon of Frances Perkins. "Okay, maybe Frances Perkins wasn't part of the original Coat of Arms," he wrote, "but it is a nice idea, considering that according to the books I've read she did more than anybody else to make Social Security the single best program of American government. The Lords of Greed will never stop trying to take Social Security away from you, because it is so simple and so helpful to those of limited means. I say again, Social Security is the true old money, the only completely magnanimous, just and workable government program that America has ever invented."

"I know you are in despair at the moral decline of America," Barnt wrote at the end of the letter. "It is very much like the situation we faced—arrogant, vulgar rich people at the top, and hardworking but powerless people everywhere else. Tell the American people what is wrong, just as William Swaim would have done. Scores of our family members were editors, journalists, scribblers, dissenters of one kind of another—that prophetic capability is part of you, whether you like it or not. Write a book that will tell the American people what is wrong, and why."

And that is what I, the author of this book, am doing. I know that many readers will particularly hate the form this book has taken, because it is in the form of a will, and in the beginning I promised you that there was money waiting for all—money of such a magnitude as to *stagger the imagination*. Don't you remember me promising you that, reader, at the beginning of this book?

Well, I lied.

I *lied*, dear American, because promising you some kind of cash reward was the only way I could get you to read this document, and consider my warning! Because instead of a fabulously wealthy relative who would solve all your financial woes, the perennial rich uncle of which Americans dream, I, the author, am instead a homeless man with mental illness, and I don't have a sous in my jeans. Furthermore, I have nothing but contempt and loathing for the way you worship money and the power to exploit others, because you will act out Barnt's mistake again and again in every generation. To the extent that you do that, the curse will always be with you.

Anthony had it right: the goal is *not* to walk away from money and power, but to use them responsibly. That would be a completely reasonable goal for most adults. But the juvenile, recurring worship of unlimited money and power for its own sake will cause you to worship bullies and demagogues, and will transform America into a horrifying cautionary tale of depravity and sadism and willful ignorance.

Was not the idea of a treasure chest of gold at the end of the quest a big part of what kept you reading? Why don't you try to imagine a life where service, kindness and spirituality are at least as important as money and power?

Grow *up*, why don't you?

**TOP HAT
BOOKS**

Top Hat Books

Historical fiction that lives.

We publish fiction that captures the contrasts, the achievements, the optimism and the radicalism of ordinary and extraordinary times across the world.

We're open to all time periods and we strive to go beyond the narrow, foggy slums of Victorian London. Where are the tales of the people of fifteenth century Australasia? The stories of eighth century India? The voices from Africa, Arabia, cities and forests, deserts and towns? Our books thrill, excite, delight and inspire.

The genres will be broad but clear. Whether we're publishing romance, thrillers, crime, or something else entirely, the unifying themes are timescale and enthusiasm. These books will be a celebration of the chaotic power of the human spirit in difficult times. The reader, when they finish, will snap the book closed with a satisfied smile.

If you have enjoyed this book, why not tell other readers by posting a review on your preferred book site.

Recent bestsellers from Tops Hat Books are:

Grendel's Mother
The Saga of the Wyrd-Wife
Susan Signe Morrison
Grendel's Mother, a queen from Beowulf, threatens the fragile
political stability on this windswept land.
Paperback: 978-1-78535-009-2 ebook: 978-1-78535-010-8

Queen of Sparta
A Novel of Ancient Greece
T.S. Chaudhry
History has relegated her to the role of bystander, what if
Gorgo, Queen of Sparta, had played a central role in the Greek
resistance to the Persian invasion?
Paperback: 978-1-78279-750-0 ebook: 978-1-78279-749-4

Mercenary
R.J. Connor
Richard Longsword is a Mercenary, but this time it's not for
money, this time it's for revenge...
Paperback: 978-1-78279-236-9 ebook: 978-1-78279-198-0

Black Tom
Terror on the Hudson
Ron Semple
A tale of sabotage, subterfuge and political shenanigans
in Jersey City in 1916; America is on the cusp of war and the
fate of the nation hinges on the decision of one young
policeman.
Paperback: 978-1-78535-110-5 ebook: 978-1-78535-111-2

Destiny Between Two Worlds
A Novel about Okinawa
Jacques L Fuqua, Jr
A fateful October 1944 morning offered no inkling that the
lives of thousands of Okinawans would be profoundly
changed—forever.
Paperback: 978-1-78279-892-7 ebook: 978-1-78279-893-4

Cowards
Trent Portigal
A family's life falls into turmoil when the parents' timid
political dissidence is discovered by their far more enterprising
children.
Paperback: 978-1-78535-070-2 ebook: 978-1-78535-071-9

Godwine Kingmaker
Part One of The Last Great Saxon Earls
Mercedes Rochelle
The life of Earl Godwine is one of the enduring enigmas of
English history. Who was this Godwine, first Earl of Wessex;
unscrupulous schemer or protector of the English? The answer
depends on who you ask…
Paperback: 978-1-78279-801-9 ebook: 978-1-78279-800-2

The Last Stork Summer
Mary Brigid Surber
Eva, a young Polish child, battles to survive the designation of
"racially worthless" under Hitler's Germanization Program.
Paperback: 978-1-78279-934-4 ebook: 978-1-78279-935-1 $4.99
£2.99

Messiah Love
Music and Malice at a Time of Handel
Sheena Vernon
The tale of Harry Walsh's faltering steps on his journey to
success and happiness, performing in the playhouses of
Georgian London.
Paperback: 978-1-78279-768-5 ebook: 978-1-78279-761-6

A Terrible Unrest
Philip Duke
A young immigrant family must confront the horrors of the
Colorado Coalfield War to live the American Dream.
Paperback: 978-1-78279-437-0 ebook: 978-1-78279-436-3

Readers of ebooks can buy or view any of these bestsellers by clicking on the live link in the title. Most titles are published in paperback and as an ebook. Paperbacks are available in traditional bookshops. Both print and ebook formats are available online.

Find more titles and sign up to our readers' newsletter at
http://www.johnhuntpublishing.com/fiction

Follow us on Facebook at https://www.facebook.com/JHPfiction
and Twitter at https://twitter.com/JHPFiction